She's a daughter of two worlds.
And those worlds are ready to collide.

BROKEN VEIL

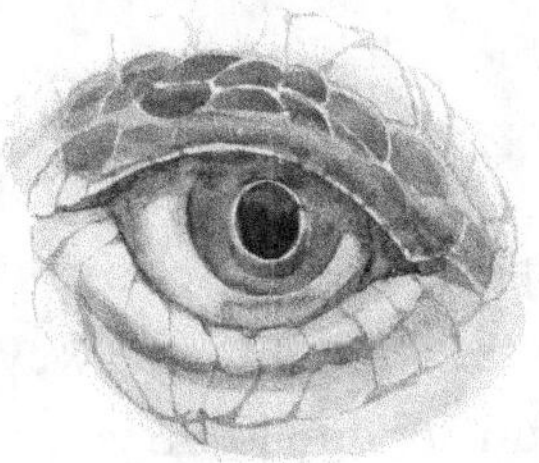

Carys Morgan is a mythology professor who walked through a fae portal and into a shadow world where myths and magic are reality. She has danced with dragons, bargained with fae, and fallen for a Scottish blacksmith with the heart of a knight.

But now both the Shadowlands and the Brightlands are in danger because Carys unleashed an ancient power, and the old gods are looking to Carys for a solution.

A goddess of war is loose in the modern world, and the fate of both realms depends on Carys correcting her mistake. To return the Morrígan to the Shadowlands and stop the worlds from colliding, she'll need the help of old gods, new gods, and every ally—living or dead—she's made along the way.

Fall into the pages of this modern fairy tale brought to life! BROKEN VEIL is the third installment in the SHADOWLANDS series by USA Today Bestselling Author Elizabeth Hunter. With vivid world-building, relatable characters, and abundant mysteries to uncover, this is a world you'll yearn to get lost in long after the last page is turned.

PRAISE FOR BROKEN VEIL

"I ran the whole spectrum of emotions while reading this book. By the end I was wiping tears away but exhilarated by the ride. The question at hand is, do you believe in fairy tales? My answer is yes!"

— SHELLY K., GOODREADS REVIEWER

"Elizabeth Hunter delivered another masterpiece that wraps up the story beautifully. Now we can only hope it won't take too long before she visits this world again."

— TANJA, GOODREADS REVIEWER

"What a fantastical conclusion to this trilogy! The imaginative narrative is truly phenomenal!"

— REALMS OF ROMANTASY

"The author is a fantastic wordsmith and worldbuilder, her writing is exquisite, her books are literally unputdownable page turners. The epic conclusion to the trilogy deserves all the stars."

— KDRBCK, BOOKBUB REVIEWER

BROKEN VEIL

SHADOWLANDS BOOK III

ELIZABETH HUNTER

BROKEN VEIL

SHADOWLANDS
BOOK THREE

ELIZABETH HUNTER

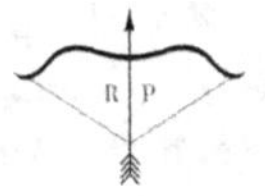

For my husband.

Driver. Personal barista. General hottie.
Every hero I write is just another facet of you.

CHAPTER ONE

Carys Morgan pulled on the heavy pine doors, then stepped into the barn to see her father working at his bench.

Light slanted through the high window that faced the west, fine sawdust floated gently in the air, and the smell of fresh cedar hit her nose along with the scent of soap, lemon, and beeswax.

Gareth Morgan glanced up. "Didn't expect to see you here."

She looked around, confused by the disordered workshop that surrounded her. There was a table leg sitting near the lathe in the corner and a half-finished spice rack that should be complete and hanging on the wall of the kitchen.

There was a nearly finished bookcase propped against the back wall. Her father had made it for her when she rented her first apartment. She'd put it in her childhood bedroom when she moved home after her parents' death.

"Dad?"

Her father wore a pair of clear goggles as he sanded a dusty piece of maple on the table in front of him. He put the sanding block down and swiped his hands over his jeans. "All right, my girl?"

Carys blinked. "You're wearing safety glasses."

"Of course I am."

"Even when you're dead?"

Gareth shook his head and frowned a little bit. "That's no reason to be careless."

She walked over and perched on a metal stool her father had scavenged from the old high school woodshop. The seat was ancient, but it didn't squeak or grind when she spun it around.

Of course not. Nothing squeaked in Gareth Morgan's workshop.

He leaned forward, propping his hands on the scarred bench. "It's good to see you."

"I'm dreaming."

"Course you are." His mouth curled in a crooked smile. "Best way to spend your time when you're asleep."

The room around her was a construction of her subconscious, an amalgamation of childhood memories, hopes, and unfinished business. The table leg was from her bedroom desk. The spice rack was for her mother, as was the cutting board her father was sanding.

"What do you need, Carys?"

"Why did we leave Wales?"

He smirked a little bit. "You never asked that when I was alive."

"I always meant to."

"Better not to leave a task unfinished, my girl." His voice grew soft. "Say what you mean to say. And if a job can be done in the moment—"

"Do it before you forget."

Gareth nodded. "Exactly."

She asked again, "Why did we leave Wales?"

He leaned back in his seat and crossed his arms over his chest. "I expect you understand better now than you would have when you were a girl."

"Because Mom came from the Shadows."

Gareth closed his eyes. "The Brightlands where I grew up was both too familiar and too foreign for your mother," he said. "Better a place that was new to both of us. You were born in Caernarfon, as agreed—"

"Agreed by whom?"

He shook his head. "I can't tell you that."

"She knew," Carys whispered. "Mom knew there would be another child."

"We both knew." Gareth blinked hard. "But we couldn't cross over. That was part of the price."

"For what? Me?"

He shook his head. "You were a gift. But we couldn't be selfish and ask for both of you. If we did, we'd be tempting—"

"The gods."

Gareth nodded silently.

"Was it worth it?"

Gareth's eyes glowed. "What do you think?"

There was nothing melancholy about this dream, which felt like far more than a dream.

"Where are you, Dad?" Carys looked over her shoulder at the open door. Light poured in from the afternoon sun, and in the distance she saw the familiar outline of Gareth and Tegan's small wooden house in the shadow of the redwood forest. "Is this heaven? Some kind of... otherworld? Is Mom here too?"

"I'm here, my girl." Gareth smiled. "I can hear her in the house. Can't you?"

Carys held her breath, but she heard nothing from the distant home. Not a song or the chirping of birds.

She whispered, "Do *you* hear her?"

"Oh yes." He nodded. "Every moment."

"Okay." She let out a slow breath. "That's what's important."

Her father smiled. "What's scurrying about your brain? Such a busy mind you have." He lifted his hand and circled his finger in the air like a wheel. "Your mother and I joked about that gear in your head. The one that never stopped turning. What are you wondering now?"

Carys looked around the shop. "Was this home to you? The house in the woods. Teaching punk teenagers. Building yet another bookcase for yet another classroom?"

"And where else would home be?" He chuckled a little. "Home is where love is. You and your mother, Carys. You were all I needed of home."

"I miss you, Dad."

"I'm right here, my girl." His voice was soft. "Don't you know? I'm just on the other side of your dreams."

SHE OPENED her eyes as the blurry memory of a dream faded away, stared into the darkness until her eyes adjusted to the dim blue light sneaking through the shutters on the windows. She focused on a dignified navy strip draped over a dark canopy held up by four mahogany posters.

Next to her, sound asleep, was the laird of Murrayshall, her knight in blacksmith's clothing, Duncan Murray.

"Mother, you should meet Carys. She's a mythology professor and she's my girlfriend, so you'll be seeing her again."

Right.

Duncan was her boyfriend.

Boyfriend.

Her boyfriend was a Scottish laird who wielded a dragon-steel sword.

That was so... kick-ass.

The bookish teenage nerd who lived inside her was squealing uncontrollably while the mature adult part of her tried to play it cool.

Duncan sucked in a breath, flopped over on his side, and let out a hard snort before he threw an arm over his eyes and fell back asleep.

Carys smiled. Okay, her kick-ass boyfriend was also just a man.

Glancing around the dim bedroom, she realized Duncan might be just a man to her, but that was probably not how the world saw him. And how the world saw him was going to be an issue.

"Oh dear. You're American."

Duncan's mother's disappointment couldn't have been more clear.

Since Carys had been born in Wales, she was—strictly speaking —a dual citizen, but while Duncan was a man of money, position, and influence, Carys was an associate mythology professor at a moderately priced state university in Northern California.

Of course, if they were getting technical, she was also a nêrys ddraig, a dragon lord, and a niece of the King of Cymru in the parallel dimension that lived just on the other side of the fae gates connecting the modern world and the magical one.

But that might be a little too complicated to explain to Duncan's mother.

She rolled onto her side and stared at the window, wishing the night away.

They had arrived in Brightlands London the night before, just as a massive earthen barrow had appeared next to Stonehenge, baffling the human world.

And in the weeks before that, she'd seen an Anglian king crowned, a fae prince declare war on the human kingdoms by stealing children, another fae prince return from exile, and nearly been in a war between human and magical armies.

And in the middle of all that, she'd not quite accidentally released an ancient war goddess into the Brightlands.

She and Duncan had returned to London because she'd sensed a trap, but nothing could have prepared her for the sight of a fae mound appearing in the human world, drones buzzing over it, and evening news presenters offering glib commentary on the supernatural activity.

"...law enforcement has been challenged by a group of neo-pagan activists who are trying to enter the site, claiming any attempt to obstruct them is a violation of their religious freedom."

The Brightlands was not prepared for what the Morrígan was planning.

She was staring into the corner, fascinated by the play of shadows against the window from the tree outside, and drifting back to sleep.

Nêrys.

Carys smiled when she heard her dragon's comforting, deep voice. *Cadell?*

I wasn't sure you were awake.

Only a little bit. Are you okay?

She and Duncan had returned to the Brightlands with Cadell, her best friend Laura, and two other magical creatures from the Shadowlands, a wolf shifter named Godrik and a fae healer named Naida.

Naida is feeling better, Cadell said.

Good. Any change in Salisbury?

Laura was watching the news until a few hours ago. She's sleeping now.

In your room?

None of your business.

She kept her eyes closed, but she smiled. *I disagree.*

Cadell had first bonded to Carys's Shadowkin, Seren, but when Seren was murdered and Carys entered the Shadowlands through a fae gate, he'd sensed her and bonded immediately to her.

Carys was the first Brightkin in history—that they knew of—to be bonded to a dragon.

And Laura was her best friend, so any relationship between her best friend and Cadell was definitely her business.

Despite your completely unnecessary interest in Laura's and my relationship, we have far more important things to worry about.

I know.

Carys had made a bargain with what she thought was a fae sorceress, only to find out that the old woman who bargained for passage to the Brightlands wasn't fae at all.

She was the Morrígan, a three-natured goddess of Celtic mythology. She was also the reason for the massive fae fort that had appeared on Salisbury Plain.

Carys didn't *know* what the Morrígan was planning, but she was fairly sure it wasn't going to be peace, love, and naked dancing under the moon.

I'm not going to pretend that the barrow near Stonehenge isn't concerning, but—

Oh no, the dragon said. *We have more immediate problems than that.*

Okay yes, the Morrígan was loose and their fae friend Naida was ill from being in the Brightlands, but they'd averted a fae war that threatened to tear Shadowlands Briton apart.

That was progress, right?

Carys sighed, wishing her dragon would shut up so she could go back to sleep. *Leave it to you to get chatty the one time I'm super time-lagged and all I want is to—*

Nêrys, I'm talking to you.

I know. And I wish you weren't.

Nêrys.

Dragon.

I am talking to you.

And?

In. Your. Mind.

Carys's eyes flew open, and she sat bolt upright in bed. "Shit!"

Duncan parked the old Land Rover in the driveway of a garage across the street from the Chelsea Bridge.

"Any other time of day, this would be asking for a tow," he grumbled.

"Which is why I would only ask you to do this in the middle of the night," Godrik muttered.

The wolf shifter and the Scotsman were equally grumbly about being woken in the middle of the night, but when Carys and Cadell explained that they were speaking to each other's minds, they both understood the urgency.

Laura had stayed back at the house with Naida, leaving Carys to jog to catch up with the three large men who strode across Grosvenor Road toward the walkway along Chelsea Bridge. There weren't many people on the streets that night, but everyone Carys saw seemed to be walking the same direction.

In the distance, she saw Cadell leaning on the railing, his long arms braced and his shoulders tense as his eagle-sharp gaze locked onto the dark water of the Thames.

Duncan halted at the sidewalk and held his hand out, waiting for Carys to catch up. "Did Godrik tell you why he wanted to come here?"

Carys shook her head. "No, I don't know what Cadell told him."

She only knew that moments after she'd realized that she and Cadell were communicating mentally in the Brightlands, the wolf and the dragon were knocking on her door, waking Duncan and asking him to drive them to the river as quickly as possible.

The night air had woken Carys up, but she was still groggy and unfocused. She could feel the bright line of energy between her and Cadell—usually muted in the Brightlands—flare to life as she approached the water.

By the time Duncan and Carys reached the bridge, Godrik was standing next to Cadell, staring downriver with a grim look on his face.

"What?" Carys asked. "What is it?"

"There is an ancient fae gate in this area," Godrik said.

"Look." Cadell pointed toward the riverbank on the near side of the river.

Carys rubbed her eyes and blinked, but all she saw was a dense stand of trees that rode along the top of the moss-covered walls of the embankment. Just beyond Chelsea Bridge was the low, arched silhouette of Grosvenor Bridge, and the lights of the city were dancing on the dark, flowing water of the Thames.

"What the hell is that?" Duncan was staring at the embankment.

"That's the gate," Godrik said. "But I've never seen one like this. Not on this side of the gates."

Carys frowned. "I don't get it."

There was nothing in the trees save for a few dancing fireflies.

"Carys, what do you think those are?" Duncan pointed at the dark silhouette of the trees along the river.

"Fireflies?" She shrugged.

"No," Cadell said. "We do not have fireflies here."

Carys blinked and looked closer. "You mean—"

"The gate is beneath those trees," Godrik said. "I don't think it's been used for centuries, not since the humans here built this embankment." He pointed to Grosvenor Bridge. "There's one a bit farther up under the bridge that's better traveled, but those aren't fireflies, Lady Carys. Those are wisps."

Wisps.

Carys's breath caught.

Will-o'-the-wisps, the dancing souls of Shadowkin never allowed to be born.

Every time a child was born in the Brightlands, their shadow self came into being on the other side of the fae gates. Created by old magic, not every child's soul was given a body. Many were born only to live in an endless limbo, food for the dark fae creatures who controlled the portals between the two worlds, destined to whisper in the night until their light flickered out.

"Wisps show up in Scotland sometimes," Duncan said. "We see them in the forests there. There have always been a few."

"In California too," Carys added. "We see them in the forests around the gates."

Cadell turned to look at Duncan. "But in all your years living in London, have you ever seen wisps here?"

"No," Duncan said. "Not out in the open like this."

Carys watched the embankment as the few humans on the bridge walked over, stopped, stared, and pointed at the lights.

A bright wisp darted out from the trees and danced across the river, disappearing under the bridge where a quiet splashing sound echoed across the water. A second later, the wisp disappeared from sight.

"What was that?" Carys whispered.

"What lives under bridges?" Duncan murmured.

"Trolls," Cadell said.

"In Brightlands London?" Carys's heart raced. "This is bad. This is so bad."

Cadell walked over, keeping his voice low. "Since the time that magic left this world and retreated to the Shadowlands, the gates have been guarded by the fae. The portals between the two worlds have thinned at times, but they have always held."

Godrik moved closer. "But now there is an ancient god in the Brightlands who has not been worshipped actively for centuries. This world is new to her, and she's been given a massive jolt of violent energy from the battle in the Shadowlands."

"She's stretching the limits of her power," Carys said. "Testing things out."

Duncan added, "And from her publicity stunt in Salisbury, it looks like she wants to make a statement."

"We can hear each other in our minds," Cadell said. "If I'm being honest, I feel like I might be able to shift if I tried."

"Please don't," Carys whispered. "I do not want to try to explain a dragon flying off the Chelsea Bridge."

Godrik shoved his hands in his pockets and shook the silver and black hair that fell into his grey eyes. "You let her cross the gate, Lady Carys. Whether you realized it or not, that was a mistake. Now one of the most powerful gods in the Shadowlands is rising in England. I might know how to fight the fae in Anglia, but this isn't my world."

Duncan looked at the crowds gathering on the bridge, the humans pointing at the flying wisps as more and more of them appeared in the trees. "From the look of the people on this bridge, the fae gates of London aren't going to remain hidden for long."

Carys heard another splash in the water. She walked to the edge and looked down. There was the distinct movement of a serpentine wave spreading as something moved under the dark surface of the Thames. Then a large ridged back became visible for a second before it slipped beneath the water and disappeared from view.

CHAPTER TWO

"I really wish my dad was here," Carys whispered.

They were sitting at a half-empty table in the morning room, waiting for the house in Belgravia to wake.

Duncan turned to her and took her hand. "Why?" He didn't look dismissive, just curious.

"I just always felt like Dad would know what to do." Carys looked up. "All the time. In any given situation, I felt like he would be able to fix it."

"Even a problem like magic creeping across fae gates and into London?"

"I mean, he figured out how to marry my mother, so he had to know about magic, right?" Carys hadn't even considered that her father hadn't known about the Shadowlands. "He had to know."

Duncan slowly shook his head. "I have no idea."

"Don't you ever feel that way? Like you just need someone older than you to figure something out?"

"I can't say I ever—"

"Duncan?"

He looked at the door a moment before his mother appeared. "Yes, Mother?"

Lady Alexandra Morrison Murray, mother of the laird of Murrayshall and current heiress to several large fortunes, appeared in the doorway leading to the hall. She was dressed in what looked like hiking pants and a bright green cardigan.

"Randall is in the kitchen." Alexandra glanced at Carys. "Does she prefer a full breakfast or a continental one?"

"*She* prefers an omelet," Carys said. "If that's something Randall can manage."

Alexandra wrinkled her forehead as if she were surprised that Carys could speak. "I see."

"We'll let Randall know what we want for breakfast, Mother. What are you doing this morning?"

Alexandra said, "I'm headed out to the garden. The roses have gone wild in the past few days. I suppose it's the heat."

"Do you think so?" Duncan murmured. "Let me know if you need any help."

It was summer in London, which according to Duncan could be cold, hot, or anything between. This morning was damp and cool, not warm at all.

Alexandra waved a hand as she pulled on a glove. "Gordon is already trimming the beds. I'm simply overseeing the pruning." She looked up, glanced at Carys for another silent second, then disappeared.

"She's cold but not naturally rude," Duncan said. "She just doesn't know what to do with you."

Carys suspected that Duncan had enjoyed springing her existence on his mother the night before, so she was inclined to ignore the way his mother spoke to her even if it felt like discourtesy. "You didn't exactly give her a heads-up that you were bringing someone home to meet her, I'm guessing."

He shook his head. "I did not. Bit too busy averting a fae war on the other side."

She could hardly fault Duncan for prioritizing that. "Well, how did she treat your other girlfriends?"

Duncan smirked. "She didn't meet any of my other girlfriends."

She pulled her eyes away from what looked like a Turner landscape hanging over the sideboard. "What?"

"She hasn't met any of the other women I've dated," Duncan said.

"Why not?"

He shrugged. "More trouble than it was worth, I suppose."

"Are you saying that I'm trouble?"

"Yes, but you're trouble that *is* worth it." He leaned over and kissed her. "Completely different situation."

Carys sighed. *What am I going to do with you?*

The question kept pinging around in her mind.

She could move to Scotland. They needed teachers everywhere, right?

But Duncan had already offered to move to California.

His workshop was in Scone.

But he could work in California.

He had a mansion in Scotland.

But she loved her cozy little house.

"I can see those questions." He tapped her temple. "Out with it."

"Our future relationship plans don't really seem like the thing to focus on right now." She had weeks before she had to be back in California. "The Morrígan needs to be stopped before we talk about anything else, and since I'm the one who let her through to this world, it's my job to stop her."

"I know you think that but—"

Nêrys.

"Cadell's coming."

She sat up as the dragon walked through the door. Cadell appeared, holding two plates, while Godrik waited behind him with a tray.

"What's all this?" Duncan asked.

"An omelet." The dragon set down a plate of eggs. "And this one has roasted potatoes, mushrooms, tomatoes, and bacon."

Duncan stared at the second dish. "Where's mine?"

"You have legs." Cadell sat across from her. "Godrik will be feeding the women upstairs."

Carys turned and watched the massive wolf duck under the doorway and back into the hall. "He got that food from the kitchen, right? I don't need to worry that there's a dead deer in Hyde Park?"

"He procured it from the efficient human in the kitchen named Randall." Cadell looked at Carys. "Who cooks in enamel-clad dishes, I might add. Important that he not use any cast-iron for the fae."

"I didn't check on Naida this morning." Carys tried to stand, but Duncan pulled her back to her seat.

"Eat, Carys. Godrik's checking on Naida." Duncan looked at Cadell. "And Laura?"

"She was up late, speaking with her brother in California," Cadell said. "I thought I'd let her sleep."

"Did her brother have anything to say?" Carys dug into the plate of food in front of her. "Are things different there?"

"Not so far," Cadell said. "Or not that he's noticed. But the gates in California were never the same as the gates here."

After Carys's first journey to the Shadowlands, she'd returned home and been startled to find that not only did her best friend know all about the parallel world, she was a shadow person—a pauwau inwe of the Yurok people—who moved between the Shadowlands and Brightlands of Northern California.

"So do you think that's what's happening here?" Carys asked. "The gates in Baywood are more porous than in London. We see more wisps. Shifters can move between them in animal form."

"Yes, and Bigfoot occasionally slips across and scares a few hikers," Duncan said. "But can you imagine a dragon accidentally shifting in Central London? Can you imagine a unicorn trotting across Hampstead Heath?"

Cadell sat down across from her. "I think the idea of letting the gates thin in Briton is a very different prospect than the thinner gates in America, Nêrys. The magical creatures of Briton are wild, numerous, and frankly, often violent. Allowing the Morrígan to break the barrier between the worlds would cause chaos on an unimaginable level."

She looked at Duncan, and she could see by the set of his mouth that he agreed with the dragon.

"Okay." She took a deep breath and let it out slowly. "Then I have to fix this. Somehow I have to figure out how to stop a goddess, get her back across the fae gate, and keep her from crossing over ever again."

And she had just over a month before her fall classes started.

No problem, right?

LAURA RUBBED her eyes as Cadell handed her a cup of coffee. "I don't know. Are we absolutely sure that it's such a bad thing to let the gates here thin? I mean, Carys and I have lived in a place with thinner gates, and yeah, it can be kind of spooky for humans sometimes, but it's not that bad."

Naida asked, "What kind of magical creatures do you have in your home?"

The fae woman was pale, but she did look stronger than she had the night before, and the abundant green salad that Godrik had gathered from the garden outside seemed to be helping.

"Most of our mythology revolves around animal spirits," Laura said. "There are the giants, of course, but they protect humans from things like the wechuge, which are very rare, and they live farther north. Wechuge prefer the cold and ice."

"There are thunderbirds," Carys added. "Those are probably the most powerful."

"But I've never seen a thunderbird who could cross a gate," Cadell said. "They almost never shift to their human form."

"So mostly animal shifters," Laura said. "And things that appear human but have other powers."

"You've been to my world now," Naida said. "What do you think it would be like if our magical creatures got lost in the human world?"

"Forget getting lost," Godrik said gruffly. "Trolls would cross the gates to scavenge almost anything from the Brightlands to sell in their markets. Shadowkin might cross just because they're curious. Shifters. Fae maybe. Magical creatures could pour into London if the gates are broken."

Carys said, "And if they don't lose their powers…"

"Chaos," Duncan said.

"Is that why she wanted to come here?" Laura asked. "Is that why she wanted to cross over? I don't know a ton about Celtic mythology, but in the fantasy books that I've read, the Morrígan is like a war god, right?"

"The Morrígan *is* a war goddess," Carys said. "But that's only one aspect of her nature. She's also about land. Sovereignty. Protecting territory. There is a guardian aspect in the myths about her."

Naida nodded slowly. "Territory. Land. Like creating more land in Briton like Orla and Cian were trying to do?"

Duncan said, "It's completely possible she was involved in that. She definitely knew it was happening."

"She's not venerated as she was in the past," Godrik said. "There is no cult among the shifters for her, and the cult that once worshipped her in Éire was suppressed by the high fae lords."

Naida sighed. "Because they are idiots."

Carys looked at Cadell. "So the Morrígan has been confined to the Shadowlands for centuries, watching as her power diminishes bit by bit."

"Stuck on a small island in a big world," the dragon said quietly.

Duncan spoke. "On a purely practical level, if the Morrígan tears down the gates between the Brightlands and the Shadowlands, she will effectively double her territory."

"That part." Laura pointed at Duncan. "Pretty sure you nailed it."

"Breaking down the fae gates would mean she's no longer an obscure goddess on a few small islands," Cadell said. "With human communication the way it is now, she could gain acolytes all over the world."

Carys put a hand over her eyes and groaned.

"What?" Duncan grabbed her hand.

"I just had an image of the Morrígan going viral."

"Oh, that would be..." Laura's eyes grew wide. "That would be bad."

"I don't know what going viral means," Godrik said. "But the dragon is correct. More acolytes means a larger cult means more power. Gods only gain power when mortals believe in them.

"We have to stop the Morrígan before she tears down the gates between the Shadowlands and the Brightlands." Carys looked around the table. "And I don't think we have much time."

"Okay, mythology prof." Laura set her empty coffee cup down. "This is your area of expertise, isn't it? How can a group of humans with a few magical friends stop an ancient goddess who wants to take over the world?"

Carys sat back with a lump in her throat and a sick feeling in her stomach. "I'm going to need a laptop and a really big library."

CHAPTER THREE

arys, Cadell, and Duncan sat at a small table in the garden outside a café in Oxford, killing time and waiting for Godrik, Laura, and Naida to reach them by car.

"Do you think she'll be sick again?" Duncan asked. "Randall is a good driver, but all cars have steel."

"Hopefully it won't be too bad," Cadell said. "Perhaps the heightened magic the Morrígan is cultivating in the Brightlands will help Naida while she's here."

"It would be one nice side effect from all this," Carys said.

They were meeting a colleague of Carys's in Oxford—a professor she'd consulted with on her doctoral thesis—and while it only took an hour by train, with London traffic, it was likely going to be closer to two hours for Randall to reach them in the car.

But the train was far too much metal for Naida's comfort. She could just barely handle the Audi in Duncan's mother's garage, so Laura had bundled her in as much wool clothing as possible and packed her in the back seat like a large woolen burrito, ignoring Randall's curious stares.

"What time do we meet your friend?" Duncan glanced at his watch.

"It's another half hour or so," Carys said. "I'm just glad Dr. Beck was able to meet with me on such short notice."

Luna Beck was a mythology professor at Oxford who specialized in early Celtic mythology, which had come in handy when Carys was doing her thesis research.

"And I'm so excited to meet her in person." Carys smiled. "We've had video chats but never actually met."

"At least you know what she looks like," Duncan said.

Cadell was perched stiffly on the wooden bench that overlooked the lawn stretching out from the café located on the back side of a church off High Street.

It was summer in Oxford, and there appeared to be more tourists than students. Carys heard plenty of American accents around her along with languages from around the world.

Duncan poured her a refill of Earl Grey tea from the Brown Betty teapot on their table, glancing at Cadell as he poured. "Try not to look like you're hunting for rabbits, old man."

Carys pressed her lips together so she didn't laugh.

Even when her dragon was in human form, Cadell still looked somewhat raptor-like. His angular cheekbones and prominent brow gave him the look of a fierce bird of prey. The piercing golden eyes didn't help.

"I'm not hunting rabbits," Cadell said. "I'm waiting for Laura and Naida."

"You look ready to eat that stray cat, man." Duncan refilled Cadell's cup as well. "Have some tea."

"I prefer coffee."

Duncan muttered something under his breath in Gaelic, and Cadell said something back in guttural Welsh.

Before they could start arguing in different languages, Carys decided to distract them. "Did you know that Dr. Beck is the current expert on the fourth branch of the *Mabinogion*? She's probably published more papers on Blodeuwedd than any other writer."

Cadell and Duncan turned to her with confused expressions.

Perfect.

"What's the *Mabinogion*?" Duncan asked.

"Who is Blodeuwedd?"

"It's a thirteenth-century collection of oral traditions and folklore that chronicles much of early Welsh mythology," Carys said. "And Blodeuwedd is the adulterous wife of a Welsh hero who plotted to kill him but instead was turned into an owl."

Cadell nodded silently. "Appropriate."

"Obviously I grew up knowing most of the stories in the *Mabinogion*, but then as I studied more, I became more interested in the links between different traditions and their common threads."

"Because the same stories reoccur all over the world," Cadell said.

Duncan smiled. "You're saying folklore doesn't repeat, but it often rhymes?"

"Exactly!" Carys smiled. "My doctoral thesis was on the parallels between Blodeuwedd and Persephone. Both women in arranged marriages who exhibited two natures, one light and one dark."

"Huh." Duncan tapped his teacup to hers. "I do enjoy listening to you fly your nerd flag, Dr. Morgan."

Carys beamed. "Thank you. Hopefully you'll enjoy meeting Dr. Beck too."

Cadell was back to staring at the cat on the edge of the lawn. "That's not a cat."

Duncan turned to look at it. "It very clearly is a cat."

"No, it's not." He stood up and started walking toward the animal, which darted into the bushes and out of sight.

"We have got to get him back to the Shadowlands," Duncan muttered under his breath.

"Maybe there's a gate nearby," Carys said quietly. "I'm still not sure it's good for Naida to be here."

"I'd agree except that of all of us, she can sense the gates more clearly on this side," Duncan said. "Even ones that are dormant. For right now we need her."

Carys spotted Godrik's silver and black hair over the top of a tour group. "I see them."

Laura and Naida were on either side, sticking close to the large man as the crowds grew busier.

"Good." Duncan finished his tea and stood. "We're headed to the Bodleian Library then?"

"No, the Weston," Carys said. "Dr. Beck has a reader card for the Bodleian, but she reserved space at the Weston for the manuscript she wanted me to look at."

"Dra— Cadell!" Duncan shouted. "We're off, old man."

They started toward Godrik, Laura, and Naida, but as Carys turned, she collided with a swiftly moving woman wearing large glasses and sent the smaller woman's massive handbag tumbling to the ground.

"Oh, I am so sorry." Carys immediately bent and started gathering up the papers that had fallen on the sidewalk. "I didn't even see you there."

"It's my fault entirely," the woman said. "I was rushing to meet a colleague and—"

"Dr. Beck?" Carys sat back on her heels, took in the woman's heart-shaped face and the mass of dark hair piled on her head, and suddenly realized who she was. "It's me! Dr. Morgan."

"Oh, for heaven's sake." Dr. Beck's Irish lilt grew stronger. "Of course you are. Your hair is longer of course. I don't know why I didn't realize—"

"I always braid it. And you usually wear yours down for meetings." Carys laughed and finished gathering the papers, shoving them into the bag. "My friends just arrived, so perfect timing."

She stood with Dr. Beck and held her hand out to the woman. "It's so good to finally meet you in person."

"And you as well. Please, call me Luna." She shook Carys's hand while wrangling her overly full handbag on her shoulder. "Welcome to Oxford." She clapped her hands together. "Finally!"

"You must call me Carys." She turned to Duncan. "And this is Duncan. He's..." Her mouth fell open, but nothing came out.

"I'm her boyfriend." Duncan held out his hand and shook Dr. Beck's. "It's new."

Luna's eyebrows flew up. "Oh, you're lovely and Scottish. Very pleased to meet you."

Carys found her voice again. "And this is my friend Cadell."

A shadow fell over the small woman when Cadell reached them, and Luna looked up and up, her eyes widening as her gaze met Cadell's.

Her mouth formed a small *O*, and she took a step back.

Cadell crossed his arms over his chest. "She's fae."

Carys blinked and looked at the dragon, then at the delicate woman to her right. "Dr. Beck?"

"You brought a dragon to Oxford?" Luna whispered. "My dear Dr. Morgan, why did you do that?"

"Fortunately it's summer." Luna Beck set down the massive bag holding her papers and books on the table in the seminar room. "If it was in the middle of term, finding space in the library on short notice would be impossible."

Dr. Beck had reserved a seminar room at the Weston. The glass windows looked out over the reading room, but once the door of the seminar room closed, even the quiet shuffle of activity in the reading room was cut off.

"We can speak freely in here." She sat at the head of the large table. "So a dragon, a wolf, and a fae are visiting the Brightlands." She looked around the table as everyone sat down. "And you..." She nodded at Laura. "You're not without your own magic either, are you?"

Laura said, "I'm pauwau inwe of the Yurok tribe in Northern California."

Luna nodded. "Wykanush Lalem then," she said. "You're from the Salmon People in the Pacific Northwest?"

"Yes."

"A shadow-walker?" Luna asked. "A go-between?"

"Exactly."

Luna glanced at Cadell. "We've needed her like for years in Briton."

"We do not disagree on this," Cadell said.

"Why are you in the Brightlands?" Carys asked. "It's probably none of my business but—"

"Oh, it's such a boring story." Dr. Beck laughed. "My fellow fae could probably guess." She looked at Naida, who was starting to regain her color as she sat near Luna.

Naida smiled sadly. "You fell in love?"

Luna shrugged her narrow shoulders. "Aren't we predictable? All that magic in our own home, and we fae end up chasing pretty faces in this one. A tale as old as the trees."

"Was he... she a human?" Carys asked.

"Of course, dear. Nigel and I were married for nearly sixty years before he passed."

Carys blinked. "You don't look older than forty."

"Of course I don't." Dr. Beck smiled. "I'm still fae." She leaned on the table. "That said, a few weeks ago, I *did* look a bit older than I do now. In the past few days, I've had a bit of what my students would call a glow up." She raised her eyebrows.

Carys immediately felt the sting of professorial judgment. "Yes. About that..."

Dr. Beck continued, "Now a wolf and a dragon are sitting in the Weston Library, a friend from California is asking about early sources on the Morrígan, and a giant barrow has risen next to Stonehenge."

Cadell's voice was blunt. "Barrows happen. Sometimes."

"Not overnight." Dr. Beck continued to stare at Carys. "Anything you want to share, Dr. Morgan?"

"So a couple of years ago," Carys started, "I met a nice man from Scotland who was traveling in California."

Dr. Beck smiled at Duncan. "How lovely."

"Not me," Duncan muttered. "My Shadowkin."

"Oh." The professor's eyes went wide. *"Ohhh."*

"Yes. Complicated." Carys nodded. "Anyway, his father wasn't very pleased about him leaving Alba, so he sent some fae to collect him, and he just... disappeared. No explanation. So I went looking for him." She gestured toward Duncan. "And met his Brightkin."

"I bet that took some explaining," she murmured.

Duncan cleared his throat. "It was an interesting conversation."

"So I crossed over the first time in Alba and found my ex in Sgain Castle, and when I was there, I met" —she gestured toward Cadell— "my dragon."

"Your dragon?" Dr. Beck leaned farther forward. "*Your* dragon? As in—"

"Carys Morgan is Nêrys Ddraig," Cadell said. "She is a dragon lord loyal to the throne of Cymru and niece of High Kind Dafydd. Her Shadowkin was Seren, my bonded human and the heir to the Cymric throne, who was killed by the fae daughter of Queen Orla. Now Carys is my lady."

Luna Beck's mouth was hanging open.

"Been a few years since you've crossed the gates?" Laura asked quietly.

"Over fifteen."

Naida said, "In fairness, things usually don't change all that much from one decade to the next. These past few years have been unusual."

"So..." Dr. Beck pointed at Carys. "*You're* a dragon lord? How? You are Brightkin."

Carys opened her mouth, then closed it. "Ummm..."

Though she'd conversed freely with Luna Beck in the past and had probably thanked her for her help countless times, she was suddenly wary of the woman she now knew was fae.

"Oh my dear" —Dr. Beck perceived the problem immediately— "I don't have any magic here. I surround myself with old books in old buildings precisely because I get as weak as your friend in this world. Even if I wanted to work magic on you—which I would not—I don't have the power."

"I'm sorry." Carys felt a wave of embarrassment. "I shouldn't have been—"

"No, no." Luna waved a hand. "If you've been navigating the Shadowlands, I completely understand."

"My mother was Shadowkin," Carys said. "So technically Laura's not the only one with a little something extra. Magic-wise."

Dr. Beck was staring. "I really want to write this down, but that would not be appropriate or wise."

"Why do you want to write it down?"

"In all my years, I have never heard of such a thing. And I study magic and myths."

"So do I," Carys said, "but can I tell you? The reality of the Shadowlands and the stories are not—"

"Oh, not at all the same!" Dr. Beck shook her head. "Which is why I'm not sure how much this is going to help." She pulled out a folder. "Obviously there is no lending at the Bodleian, but I was able to locate the earliest manuscript we have on the Morrígan. Older stories tend to be a little more accurate. Less French influence and all that." She slid the file over to Carys. "I was able to acquire some scans of the manuscript, but they are in medieval Irish."

"I can help with the translation," Naida said.

Carys flipped open the folder and saw color scans of a manuscript in very poor condition. "It's a partial manuscript?"

"*Very* partial. It's eleventh century. Authorship unknown. It's still being restored and translated. We only received it last year when Trinity passed on acquiring it. They have the majority of medieval

Irish sources obviously, but this is early and it does mention the Morrígan." Dr. Beck leaned forward. "Macha, to be exact. One of her aspects."

"Yes," Cadell said. "That is the one who was living in Gorne Wood until a few days ago."

"Macha?" Dr. Beck asked. "The Morrígan is in the Brightlands?"

Carys nodded. "She's the reason the barrow rose in Salisbury Plain. There was a battle there a few days ago, and Fomorian and fae blood was spilled."

"Blood on Sarum," she murmured. "That's never a good thing. The Morrígan was bound by Epona's daughters. She wasn't supposed to be able to cross into the Brightlands."

Every eye in the room turned to Carys.

"Yeah, that was…" She sighed. "That was my fault."

Dr. Beck leaned closer and took a long sniff. "Now that I'm thinking of it, you smell of Epona."

Carys blinked. "H-how?"

Luna Beck and Naida shared a glance, and both of them shrugged.

"You just do," Naida said. "I noticed it immediately."

"And you didn't say anything?" Carys asked.

"Why would she?" Godrik spoke for the first time. "What would be the point?"

"I don't know, maybe if I'd known that it was the job of Epona's cult to keep the Morrígan in the Shadowlands, I wouldn't have made a deal with the Crow Mother to get Seren's journal!"

Everyone in the seminar room was silent.

Duncan grimaced. "That's… a bit of a stretch, darling."

"Okay, yes, but obviously…" Carys sighed. "I didn't know that the aspect that I met—the Crow Mother—was a goddess. I thought she was a fae sorceress who wanted to see the Brightlands to look at the sun. And a fae sorceress—"

"Would lose her power here." Dr. Beck nodded. "Of course. That makes sense, and you can only make decisions with the knowledge that you have, Dr. Morgan. You had no way of knowing she was a goddess. The Morrígan is known for her cunning. She's a very old and shrewd divinity."

"And you are a young and stupid human," Godrik said. "It was not an even negotiation."

Cadell nodded. "Ignorance is expected from humans."

"Okay." Carys lifted a hand. "That's—"

"It's true," Naida added. "You can't dwell on your foolish actions that have put the fae gates in danger. You didn't intentionally put the magical barriers in jeopardy; you just didn't know any better."

"Hey!" Laura barked. "All the negativity is not helping, okay?" She turned to Dr. Beck. "The Morrígan was bound to the Shadow-lands once, right? That means it can be done again."

"Honestly, I do not know," Luna said. "But though the Morrígan has never been defeated, per se, there is one hero in stories who thwarted her, and he was half-human."

"See?" Laura spread her arms and looked around the room. "Humans do not suck. Humans can do things. Even against the gods."

"He was also half-divine," Luna added. "A demigod, if you will."

Laura hissed, "*Not* helping, Luna."

Duncan had reserved three rooms in a beautiful historic inn that overlooked the River Thames near the Folly Bridge. Carys was lying on the bed, staring at the plastered ceiling and listening to Duncan, who was speaking to his foreman at the smithy in Scone.

"No, that sounds workable," Duncan said quietly. "When? Probably a couple of weeks at least. Not sure, but I'll let you know. If there's a project..."

Carys rolled over to look at him.

"No, that's fine. I trust you, Valentin." Duncan sat on the edge of the bed and reached out for Carys's hand. "That's why I put you in charge. Ignore Robby; he second-guesses *me* most of the time."

Duncan folded her fingers in his massive, callused palm. "Yes, good." He cleared his throat. "Good man, Val. Talk to you soon." He ended the call and tossed his phone on the bedside table. "Sorry about that."

"Don't be sorry. This is one hundred percent not how I imagined my first trip to Oxford."

"Eh." He shrugged his massive shoulders. "It's not the worst. I had to visit a mate here when he was in university, and it was much worse being surrounded by a crowd of snobby public school lads with more money than sense."

"Weren't you a snobby public school lad?"

He put his hand over her mouth. "Hush."

Carys laughed and pulled his fingers from her face, kissing his knuckles.

She hated the idea of facing all this without him, but she had to be honest. "Do you need to go home? You have gone above and beyond trying to fix my screw-up, and at this point—"

"Don't be daft." He stretched out next to her. "Besides, none of these magical tossers have any money. You don't need to be paying for their room and board when you have a rich boyfriend."

Carys groaned and pressed her face into Duncan's chest. "I'm officially a freeloader. My father would be horrified."

"No, he wouldn't." Duncan ran a hand over her hair. "You're trying to right a mistake, Carys. And we're making progress, aren't we? None of us knew a fae was hiding in Oxford and teaching Celtic mythology, did we?"

"And somehow it's just not that hard to believe."

"No, it isn't."

She relaxed as Duncan stroked her hair. "I've written back and forth with her for years, but I never expected that."

"Why would you?"

What had she done to deserve friends like Duncan and Laura who crossed oceans to stand with her?

I think that when you love someone—really love them—you'll cross an ocean to find them again. Maybe even cross a world.

She looked up. "You really love me, don't you?"

"Aye, I do." His accent got thicker. "Even though that scaly arse is always following you around."

"Don't call my arse scaly. I just need some moisturizer."

Duncan burst out laughing and hugged her tight. "You're going to fix this. We'll figure it out."

"And if we don't?"

"You can't think that way."

"No, but I have to." She gripped the front of his shirt with her hands. "It helps. If I imagine the worst thing that can happen, take it in, and really process it, then I feel like I can tackle anything."

Duncan grumbled, "That makes no sense to me."

"For the longest time, the worst thing I could imagine was losing my parents and being completely alone." She blinked hard to battle the tears that wanted to come out. "But then it happened. I lost my parents, and I was completely alone. So the worst thing that could happen *happened.* And I survived. See what I mean?"

"No, that's not the way of it though, darling. Because yes, you lost your mum and dad, but you're not alone, Carys." He kissed the top of her head. "You're never going to be alone. I promise you. Laura and Kiersten were with you. And now you have Cadell. And better than that fire-breathing numpty, you have me, don't you?"

She wanted to kiss him, but she needed to make a point. "What happens if we don't stop the Morrígan?"

"Then this world—our world—discovers that magic is real, and an ancient goddess of war creates a cult of neo-pagan acolytes to do her bidding, only instead of spears and swords, this generation has bombs and drones."

Carys took a deep breath and let it out slowly. "Okay, that sounds like a really bad outcome, and I don't feel better."

"I'm not a fan of this coping mechanism." Duncan reached down, grabbed her knee, and hiked her leg over his thigh. "Know what coping mechanism I do approve of?"

She put her arm around his neck. "What's that?"

"Making you come so hard that you pass out for around eight hours."

"That sounds good." Carys scooted up and kissed him. "Let's try that one."

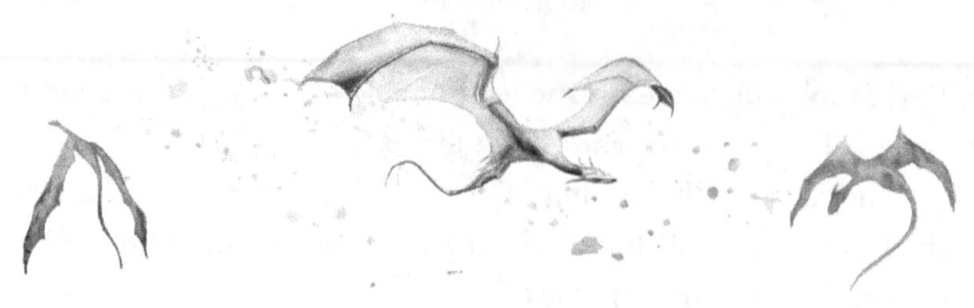

CHAPTER FOUR

"You're looking very *refreshed* this morning despite the possible coming of a mythological catastrophe." Laura sipped a large mug of coffee in the hotel restaurant.

The meal that morning was a full English breakfast with eggs, roasted tomatoes, baked beans, black pudding, and fried mushrooms. Carys had eaten the lot.

Laura pushed the black pudding to the side and raised her eyebrows. "Did you get a quick massage at the spa? Maybe a… treatment of some kind?" She lifted her coffee mug for another sip.

Carys smiled innocently. "Sheet mask."

Laura nearly snorted her coffee. "Wow." She tried to cover her smile. "Those brightening serums are really upping their game."

"They're amazing." Carys felt her cheeks flame. "Sometimes I use two or three of them."

"Really?" Laura's eyebrows went up. "On the same night?"

"I mean, if one sheet mask is good, two is better, right?"

Laura bit her lip. "Hey, if that's what is keeping you fresh, I'll try not to be jealous."

"Why be jealous?" Carys reached for a piece of toast. "You could always try a... sheet mask of your own."

Laura pursed her lips. "You know, I've been a little busy for sheet masks lately."

"That's probably not healthy."

"Some of us don't have multiple sheet masks vying for our attention."

Carys shrugged. "I don't know. I feel like if you looked around, you might find one closer than you think."

Laura narrowed her eyes. "Carys?"

"Yes?"

"Shut up."

It wasn't lost on Carys that Laura and Cadell had both been keeping their distance. One might even say they were avoiding each other.

A difficult feat when they'd been thrown together on a fantastical quest to stop a rogue goddess let loose in the Brightlands.

"Changing the subject from sheet masks—"

"You're the one who brought them up."

Laura shook her head and laughed. "I called Kiersten and my brother again."

"Anything getting weird in Baywood?"

"So far they haven't noticed any changes in the gates in Baywood," Laura said. "My brother has been across the gate, and while the old gods in Wykanush have always been more present than the ones here, the Shadowkin in the village seem to feel like things are basically the same. And Kiersten says she hasn't noticed anything off in town." Laura lifted a finger. "Check that. Old Mr. Harris at the bookstore said he saw Bigfoot fishing on Moore's Pier, but that's the third time he's seen that this year."

"I think he needs new glasses," Carys whispered.

"The man is eighty-three. I'm taking any Bigfoot sighting from him with a grain of salt."

Carys thought about the old proprietor of Redwood Pages, the lone bookstore in Baywood that didn't only sell textbooks for the college. The younger Mr. Harris—a spritely sixty-two—had taken over the day-to-day running of the bookshop, but Old Mr. Harris still lived next door.

"Okay, if we ignore Bigfoot sightings from old men with delightful imaginations," Carys said, "I'd argue that the rest all sounds normal. The gates in California are all more porous than the ones here. All in all, it's probably a healthier system to have a bit more..."

Laura wrinkled her nose. "Permeability?"

"Yeah, maybe."

"So what are you thinking?"

Carys sat back and took a deep breath. "I don't know. Think about what Dr. Beck said yesterday. She thinks Briton needs go-betweens like North America has. What if the high fae in Briton loosened their grip on the gates a little bit? It might make things... I don't know, more balanced maybe."

"With Dru taking over the throne, if there was a time for change, it's probably now, but I still think it's debatable." Laura lowered her voice as a group of tourists entered the dining room. "Think about it, Carys. Northern California has a lot of woods and a very small population."

"Good point. Trolls randomly popping out from under London bridges is probably not going to lead to peace between dimensions."

Laura nodded. "And let's be honest, I don't think balance and harmony are the Morrígan's end goals with" —she waved her hands around— "all this."

"You're probably right." She felt Cadell approaching. His energy was a heat signature on the dark, cool ground floor of the hotel.

"I think stopping the Morrígan has to be the goal." Laura glanced at the door. "Hopefully Naida has some success translating those documents that Dr. Beck gave you."

Cadell sat down a few moments later, a steaming coffee cup in his hand. "Good morning. Nêrys, you look well rested. I'm glad the cross human didn't keep you awake all night having sex."

This time Laura did snort coffee through her nose.

"My apologies." Cadell handed Laura a napkin. "Was my statement too direct?"

Carys had gotten used to Cadell having zero boundaries and many opinions. "It's fine, Cadell."

"What were you two talking about when I came in? Your expressions were serious."

Laura wiped her face and crumpled the napkin in her fist, barely holding back laughter. "Skin-care routines. Sheet masks actually."

Cadell frowned. "And this is a subject for serious debate?"

"Dragon, you have no idea."

THEY WAITED in front of the hotel after breakfast, and Laura was tapping her foot as she stared at Duncan, who was scrolling through the mobile phone he'd picked up in London two days before.

"So you're telling me you can just call someone and have a van delivered?" Laura asked.

Duncan glanced up. "What part of disgustingly rich did you not understand?"

"To be fair," Carys said, "I'm pretty sure rental car services will deliver minivans to your hotel in the States too."

Laura raised an eyebrow. "You think he rented one?"

"Of course he did." She turned to Duncan. "You rented a van, right?"

He frowned. "Why would I do that? I don't know how long we're going to need it, and the rental vans all had too many steel components." He lifted his chin when he spotted something over her shoulder. "See? This is preferable."

Carys followed Duncan with her eyes as he strode toward a sleek grey Mercedes van that slid to the curb in front of the hotel.

A driver hopped out. "Mr. Murray?"

"You've found him."

Gone was the blacksmith, the smooth-talking laird sliding into place as the driver opened the side door and explained the features of the luxury vehicle.

Laura sidled up to her. "It's very convenient, you having a rich boyfriend."

"Laura—"

"Lachlan is charming, and admittedly he has a castle and stuff on the other side, but Duncan has a castle *here* and he probably just bought this Mercedes with cash."

"That is so much money," Carys whispered.

"Just saying" —she slapped Carys's shoulder— "if we're going to save the world from an immortal war goddess, it's good to have a bankroll."

"...real wood trim, as you requested," the driver was saying. "All leather seats and very little exposed metal."

"Thank you, Derek." Duncan held his hand out. "Is your card in the glove compartment?"

"It is."

"I'll give you a call if I have any other questions."

The driver dropped the keys in Duncan's palm and nodded. "Enjoy, Mr. Murray."

"Thank you." Duncan turned to Laura and Carys. "Your chariot, my ladies."

Carys picked up her duffel bag and stepped forward. "Duncan, this is a *lot*."

"Yes, but Naida should be able to travel in this one, and it's big enough for the wolf and the dragon." He spun and looked at Laura. "Any arguments from you?"

"Nope. Do you know how to drive it?"

He nodded. "I do. Had to get a commercial license a few years ago. It comes in handy at the smithy."

Laura shrugged. "Sounds good to me." She threw her backpack through the open van door. "I'll go grab Naida and Godrik. She was taking a bath before I came downstairs, and Godrik…" Laura sighed. "He's probably hunting deer in the park."

Laura left Carys and Duncan on the curb. Carys was staring at the van while Duncan examined it.

"Is that real walnut burl?" Carys stared at the fold-down tables next to each leather armchair.

"Probably?" He tossed his satchel into the back. "I told them no metal. So it's leather and wood on the interior. There is a small kitchen in back with aluminum fixtures. I'll have someone from the hotel run out to the market and grab some food before we go."

"Always with the feeding me," Carys murmured.

"Is this our transportation?" Cadell's voice boomed from behind Carys. He braced his hands on his hips and glared at the van. "There does not appear to be an excess of iron."

"So glad to meet your approval," Duncan muttered.

"Naida was up late translating the manuscript," Cadell said. "I believe she has finished, but she will need rest and a place to gain her strength back. Is there a wild forest nearby?"

"There's a forest about ten miles from here," Duncan said. "We're ready to leave when she is."

Cadell climbed into the van and—to Carys's astonishment—the dragon's large human form actually fit.

"We need one of these in California," he said.

"If you want one of these in California," Carys said, "then you better start looking for a job."

THE ROAD to Bernwood Forest wound through the city, passing parks and quiet neighborhoods, following the main road until it didn't. Carys watched from the passenger seat beside Duncan as the road narrowed, turning from four lanes to two lanes to one.

Civilization fell away, and the countryside emerged. Houses grew smaller and the trees loomed larger until finally all signs of urban life were left behind and the quiet English countryside surrounded them.

Rolling fields of verdant green and high hedgerows damp with morning mist. The lushness of England surrounded her. Barley fields nodded, and small orchards waved their leaves in the breeze.

Duncan pulled the van into an empty parking lot far off the main road, and every creature in the vehicle, magical and mortal, heaved a unanimous sigh of relief.

Godrik opened the van door, and Cadell bolted out.

Moments later, Naida was outside, kicking off her shoes and running for the trees. She didn't even look back before she disappeared into the forest.

Laura, Duncan, and Carys left the vehicle and walked over to the sunny spot where Cadell was basking in the light and Godrik was taking deep breaths of fresh country air.

He glanced back at Duncan with a slightly abashed expression.

"The van is comfortable," the wolf said. "Far more comfortable than most vehicles here. Thank you for procuring it and driving us to the woods."

Laura squinted as she looked into the forest. "Does anyone see Naida?"

Godrik walked to her side. "Do not fear. The fae woman must be with the trees after so much time in town." He glanced at Duncan. "I'm sure she means no offense."

"I'm not offended." Duncan locked the car and started walking toward the trees. "I know how hard it is for her to be on this side."

Godrik handed Carys an envelope as the party headed toward the forest. "She was working on the translation last night. I escorted her to the park so she could concentrate away from the distracting human environment."

Cadell whipped his head around to look at Godrik. "Did you try to change?"

Godrik smirked a little. "Perceptive." He looked back at Carys and Duncan. "I tried. I wasn't able to, but I did feel *something*. The dragon's thought is not without merit. If the Morrígan's magic continues to grow, there may come a time when shifters on this side of the gates are able to take their true form."

Laura grimaced. "Well, that would be exciting."

Carys walked across a grassy berm and paused next to a spiky blackthorn hedge where pale purplish-green berries hung from the branches. Honeybees buzzed around the leaves, and butterflies flitted along the top of the hedge.

No, not butterflies.

Or yes, butterflies, but... more.

It was just a flash, but Carys spotted a flutter of long wings as a purple-headed sprite danced from inside the hedge, popped its head out, then zipped away, disappearing into the shadow of the trees.

"Sprites in the Brightlands," she whispered.

If sprites were on this side now, what else was coming through?

Laura walked over, copying Naida and removing her shoes when she reached the grass. She dug her feet into the earth and crouched down, putting her hand in the grass. "The ground here feels really alive. I think there's a gate nearby."

"I saw a sprite," Carys said.

Laura looked up. "Really?"

She pointed at the hedge and nodded. "With the butterflies."

There were more butterflies now, masses of them, dipping and dancing in the sunlight as Naida walked out from between the trees.

"There is." Naida paused and leaned against a birch tree. Her color was the best it had been in days. "Sprites and nymphs in a nearby spring. The gate is small, but it's very alive. Do you want to go through?"

Godrik, Cadell, and Duncan walked over when they saw Naida return.

"Elf, you look recovered," Godrik said.

"Thanks—I found some mushrooms." Naida smiled. "They are like medicine for my kind."

Cadell stared into the trees. "There is a gate in this place."

"Yes, we're on the light side of the Great Bern Wood," Naida said. "I was just telling Carys and Laura that there is a fae gate nearby. We could go through it if you want. It's very well-traveled."

Walking through fae gates was never Carys's favorite thing. It was as if the fae portals knew she wasn't truly a creature of either world. They always tried to grab her and hold on even when she was with Cadell.

Duncan was watching her. "It's up to you, Professor."

"Maybe we should," Carys said. "Naida, I'm sure you'd feel better."

"It's not about me," Naida said. "But things might be happening on that side of the gate too. We don't know if the Morrígan's power might be felt in both the shadow and the light.

"It might be advantageous to go even if it was only for a few hours," Cadell said. "We could send a message to your uncle and to King Harold, Nêrys. Let them know what is going on this side of the gates."

"It's the middle of the night there," Duncan said, "but Cadell, you can still speak to any dragon who might be around, right?"

Dragons had a kind of mental communication that stretched across large distances. While Cadell could speak to Carys in his mind, he could also call out to any of his clan who were within range.

"I can," Cadell said. "And it would be wise to let Mared and Demelza know what we think the Morrígan might be plotting."

"Fine." Carys nodded. "We'll go."

Without another word, Naida turned and started walking farther into the forest, not looking back once as the trees grew thicker.

Carys tucked the envelope that Godrik had given her into her pocket and followed Godrik, Laura, and Cadell. A moment later, Duncan took her hand in his.

"Did you leave your phone back in the van?"

He nodded. "I did."

"Okay, good."

He squeezed her fingers. "Are you nervous?"

"I'm nervous at every gate," she said. "They always feel... sticky."

"Sticky?"

She nodded. "Like they're trying to grab me and keep me."

"Oh, but I can't blame them for that, lass." His brogue grew thicker. "You're a tasty morsel."

She smiled. "Are you trying to distract me?" She could feel the gate nearby. The trees grew dense, and the light above them dimmed as the sky disappeared.

"I am—is it working?" Duncan pulled her closer.

The first branch reached out for her ankle and slapped it.

Carys sucked in a breath. "Uh-huh."

"You're lying."

When Carys looked down, the moss was up to her ankles, and a whooshing blue light darted between her legs.

"Keep walking," Duncan whispered. "Keep your eyes on Naida."

Between Godrik's and Cadell's massive shoulders, Carys could see the small fae woman tripping along the path, clearly delighted to be heading back to her native realm. Unlike the vines and branches that reached out to clutch and grab at Carys's ankles, the thick vege-tation seemed to bend toward the tiny fae as if waving and welcoming her home.

"I have you." Duncan locked her arm with his. "I can feel them."

Duncan might have felt them, but Carys could hear them now, the whispering voices, the childish laughter, the high-pitched squeals that sounded somewhere between an excited baby and a rare bird.

They walked the narrow pathway between two oaks, and as soon as they passed through, a shower of butterflies burst from the trees, whirling around them with bright purple-and-orange splendor, and between the fluttering creatures, the wisps were everywhere, darting here and there, cascading through the canopy and dancing in the dim, slanted light.

The sky grew darker, and the wisps glowed brighter.

The shrieks of laughter pierced her ears.

She clung to Duncan's hand as if he was her lifeline, her eyes fixed on Naida even when ominous shadows loomed in her peripheral vision and she heard the flap of bird wings behind her.

Keep going. Keep walking. Don't follow the wisps, Carys. They want to lead you away.

The last of the light fell away, and the darkness in the woods wrapped around them like a blanket. The air took on the bite of nighttime cold, and the wisps flew back to the safety of the gate, falling into the shadows as Naida led them through the tunnel of trees and into a meadow lit with the blue-green glow of luminous mushroom caps.

Carys took a deep breath, and the damp mist of the Shadowlands entered her lungs.

They were back.

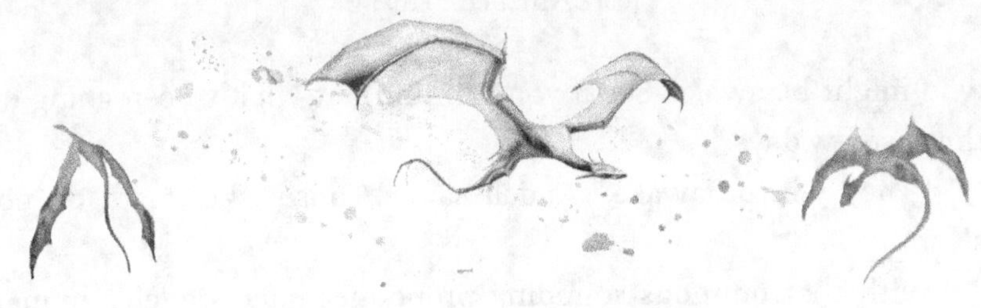

CHAPTER FIVE

The party walked through the meadow and onto a forest path that Naida chose, weaving between the trees and heading up a small hill where white flowers nodded in the evening breeze.

"We'll head to the human road," Naida said. "This wood is small in the Brightlands, but it stretches across a massive territory here."

The trees around Carys were twisted and ancient. Oaks reached to the sky, spreading their leafy branches and blocking out the sky.

The path was narrow and the forest dense, but long grasses grew beneath the trees, and luminous mushroom caps lit the way.

Glowing sprites jumped up from the grass as they passed, whizzing by Carys's head and distracting her from the crawling sensation that lingered on her skin.

As soon as they reached a part of the forest with open sky, Cadell looked back at Carys.

"Go," she said before he could ask.

Cadell looked silently at Duncan.

"I have her, lizard. Go and shake off your human skin for a bit."

"I'll be fine," Carys said. "Stretch your wings and look for anyone who might be awake. See if you can find out what's been going on the past few days."

"They will be awake," Cadell said. "Those who guard do not sleep."

With that ominous-sounding pronouncement, Cadell's human body shimmered into a gold shower and his true form emerged. He spread his wings and took to the sky.

Carys sucked in a quick breath at the lightness that filled her chest.

Duncan squeezed her hand. "You doing all right?"

Carys nodded. "I'm good."

He leaned over and kissed her temple. "You want to go with him, don't you?"

"Yes." She didn't even try to deny it.

Duncan angled his head and looked at her. "So go. Call him back. Go fly with your dragon for a bit."

It was tempting. So very tempting. She looked down at her thin cotton shirt and laughed a little bit. "When I walked through that gate, I was dressed for summer in England. Do you know how cold I'd be if he was carrying me?"

"Fair point." Duncan smiled. "You know, they say layering is the key when you're a supernatural dragon lady."

"Shut up."

That only made him laugh.

They moved on, up the path out of the trees. Naida was practically skipping.

They had reached a large berm of land sticking out of the ground. By the time they climbed it, Carys could see it was a raised walkway built up by rock and soil with a path along the top that was wide enough for a wagon and a team of horses.

"This is a high road," Godrik said. "The Anglian kings built them centuries ago to connect the towns and keep humans out of the forests."

Naida turned and winked at Carys. "Keep those poor humans away from the dangerous fae."

"You may mock me, elf, but we just passed through the Great Bern Wood. There's a reason children in the Shadowlands are warned away from it."

From the top of the high road, Carys could look out and see a nearly endless sea of dark treetops. Mile after mile after mile of nothing but woods and low fog, illuminated sporadically by colorful dancing lights that jumped from tree to tree.

Naida said, "There is a village up the road a little bit. There will be an inn to rest if you want, or we could find something to eat."

"How long are we staying?" Carys was starting to wonder if all this had been a ploy by Naida to get home. She pulled out the envelope Godrik had given her. "If we're just going to wait for Cadell to return with news, I—"

"What is that?" Laura squinted at something in the distance.

Carys turned and looked ahead. There was a soft white glow illuminating the road in front of them, almost like a pair of headlights coming through fog. But she'd never seen anything in the Shadowlands that used headlights.

A few moments later, a silver-white unicorn emerged from the low-lying clouds, slowing its trot to a walk as it approached Naida. The creature lowered its horn a moment before it transformed into a shower of sparkling silver rain.

Seconds later, a tall woman with silver hair and a glowing blue sigil on her forehead appeared from the shimmering light. "You've returned." The unicorn's round face lit up when she looked at Naida. "My lady, your king has been searching for you."

Seconds later, a man on a horse followed the unicorn, dismounting and throwing back his hood to reveal a rich mane of reddish-brown hair. He smiled. "Hello, Carys."

Carys blinked at him, looked at Duncan, then back at her ex-boyfriend. "Lachlan? What are you doing here?"

"KING ROBB HAS SENT me to Temris." Lachlan walked beside his mount as they continued along the highway. "I've been in the fae court ever since you left."

Lachlan and the unicorn were leading them toward a fae stronghold controlled by King Diarmuid that could act as a magical portal to Temris, the fae capital in Éire. It was intradimensional travel and —according to Naida—much less stressful than gates between worlds.

"So you're finished in Anglia?" Carys was walking hand in hand with Duncan while Lachlan walked on her right, leading his horse behind them.

"For now," Lachlan said. "My younger brother appears to be the heir apparent—and I don't envy him the position. It leaves me free to travel to different courts as needed."

"I feel like you'd really excel in that," Carys said.

"I appreciate your confidence." Lachlan smiled as he looked at her. "It's important work. With the new king in place, my father wants to make sure that Alba and the high fae court have better relations going forward."

"I bet the high fae in Temris *love* you," Duncan muttered.

Lachlan laughed, seemingly unconcerned with his Brightkin's mood. "They appreciate a song, so I'm in good company there. And I can put some of my... What did you call it once, Carys? At the pub in Baywood?"

"Uh... charm?" Carys flashed back to one of the numerous nights in California when Lachlan held an entire pub in the palm of his hand with one of his stories or songs. "People skills?"

Lachlan smiled. "That's the one. I can put my people skills to good use in the service of my country."

Duncan dropped Carys's hand and stepped in front of Lachlan.

The entire party stopped walking, and tension sparked in the air around her. Lachlan's horse stamped a foot, and Naida and the unicorn, who had been chatting with vigor, fell silent.

Duncan stared at Lachlan. "You're singing songs for the people who killed Seren."

The bright expression fell from Lachlan's face, and a muscle in his jaw twitched. "*Regan* killed Seren. In concert with her bastard of a father, Cian, whom Dru killed in the Battle of Saris Plain. Did you already forget?"

"And did Dru kill all of Cian's allies in the court?" Duncan asked.

"Hey, Murray brothers." Laura tried to keep her voice light. "Let's keep walking."

It was like watching two stags face off in a forest. Their attention was locked on each other, and neither one was going to back down.

Lachlan's eyes flashed. "He's killed more than one, yes."

"So he's rooted out that arrogant streak they have, right?" Duncan sneered. "All the superiority that makes the high fae think they should be the ones ruling everything here."

Naida stepped toward them. "Duncan, if this is about—"

"I'm not blind to reality." Lachlan spoke over Naida. "There is still prejudice. There are still those who think that Cian was right, but with time—"

"We have a saying in the Brightlands." Duncan lifted his chin. "A leopard doesn't change his spots."

Lachlan stepped forward. "So no redemption, hmm? No reform? An enemy is always going to be an enemy?" Lachlan's accent grew thicker. "So how do we move forward, Duncan?"

Carys wasn't going to get between them, but she tried to calm them down. "Lachlan. Duncan. You're brothers, and you both want—"

"Maybe you demand accountability from the people who killed your wife! Who kidnapped innocent children. Who tried to start a bloody war less than a month ago!" Duncan shouted. "Have some bloody principles, Lachlan."

Laura spoke up. "Hey, Duncan, no one is excusing that, but—"

"Cian was their leader." Duncan's eyes never left his brother's. "The high fae lords could have rebelled against him, but they didn't really want to, did they?" Duncan's face was red. "Because deep down, they agree with him. You know it. I know it. And every human in this place—"

"Every human in this place has to live with them!" Lachlan shouted. "They control our future, Duncan. Without them, not a human child exists in Alba. Without them, the gates are locked tight. My people don't have the luxury of skipping back to the Brightlands to avoid the fae. We have to live with them." Lachlan glanced at Naida. "We all have to live with each other here. The magic and the mundane. Albans and Éirans. What do your high-minded principles say about compromising for the good of—"

"Enough." Godrik's voice was a low roll of thunder. "Both of you, be quiet. This is a stupid argument." He stepped between the two brothers and looked at Lachlan. "It seems frivolous to sing and dance in a fae court in order to make friends, but I am not a diplomat, and that's what diplomats do." He turned to Duncan. "Dancing and singing are better than war. If it takes dancing with an enemy to keep my people from dying, I'll put on a party dress and spin in circles."

Laura whispered, "Actually, I'd really like to see that, Godrik."

He looked over his shoulder and winked. "I look great in blue."

Naida left the unicorn's side and walked toward them. "It seems that King Diarmuid summoning me has led to conflict, and I don't want to bring that into your party," she said. "There is no reason for all of us to go to Temris when Dru is asking for me. Why don't all of you stay here and—"

"No, he's asking for all of you." Lachlan looked at Carys. "He's particularly asking for Carys."

Duncan walked back to her and took her hand. "Why?"

"I don't know." Lachlan shrugged. "Perhaps it's because she led an old god into the Brightlands and now the Morrígan is attacking the fae gates and trying to break them open from the other side."

Carys's stomach dropped.

Nêrys? Cadell spoke into her mind. *I feel you. What is wrong?*

The knot in her stomach loosened as soon as she heard Cadell's voice. *Dru—King Diarmuid—wants to see me in Temris. He wants to see all of us.*

Laura said, "She's talking to Cadell. She gets that look on her face when they're talking."

I'm coming now. I'll fill you in on what the others told me when I return.

"Cadell is coming back." Carys refocused on the group. "How far are we from the fort?"

The unicorn said, "Maybe forty minutes?"

Cadell, forty minutes to the gate. She had a sudden picture in her mind. *Wait. Have you been to Temris before?*

Yes. I know it.

Then don't come here.

Why not?

Because I want you to make an entrance.

THE GATE through the fae fort was nothing at all like the gates the dark fae opened to the Brightlands. After descending into an immaculate earthen structure, they entered a passage lit by blue fae torches and lined with intricately carved and dressed stone. Painted columns held up the ceiling, and the portal itself felt like walking through a soft, shimmering curtain.

When Carys reached the other side, she was greeted by the scent of rosemary and the sound of trickling water in the distance. Naida and the unicorn led the way up from the earth and into the open air through another passage carved with even more intricate stonework.

Night was turning to day, and though the Shadowlands did not see the sun, a pearlescent dawn touched the edges of the horizon as they emerged from the earth. The light was a wash of pink in a deep blue sky.

Carys looked around her and knew this portal to the fae capital was intended to make a statement.

"Wow," Laura said. "Just... wow."

The unicorn turned and faced them. "Welcome to Temris, guests of High King Diarmuid mac Lir, ruler of the aes sídhe, son of Aíne the Wise."

It was a greeting designed to impress, and it worked.

They were on a rise overlooking a glittering city, and rolling green hills surrounded them. Narrow spires pierced the sky, and the city, built from stone and wood, was trimmed in gold and silver that made buildings and towers shine in the low light.

There was a spring flowing down from the hill, channeled via a stone canal that carried springwater into the city center.

Laura stepped closer. "So like... Tolkien's books—"

"Not that far off." Carys shook her head. "I'm starting to wonder if he'd been here."

Lachlan asked, "Are you talking about the English professor?"

Carys turned to him. "Maybe?"

"Frequent visitor." Lachlan took a deep breath. "Obsessed with languages, apparently. Gods, the air is so much better here."

It was true. The air around them was sweet in a way that Carys had never smelled in her life. A delicate perfume wafted on the breeze, but nothing about the scent was false or chemical. It was herbaceous and refreshing.

The unicorn shifted to her true form and lifted her head in a high whinny, a call that was answered by a bright, echoing sound in the distance. Naida started walking after their escort, and Carys noticed that the ellyllon hadn't said a word from the moment they stepped into the fae fort in Anglia.

Carys loosened her hand from Duncan's and walked over to Naida.

"Sut wyt ti?" she asked in a soft voice.

The sound of Carys's very rudimentary Welsh brought a fleeting smile to Naida's face. "How am I?" She shrugged one shoulder. "I'm wishing I was home. But I can't hide from him there either."

"Yeah, I remember." Naida had told her how Dru—when he was still *Prince* Diarmuid—had raised a barrow in the valley in Cymru where Naida came from and parked himself for a decade until she agreed to let him court her. "Do you love him?"

"Yes," Naida said simply. "Or maybe no. I love who he was. I don't know who he is now."

"You think he's changed that much?"

"He has always hated the court, and now he is king of it. And a fae king does not die." She glanced at Carys. "Especially one who is also the son of a god."

"He could give up the crown someday."

Naida nodded. "He could."

"Or you could join him," she said softly.

Naida looked at Carys with a smile. "Your men were both right, and they were both wrong. Lachlan is not wrong to try to negotiate and make peace with the high fae. That has been the policy of my own people for as long as I can remember."

The ellyllon of Cymru were what the high fae considered "wild fae." They didn't recognize a king or a queen, neither human nor magical. They were connected to the earth and rarely left the place where they were born. Naida was most definitely an exception among her people.

"That said, Duncan was right too. They do think they're better than everyone else," Naida said. "They consider me inferior, and they would never accept me as a consort to their king. The moment Dru accepted that crown, I knew any hope of a future with him was gone."

The ellyllon were simple fae and decidedly nonpolitical. Shorter than the tall children of the Tuatha Dé Danann, they usually had curly hair and darker skin. Carys hadn't ever been to Temris, but if the high fae she'd seen in Anglia were any indication, Naida would not blend in.

"So stick with me." Carys bumped her shoulder against Naida's. "You're our friend, and we're not going to let a jumped-up bartender from Scone push you around."

Naida threw her head back and laughed. It was far better than the morose expression she was wearing before, so Carys didn't care if both Lachlan and their unicorn escort looked at Naida with slight disapproval.

Moments after they entered the outskirts of the city, the day was dawning and the citizens of Temris began to wake.

It was far more diverse than Carys had anticipated from her previous interactions with the high fae of Briton. There were short, dwarflike fae and stocky creatures that looked like trolls. There were tiny sprites flying around and putting out the streetlamps still burning from their night watch.

And yes, there were tall, beautiful, otherworldly creatures who looked like supermodels from a fantasy convention. There was very little metal other than hints of gold or silver. Carys saw no weapons and nothing that looked like it was smuggled from the Brightlands.

"I'm guessing no grey market for Brightlands stuff around here," Laura said.

Duncan let out a low grumble. "That means no coffee."

"But we're not staying long," Carys said. "Remember? We'll survive without coffee for a few hours."

"At least our bodies think it's nighttime," Laura said.

"Speak for yourself." Duncan pointed at the sky. "My brain may know it's night in England, but my eyes say it's dawn. I know which one my stomach is going to listen to."

As if on cue, Carys's stomach rumbled.

A second later, Duncan was shoving a bag of trail mix into her hands. "Eat."

Carys smiled at him and lifted on her toes to kiss his cheek. "I love you."

Duncan's cheeks grew ruddy, and Carys tried not to notice when Lachlan lost a step on the path.

Nêrys.

"Cadell is here." She smiled. "Perfect timing."

No fire, she said to him in her mind, *but you can yell a little bit. Circle the city. Make a show.*

Carys stuffed the trail mix in her pocket and jogged up to Naida. "Cadell is here."

The ellyllon looked confused. "Okay."

"Hey." She took Naida's hand. "Duncan told me something when I first came here that I think you need to remember."

"What's that?"

Carys looked up when the first thunderous roar sounded from behind a grey bank of clouds. "In the Shadowlands, nobody messes with Cymru."

Cadell burst through the clouds, his emerald-green wings spread wide as he soared into the valley of Temris. He banked to the right and followed the hills surrounding the city before he let out another roar, sending residents running back to their houses as they gasped and cried out.

"Remember that." Carys squeezed Naida's hand. "No one messes with Cymru or her people."

Naida smiled. "Because we have dragons?"

"That's right." Carys nodded. "Because we have fucking dragons."

CHAPTER SIX

Diarmuid mac Lir, high king of the fae, son of the sea god and Queen Aíne the Wise, sat on a throne layered in gold and gemstones. "Carys Morgan, I extend my welcome to Temris, seat of the Tuatha Dé Danann and stronghold of the children of Danu."

They were in a throne room filled with light. Whatever fae magic powered this castle, it looked like midday sun shining through milky alabaster windows that stretched from the floor to the ceiling.

"You arrive here at my request," Dru continued, "and are under my protection for as long as you reside in this place."

In a nod to his sea-god father, Dru wore a crown of twisted blood-red coral set with pearls and threaded with silver. The blue sigils on his face were the same ones that Carys had seen when she first crossed into the Shadowlands, when she was a wandering mythology professor and Dru was a strange bartender at the Four Crowns Pub.

"King Diarmuid," Carys said, "we have accepted your invitation." She couldn't say thank you, but she was aching to be polite. "Your city... is very beautiful."

"Yes, and your dragon is very loud." Dru smirked. "Cadell." He offered a short nod. "Good to see you."

"Fae." Cadell acknowledged Dru and nothing else. He stood behind Carys and Naida like a stoic pillar, guarding their backs.

Perfect, Carys said in her mind. *I want to know what he's up to. We're not friends here.*

I never considered this fae a friend.

Okay, well... good.

Lachlan, Duncan, Laura, and Godrik were all standing along the side of the throne room with the courtiers of Temris. Most of the curious onlookers were fae, but there was a good mix of unicorns in the mix and a fair number of humans wearing green sashes. Carys guessed they were diplomats from Éire.

There were no dragons other than Cadell. And no wolves save for Godrik.

"And Naida." Dru's voice softened. "It has been too long since a healer of your skill has visited my court." He looked at the silent and watchful fae. "All of you, bow to the healer Naida of Gwenlais, for she saved the life of your king."

Oh shit.

After a second of hesitation that had the fae king leaning forward on his throne, the entirety of the high fae court bent and took a knee, bowing their heads toward Naida as she stood before Dru's throne.

This is appropriate. Cadell was quick to speak to her mind. *He is making a statement. This makes me like him slightly better.*

Naida is going to hate the attention.

This is only partially about her.

"Our gratitude, Naida of Gwenlais, for your service to the throne," Dru said in an eerie voice. "The court of Temris honors you."

Naida spoke cautiously. Her eyes were narrowed on Dru. "I am pleased to see the king has healed so well. No doubt your decisive victory over your brother has added to your health."

She is more skilled in politics than she realizes, Cadell said.

She's not wrong though.

Dru had never looked more powerful. Though he'd always held a mysterious aura, even in the Brightlands, now the magic fairly oozed from his pores. While Carys could feel power among the watching court, it was dwarfed by the wild strength of the sea god's son.

Cian's magic had been refined and controlled. Dru's felt like he was barely keeping his in check. Even the stones beneath her feet held a decided hum.

Fae magic was elemental in nature, which was why they detested most metal and hated forged iron in particular. Something about it blocked their power. The castle around them was built of stone and wood. Vines grew around the pillars that held up the gallery and crawled across the vaulted ceiling.

"Rise and leave us, courtiers of Temris. I have dealings with this dragon lord and this healer." Dru waved a hand. "I do not need your counsel today."

An older fae with long silver hair stepped forward. "My lord, the Kingsguard—"

"Is not needed." Dru was quick to answer. "Not even when a dragon has come to call." He looked at Carys and smirked. "I know this wyrm of old, Rowan Dún Nath."

The old fae bowed. "My king." He backed out of the gallery, following the other whispering fae courtiers and humans.

Carys looked at Duncan, who shook his head.

Not leaving. The message was clear.

"The rest of your party may stay if they like." Dru looked to his right, where the unicorn with silver hair was standing at attention. "Setare, tell the kitchens to ready a meal for my guests."

Duncan huffed. "We can't eat it, Dru."

"I think what my Brightkin means," Lachlan said, "is that your guests are representatives of foreign courts and must be cautious in an unfamiliar place, King Diarmuid."

The corner of the king's mouth turned up. "Drinks then. Some mead."

Cadell growled. "My nêrys will eat no food and drink no mead from the fae king's table."

Dru wasn't pleased. "You reject my hospitality, wyrm?"

"Decidedly yes."

Laura spoke up. "Okay, but hear me out…"

Cadell angled his head toward Laura but kept his eyes on Dru.

"People have to eat here, right?" Laura continued. "I mean, it's a city. You have to feed people." She looked at Lachlan. "How does that work? Is there some diplomatic protocol we don't know about? How do you eat and drink here without falling under a spell?"

"Setare, bring food for my table." Dru raised his voice. "And mead."

"Yes, my lord." The unicorn bowed and backed out of the room.

Dru heaved a sigh, then stood, took off his blood-red crown, and set it on the throne behind him before he walked down the steps. "The chefs are unicorns. The servers are unicorns. And I pay a mountain of gold and healing herbs to have them here." He walked up to Cadell and stared. "I don't trust the fae in this court either—not a single one of them—but I trust the unicorns." Dru looked at Naida directly. "So eat and drink. I offer it freely. You are under no obligation to me or any other in this city."

Lachlan stepped forward and spread his hands. "And that's all we needed." He smiled. "It's fine. We're fine."

Carys stuck her hand in her pocket and grabbed a handful of trail mix before she looked at Cadell. "You're still not going to let me eat anything, are you?"

"Absolutely not."

"The Morrígan is testing the gates, but we will keep them secure." Dru picked up a gold goblet and drank. "She's powerful, but so am I, and every fae in Briton has a vested interest in keeping our gates from breaking.”

They were sitting in a small dining chamber, and unicorns with bright silver sigils on their foreheads came and went silently, serving them giant platters of fruit and bread. Steaming vegetable soups simmered in tureens, and roasted platters of vegetables wafted delicious aromas into the air.

“So the high fae have enough self-interest to keep the Morrígan at bay?” Duncan asked.

“Obviously, we don’t want human technology leaking into the Shadowlands and damaging our refuge.” Dru continued talking with Duncan. “How are things on the other side?”

“Things aren’t chaos,” Duncan said. “Not yet. A little strange, but steady so far. The biggest story in England is that massive barrow she’s raised in Salisbury.”

Dru set down his goblet. His eyes were fixed on Naida even as he spoke to the others. “Do the humans suspect anything supernatural?”

“Not yet,” Godrik said. “A few of the superstitious are making noise, but they’ve trained themselves thoroughly to not believe in magic.” The wolf looked around the chamber with obvious discomfort. “Did Cian eat here?”

“No,” Dru said. “I destroyed most of the parts of the castle that Cian lived or ate in. This was my mother’s chamber. I will rebuild the rest within a year.”

Dru’s brother Cian had hunted the wolves of Ireland to extinction. It was a genocide that still scarred Anglian and Éiran relations.

Cadell spoke silently. *It is likely that Godrik is the first wolf in Éire in hundreds of years.*

That’s horrible.

That is Temris.

Laura looked up from her bowl of soup. “You can rebuild a castle in a year?”

“Only with magic.” Dru spread his hand on the stone table.

"When you build of the earth and not with bones of trees, the earth does not fight you." He was still staring at Naida. "You will not eat of my table, Naida Brightwater?"

Every eye turned to Naida, whose cheeks were slightly red.

"I am not hungry." Naida glanced at Laura, who was sitting on her right. "But please enjoy the food. If the unicorns have prepared it, I'm sure it is safe and wonderful."

"But you will not eat of it, though I know you are hungry." Dru's voice was sharp. "Am I so hated by you now?"

"Watch your tone." Godrik's voice held the menace of his wolf. "We are not your subjects."

Dru turned to Godrik and cocked his head. "Acknowledged, wolf."

"I hate no one." Naida picked at the tablecloth, keeping her voice soft. "You should know that better than anyone."

"Daughter of the Valleys," Dru whispered, "Singer of my song, will you not even look at me now?"

Naida finally looked up. "I can look at you, King Diarmuid."

Dru was silent for a long moment. He seemed to drink in Naida's attention like a parched man.

Carys reached for Duncan's hand under the table. He squeezed her fingers and knit them with his own.

Dru finally spoke. "And what am I to your eyes, Naida of Gwenlais, Brightwater of the Valleys?"

The room went so silent Carys heard nothing but the crackle of blue flames in the fireplace.

"Son of Aíne ," Naida said, "I... acknowledge your crown." Without another word, she stood from the table, set her linen napkin on the table, and walked out of the room.

Dru watched Naida leave with hooded, hungry eyes, then narrowed them when Godrik stood and followed the small fae woman out of the room.

"Dru," Carys said, "I don't want a favor, but I was wondering if I could ask for some advice without forming an obligation."

Dru looked away from the door where Naida had disappeared and shook his head as if waking from a dream. "About the Morrígan?"

"Yes."

The corner of his mouth turned up. "Why do you think I brought you here?"

Carys and the high fae king met privately after the meal while the rest of her friends waited in the library with Dru's private retinue of unicorns.

"How do you defeat a goddess?"

"Defeat one?" Dru sat across from her in a wingback chair, his head resting on the back of the chair and his legs stretched out before him. "You don't."

They were sitting in what looked like a woman's morning room. There was no art hanging on the walls, but the round chamber was decorated with enamel, inlaid gemstones, and rare metal, creating a floral pattern that grew from streaked green malachite, forming grass and ferns at the base of the wall to soaring tree branches that stretched nearly to the ceiling.

"You don't defeat a goddess?" Carys was perched in a chair where her feet almost didn't touch the ground. "Like, at all? Then what is the point of all this?"

Dru opened his mouth, closed it, and sighed. "You're accustomed to thinking of gods as something from legends and myths. But gods are not fictional characters. Except when they are."

Carys closed her eyes and rubbed her temple. "Why did I think I could get a helpful answer from you?"

"Gods are born when humans adore." He crossed his long legs at the ankles. "It's always a relationship."

"Gods exist because humans believe in them."

"Yes. And all gods are fictional, but that doesn't mean they're not also real."

Carys grasped the tail end of what she thought Dru was trying to say. "You can't kill a god because they exist as a result of human belief."

"As long as the Morrígan has a single acolyte, she lives," Dru said. "As long as the idea of her exists in a *story*, she survives. So you cannot kill a god. You can't *defeat* them."

"You and your brother are half gods. Demigods. You can be killed."

Dru pursed his lips. "Can we?"

"Isn't your brother dead?"

"No, he's simply not in the Shadowlands anymore."

A terrible thought jumped into Carys's mind. "Is he—"

"He's not in the Brightlands either." Dru smirked. "He's... else-where. There are places other than the mortal realm. There are worlds other than the two that you know."

"So..." Carys tried shifting to get comfortable, but it didn't work. "It's pointless? The Morrígan is just going to keep leaking magic into the Brightlands, and there's nothing we can do to stop her?"

Dru raised a finger. "I didn't say that." He pointed to Carys's side. "You have something from Naida. I can smell it on you."

"That's so creepy." Carys had nearly forgotten about the papers in her pocket.

"You say creepy, I say focused." Dru flicked his fingers. "Give it to me."

She pulled out the now-bent envelope. "I don't know if this will help. A professor at Oxford researched the oldest stories they had about the Morrígan. Doctor..." Wait. Did Dru know about Luna Beck? Should she not mention Luna to the fae king if she was in hiding?

"Are you referring to Luna Beck?" Dru reached out and took the envelope. "I know Luna."

"Of course you do."

"Luna is highly intelligent and an excellent researcher. She's also quite wise, which is not a given with my people. I'm sure if she offered you a boon in your quest, it will be useful."

"Do all the fae living in the Brightlands get together for bingo night or something?"

"Trivia weekend in Manchester." Dru's eyes skimmed the papers. "Every Beltane." He flipped the scans over and read Naida's translations. "Her Old Éiran is good, but not as good as mine. Still..." He set the papers on the table between them. "It's nothing you don't know already."

Carys's eyebrows went up. "What do you mean?"

"I assume that in your studies, you've read *The Cattle Raid of Cooley.*"

"*The Táin Bó Cúailnge?*"

"Yes." Dru rolled his eyes. "The great Irish hero Cú Chulainn—who was an absolute asshole, I want to add—single-handedly defends Ulster for months... until he loses, and two perfectly good bulls die in the end."

Carys opened her mouth, unsure of how to counter that stunningly abrupt yet not entirely incorrect summation of the greatest Irish epic poem ever written down.

"Uh... pretty sure there was a lot else that happened. Wait, you knew Cú Chulainn?"

"Trust me, *everyone* knew Cú Chulainn even if they didn't want to," Dru muttered. "This part of the poem does mention the Morrígan, but it's the part where she tries to seduce Cú Chulainn." Dru raised an eyebrow. "Did I miss something exciting? Has the goddess tried to seduce you?"

"Don't be ridiculous." Carys snorted.

But...

She flashed back to the image of a naked redhead lounging in a tree in Gorne Wood.

"Oh, the oak and the ash and the bonny ivy tree. They flourish at home in my own country... how I wish once again in the west, I could be..."

"She didn't proposition me," Carys said. "Exactly. But she was naked. Lounging in a tree, and it was impossible not to look at her. She was probably the most beautiful woman I've ever seen."

The corner of his mouth turned up. "She can be."

"We left," Carys said. "But she did try to get us to stay. You could tell she was trying to waste our time, make us linger in the woods..."

Lotus-eaters.

Sirens.

The irresistible firebird, lulling her to sleep in a comfortable hideaway.

"She did try to seduce us in a way."

Dru spread his hands. "It's not the same story, Carys Morgan, but it just might rhyme."

She sighed and swung her legs to the side, wishing she could get comfortable. "Again with the riddles."

"Not a riddle. Luna gave you a clue. She gave you a piece of a poem where the Morrígan is defeated. In a sense."

"Yeah, by a demigod." Carys pointed at Dru. "Like you. Cú Chulainn was a demigod, and I am not. Someone like you could defeat her."

He shrugged. "This is not my path."

"Are you saying it's mine?" She nearly laughed. "If the Morrígan was in the Shadowlands, I might stand a chance. Here, I have a *dragon*." She pointed at the door. "On the other side, I have nothing. I can shoot a bow half decently, but that's not going to stop a deity. I don't have magic there. I don't have..." She snatched the papers off the table. "I don't have *anything* there."

Dru tsked, a smile flirting around his mouth. "How shortsighted of you, Carys Morgan. You have many things in the Brightlands."

"Like what?"

The smile fell from his face. "You have two lovers who would do anything for you, cross a world to bring you a draft of water. Two parents who defied a goddess to bring you into the world. You are surrounded by love. Do you have any idea how powerful that is?"

Carys couldn't help but think of Naida. Dru had crossed into the Brightlands to prevent a war among the fae and only returned when his brother proved immeasurably corrupt. And yet all the time that he was living in the Brightlands, Naida had never crossed over.

She'd only crossed over once Dru had taken the throne.

"She loves you," Carys said softly. "She only came with us for a little while. She knows she could never stay."

"I never asked her to."

"What do you want from her?"

"She knows." He lifted his chin. "And she is the only one who needs to know."

Carys nodded, folded the papers in her hand, and stuffed them back in her pocket. "Th—" She caught herself. "I appreciate the meeting." She glanced at him, still stretched out in the chair, his eyes fixed on the wall behind her. "And it is good to see you, Dru."

"I miss my pub." He pouted. "Some days I am tempted to tear open the gates and let the flood of iron and wires and plastic pour into this place." His eyes gleamed. "It would slowly kill all the fae here until they were as dead as they are in the Brightlands."

Scary. That was obviously something he'd thought very clearly about.

Carys leaned on the chair. "Okay, so... you wouldn't do that."

Diarmuid mac Lir probably had the power for it if he wanted to, but he wouldn't do it.

Dru lifted an eyebrow. "Wouldn't I?"

"No, because that would hurt Naida."

He sneered. "Love is a weakness."

"No, it's not." She walked over and ruffled the long and lustrous hair of the high fae king. He was acting like a toddler, so maybe she should treat him like one. "Love isn't weakness. You just got finished telling me to use my two lovers—which... technically correct, but it doesn't reflect the current situation."

"They both love you."

"Not the point. You just got finished telling me that being surrounded by love made me strong."

"You have a dragon and a shaman as well. Use them."

The corner of her mouth inched up. "Not the wolf, Dru?"

"That wolf..." He narrowed his eyes. "Do you think if I—"

"Do not finish that thought." She started toward the door. "Leave the wolf alone. He's kind of my friend now. Kind of."

"Am I?"

She stopped and turned, leaving her hand on the door. "Do you want to be?"

Dru shrugged.

The corner of her mouth twitched. "Yes, Dru. I consider you a friend. Don't tell the dragon."

Dru smiled, and it softened the hard planes of his face. "I will hold the gates, Carys Morgan. Until you find a way to bring the Morrígan back to the Shadowlands, I will hold the gates from this side."

CHAPTER SEVEN

When Carys returned to the dining room, Duncan and Lachlan, Laura, Naida, and Godrik were all still there, but they'd been joined by a massive silent man standing in the corner.

He reminded Carys of the old fishermen who docked their boats in Baywood. He had on a pair of muddy boots, a knit sweater, and canvas cargo pants.

He didn't look fae. He didn't look like a wolf, though he was sized like one. And he wasn't talking to the others. He was just staring out a window.

So... normal human? What was he doing in Temris?

"Carys." Duncan walked over. "So the thing is—"

"Ey up," the man blurted as he turned to Carys. "I'm Wade."

Oh no. Not human. At least not a normal one. This man radiated power in the same way Duncan's friend Angus did. Cold and old and enigmatic.

"Hello, Wade." Carys looked at Duncan, then at Lachlan, who simply shrugged.

Wade moved from the window over to Carys, his massive arms crossed over his chest. "Don' like your accent." His face barely moved when he talked. "But I like his less." He angled his head toward Duncan.

Duncan muttered, "Fuck off." He looked at Wade. "Yer askin' me to carry ye somewhere and insulting me at the same time?"

Wade kept looking at Carys as if she was the one in charge. "Dru's people said you c'd give me a lift back in the Brightlands."

"A lift? I mean, we don't have a coracle, so we're just walking back and—"

"Nah, not with the wyrm," the man mumbled. "I mean, *in* the Brightlands, you know."

"You want to go through the gate with us?"

"Aye."

"To England?"

"Aye."

Carys shook her head. "Sorry, but I don't know you, and I recently made a very bad decision about taking someone through a gate who really shouldn't have been there to begin with. I'm still trying to clean up that mess, so—"

"Ah, be reet. I c'n go through the gates," he said. "Ask the little one over there. She knows me. Just need a lift to th' Great Ouse."

Carys blinked. "The great house?"

"No, th' Great Ouse." He huffed. "This is the problem with the accents."

Yes, because his was so easy to understand.

Lachlan stood and walked over. "I believe he's referring to the Great Ouse." He looked at Duncan. "The River. The Great Ouse River."

"Oh."

"Aye." Wade pointed at Lachlan. "See? Better accent."

Carys frowned. "They have the same accent—what are you talking about?"

Duncan coughed. "What?"

Lachlan's eyes went wide. "I beg your pardon, mo chridhe, but Duncan's and my—"

"Don't call her that," Duncan snapped.

"I apologize." Lachlan's cheeks went red. "It's a habit, and I—"

"It's a habit you're breaking today or it's your face I'll break," Duncan rumbled. "I'll not hear it again, Lachlan."

"Will you calm down?" He sighed. "Honestly, you've won the contest, all right?"

Carys cocked her head. "Excuse me? Contest?"

Lachlan spread his hands. "You've won her *heart*. Can you let me—"

"I'll not fucking let you do anything when you…"

Duncan and Lachlan descended into an unintelligible argument in Gaelic while Carys took a step back and closed her eyes, trying not to lose her temper.

Wade took a step closer, a frown set on his face. "So ya fucked both of 'em then?"

"What?"

The old man shrugged. "No shame in it, girl. They're fine-lookers. But fuckin' a Shadowkin and a Brightkin—"

"Okay. One, there is a lot of context you're missing with all this, and two, there was over a year between…" She shook her head. "I'm not explaining this to you. What do you even want?"

"Ya got an automobile, do ya?"

"A car?" She blinked. "Yes, we have a car. A van."

"And the little one there said ya came across from the Great Bern Wood. That's close to where I need t' go. Just up the road from Wappenham."

"I have no idea where that is."

"Just saving some miles on the old feet, girl." He nodded at Lachlan and Duncan, who were still shouting. "And you know the Shadowkin is coming with us."

Carys blinked. "What?"

"Oh aye. Heard the wolf and 'im talking about it. Settled business that." Wade's eyebrows went up. "Course maybe 'tisn't." He looked down at Carys. "Context and all that."

Carys decided Wade probably had the right idea after all. She crossed her arms over her chest and let Duncan and Lachlan bicker at each other while she and Wade struck a bargain.

"So you want to go to Wapa..."

"Wappenham. It's about forty minutes from the Bern Wood gate as the humans drive it."

Okay, so Wade was not human.

What was he?

She looked for Cadell, but the dragon was obviously back in beast form and she didn't want to bother him. "So you want a lift in our car?"

"Metal don't bother me, if that's what you're wondering. I c'n pay ya."

"In what?"

"Good old English money, girl." Wade opened his palm, revealing a handful of gold coins. "Of the old-fashioned variety."

Carys nodded. "I'm going to make an executive decision that you can come as long as Godrik and Naida say you're okay."

"Nowt. Like I said, they know me."

"Okay." She tried to catch Naida's eye, but she was deep in conversation with Godrik. "So what do you do in Wapping—"

"Wappenham."

"Right. That place."

Wade shrugged. "Ah, nothing much, but it's the source of the Great Ouse, and I'm working on an environmental reclamation project on the river."

"Oh yeah?" That was strikingly normal for someone she'd met in the Shadowlands. Sort of like meeting a unicorn who bused tables at a vegetarian café on the weekends.

Wait, would a unicorn do that?

"So what's the focus of the reclamation project? Industrial pollution or something?"

Duncan and Lachlan seemed to be coming to some kind of truce, but Carys was irritated with both of them, so she ignored them.

Won the contest? She would be having a conversation with both of them later.

"Eels."

She turned to Wade. "Pardon me?"

"You asked what the focus of the reclamation project is," Wade said. "It's eels."

"Huh." Carys blinked. "Eels."

"Fascinating creatures, eels. Very important for the ecosystem."

THE MYSTERIOUS WADE sat in the first row behind Carys and Duncan with Cadell sitting next to him as they drove off the small country roads around Bernwood Forest and up the dark roadway through the English countryside.

The dragon was glaring at the stranger. "Nêrys, I thought we agreed that you bringing magical creatures from one world to the next was a bad idea."

Wade muttered, "Not a magical creature."

"Then what are you?" the dragon asked.

"Not your business, wyrm."

Wade had kept mostly silent when they walked back through the portal from Temris, then back up the road to the Bern Wood, and through the gate—which again tried to grab Carys—and he walked with ease.

So whatever he was, he felt comfortable enough in both worlds.

Naida kept her eyes closed but let out a sigh and said, "He's more trustworthy than a unicorn, Cadell. You don't need to worry about Wade."

Wade muttered something under his breath.

"Be polite, ferryman," Naida said softly. "The humans have granted you a favor, and now you owe them one."

"Don't owe nothin' to nobody," Wade muttered.

"That's not what we agreed." Naida still had her eyes closed. "Be nice."

Whatever bargain Naida had struck with Wade, she hadn't shared it with the rest of them.

They'd returned to the Brightlands in the middle of the night, and Duncan had to break a chain on the gate of the Bernwood Forest parking lot to get the van out before dawn.

Carys was not going to pretend that the blacksmith twisting open that chain with his bare hands was not hot as hell. It helped a little to assuage her irritation with Duncan and Lachlan's pissing contest in Temris.

So now they were eight instead of six, packed into the van in the middle of the night while Duncan drove, his expression locked down tight.

He gripped the wheel with both hands, very pointedly not looking at his Shadowkin, who was sitting silently in the back. The night flew by, and the clock on the dashboard read 1:00 a.m.

Cadell was still staring at Wade with piercing gold eyes. "Lady Carys is my business, and you are in the same vehicle as she is. Therefore, you are my business."

The dragon was not good at letting go of arguments.

So Wade decided to ignore him. He leaned toward Duncan in the driver's seat. "Yer Angus's smith, aren't you?"

Duncan glanced in the rearview mirror. "You know Angus?"

"What kind of question is that?" Wade grunted, then sat back and stared out the dark window. "Course I know Angus."

"Naturally," Duncan muttered. "Why wouldn't you know a magical creature from Scotland who works at my forge? What a completely obvious answer."

Carys reached over and took Duncan's hand. "Are you tired?"

He glanced at her, and his expression softened. "Honestly, I don't know what day it is or what time my body thinks it is. And I'm hungry. But I'm fine for now." He lifted her hand to his lips and kissed her knuckles. "Are *you* tired?"

"I'm okay." She was also exhausted and hungry, but she wanted to get rid of the giant who'd hitched a ride.

"Tell me when you're tired, and I'll find us a hotel," Duncan said. "Wade and his eels can fuck off."

"I heard that," the old man said.

Carys looked over her shoulder for a moment, then looked away.

Lachlan was silent and brooding in the middle row behind Cadell and Wade. Every now and then, Carys caught him staring at her.

She tried to keep from looking, but it was as if she could feel his eyes on her even when she fixed her gaze ahead.

None of this was ideal.

Not the Morrígan in the Brightlands.

Not Dru's cryptic advice.

Not a strange giant in rubber boots hitching a ride in the van.

And definitely not Lachlan being back.

Once, Carys had been so in love with the man that she'd flown to a strange country to figure out where he'd gone. And now?

Looking at Lachlan was painful. It was just... painful.

"You should try to sleep," Duncan said. "It's another half hour to Wappenham at least."

Carys nodded and reclined her seat. She could feel her stomach groaning, but she was out of trail mix, and the other food was in the back of the van. She didn't want to wake Laura and Naida, so she closed her eyes.

"The eels'll be hunting this time of night." Wade's voice boomed in the silent van. "European eels are nocturnal. Fine summer night like this, they'll be hunting."

"What do eels eat?" Lachlan asked.

Carys opened her eyes; she was not going to be able to sleep.

"Opportunistic feeders," Wade said. "They like mudworms."

She had a vivid picture in her mind. It was not pleasant.

"They eat fishes," Wade continued. "Crayfish. Slugs."

"So lots of different things," Carys said. "That's fascinating."

"Oh aye, they're fascinating creatures, the old *Anguilla anguilla*." He looked at Cadell. "That's what the humans call 'em. They migrate to breed. Kind of like your kind."

Carys blinked and turned around. "What? Dragons migrate to—"

"That is none of your business," Cadell said. "Ignore him."

"Eels swim to the Sargasso Sea." Wade smiled, clearly enjoying poking the dragon. "But that's not where the dragons go, do they, old man?"

Carys looked back and saw that Laura's eyes were open even though she was staying silent.

"No," Wade continued, "you fly to the fire islands, don't you? Breed. Hatch your—"

Cadell's hand shot out and gripped Wade's throat. "Whatever you think you know of our young, forget it, old one."

"Hey." Laura sat up and put a hand on Cadell's shoulder. "Hey, hey. Everyone calm down."

Carys felt a burning knot in her chest, and she knew she was feeling Cadell's simmering rage.

The fae had stolen young dragons only weeks ago, hiding them in fae forts that were only found because the dragon children broke the magical wards with their own blood.

Carys had seen the little ones, some no older than six or seven, their hands and arms bloodied from cutting themselves with sharp rocks in order to rescue the sleeping human children taken with them.

Cadell. Carys spoke in her mind, hoping that he could hear her. *Leave him alone.*

There was nothing in her mind but a low, angry buzzing sound.

Cadell.

"Old man!" Duncan called out. "We all right back there?"

Despite the dragon's grip, Wade chuckled. "Aye, be reet, old wyrm. I've no desire to harm your kind. I've known more than one sea wyrm in my time."

Cadell took his hand away from Wade's throat, but the dragon never stopped glaring.

Godrik leaned toward Cadell and muttered something under his breath in Cymric.

"You think I don't speak that one?" Wade chuckled. "Brightkin, how's old Angus these days?"

Carys glanced at Duncan, then at the clock.

Ten more minutes to their destination.

"Angus is fine, last I checked. He doesn't need me holding his hand," Duncan said.

"Never heard a thing more true."

Laura yawned loudly from the back seat and made a show of stretching and leaning forward. "Can I ask something? Why is every man we meet in the Shadowlands a giant? No offense, but it makes the van really crowded. And this is a large van."

Wade, Cadell, Godrik, and Lachlan all turned to look at her.

"I'm just saying," Laura said. "Shadowlands men back home are normal-sized. Is it the Viking blood or something? Why are you all so tall?"

"Viking was a job, not a people," Wade said.

Laura pursed her lips and sat back. "But do they like... stretch you or something?" She yawned again. "Just wondering." She blinked and folded her hands on her lap before she let out a long sigh. "So much testosterone."

CARYS WATCHED Wade move toward a dark, flowing river as they waited in the van. Naida had exited the car with the old man and walked part of the way with him, exchanging words while Wade gestured animatedly and pointed at the water in the distance.

Lachlan sighed. "What are we doing?"

"Waiting for Naida," Duncan said.

After a few moments, Naida turned and walked back in the car.

"Start the car," Godrik said. "I want to get far away from that old one."

"Do you know what he is?" Carys asked.

"I have my suspicions." Godrik opened the van door and let Naida inside.

She sat in the front-row seat where Wade had been and held up a hand. "Wait."

She watched the old man through the windows, and Carys decided she'd waited for food long enough. She walked to the back of the van and the small kitchenette. "Anyone want some food?"

"Is there meat?" Cadell asked.

"Not enough for you." She held up a bag of sliced roast beef. "Want a sandwich?"

Cadell sat back and grumbled, "No."

"I'll take one," Laura said, "if you're offering."

"Cool." Carys set about making two quick sandwiches, then grabbed a bag of pretzels for Duncan and walked back to the front.

Naida was still staring at Wade.

"Why are we still here?" Carys looked at Duncan, then at Naida.

"I don't know," Duncan said. "To make sure he... gets to the river safely?"

Naida's eyes were narrowed, but rain had started to fall, and Carys could barely see anything out of the windows. "Naida?"

"The old one is safe," Godrik said. "We should go."

"He's still walking," Duncan said. "Where the hell is he going?"

"And he's walking to nowhere." Lachlan buckled his seat belt. "Let's go. Let him go play with his eels."

Carys leaned toward the window and saw Wade, his head turned to the sky, shouting at the rain. And that wasn't even the strangest part of the scene.

The river was *glowing*. Not just sprites and wisps like they'd seen on the Thames. The entire river held an otherworldly greenish-blue glow.

"What the hell?" Laura pressed her face to the window. "Carys, you seeing this?"

"Yes." She glanced at Cadell. "You feel it?"

Yes. He spoke to her mind. *There is strong magic here.*

"Is it growing?" Godrik asked. "I feel like the magic is getting stronger."

"Maybe it's just the place," Naida said. "Wade is very strong around rivers and other bodies of water."

"What is he?" Lachlan asked.

"Not my place to say," Naida said. "But you can trust him."

"He's walking" —Duncan craned his neck— "and he's turning around. He's walking back to the car."

"We should leave," Cadell said. "Right now."

Lachlan opened the door, and rain spattered inside the van.

"What are you doing?" Duncan asked. "He's not getting back inside this—"

"Ey up." Wade hopped back inside the van, forcing everyone to shift around to make room for the burly and muddy dripping giant. "Eels are fine. We need to go to the Ouse."

"We're at the Ouse," Carys said.

"This is the Great Ouse." Wade pointed his chin at the river. "We need to go to the other Ouse."

Laura asked, "How many Ouses *are* there in this country?"

"Four." Duncan, Godrik, and Lachlan all spoke at once.

"That's so many Ouses," Laura said.

"Yorkshire Ouse," Wade said. "That's where we need to go."

Duncan glared at him. "Why?"

"'Cause my daughter called me, told me we need to go to the Ouse, that's why."

Lachlan frowned. "You don't have a phone."

"And? She called me, didn't she?" Wade rolled his eyes as if Lachlan was an idiot.

Duncan turned. "You want us to drive you to Yorkshire? Yorkshire is three hours from here."

"Aye." Wade looked around the van. "Good thing ye have this comfortable caravan."

Duncan looked at the small fae squished between Cadell and Wade. "Naida?"

She sighed. "If Wade says we need to go to the Ouse, we probably need to go to the Ouse."

"Ye definitely need to go to the Ouse," Wade said. "Most importantly" —he pointed at Carys— "*she* needs to go to the Ouse."

Cadell growled. "Why?"

Wade's eyes glittered. "Well, 'cause she's the hero of this story, isn't she?"

CHAPTER EIGHT

"Why did you call me a hero?"

Wade opened one eye.

They'd shuffled around in the van for the three-hour drive to Yorkshire and the deep waters of the River Ouse. Carys had switched with Cadell so the dragon could stretch his long legs in the front passenger seat. Godrik and Lachlan's broad shoulders blocked the row behind the driver, and Naida and Laura were sleeping in the middle, leaving Carys in the far back with the strange old man.

"Who are you?" Wade asked.

Naida said he wasn't fae, so she offered her name. "I'm Carys Morgan."

Wade just stared at her. *And?* his eyes seemed to ask.

"I'm... a mythology professor," Carys continued. "I was born in Wales, but I grew up in Northern California."

Wade narrowed his eyes. "You're telling me where you were born, not who you are."

"Okay." Carys shook her head. "Um... I'm an only child. My parents never had any other kids, so Laura is kind of like my sister."

Wade was still silent and staring.

"My mother was an artist, and my father was a teacher like me. And a carpenter. And then a few years ago, my parents died in a really horrible car accident." Carys looked out the window. "And I miss them every day."

"So that's all you are?" Wade lifted one eyebrow. "Just an ordinary teacher from California with a sad story about her parents?"

"Okay, fine." She felt the corner of her mouth lift in half a smile. "I'm a professor *and* a dragon lord." She plucked at her jeans. "A nêrys ddraig of Cymru." She laughed quietly. "Still working on that part though."

Wade kept staring. "What else?"

"I'm..." Carys's voice dropped to a whisper. "I'm the daughter of a Brightkin and a Shadowkin. My mother served Epona. But I don't really know what that means. And I don't really know anything about how they met or what it means when people mention Epona's—"

"You're a sage." Wade's voice dropped and his folksy accent disappeared. "A teacher and a storyteller. That's the obvious part, Lady Carys. But what else are you? Why do you think I called you a hero?"

Carys shook her head. "I don't know."

"Yes, you do."

Her heart raced, and she saw Cadell turn around in his seat.

Nêrys.

I'm fine.

She couldn't take her eyes from Wade's. She would have sworn earlier that they were a greenish color, but now they were deep blue.

I'm fine, Cadell.

"Stop talking to your dragon," Wade said, "and answer the question: Why did I call you a hero?"

Carys whispered, "You called me a hero because I shouldn't exist." She let out a soft breath. "Because I'm the daughter of a Shadowkin. Because I'm a human born from magic."

THEY LEFT the M1 east of Sheffield and headed northeast on the highway. Carys tried to sleep, but she couldn't. She moved to the front seat to keep Duncan company, but the blacksmith seemed to be running on pure annoyance with their unexpected passenger.

Wade would bark out, "Turn here, jock!" Or "Not that way, eejit," causing her boyfriend to bare his teeth until Carys reached over, took his hand, and breathed deeply until Duncan no longer looked like he was seconds away from murdering Wade.

It was over three hours of driving before they turned off the highway and reached a wide spot in the road just ahead of a bridge and Wade yelled, "Stop here!"

Duncan slammed on the brakes and turned to growl at Wade, but before he could even speak, the old man had yanked the door open, climbed over Godrik, and jumped out of the van.

"What the hell?" Duncan looked furious.

Godrik said, "I have no idea."

The strange man was halfway toward a long, straight river that shone silver in the moonlight before he turned and yelled, "Meet me at Shipp's Inn tomorrow night."

Then in a blink, Wade walked into the river, sank beneath the surface, and disappeared.

Laura leaned toward the window. "Did he just go *in* the river?"

Cadell was staring. "Mm-hmm."

"I believe he did," Lachlan said.

"He's not..." Laura frowned. "He's not coming up."

"Do you think *he's* an eel?" Carys asked. "And he studies them because he's just like a really giant eel? Are there eel shifters?"

No one in the van answered, probably since Carys was talking nonsense because she'd been awake for over twenty-four hours.

Lachlan asked, "Did he tell us to meet him at Shipp's Inn tomorrow night?"

Godrik nodded. "Yes."

"Does anyone have any idea where this Shipp's Inn could be?"

Laura raised her hand. "Do any of us have any reason to follow the instructions of a weird guy from Temris who talks to rain?" she asked. "Because I feel like that's the more important question."

Lachlan said, "He told us that Carys needed to go to Yorkshire with him. That she is the hero."

"And?" Laura shrugged. "Who the hell is—"

"Fine!" Naida sighed from the far back row. "He's a sea god."

Every eye turned toward her.

"He asked me not to say anything, but this is ridiculous." She closed her eyes and muttered, "Wade is Wada. He's a sea god."

Godrik's eyes went wide. "*That* was Wada?"

Naida nodded slightly.

Godrik started muttering something under his breath in what sounded like an incantation.

"That man" —Duncan pointed at the river— "is a god?"

"Yes, one of the oldest gods in Britain," Naida said. "So we should probably meet him tomorrow like he asked."

Cadell nodded slowly. "So he is not an eel after all."

That meant a god had told Carys she was a hero.

That was... something. She was too tired to think about what, but it was definitely something.

"Gods don't always look how you think they might look," Naida said softly. "Especially in the Brightlands. What did you think a sea god looked like? Long hair tangled in weeds and a fish tail?"

If Carys was honest with herself, that was kind of what she'd pictured in her mind. Probably because of Disney movies.

"Fair point," Laura said. "I mean, our sea gods look like fishes and whales, so why not a weird old guy in rubber boots?"

Carys murmured, "Did I say that out loud?"

"Did you say what out loud?"

"Sea gods look like Poseidon in cartoons."

Duncan looked at Carys with a smile. "You are very exhausted, aren't you?"

"A little bit."

Lachlan said, "She doesn't sleep well in cars."

Duncan shot him a look. "I know."

"How do you know?" Lachlan asked. "You've only spent time with her in the Shadowlands, and there aren't really any cars—"

"Did you forget that I live here?" Duncan asked. "On this side. Where Carys was born and she lives? You don't have any idea—"

"I understand that both of you are still vying for the affections of the nêrys ddraig," Godrik said, "but we have been traveling for many hours and all of us should sleep. We need to find an inn or some other kind of lodging."

Duncan whipped out his phone. "I'll do it." He glared at Lachlan. "And there is no vying. The vying period is over. Done."

Lachlan said something, but Carys didn't really hear any of it because she was staring out the window and watching the surface of the river, which was now shimmering a brilliant green and blue.

IT TOOK them another twenty minutes to find a hotel with enough rooms, and it was nearly dawn by the time they pulled into the long drive of a large country house that sat on the turn of the River Ouse.

Carys didn't care about the grand entryway or the hushed tones of the butler who showed them to their rooms. She only cared about the bed.

She collapsed onto the down-covered mattress fully clothed and barely registered when Duncan pulled her shoes off, then gently undressed her and pulled one of his large T-shirts over her head. He tucked her under the comforter, turned off the lights, and everything in Carys shut down.

She didn't know how long she'd slept, but she woke sometime midmorning, saw Duncan sleeping beside her, and tucked herself into his side before she closed her eyes again.

His heavy arm wrapped around her, pulling her close, and his shirt smelled of wood with a slight hint of vanilla.

She closed her eyes and saw dancing lights before she walked toward the forest. The night folded around her, and it was warm and cold at the same time. Fog kissed her cheeks, and the smell of damp pine and eucalyptus filled her senses.

She was deep in the forest.

Birds watched from the trees as a doe lay on her side, her chest heaving and her legs kicking out as her mother laid her hand on the animal's belly.

"Shhh."

"Mama?"

"Wait, cariad. Shhh." Tegan stroked the deer's belly. "You can do this, my sister."

Carys walked around the clearing, picking up sticks and tossing them in a small pile in the middle of the trees, but her eyes kept returning to her mother. "What is she doing?"

"She's ready to have her baby, but she's a little bit scared." Tegan kept stroking the side of the deer. "She doesn't know that she already knows how to do this."

"If I don't know how to do something, I ask you or Dad." Carys jumped across the pile of sticks, then went to gather more. One of the birds flitted down and playfully flew around her head, making Carys laugh.

"I can't tell her how to have her baby," Tegan said. "Not with words." Tegan stroked her hand down the doe's side. "Come on, sister. You need to stand now."

As if she understood every word, the deer flailed a little bit but managed to get to her feet. Her sides were still heaving, but Tegan stroked her hand down the deer's neck.

"Good, good." She whispered something in Welsh.

Carys didn't speak Welsh like her parents did. Sometimes they tried to get her to talk to them in Welsh, but Carys felt shy. No one at school spoke Welsh. She wished she could learn Yurok like Laura and her sisters.

"Carys, do you want to see?"

"No." There was blood on the ferns, and it made Carys nervous.

"Birth is nothing to be afraid of. It's natural." Tegan soothed the deer with long strokes down her neck as the deer leaned forward, then back again. "Remember, sister, your body knows what to do."

The doe stumbled back when the small bloody creature fell into the fern patch, nearly stepping on the tiny fawn.

Carys winced, but seconds later she saw tiny hooves kicking through the bloodstained mess.

"Good girl!" Tegan praised her. "I'm so proud of you."

Despite Tegan's words, the doe's body kept heaving.

"Another?" Tegan's voice went soft. "Of course you have another." She bent to the deer's head. "Would that I were you," she whispered. "Mother of two souls."

Her mother's voice made her sad.

Carys wished she had a sister. Laura had four sisters. Sometimes she complained about them, but Carys could tell she really loved them, and if Carys was her best friend, then Laura's sisters were her second-best friends.

When Carys asked if she could have a sister, Tegan smiled and said that she was as lucky to have Carys as if she'd had a hundred children.

That made Carys laugh. A hundred children didn't sound very lucky to her. That sounded loud.

As the doe labored to birth the second fawn, Tegan sang something in Welsh. It was an old song, a lullaby her mother sometimes sang when strange dreams haunted Carys and she couldn't sleep.

Pan elei dy dat ty e helya
Llath ar y ysgwyd llory eny law
Ef gelwi gwn gogyhwc
Giff gaff dhaly dhaly dhwg dhwg

Sometimes Carys dreamed of running across green hills and jumping in streams she didn't recognize. The place in her dreams was soft and green and foggy, but it wasn't home.

And sometimes when she was sleeping, she heard her mother singing. But when Carys heard the song in her dreams, she understood every word. She saw her father going out to hunt, a fur cape on his shoulders and a spear in his hand.

Tegan urged the doe on. "There you are, mother, there you are."

The second fawn fell into the ferns, and a flock of birds took flight.

A branch broke behind her, and Carys turned with a gasp.

Carys woke with her hand clutched over her heart and a harsh breath sucked into her lungs.

There you are, mother. There you are.

"Carys?" Duncan sat bolt upright. "What's wrong?"

"I had a strange dream."

Mother of two souls.

"My mother…" She blinked the tears from her eyes. "She knew. I've never let myself really think about it, but of course she knew. She knew when I was born that Seren would be born in the Shadowlands. She knew that she had another daughter she would never know." Something in Carys's chest folded in on itself. "And if I ever have a baby…"

She'd always wanted children… but maybe she didn't now.

"Shhh." Duncan gathered her into his arms and rocked her as silent tears fell from her eyes. "Carys, we don't have any control over that."

"We give birth to life and death at the same time," Carys murmured. "To light and dark. That's why the fawn is covered in blood."

He stroked her hair back from her forehead and kissed her temple. "I think you had a bad dream, lass."

Not a bad dream. Not a bad dream. It was a memory.

"You can't think about it that way," Duncan whispered. "If there was no life here, there would be no life there."

She blinked. "Lachlan is alive." She pulled back so she could look at Duncan. "If you have a child, the fae would give the other twin to your brother. But Seren is dead."

Duncan rubbed a hand over his face. "It's too early for this."

"I know." She closed her eyes and rubbed a hand over her face. "I'm not even making sense to myself. We're both exhausted and I'm still tired but I had this dream and I woke up thinking—"

"Not that kind of early." Duncan's voice was hoarse. "Carys, you know I love you. I loved you before I even met you. And now I'm just… I'm mad for you, woman."

She melted into his chest and slid her arms around his waist. "I love you too."

"So what makes you think I'd want children with anyone but you?"

Carys froze.

"See?" He laughed a little bit. "It's too early to have this conversation."

"Oh." Her face heated. "Yeah. It is."

"I understand why you had the thought. I've thought about that most of my adult life, but I always took comfort in the idea that if I had children, Lachlan and Seren would raise their other selves."

"But Seren is gone."

"And? Lachlan is still around. As much as my Shadowkin annoys me at times, I trust him like no one else." Duncan took Carys by the shoulders and turned her to face him. "Would you want that world to not exist? Would you want the Shadowlands to fade away? To have no more nêrys ddraig. No more alchemists or healers to learn from *unicorns*. No more human children who grow up... dancing with pixies in the meadow! Not even a little part of humanity to live with all that magic?"

"Of course not." She wasn't sure if she wanted to stay in the Shadowlands, but she would never want it to fade away.

He stroked her hair. "Know that whatever happens with us, any child you have—either here or in Baywood—their Shadowkin would be treasured."

"You're right." She hugged him hard. "I know you're right." She sat back and took a deep breath. "I'm sorry."

"Carys, you've been hit with about ten different realities crashing in on you over the past month." He held her tightly. "You've nothing to apologize for."

"I just had all these realizations hit me at the same time. I'm remembering dreams and things from my childhood in an entirely new way, so I try to remember more and then I wonder—"

"Carys."

"I know." She gave him a shaky smile. "Spiraling again."

She blinked and looked at him.

Then she *really* looked at him. "Hey."

"Hey yourself." Duncan was shirtless and rumpled. He had pillow marks on his forehead and hooded eyes that still hadn't woken up entirely.

And there was a very prominent bulge in his boxer shorts.

He saw her looking and sat up against the headboard. "Ah, lass, it's morning. He has a mind of his own."

Carys pushed Duncan back against the pillows. "I feel like he might be trying to distract me."

The corner of his mouth turned up. "I'm sure that's what it is."

She threw her leg over his thighs and straddled him. "He's probably trying to keep me from spiraling about things I can't control."

"There's no use in it, is there?" His voice was hoarse again. "Take your mind off it."

Carys reached down and gripped him over his boxers.

Duncan let out a short groan. He shifted, easing the shorts down his legs until he was sitting with his manhood proudly displayed, and Carys wrapped both hands around it.

She stroked him slowly, deliberately teasing him with a firm grip.

Duncan reached for the oversized shirt she'd worn to bed. "That needs to come off."

She kept her right hand on his cock but lifted her left so he could pull off her shirt. Then she switched sides until she was naked, still straddling Duncan, her hands still wrapped around his erection.

A groan rumbled in his chest when she scooted back and took his cock in her mouth, circling her tongue around the head and humming as she continued to stroke him firmly.

"That's enough of that." Duncan reached for a condom, then tugged her up until she was poised over him, her breasts in front of his mouth. "Now that sight will wake a man from the dead."

Carys guided him into her body and shifted until his erection filled her. She let out a soft sigh, Duncan's cock filling her, his hands at the small of her back. She let her head fall back when he put his mouth on her breasts, and the roughness of his beard scraped against the tender skin.

He teased her nipples with his tongue as Carys began to move, riding him slowly, her legs pushing her up and down as Duncan's fingers dug into her hips.

He lifted his head and licked his lips, which were flushed and swollen. Duncan bit his lip, his eyes closed. He took one hand from where he gripped her hips, moving it to where they were joined, stroking her as her body stroked him.

Carys braced her hand on his shoulder when she felt herself start to come. It started at her thighs, radiating up and to the center of their joining until her climax took over, her muscles contracting and releasing in rapid waves as Duncan braced his hand on the bed and drove up into her body as she shook.

She felt like the top of her head floated away, and she could barely see.

Duncan flipped them over, his body still driving into her, and moments later he nearly shouted when he came.

He braced himself on his forearms, capturing her mouth with his, kissing her over and over as her body relaxed and stilled. Her chest rose with rapid breaths and she closed her eyes, floating in the feeling of his fullness in her, the scent of his skin, the awareness of air brushing over her skin.

She opened her mouth to speak, but nothing came out.

"Shh." He kissed her chin. "I don't need words right now."

"I love you so much." She felt her heart ache with it. He had been the fire that burned so bright she could barely look at him.

"I suppose I'll take those words if you're offering them." He brushed his lips over her temple and rolled to the side before he gathered her up in his arms and pulled her against him. "Love you, Carys."

And now he was the rock that she could depend on. The mountain who kept her feet from slipping when everything around her felt like chaos.

"We'll figure all this out." He kissed her temple again. "I promise you. We'll make it all right."

CHAPTER NINE

Shipp's Inn was an old pub directly on the river that Carys was guessing hadn't been updated since the mid-seventies. It had Formica tables, red-and-brown-checked carpet, and framed photos of fishermen on the walls along with various trophies and a large blue-and-white football club banner.

Despite its dated appearance, Carys could smell that the pub was clean as a whistle, and whatever food they were cooking in back had her mouth watering.

Cadell noticed too. "I need to eat whatever it is that they are making."

"Agreed," Godrik said.

Not a minute later, a stout woman with red cheeks and a grey bun on top of her head walked out of the back. Her eyes went wide at the four massive men and three women in her bar.

"Now there's a group of lads. I'm Bess, and I'm making shepherd's pie. You hungry?"

"Yes." All four men spoke at once.

Bess beamed. "Good thing I made extra tonight. You're early for dinner, so you get the first batch."

There were two men in a booth and one at the bar, but none of them seemed interested in anything but the drinks in front of them. And none of them looked like Wade.

Wada.

The sea god.

Laura said, "We're meeting someone. A guy named Wade. Do you know him?"

"American!" Bess said. "Are you all American?" She looked at Duncan and Lachlan. "You two aren't."

"Scottish," the brothers said in identical voices.

"Oh yeah. Ya sure are." She looked at Godrik.

"Ang-lish," he said. "English."

She nodded. "Essex boy, I'd bet." Her eyes moved over and up to Cadell. "And you're a tall one, aren't you?"

"I was born in Kernow."

"Cornwall," Carys said.

"Kernow," Cadell said again.

"All right then." Bess brushed her hands on her apron. "Why don't you sit where you like and I'll bring you seven servings of shepherd's pie." She glanced over her shoulder. "As soon as my man gets out here, he'll get your drinks sorted."

They sat at a booth and pulled over an extra table. Laura positioned herself so she could see the door.

"He didn't tell us a time," she said. "So we may be waiting awhile. Hope you guys really are hungry."

Carys watched all four men staring at the kitchen door like baby chicks waiting for their mother to return.

"I don't think that's going to be a problem," Carys said.

Naida had been silent since they'd loaded into the van, but her eyes were bright even if she looked a bit wan. "Did Dru's pub in the Brightlands look like this?"

"Is this the first time you've been in a pub?" Lachlan asked.

"I've been inside a human pub in the Shadowlands. They don't look like this though." She was looking at the fishing photographs on the walls. "Is it a contest?"

"I think so," Carys said. "Looks like it."

"To catch the biggest fish." She smiled. "That's not bad."

"Dru's pub in Scone was more old-fashioned than this," Duncan said. "It was in a very old building, so it was all plaster and wood. Beautiful old bar."

Naida was still staring at the photographs on the walls. "Did he have fishing pictures?"

Duncan smiled. "No, but the Four Crowns did sponsor the local football club, so there were banners like that." He pointed to the blue-and-white flag.

"I tried to picture him there so many times," she said softly. "What would a prince do in a place like this?"

"He worked hard." Duncan kept his voice low. "He made people happy. He liked making people happy."

"Yes, he did." Naida kept her eyes on the flag. "Wade is coming."

Carys scooted closer. "You can feel him?"

"I can smell him."

It wasn't more than three minutes later that Wade walked through the door and made a beeline for their table. He was followed by a tall, bushy-haired woman wearing clothes that were nearly identical to his.

Bess was just bringing out the first of the shepherd's pies when Wade and the woman sat down. "Can I get you two some food?"

Wade eyed the pies. "Two o' those, Bess."

"Course, Wade." She beamed. "Good to see you again."

Carys watched the woman walk away and looked at Wade. "We asked if she knew you."

Wade shook his head. "She doesn't remember me unless I'm here."

"How does that work?"

He shrugged. "This is my daughter Frida." He barked something at her in a strange language, and Frida sat down.

"I am Frida." The woman looked even less comfortable around humans than Wade did. She would have been in middle age if she was human, but if Wada was her father, she was a demigod at the least. She was tall and nearly as broad as the sea god, but there was a distinctly feminine curve to her features and her bearing.

Carys looked from her to Wade, then back again. "So you're Wade's daughter, which means you're also a…"

Frida's eyebrows went up. "A river reclamation biologist?"

"Yes." Carys nodded. "A river reclamation biologist."

"I am."

"Great. That's great." She looked at Duncan, who paused long enough in devouring his pie to raise his eyebrows and shrug.

Wade was the one who cut to the chase. "We have a problem here. That's why Frida called."

Cadell was also devouring his pie, but he paused and looked up. "What is the problem?"

"There is a sea serpent," Frida said. "He's swimming up the Ouse and destroying boats. Eating pets. Things like that."

The moment Frida said *sea serpent*, everyone stopped eating and looked at her.

Laura said, "So when you say *serpent*—"

"Monster," Wade said. "Giant beastie-like. Not as big as the Great Serpent in London, mind, but not much smaller either."

Laura's eyes were as big as saucers. "Are you serious?"

"Serious as Sam," Wade said.

"Who's Sam?"

"That's what they called him last time. The humans, that is. He slipped through a gate 'bout a hundred years ago. Mortals here tried to make a mascot of him, they did. Like that lovely beastie up in Loch Ness." Wade nodded at Duncan. "But this un's a bit more… feral."

Naida said, "So a sea monster got through an underwater fae gate and is now eating human pets in Yorkshire." She sighed. "Wonderful news."

"Really not wonderful." Frida narrowed her eyes. "Quite harmful.

The humans on this side don't know about sea monsters. If they did, I imagine they would find it quite upsetting."

Apparently river reclamation biologists were not keen on sarcasm.

"You've got to stop it." Wade pointed at Carys. "Got to stop it from getting farther upriver. Once he passes the Naburn Locks, he'll have a clear shot to York city. And after that, there'll be no stopping him."

"Me?" Carys shook her head. "What are you talking about? I don't know how to stop a sea monster."

"Well." Wade slapped his hand on the table. "It's about an hour drive if we follow the river. You'll have time to figure it out."

"FIGURE IT OUT?" Carys was nearly shouting. "I'm supposed to just *figure it out*? What the hell?"

They'd piled into the van so they could follow the old truck Frida was driving, heading upriver toward the Naburn Locks where the tidal River Ouse stopped and the river evened out.

"Calm down, Nêrys." Cadell tried to soothe her. "There is one sea serpent and seven of us." He grumbled. "Which is far more than we need, in my opinion, but no one listens to me."

"I listen to you," Laura said.

Cadell raised an eyebrow.

"I mean…" Laura continued, "I also ignore you a lot of the time, but I do listen to you."

The dragon smirked.

Despite Cadell's confidence, Carys had the urge to sit under her dragon's long arm and hide.

"You have to do this," Godrik said. "The god said that it was your task, and we will help you, but it must be your victory."

"Why?" Laura asked. "Carys didn't ask for any of this."

"Because she's the one who let the Morrígan into the Bright-lands," Naida said. "And she is the one the gods have named as the hero."

Naida wasn't wrong, and that was the most terrifying part.

Carys knew that none of this was going to stop until she figured out a way to get the Morrígan back across the gate and locked out of the Brightlands.

But first she had to figure out how to stop a giant serpent from destroying the city of York. Because *that* was completely in her skill set.

Laura was looking at her phone. "From what I can tell from reading online, once you get past the Naburn Locks, the river is no longer tidal. So the water levels are more even and recreational boats are more common."

"That means more houses." Duncan chimed in. "If the water is calmer upstream of the locks, there'll be more farms and businesses too."

"And far more opportunities for Sam the Serpent to cause chaos," Godrik added.

"Locks," Naida said. "How can they put a lock on a river?"

"Not a lock like on a door," Lachlan said. "Locks are a Brightkin technology to move boats upstream. We don't use them in the Shad-owlands because they disturb the river spirits. But here, they build a series of walled channels where the river flows."

"When the tide is high," Duncan continued, "a boat can enter on one end of the lock, then a door is shut and another door opens on the opposite side to flood the chamber and even out the water level. That way a boat can move upriver even if the elevation changes."

"So clever." Naida smiled. "But yes, the river spirits would hate anything that disturbs the natural body of the river."

Carys had already seen the map. There was a weir on the Ouse, a low dam to control the flow of the water and operate the locks, but that weir would be nothing against a massive sea serpent.

If Sam the Serpent followed the river far enough upstream, it would put him right smack in the middle of York, one of the most historic cities in the UK, where over 140,000 people lived and worked, completely oblivious to the fact that apparently a cranky and confused sea monster was heading their way.

"I wonder why he is doing this," Cadell said. "Sea serpents are usually quite peaceful. Shy even. They would not eat dogs, cats, or humans when there is plentiful fish to eat."

"Maybe that's the problem," Duncan said. "Slipped through that gate to the Brightlands, tried to hunt, and got confused because the ocean on this side is different."

"Is it though?" Laura asked.

"Significantly," Godrik said.

"Humans have engineered the river systems in the Brightlands," Lachlan said. "A creature from the Shadowlands would likely be very lost."

"Lost, confused and—in the end—innocent," Carys said. "It's not Sam's fault that he took a wrong turn and got caught up in the Morrígan's plans."

"True, but it is still a sea monster," Godrik said. "Not a bear cub or a hound. Chances are high that in order to stop it, you will have to kill it."

Carys hated that idea.

They were driving up a combination of highways and surface streets, following the river, but their view was blocked by tall hedgerows that bordered the fields and farmland of Yorkshire.

Frida's pickup truck finally turned left near an RV park, and Duncan followed, navigating the narrow green-bordered road that led away from the agricultural land and toward the river.

Boats large and small were dry-docked in a marina by the RV park, and Carys saw everything from tiny sailboats to massive powerboats sharing the yard.

The sign by the gate said YORK MARINA. Frida pulled in, waved to a man in a guard station, and pulled her pickup truck into a parking spot.

Carys let out a slow breath. "Okay, I've had an hour, and I am no closer to figuring out a plan."

Duncan parked the van, then Cadell hopped out and opened her door.

"What did I teach you about going into a battle?" The dragon's eyes bored into hers.

Carys took a deep breath and tried to think. "Uh... the most important aspect is terrain. Getting an understanding of where the fighting will happen so you can understand your plan of attack."

"Correct. You have not been able to see the terrain where this battle will take place," Cadell helped her out of the van. "Therefore, it is understandable and wise that you do not have a plan."

Carys nodded. "Okay, that makes me feel better."

Duncan came to stand beside her. "What can we do to help?"

"Right now I just need to get to the river and..." She glanced at Cadell, who nodded. "I need to see what I'm working with, and I need to see how big this thing actually is."

"I wish I could shift to my true form," Cadell said. "But I tried when I exited the van, and I am not able to change."

Frida and Wade were leaning against their truck, staring at the river like two old fishermen chatting about the weather.

Laura marched over to them and pointed at Wade. "Hey, you."

Wade lifted one eyebrow.

"We need a boat," Laura said. "Can you do that?"

Wade shrugged. "I suppose."

"Okay, let's go." She tugged his arm and started walking toward what looked like an office.

Carys asked Frida, "How far away is this thing?"

"It was in Goole this morning."

"Goole was where we just were?"

"Yes."

"So it's probably here or almost here." Godrik looked over his shoulder at Naida. "Fae, can you sense the creature?"

Naida shook her head. "If it was on land, probably, but not in the water." She cocked her head. "However, when we were in London, there were water fae who had crossed the gates and traveled along the Thames. It's possible the same thing happened here." She nodded. "I'll go to the water and look. If any nymphs or sprites are around, I imagine they will talk to me."

"Good," Godrik said. "Do that."

Lachlan stood in front of Carys as if reporting for duty. "What can I do?"

What was Lachlan good at?

Hunting.

"When Wade gets us a boat," Carys said, "I need you on it. If we need to kill that thing, you're the only one with a sword."

"True." Lachlan put a hand on the short bronze sword he'd brought from the Shadowlands. "But I should stay near you in case all this is a ruse by the Morrígan to attack you."

Well, shit. She hadn't even considered that this was all a distraction to make her vulnerable. Unfortunately, it was as likely as any other explanation.

"You go on the boat," Duncan said. "I'll stay near Carys and keep her safe."

"With what?" Lachlan lifted his chin. "In case you've forgotten, you don't have a blade."

"*With* me, you mean?" Duncan crossed his massive arms over his chest. "That may be, brother, but I guarantee I can find something around this boatyard I'll be able to swing far better than you can. I've a mind to see what an anchor would do to your thick skull at the moment."

"Both of you need to stop." Carys started walking toward the river, following Naida. "Lachlan, I know open water isn't your favorite, but you have good eyes. You're the best I know at spotting animals that are trying to hide."

"Carys—"

"You asked me what you could do to help, and I'm telling you."

He gritted his teeth but muttered, "Fine."

Even when they were hiking in the forests back in Baywood, Lachlan always seemed to have a preternatural sense of where animals were. He could avoid a bear and sneak up on a buck. He didn't hunt in the Brightlands, but he was a hell of a spotter.

"Does anyone know how to pilot a boat?" Carys looked at Godrik and Duncan. "Either of you guys?"

Godrik shook his head.

Duncan looked stormy, and Carys knew she had her answer.

"Don't tell me you didn't have boating lessons at that fancy boarding school." Carys stepped toward him and smiled. "Duncan?"

"I don't want to leave you to fight that thing alone," he said. "Right now all you have—"

"I'm going on the boat with you," she said.

Duncan curled his lip, but Lachlan brightened.

"Like Cadell said, I need to know what the territory is." Carys looked at the square building where Laura had disappeared. "Cadell can't fly me over the river, and I can't see the territory if I'm on shore."

"Fine then." Duncan nodded. "I don't know what boat the old man is going to procure, but I can probably figure it out."

"Good." She turned to Godrik. "You, Cadell, and Laura stay on shore." She walked to the edge of the embankment and looked at the slowly moving water as it flowed toward the twin channels of the locks. "I may have an idea."

CHAPTER TEN

The sun was setting on the horizon, and giant flocks of black starlings dipped and danced across the purple-edged sky as Carys and Lachlan stood on the bow of the small river cruiser that Duncan piloted down the Ouse.

"There." Lachlan pointed. "I see it."

"I don't see anything."

Lachlan leaned close to her and bent down. She could feel his breath on her neck, and the scent of cedar and sandalwood mixed with the breeze.

"Look at where the current is moving," he said quietly, "then look for the interruption where the—"

A massive snake with a head at least a meter wide breached the water, letting out a sharp scream and bashing its body against the wood-and-concrete embankment.

Carys nearly fell over. "Holy shit."

"Think we all see it now," Duncan said from behind the windshield where he was piloting the boat. "Good spotting, Lachlan."

The massive beast dove beneath the water, and as it did, the concrete embankment that separated the land from the river collapsed and crumbled into the water.

"Get to the right!" Lachlan yelled. "It's heading straight toward us!"

Duncan managed to move them over to the far bank, barely avoiding Sam the Sea Serpent as a massive wave hit the side of the cruiser, splashing muddy water across their legs and feet as the snake's body undulated side to side past their boat and up the river.

Lachlan grabbed her and wrapped one arm around her waist, steadying Carys against his chest as he braced his legs wide and hung on to the side of the boat.

There were fishing lines and clotheslines wrapped around the serpent's body, and a bright orange kayak floated up as he passed, smashed against the side of their cruiser, then sank again as Sam dove deep.

"He's heading toward the locks," Duncan yelled. "Carys, d'ya have a plan yet?"

Sam was larger than Carys had imagined but not as big as she'd feared. "Duncan, how many meters do you think that thing is?"

She heard Cadell in her mind before Duncan could answer.

I would estimate that the beast is around thirty meters long.

Ask Laura how long the locks are.

"I'd say it's twenty-five, maybe thirty?" Duncan wiped his forearm over his eyes to clear them from the muddy water. "What do you want to do?"

Thirty meters long meant that old Sam was a little longer than a basketball court. In the vast Atlantic Ocean, he was in his element, but the creature was probably panicking in a river like the Ouse.

"Can you turn this thing around?"

With a quick nod, Duncan eased the wheel around and moved the boat forward, creeping into the wash of debris and waves the sea monster had churned up.

Carys saw dead fish floating in the water, and along the top of the embankment, a sleek, black cat reared back, hissing at the monster before he slunk into the bushes.

Nêrys.

"Cadell?" She could hear him in her mind, but his voice was faint.

I am near the weir with Laura. She says the locks are forty meters long.

"Forty meters," she muttered. "If we can get it inside..."

Duncan shouted, "What are you thinking?"

"It's turning around," Lachlan said. "Carys, it's heading straight for us."

Carys looked away from the grey-walled locks and saw a white ridge of water heading straight toward them.

She felt Cadell's panic in her mind, the intense need for his dragon form.

"It's going to ram us." Duncan kept his voice steady. "Lachlan?"

Before Carys realized what was happening, Lachlan spun her around, yanked a life vest over her head, and snapped the top clip just before the boat rocked to the side and Lachlan went tumbling into the water.

"Lachlan!" She screamed as she fell to the deck.

Duncan shouted something that was drowned out by the roar of the engines, and Carys braced herself as the white water roared toward them.

Something orange went flying over her head, splashing into the river as the dragging tail of the serpent spun the small cruiser into the center of the Ouse.

"Lachlan, buoy's in the water!" Duncan yelled. "Carys, stay down!"

Nêrys, I am swimming to you.

Stay on the shore!

Nêrys, I cannot.

She heard a distant splash, and Cadell must have grabbed the attention of the serpent, because the boat stopped spinning. Duncan steadied it, then ran to the side to look for Lachlan.

"Duncan, go!" a voice called.

Carys heard Lachlan's voice coming from a distance.

"I can swim it," Lachlan shouted. "Get her out of the water!"

The swiftly moving current of the River Ouse caught Lachlan and snatched him away, but before he disappeared into the darkness, Carys saw him clutching the bright orange ring Duncan had thrown.

Duncan ran to the wheel, gunned the engine, and pointed the bow of the cruiser toward the dock where Carys could see Godrik and Laura waving their arms.

They were getting closer.

Closer.

Thunk.

Carys, who had been on her knees in the bow of the boat, peering into the darkness, was thrown back.

"Carys, lie down!" Duncan shouted. "Get on the—"

The bow tilted up, rocked to the side, and moments later, she felt the freezing, muddy water of the river swallow her.

SHE WAS SUCKED INTO DARKNESS, water shot up her nose, and something grabbed her ankle, pulling her deeper into the river.

There was a roar in her ears and muffled shouting in the distance.

Just as suddenly as she'd gone under the water, she popped up, her lungs exploding as she gasped for air. She blew the water from her nose and hung on to the straps of the life vest that was keeping her afloat.

"Carys!"

She searched the darkness for the voice that called her name, but just as her vision cleared, something that felt like a rope wrapped around her ankle.

She went under the water again as high, snickering laughter surrounded her and angry caws sounded in the sky above her.

What death do you choose, daughter of Epona?

The whispering voice made Carys stop struggling. She listened and she stilled, waiting for more.

What death do you choose, daughter of two worlds? The voice was familiar. *For death comes for all your kind—* it was tinged with the cackle of crows *—and I am guarding yours.*

Carys's lungs were on fire, but the darkness of the river was suddenly lit with an eerie blue light, and creatures emerged from the darkness.

Wide black eyes set in moonlike faces. Wide mouths as much fish as faerie. The creatures in the river grinned, revealing sharp, pointed teeth as their long, bony hands reached out and the Morrígan's laughter echoed in her mind.

There was a crashing sound overhead; then a hand plunged down and grabbed Carys by the braid, yanking her up and out of the water with a roar.

Duncan wrapped thick arms around her as Lachlan dove underwater with his sword drawn.

"Grindylows!" Duncan shouted. "They've come through the gates, and they're everywhere." He kicked out, stretching one arm toward the shore.

Cadell was there, pulling her up by her arms and dragging her onto the grassy riverbank.

"Give me a knife, dragon!" Duncan said. "Anything you have!"

Cadell reached into his tall boot and grabbed a silver blade, flipping it toward Duncan, who caught it by the handle and dove back where Lachlan was still fighting with the water fae.

Carys lunged toward the river even as Cadell held her back. "Duncan!"

"Nêrys, the wyrm—"

"I'm not worried about the fucking sea monster!" she screamed.

Neither of the men had life vests. The unearthly creatures lurking in the Ouse would kill them both.

Only Cadell held her back.

"I can hear him," Cadell shouted. "She has possessed his mind."

"You're not listening!" She wrenched her body around as Cadell held her. "There are things in the water that are going to drown Duncan and Lachlan!"

"You must trust your men to battle the water fae. They are not as powerful on this side of the gate, and that dagger has a steel core."

Carys felt hot tears on her freezing-cold cheeks, but she choked back a sob and nodded.

"Nêrys, I can hear the wyrm's mind." Cadell's eyes drilled into hers. "It is confused, unhinged, and he does not know what is happening."

"The Morrígan has... possessed it?"

"I believe so."

Carys looked around to see a thick fog pressing around them. "What's happening?"

"Laura created a fog to keep any humans away," Cadell said. "Naida is trying to call friendly water fae to help us. There are some, but they are frightened and confused."

There was a giant splash, and Carys turned. She saw Lachlan swimming toward the edge of the river, dragging Duncan under one arm.

"Bloody massive idiot." He grunted as she and Cadell raced over to help him pull Duncan up the slope. "Nearly got himself killed."

"Is he breathing?" Carys ran to Duncan's side and knelt down.

Just as she reached him, Duncan started to cough and retch, spewing river water from his mouth and nose.

Carys turned him on his side, and Duncan gripped her hand as he expelled the water from his lungs.

"How did you get away?"

Lachlan had red marks around his throat and a slice on his shoulder. "Never seen grindylows in a river before." His shirt was half gone, and it looked like there were teeth marks in his side. "Don't care to see them again. But they can bleed, the bloody little monsters."

As Duncan coughed and gripped her hand, she heard splashing in the water and a low thump as the serpent hit something beneath the surface. The dense fog shrouded everything from her view, but she could see the muddy water washing up like waves on the grass.

"He's turned at the weir," Cadell said. "But he's not leaving. The Morrígan is telling him to keep going."

Lachlan pulled off the remains of his shirt and used the scraps to clean his blade before he set both down on the ground. "We have to stop it from going over that dam. It's a meter or two at most."

Duncan was as beaten up as Lachlan and had a red slash right across his throat, but he pointed at the river. "That monster is powerful enough to go over that dam," he rasped. "But how the bloody hell are we supposed to stop it?"

With every turn of the serpent's great body, another massive wave hit the riverbank. There was a muffled roar from beneath the water, and Carys knew the Morrígan was losing patience.

Flying through the fog, flocks of crows and starlings circled overhead, cawing and raining black feathers down on them.

Carys pointed upriver where she remembered the two narrow channels in front of the embankment. "The locks. The longest one is bigger than Sam. If we can get him in the lock and shut the gate, I don't think he'll be able to get out."

"He could bash them to pieces," Lachlan said. "I think he's strong enough."

"If the serpent destroyed the locks, the concrete would fall in on it and kill it," Cadell said. "It is not stupid."

Duncan rasped, "There's the problem, dragon. It's not stupid. So how are we going to get it in the lock?"

Carys looked at Cadell. "You can talk to it?"

"I can. The Morrígan has possessed it, but underneath her influence, the wyrm's mind is intact. Confused but intact."

"Tell it to start swimming toward the lock," Carys said. "But don't tell it why."

"I can try." Cadell walked toward the river and started pacing along the bank, clearly trying to communicate with the serpent circling in front of the weir.

Carys strode up the riverbank and toward Wade and Frida, who still appeared to be hanging out and chatting like a giant serpent swimming up the River Ouse was something that happened every Sunday afternoon.

The crows and starlings swooped low over their head as if trying to eavesdrop on the sea god and his daughter.

"You!" She pointed at Wade. "I need you to open the lock gate. Or someone. Someone has to open the gate." She could tell that a mechanism of that size was not going to be cranked open by hand.

Wade's eyebrows went up. "You're asking a favor of me?"

Damn. The crows flew lower. Listening. Probably reporting back to their mistress.

She stepped closer and kept her voice low. "Not a favor. You told me I needed to get rid of the sea serpent before it got to York."

Wade glanced up and kept his voice as low as hers. "And you're proposing that I open the gate that could take it upstream."

Carys was starting to fume. "I'm not telling you to open both gates, Wade. I'm telling you to open the downstream gate so the giant snake can go inside so" —she spoke through gritted teeth— "we can figure out what to do." *Before it jumps over the tiny dam that would barely hold back a salmon.*

She didn't say that part out loud.

Wade smirked. "So you're asking me for a favor."

"I'm trying not to kill it, okay?" She threw up her hands. "Do you want me to just fire arrows at it until it's dead? We can go that route if you want. I have my gear in the van."

"Oh, stop bein' an arse, Da." Frida shoved away from the truck they were leaning on. "She's tryin' to help and you're bein' an arse." She shoved her giant shoulder in the direction of a small house on the edge of the embankment. "Come with me, human."

Carys fell into step beside Frida, practically running to keep up with her long strides.

Frida muttered, "You think you can get it back out to sea?"

"Cadell can speak to it. Serpent mind to serpent mind or something. He says the Morrígan has possessed it, but underneath that, it's just confused."

"Figured it was her" —Frida glanced at the crows and starlings overhead— "what with this bloody racket."

They walked over to what Carys was guessing was the lock-keeper's house.

"Wait here." Frida disappeared into the thick fog.

Moments later, Carys heard a creaking sound and then a groan from the direction of the locks.

"You're lucky!" a voice called out. "The water was already in your favor."

Carys took that to mean the lock gate was open.

Cadell. She paged the dragon in her mind.

Nêrys.

The gate is open.

I am with Naida and Godrik. The fae woman is speaking to the river fae.

Not the grindylows?

The grindylows should not be here. The wild fae are quite angry that the Morrígan called them, and they appear willing to speak to the serpent.

Carys walked back toward the edge of the river. The embankment was high next to the locks where the land sloped down to the left. She saw Naida and Godrik like specters through the fog, and somewhere in the distance, she heard Laura singing a low song.

Frida appeared beside her, and Carys nearly jumped out of her skin.

"Your friend is gifted with elemental magic."

"Yes, she's a pauwau inwe of her people." Carys kept her eyes on the water, hoping that Cadell could speak to the giant snake. Hoping that the water fae would be irritated enough by the Morrígan to guide the giant serpent to the lock. "Kind of a Brightlands diplomat to the Shadowlands."

"What an excellent idea." Frida put her hand on a large black wheel. "I've switched it to manual operation, so one of you can close it when the creature is inside. Good luck."

Carys's eyes went wide when she saw the giant black wheel mounted on the ground. It looked like it would take two grown men to even budge it.

"Wait, you want me to..." She looked around, but Frida had already disappeared.

Who did she know with the strength of two grown men? "Godrik!"

CHAPTER ELEVEN

Carys ran down the grassy verge and listened for anything that sounded like the wolf. "Godrik?"

The ground dipped, and Carys nearly tripped into the water, which would have been a very bad thing because the green-skinned grindylows were now crawling up the banks.

Naida had stepped back, speaking to some small glowing thing that hovered around her. Laura was backing away, her arms up and holding the fog as she chanted. Duncan and Lachlan were swiping at the scaly creatures with black-stained blades, trying to hold them back.

Cadell was pacing on the edge of the river, staring into the fog and occasionally punting a grindylow's head like a football anytime one got too close.

"You called for me?" Godrik appeared from the fog, holding what appeared to be a massive anchor. He was eyeing the grindylows. "These little bastards are stubborn."

"I need you to close the lock gate when the snake is inside."

He frowned. "I know nothing of your Brightlands technology, Lady Carys."

"Can you turn a really big, heavy wheel?"

Godrik flexed his shoulders, and Carys was reminded of a bear. "Yes. I can do that."

"Good, then come with me."

Cadell, is he moving?

He is quite confused, but the water fae will try to guide him into the lock.

Does the Morrígan understand what is going on?

She only sees through his eyes, and he is still thinking this is a way upriver that will avoid the rocks and metal of the human weir. He knows that going over it will be painful.

Good.

"Laura!" she shouted.

A moment later, she heard a response.

"What's up, buttercup?"

"Need a little less fog."

"Uh… I can just do fog or no fog."

"Tell her no fog then," Godrik muttered. "Because this mess is as thick as pea soup. I can't see a thing." He stepped up to the thick iron wheel. "This is the one?"

He tested it, and Carys heard the door creak a little bit.

"Yes." She kept her voice soft. "So when the fog lifts and you can see the serpent swim into the lock, close that gate. As soon as he's through, close it."

Godrik nodded. "Yes, my lady."

Carys shouted at Laura. "Okay, Laura, let the fog go!"

Almost as soon as Carys spoke, the wind picked up and blew the heavy, low-lying clouds away. The river revealed itself, as did the full moon overhead, which glinted off the churning white water flowing over Naburn Weir and the large creature swimming in circles.

The wind didn't clear the crows away, but the starlings seemed to have disappeared, and the crows were no longer whirling overhead but were cawing from the branches of the trees and perched on the bridges and railings all around.

"Okay, Sam." She walked to the edge of the embankment. "Let's see if we can get rid of your hitchhiker."

The grindylows were still trying to crawl onto the riverbank, but as the fog cleared, they turned their eyes toward the full moon, distracted by its light. They blinked and stared, which allowed Lachlan and Duncan to slash and kick at them, sending them back into the black water from where they had emerged.

Naida was watching blue glowing lights that darted underneath the surface, two growing to four growing to eight, and then there were so many lights they looked like fireflies swimming in circles around the great sea monster.

Slowly the snake stopped swimming in rapid circles and stilled. He stretched his body and followed the blue lights, which led him in wide, arching whorls under the water. The glowing water sprites teased the wyrm, drawing it one way, then another, until the creature followed them around the wide river like a dog following its master.

"There it is." Carys watched the serpent move along the banks downstream, then upstream and toward the Naburn Locks. "There it is. Godrik?"

"I see him."

It was impossible to miss. The serpent was riding shallow in the water, a large ridge visible on its back. She glanced around, hoping no humans were around to see the monster, but she was more focused on where the sprites were leading it.

Whatever trance the Morrígan had over the serpent, it wasn't strong enough to combat the glowing lights and the draw of the water fae on the water serpent's primordial brain.

They led the wyrm in a long, curling pathway downriver, upriver, and right into the longest of the Naburn Locks.

"Now!"

Godrik grunted as he turned his shoulder into the wheel, and within moments the heavy wood-and-concrete doors swung shut.

And Sam the Sea Monster was trapped in Naburn Lock.

THEY STOOD ON THE EMBANKMENT, watching the serpent twist and roll in the locks, bashing his sides against the concrete. Sam prodded the gate with his nose, then tried to turn, but the lock was too narrow.

"We really caught a giant snake, didn't we?" Laura grabbed her mobile phone from her pocket. "Good thing my night camera is excellent."

"You are not taking a picture of it," Cadell said. "Laura—"

"Relax, O fiery one." Laura rolled her eyes. "I'm not going to post it on my dating profile or anything." She pursed her lips. "Even though that would be the best profile pic ever."

Carys couldn't stop her smile. "The problem is, what do we do with it now?"

"Let us hope the Morrígan has a short attention span," Cadell said.

Frida appeared with them, staring at the serpent in the lock. "She will tire of occupying his mind soon, and then I will sing a song to guide him back to the ocean."

Sam pushed on the upstream gate, but the solid wood-and-concrete structure didn't budge. And just as Cadell had said, the beast was smart enough to realize that pushing through the lock and destroying it would bring an avalanche of concrete and steel.

The monster's tail whipped around behind him, but it wasn't enough to break the downstream gate; he could not navigate the lock from either direction.

The crows surrounded the watery prison, hopping and shouting their displeasure at the unexpected turn of events.

"So we just wait?" Laura asked.

Duncan and Lachlan were both sitting on the grass, tying scraps of their bloodied shirts around various wounds.

Naida stared at the giant serpent with sad eyes. "It does not belong here."

Duncan nodded at the lock, wrapping a red gash on his wrist. "I say we go talk to that sea god and see what he has to say for himself. This is one of his creatures, isn't it? The Morrígan possessed it. We trapped it. Seems like he might owe us a favor for trapping this beastie before he reached York."

Frida raised her eyebrows. "I will go with you. I would like to hear what he says."

Duncan and Frida walked back to the parking lot to find Wade, and Carys walked over to Lachlan. He was struggling to try to tie a bandage around a slice on his lower back.

"Here." She took the strip of shirt from him and motioned him to standing. "I'll get it. Don't want you bleeding all over the van."

The giant snake hissed and arched against the side of the lock. There was a shriek, a strange gurgling sound, and then silence.

Lachlan smiled a little bit and handed her the piece of shirt. "Duncan bought that van, didn't he?"

"Yes. I kind of gave him a hard time, but considering the unexpected amount of blood on both of you, probably a good thing he didn't go for the rental."

"He always thinks ahead." Lachlan nodded. "It's good. In this world, he can give you the things that I could not."

Carys looked up and met his familiar green eyes. "I never cared about any of that, Lachlan."

The corner of Lachlan's mouth lifted. "I know. I shouldn't have said—"

"I had enough. We had enough. If you'd stayed, I never would have—"

"It wasn't my choice to go." His voice dropped. "You believe me, don't you? That I was happy in Baywood. That I would have stayed with you forever."

Carys couldn't look away. "I don't think it matters now, does it?"

"It matters to me." Lachlan was staring at her, and it was like years slipped away.

It had been almost two years since she'd first encountered his brilliant green eyes, his smile that made her feel like the sun shone on her.

Do you believe in fairy tales?

Two years. And a thousand truths hidden and revealed.

Nêrys, Cadell said in her mind, *the cross human and the demigod return.*

Carys shook her head and touched Lachlan's arm. "Turn around. Let's get that wound covered before you start attracting vampires."

Another round of hissing and thumping from the lock, but the gates both held.

"There are no vampires in Anglia." Lachlan turned around. "Eastern Europe and India are another story."

"India?"

"Oh yes."

Carys placed the bandage center over the red wound. It was a red, raised welt with a slice taken from the center, as if something had peeled off a strip of Lachlan's skin.

She winced when the bandage touched the open wound even though Lachlan didn't move.

"Good news," Duncan said. "Well... news anyway."

"Wade says that I have his permission to sing this creature back to the sea." Frida turned to Carys. "And that after that happens, you will know what you must do next."

Carys finished wrapping Lachlan's bandage and tied it off. "I'll just... know what I need to do next?"

Frida nodded. "Yes."

The crows hopping around the riverbank cackled. But then the cackling turned to squawking that turned to shrieking as the flock of birds took to the air, circling the serpent twisting in the lock. The creature let out a roar that sounded halfway between pain and rage.

It pierced Carys's ears, and she slapped her hands over them.

"Fuck!" Laura exclaimed. Her hands were covering her ears too. "If there are any humans in a five-mile radius, they're going to hear that shit. It's louder than a train whistle."

The sound went on and on until suddenly—

It died.

The beast shuddered through its whole body, and the murder of crows screamed and took to the air, disappearing into the night.

Cadell stared at the sea serpent. "She is gone."

Carys and Naida ran to the side of the lock, and the sea serpent named Sam was still as death.

Frida touched Godrik's arm. "Wolf, open the gate to the river."

Godrik walked to the gate, and with Duncan's help, they easily opened the doors.

Sam didn't move.

Without a word to any of them, Frida walked down the edge of the water and waded into the long grass. The moment her feet touched the river, she grew taller and her hair grew longer, longer, longer until the waves touched the grass and her hair drifted as one with the rushes.

The water sprites danced around her, and the current stilled.

When Frida opened her mouth, gone was the blunt and practical human woman they had met the day before. Her song was like water rippling over rocks, and as the music rose, the water pulled the sea serpent back and into the flowing depths of the river.

Frida walked to the great beast, her godly form twice as tall as the creature, and ran her hand over its rippling skin. Not scales like a fish, but much closer to the soft, pebbled skin of Cadell in his natural form.

When the glowing water sprites landed on the serpent, his skin seemed to come alive with a pearly grey light.

Then Frida sang a different song, and it was as if the music was a rhyme that Carys had always known, a song her mother sang to her in her cradle, a song her father caroled as he returned from the hunt. It was a marching rhythm, and the melody was as familiar as her own voice.

Though Carys had no idea what language the demigoddess sang in, the words formed in her mind as if Frida sang directly into her ear.

> *A single choice shows the path you must follow.*
> *Over the hill and down in a hollow.*
> *Gather an offering of milk and clay*
> *Cross the bridge and*
> *Wait for the shepherd*
> *And when the birds sing the light will array.*
> *One choice is waiting to show you the way.*

Sam drifted into the center of the river, and Frida walked with him. She climbed on the great serpent's back, wrapped her arms around his body, and without another word, they slipped beneath the surface of the water.

Naida let out a relieved sigh. "He is so happy to be going home."

Cadell nodded. "His mind is still tormented by the goddess, but Wada's daughter can heal him."

"Will she be able to guide him back to the gate?" Lachlan looked at Duncan. "I need to find a fae gate and get word to the other side. Dru's people need to pay more attention to any portals open underwater."

Duncan nodded. "He's probably not even thinking about sea gates, but they're there."

"He's the son of the sea god," Naida said. "He can set the mermen and the other water fae to strengthen the gates. They have always listened to him above anyone else."

Wade appeared next to Cadell. "The wyrm will be fine." He stared at Carys. "Did you get the message, girl?"

Every eye turned toward Carys.

"What message?" Duncan asked. "Was she singing words? All I heard was a melody."

"Yeah." Carys nodded. "I heard."

"But did you understand?" Wade asked.

Carys nodded. "One choice."

The sea god smiled. "Good. So you did understand." He started walking away. "You know where to go."

Cadell walked to her. "One choice?"

Frida had repeated the phrase. It couldn't be a coincidence. "One choice will show me the way." She started walking back to the van. She wanted a bath, a bed, and a hamburger, but she'd settle for two of the three.

"One choice is what?" Cadell shouted.

She turned. "Ask the Scotsmen."

Carys kept walking, but she heard Lachlan groan.

Cadell was silent for a moment, then said, "Ah! Of course. After all, he was never a fae."

Laura ran to catch up with her. "Okay, everyone knows what's happening except me, and that's not right."

"The gods like riddles. One choice." She glanced at Laura. "It's not an idea—it's a name. It's a famous name in Scotland actually. Lots of famous kings and chiefs loved it. Aonghas. One. Choice. A play on words."

"Aonghas?" It took Laura only a second to get it. "Let me guess—"

"Fucking Angus?" Duncan shouted. "Absolutely not."

"Are you kidding me, Carys?" Duncan was not pleased.

He had obtained rooms for all of them at a very decadent hotel that looked a little bit like a castle in the middle of York's Minster quarter. It was fancy enough that when he told the front desk that his girlfriend wanted a hamburger and chips, the concierge just nodded and said, "Right away, Mr. Murray."

Now Carys was staring into the en suite fireplace with a full stomach and drooping eyes. "Was the tub in the bathroom copper? I don't think I've ever seen a copper tub before." She was about five minutes away from falling face down on the fluffy, down-filled duvet.

"What does a copper tub have to do with going all the way back to Alba so you can get the damned ùruisg involved in all this..." He waved his hands. "I don't even know what to call this."

He was staring at the television where the early-morning news had already picked up the story about some kind of unexplained disaster in Yorkshire along the River Ouse.

Unfortunately, a teenager from Barlby had watched his golden retriever get eaten by a giant snake, and instead of fainting straight-away, he'd taken out his drone and sent it after the monster who had eaten his dog, posting the footage on social media as soon as he saw it.

While the internet couldn't seem to agree if the video was genuine or fake, Carys would recognize Sam the Sea Serpent anywhere.

The video was fuzzy, but the on-air presenters were clearly having a hard time avoiding the phrase "river monster" while trying to explain what had caused all the destruction.

"At this point I feel like you could probably call it a quest." Carys stared at the drone footage and turned the volume up on the television as Duncan came to sit next to her on the end of the bed. "I just don't know why you're so upset about getting Angus involved."

Someone in the control room at the local news station clearly wasn't buying the excuses the presenters were trying to make, because every time someone mentioned flooding, they cut to the unmistakable drone footage of a giant snake as long as two school buses.

"Of course it's impossible to avoid all speculation," the female presenter was saying in a very calm voice, "with the continued and unexplained occurrence of the... very large earthen berm in Salisbury."

"I believe it's a fairy fort," the male presenter said. "Or at least that's what the current theory is among the neo-pagan community in Britain."

The early-morning traffic reporter was clearly having fun with it. "Better watch for kelpies if you're taking a walk along the river."

"At least this gives the boys in Leeds some kind of excuse for that devastating defeat last night," the sports reporter said. "Just blame it on the fairies, John."

The male presenter and Traffic Guy laughed, but the woman at the desk didn't look amused.

Someone decided to play the drone footage again.

Carys grabbed the remote and turned off the television. She needed to figure out why Duncan was so upset. "Okay, why are you mad about getting help from Angus?"

"Because he's Angus," Duncan said. "And he'll make you pay for it. Somehow he'll make you pay. Angus never does anything for free."

Favors and obligations were practically their own currency in the Shadowlands, so Carys couldn't be surprised. "How long has Angus worked with you, smithing in Sgain?"

Duncan shrugged. "Around fifteen years."

"And how much do you pay him for helping you at your forge?" It was probably a bucket of milk every week and a goose at Christmas.

Midwinter. Yule. Imbolc. Whatever their winter festival was.

"How much do I pay Angus?" Duncan crossed his arms over his chest. "Two hundred gold sovereigns a year."

Carys blinked. "Wait, really?"

"Did you think the old bastard worked for free?"

Maybe she shouldn't have been surprised, but she was. "You pay Angus in gold sovereigns?"

"You think he'd take pound notes?"

Obviously not. "Okay, but you're still his favorite. I remember Lachlan's father saying that you're his favorite." King Robb might not have said that Duncan was Angus's favorite out loud, but it was definitely implied.

"Sure I am!" Duncan snorted. "Do you see Robb and Lachlan paying the old bastard in gold coin?"

Okay, that was fair. But Carys had a feeling that Angus didn't really work because he was hard up for money. The magical creature wasn't a fae. Not really. He might be a demigod of some kind, but he was ornery, opinionated, and tremendously powerful.

"If Cadell is right and Angus is some kind of demigod related to Pan, asking him to serve as a guide during this…"

"You just said we should call it a quest."

"I have to get rid of the Morrígan. Or at least make her go back to the Shadowlands, right?" Carys shifted and angled herself toward Duncan. "Angus is powerful, he's magical, and according to Cadell, he is really, really old. Maybe even older than the Morrígan."

"Carys—"

"He has a fondness for you." She took his hands, leaned forward, and kissed Duncan softly on his grumpy, pouting mouth. "And you love me, right?"

Duncan's voice was rough. "I love you like mad, woman." He wrapped his hand around her wrist where a red welt from the grindylows still lingered. He brought her arm up to his lips and kissed the angry wound. "I love you so much I want to take you back to California and forget all this is happening."

"And let more golden retrievers get eaten?" She glanced at her arm. "Imagine it wasn't you and me and Lachlan in the water. Imagine a little kid fell in." She shook her head. "Dru may be guarding the gates, but things are still creeping across, Duncan. They're drawn to her magic. I have to do something before anyone else gets hurt, and if Wade says Angus is the one who can help me, I'll figure out how to buy some gold sovereigns even if that means selling my house."

"Fuck that." Duncan wrapped his arm around Carys and sighed. "You're not selling your house. We're going back to Alba, and if that old bastard doesn't offer to help you, I'll sic Auld Mags on him."

CHAPTER TWELVE

They drove all afternoon, hitting rest stops and byways where average citizens of the Brightlands eyed the odd group of shifters, fairies, and humans.

Carys was leaning on Cadell's shoulder in the back of the van, watching as Lachlan and Duncan argued over who would pump the fuel for the van at the service station just off the A1 in Barton Park. Eventually Laura dragged Lachlan by the arm to take him inside the market attached to the service station.

Godrik and Naida walked into the market behind them. The wolf was hovering over the small fae woman, glaring at anyone who looked at them sideways.

Carys spoke to Cadell in her mind. *Do you think he realizes most of the people are staring at him and not her?*

"Unlikely." He answered aloud, his voice low and sleepy. "Godrik is not particularly sizable for an Eskari wolf."

Her eyes went wide, and she turned to look at him. "Seriously?"

Cadell nodded.

"I'm afraid to think what the big ones look like in human form."

"Many wolves rarely take human form." He leaned back and closed his eyes. "Not unlike dragons."

She leaned back on his shoulder and took a deep breath. "Thank you."

"For what, Nêrys?"

"For being here and spending so much time in the Brightlands." She shifted her head against his shoulder. "When we get to Scotland and get through the gates, you'll be able to shift again."

"I go wherever you go," he said. "There is no need to thank me for that."

She watched as two men on the other side of the fuel island began to shout at each other. The volume increased until Carys could hear them through the excellent soundproofing in the van.

Duncan walked over, his hands in his pockets, and Carys watched as he quickly defused the situation.

"Weird," she murmured. "I kind of think of road rage being an American thing."

"It is not, but that was likely because of the Morrígan."

"What?" She kept her eyes on the two retreating men. "Why do you say that?"

"Can you not feel it?"

She shook her head.

"She excels in fomenting discord," the dragon said. "I suspect human law enforcement will see a steady increase in violence until we find a way to rid her from the Brightlands."

Carys kept her eyes on Duncan, who was also watching the two angry men.

Tall, steady Duncan. As massive and immovable as a rock.

"There was a moment between you and Lachlan yesterday," Cadell said. "When Duncan was gone. You felt... unsettled."

She turned her face into his arm, dragging her eyes away from the blacksmith. *You know those moments when you have a memory of another time, and it somehow feels more real than the moment you're in?*

He responded to her inner voice. *You were remembering how you loved him.*

Yes.

That does not mean you love Duncan any less.

You can't love two people at once.

What a ridiculous thing to say. Cadell's inner voice was as cutting as his audible one. *Of course you can. Do you think either Lachlan or I stopped loving Seren after she died? We both still love her; we simply love you too.*

It was such an odd connection to realize that the three most important men in her life were all grieving her Shadowkin, a woman who looked exactly like her. A woman Carys had never known.

"I feel like a very poor replacement for Seren most of the time." She whispered the admission, almost hoping Cadell hadn't heard.

"That's as ridiculous as saying that you cannot love two people at the same time." Cadell stretched out his legs and crossed them at the ankles. "If anything, she was a shadow of you."

"I know that is technically true, but it feels like she was more alive than me somehow. She was a warrior, a princess, a—"

"She was exactly who she was raised to be," Cadell said. "And yes, she was all those things, but she also…"

"What?"

I don't want to be disloyal, Nêrys.

You could never.

She was sad. She was deeply lonely, and she never wanted anyone to know it.

Carys looked over her shoulder again, continuing the conversation in her mind. *Why do you say that?*

She knew that by marrying her, Lachlan was giving up the crown of Scotland, and she felt like he was sacrificing too much. She was angry that she didn't like Eamer more. She never had a mother. She wanted to like her father's wife, but she didn't. She didn't know how to relate to her. She had no true friends.

She had you.

Cadell nodded slowly. "Who is your best friend?"

She opened her mouth, then closed it.

"It is not me." He smiled gently. "It should not be me. Our bond is far deeper than friendship and far more complex. Your best friends are Laura and Kiersten. And Seren had no one like that in her life."

"She was a princess in a tower," Carys whispered.

"No, she was a woman and a leader," Cadell said. "And that can be very lonely in either world."

Carys thought about her uncle, who would probably make her heir to the throne of Cymru if she showed even the slightest inclination for it.

"I never want to be a queen."

"I know you do not." Cadell lifted a massive hand and patted the top of Carys's head. "Therefore, it is good that you love the blacksmith more than the prince."

"I do." She might have felt a sad kind of yearning for the simplicity of her love for Lachlan, when she was a teacher and he was a wandering musician in a small town by the sea. But Carys barely recognized that woman anymore. Her life was full of magic she had once only read about in books.

Godrik yanked open the door to the van, nearly shoving it off its hinges in his inadvertent enthusiasm. He held up a blue cup with a cartoon dog on it. "It is both frozen and bubbly. A wizard must have created this."

Carys squinted. "Is that a slushy?"

Godrik waited for Naida to climb into the van, holding the door for her.

The fae's eyes were round and bright; she was holding her own blue cup. "I have never seen a blue raspberry before, but they must be the sweetest berry in the Brightlands to be flavored in this way."

It took over five hours to drive from York to Scone, but Carys was hit with the most curious sense of homecoming when she saw the bright green roof of the Murrayshall Garden Center. She glanced to her right to see Duncan nearly grinning.

"Excited to be home?"

"Yes, it feels like it's been a year since I've been back, not two months." He reached over and took her hand. "Mary'll be excited to see you. Andrew too. They've been itching for you to visit again since you left last year."

"Really?"

Mary and Andrew were Duncan's friends and the couple who managed Murrayshall House for him when he was away. Carys had only met them as Lachlan's ex-girlfriend, so returning to Duncan's home as his girlfriend was going to feel completely different than her first visit.

"Are you kidding?" Duncan glanced at the rearview mirror, and Carys wondered whether Lachlan was looking at his Brightkin. "You've had a fan in Mary since the first day you met. Nothing makes her happier than someone putting me in my place."

Carys turned to look at Laura, who was sitting next to Cadell in the first row. Lachlan and Godrik were behind them, with Naida curled into the far back. "Mary is Duncan's housekeeper."

"House manager," Duncan said. "Honestly, the hall is more her house than mine. And her husband Andrew manages the grounds. They live on the property, so there's always someone there."

"Do they know about..." Laura looked around the van. "All this?"

"Oh yes." Duncan chuckled. "Mary, Lachlan, and I all played together as children. She knows all about the Shadowlands, though she's never been on the other side."

"One could say," Godrik said, "that though your friend has never been to the Shadowlands, we are bringing the Shadowlands to her."

Laura looked out the window at the green hedgerows that lined the road. "A wolf, a fae, and a dragon walked into the Brightlands."

"Don't forget the shaman," Cadell said quietly.

Laura looked at him, and the corner of Cadell's mouth turned up.

Carys couldn't help but notice that behind Laura and Cadell, Lachlan was staring out the window, his eyes fixed on the landscape, his lips pressed shut in a firm line.

She felt a tug of something in her chest.

Lachlan was home but not home. Carys wanted him to be happy, and she knew it wasn't her responsibility. She knew that, but she still felt the urge to comfort him.

Do you think either Lachlan or I stopped loving Seren after she died?

A part of her still loved Lachlan. She had to admit that to herself even if that made things with Duncan more complicated. You didn't just stop loving someone who had turned your life around the way Lachlan had with her.

She'd been drowning in depression when she met him. In many ways, Lachlan had saved her life. He'd forced her to think about the future again. He'd made her laugh and made her believe things could get better on days when the darkness wanted to swallow her.

Meeting Lachlan had made Carys believe in hope.

She turned and forced her eyes back to the winding road. She caught Duncan looking at her and knew he'd spotted her watching his twin.

She reached across the van and took his hand in her own.

She loved Duncan. He was the fire, the spark, the man who held her heart.

But that didn't mean she didn't remember what it felt like to love Lachlan too, and she only hoped that Duncan was able to understand.

"Look at you!" Mary enveloped her in a massive hug. "Oh, look at him too." She reached up and tugged on Duncan's ear. "You two look so happy. I knew it was meant to be."

"Mary," Duncan growled. "We have guests."

"Oh aye, my laird." Mary, dressed in a blue work shirt and worn green trousers, pretended to curtsy. "I shall see to your guests right away, my laird."

"Och, haud yer wheesht, woman." Duncan rolled his eyes.

Laura nodded. "Yeah, I like her."

"I like you too." Mary grinned. "I can tell already. This one'll take the piss out of a dragon, won't she?"

"I'm really not sure what that means, but context leads me to believe it's a compliment," Laura said. "So thank you."

Mary clapped her hands and walked over to Lachlan. "Here's the golden boy." She pinched his cheek and drew him into a hug. "It's been too long, Lachlan." She kissed his cheek. "Why have you been a stranger? Andrew's had three seasons of hunting without your company."

"Mary, you're looking well." Lachlan hugged her tight and whispered, "Leave your ogre of a husband and run away with me, won't you?"

Mary hooted and slapped his shoulder. "Listen to you." She turned to Naida. "You might be a stranger, but not for long. I'm Mary, and if you need anything, you've only to call on me." She took Naida's hand, and the moment their skin touched, Mary stilled. Her smile fell. "Mother of God, what've I done?"

"You are right—I am not human," Naida whispered. "But you've no obligation, Mairi a gael. I can see that your heart is as bright as your smile."

Mary seemed to relax, but her joy turned to suspicion when Godrik and Cadell walked from around the back of the van, carrying duffel bags and an odd collection of weapons. "Duncan, what's going on?"

"Och, Mary." He scratched his beard and winced. "I don't suppose Andrew's noticed anything... odd about the place, has he?"

"Not that he's mentioned to me, but you know how tight-lipped the man—"

"Duncan!"

A man half as tall as Godrik but nearly as wide walked out from the side of the house, pointing at Duncan.

"You arse!" the burly man said. "You bring a dragon, a wolf, and a fae to this house and you don't even call to warn us?"

Naida turned to Mary with wide eyes. "Your husband is an ogre?"

Laura and Carys spoke at once. "A what?"

Duncan regularly referred to his grounds keeper as an ogre, but Carys had always considered it a playful insult or a figure of speech.

"Oh, he's quite tame." Mary scrunched up her nose. "Tame-ish."

"Tame... for an ogre?" Naida murmured.

"Wait, ogres are real too?" Laura's face was a picture of delight. "This country is fantastic!"

"Andy, I can explain." Duncan raised his hands. "There was a misunderstanding, and Carys thought she was making a bargain with a fae—a dangerous but reasonable bargain—and it ended up being... a little more complicated."

"There's a damned fae fort rising in the south. There's a sea monster in Yorkshire." Andy pointed his finger and shoved it under Duncan's nose. "And now you're bringing a Shadowlands menagerie to my woods, and I find imps and redcaps sneaking through the trees. I had to smash two of the buggers this morning. What the fuck is going on?"

"Technically they are my woods," Duncan said. "But you're correct. The Morrígan is loose in the Brightlands and trying to weaken the gates from this side."

Andy's face went pale, and Carys wasn't sure, but there might have been a slight greenish tinge to his skin.

Lachlan added, "So things are starting to sneak through. That sea monster in Yorkshire was one of them."

Mary walked over and Andy grabbed her around the waist, gripping her to his side as he bared teeth that were distinctly less human than Carys would have expected for the average Scottish groundskeeper.

Right. So ogres were definitely a thing that existed.

"Andy, calm down," Duncan said. "That's why we're here. We need help and—"

"I had enough of the bloody fae when I left that place." Andy glanced at Naida. "No offense."

"None taken." Naida already had her shoes off and had walked onto the lawn in front of the manor house. "Your woods are very beautiful. I can tell the trees are deeply happy with you as their steward."

Andy said nothing, but his expression softened.

"This is my fault." Carys stepped forward. "And I'm so sorry that I have brought anything bad to Murrayshall House. Or the woods. But I'm trying to figure out a way to get the Morrígan back to the Shadowlands so the Brightlands stay safe from giant serpents and ancient Celtic war gods."

Andy nodded. "Appreciate that."

"We should go through the gate tonight," Duncan said. "But right now I need something to eat and bed." He grabbed Carys's hand and led her inside the house. "The rest of you, make yourselves at home."

DUNCAN HAD his eyes closed and his feet sticking out of the tub in the bathroom of the vast suite that was the laird's bedchamber at Murrayshall House.

"Carys?"

"I'm here."

"Come and join me."

She would. As soon as she could take it all in. If Carys had ever pictured the lord of the manor's bedchamber, this was it.

There was a vast four-poster bed with a coat of arms carved into the headboard. There were framed landscape paintings on the honey-brown wood paneling, and a large rack of antlers decorated the wall behind a truly massive wardrobe.

Carys perched on a bench at the foot of the bed, peeking at Duncan as he hummed in the bath.

His voice echoed in the marble-tiled bathroom. "Professor Morgan, the tub is big enough for two."

"Is this entire room yours?"

"This entire estate is mine," he said. "Every room. Every bathroom. Every library."

She jumped to her feet. "There's more than one library?"

Duncan chuckled and stretched out an arm. "I should have led with that." He opened his hand, palm out. "Come on now. You look a bit tired, lass. Come relax in the tub with me."

Relaxation was the last thing on her mind.

All she had to do was see the drops of steaming water rolling down his massive shoulders and she was convinced. Carys toed off her shoes, pushed down her jeans, and walked barefoot to the bathroom in an oversize button-down shirt and a pair of pink panties.

She walked across the cool tile and put one foot on the edge of the tub, right next to Duncan's shoulder. "You think I need to relax?"

His head fell back, and his eyes went straight to the juncture of her thighs. "Did I mention that everything in this house is mine?"

Carys raised one eyebrow. "Including that?"

Duncan trailed a wet finger from her anklebone, up the inside of her calf, behind her knee, and up her thigh before he dipped two fingers under her panties and into her sex, which was already damp and needy.

"Yes," he murmured. "Especially that."

He eased her leg into the water, spreading her wider as his fingers stroked and teased her beneath the silk.

Carys could barely breathe. The air was damp with steam from the bath. One foot was held firm in Duncan's hand while the other was planted on the cold tile.

The sensations were a riot of contradictions. Hot and cold. Soft and firm.

Duncan stroked the arch of her foot where it rested between his legs, and Carys felt the hard length of his erection against her ankle. He licked up the inside of her knee and her thigh; then her hips arched toward his mouth as he took his fingers away, gripping her backside as his tongue stroked her clit over the thin silk.

"Duncan—" She choked on his name. "Oh God."

She braced her hand on his wet shoulder as he scraped his teeth over the soaked material.

"I'd say take them off" —he spread his tongue and licked her over the silk— "but then I'd have to let go of you." He pressed the tip of his tongue to her swollen clitoris and hummed. "And I like you right where you are, Professor Morgan."

The wet silk only made her flesh more sensitive. Her desire was so close to the surface, she felt like it was seconds before his teasing tongue had her falling over the edge of climax.

Duncan pulled her into the tub, ripping her panties down her legs as she fell into the water. He caught her in his arms, fumbling with the buttons on her shirt in an attempt to bare her breasts to his hungry mouth.

"Big tub," she managed to gasp. "This is a very big tub."

"Oh aye." He gave up and tore the shirt down the center, sending buttons flying as Carys straddled his legs. "Big tub. Cast it myself."

"Oh, that's... great. Good." She could barely think. She wanted him in her. She wanted his thick erection filling her up, and she wanted it so much she could cry. "In me. Please. Please."

"Shhh." He put his hands on her hips, lifted her up, and slid her slowly down his erection, impaling her on the length of his rock-hard cock.

A sob caught in her throat. It was so good.

So, so good.

"That's a lass," he growled. "That's my Carys."

Her flesh was still swollen and sensitive from her first orgasm, and Carys could feel another wave coming as he lifted her up and down, helping her to ride him in the water.

She came all over him, her body tightening around his cock, and fell forward. She wrapped her arms around his neck, crying out against his neck as Duncan thrust up, over and over again until he groaned out her name and dug his fingers into her thighs so hard he might have left bruises.

"Fuck me," he choked out. "Oh, fuck me."

"I just did." She laid her head on his shoulder, and there were flashing lights behind her closed eyes. "It was great."

"Professor Morgan?"

She kissed his neck. "Yes, Laird Duncan."

His voice had a tinge of dread. "Condom. We forgot a condom."

Her breath hitched; then she let it out in a whoosh. "Good thing Laura reminded me to go to the pharmacy when we were in London." She kissed his shoulder again. "I'm good."

"You're more than good." He stroked his fingers up and down her spine. "You're amazing."

"And you have a thing for bathtubs."

"Only since I met you." He pressed a kiss to her temple. "Just so you know, there's a bathtub in every suite in this house."

"How many suites?"

"Eleven."

She nodded. "Then we've got our work cut out for us."

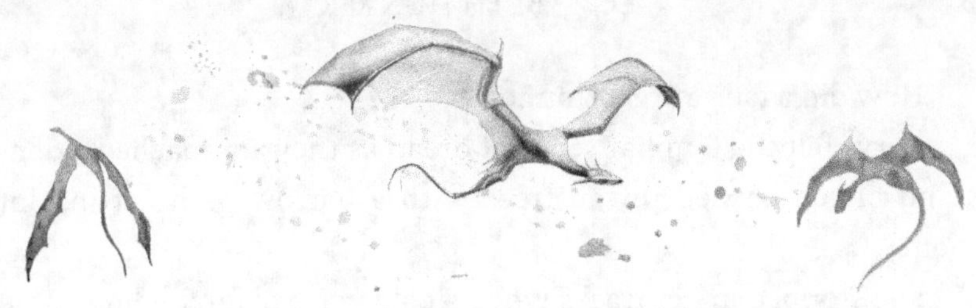

CHAPTER THIRTEEN

It was dusk when they followed the narrow trail in the forest behind the house, weaving between the cedars and the pines, the rowan, birch, and the underbrush that grew over the worn path where deer tracks mixed with human.

Andrew walked with them, speaking with Duncan as Lachlan led the way.

"Two imps there." He pointed at the base of a twisted pine. "Smashed against the roots. Nearly bit my hand in half, vicious little things."

"Has there been anything besides the imps?" Duncan asked.

"Redcaps, the nasty bastards." Andrew looked up, and Carys followed his eyes. "More wisps than usual," he murmured. "Far more."

Carys saw what he was talking about. They were still quite a ways from the gate, and yet the glowing blue wisps that marked it were dancing overhead like fireflies. There were way more than Carys had ever seen before.

"What does that mean?"

Cadell said, "I can feel the gate even from here. It feels... thinner."

How did a fae gate get thinner?

Carys felt the familiar sense of dread as they approached a dense stand of red-berried rowan trees with a narrow path cutting into them.

She stopped in her tracks when a cold wave of foreboding passed through her.

Whispers and hissing sounds teased her ears as shadows reached toward them like fingers cut by the setting sun.

Carys forced herself to put one foot in front of the other, walking into the shadows whether she wanted to or not.

One choice. Angus.

But was it her choice or his that would decide her fate?

One choice.

Behind her, Naida began to hum, and it was the same song Dru had sung the first time he walked Carys and Duncan through the gate. The ellyllon might have found the melody soothing, but it did nothing to calm Carys's fear.

"This is as far as I go." Andrew stepped to the right of the path and crossed his arms over his barrel chest as his eyes reached Carys. "Be careful. It's her they want."

Carys paused in front of him. "Why?"

He shrugged. "Why do you think?"

Because you are of the Shadow, Cadell said in her mind. *Your mother was born within it. By fate, you should not exist.*

Duncan paused to lean closer and say something to Andrew; then he joined Lachlan on the path, reaching his hand back for Carys to hold.

"Do you think they resent me for it?" Carys put her hand in Duncan's but turned to look at Cadell.

The dragon was already growing more inhuman, his eyes glinting gold, his wild nature emerging with every step they took.

Yes. His voice was a low rumble in her mind. *That is why they want you.*

"Who would resent you?" Laura piped up. "Wow, this gate feels weird." She was looking around like the professional she was. "Carys, this is the first gate you went through?"

"Yes." And the cold dread hadn't let up.

"No wonder you were so freaked out."

As they walked closer, the shadows grew deeper and the wisps circled. Carys heard them before she felt them, laughing whispers coming from low-hanging branches as dark and creeping shadows reached across the narrow path to trip her.

She felt a chilly finger reach across her ankle, and something cold and fluttering tickled her ear, as if an icy moth jumped from her shoulder and flew into her hair.

"Duncan." She squirmed at the feeling of cold fingers running over her.

He must have heard the fear in her voice because he turned and grabbed her, tugging her in front of him and surrounding her with his solid embrace.

"Walk with me now, lass." He put his mouth by her ear. "They can't have you, can they? That's why these wild fae are angry little bastards—because they know you're mine."

Lachlan had his sword drawn, his footsteps steady but relentless as he pushed through the hanging branches and thick darkness. "There are imps in the trees. And I saw a redcap watching from the roots of an oak tree we just passed."

"So Andy is right," Duncan said. "The woods are wilder now."

Carys saw a shadow darting forward to her left. When she turned to look, she realized it was Godrik, dissolving into a dark mist as his wolf form took hold of him and he bounded into the thick woods with silent ferocity.

"Godrik?" Naida's eyes went wide. Her mouth formed a small *O*; then she went silent and her eyes were sad.

"Hey." Laura held her hand out to Naida. "He probably just needs to stretch his legs. He's been human for a really long time."

Naida took Laura's hand, and the two women continued walking with Lachlan and Cadell bringing up the rear.

The whispers were everywhere in Carys's mind, tugging at her ears and fanning their cold breath down her neck even as Duncan held her safe in the cage of his warm arms.

It didn't seem to matter. She stumbled on a root that stretched toward her, nearly sending both her and Duncan tumbling.

"That's it!" Duncan lifted his head and shouted at the trees. "You little bastards, just let us pass. You know us, remember?"

Whatever was in the trees laughed. Then another laugh. Another and another until wicked laughter echoed up the branches of the ancient forest. Vines swayed with the darting movement of the wisps.

There came the sound of crackling wings, and a buzzing sound filled Carys's ears.

Lachlan turned and shouted, "Imps!" He waved an arm at Duncan. "Get her out of here now! Run!"

Without a word, Duncan hoisted Carys into his arms and followed Lachlan's advice.

HER TEETH CRACKED together as Duncan ran with her in his arms. Naida moved like a shadow in front of them, and Carys could barely see her.

Laura was behind—Carys spotted her friend running when she turned and looked over Duncan's shoulder. Laura held one hand up, and there was a golden glowing light that lit the forest around them and illuminated Cadell, who ran beside her with flashing gold eyes. Lachlan guarded their rear, occasionally turning to sweep his short bronze sword through a thick cloud of what looked like buzzing insects.

Carys knew they were not insects.

An imp surged forward and buzzed her ear, snapping at the edge of it until she smacked it away. She heard a crunch and a squeal.

Nêrys, Cadell shouted in her mind. *Hide your face if you don't want them to make you bleed. Your blood will only excite them more.*

She hid her face in Duncan's shoulder and held on tight, but she could feel a line of blood dripping down her ear and neck.

When she heard the roar and felt the crackling fire within her, she knew Cadell was shifting. A moment later, her heart lifted in her chest, and she knew her dragon had taken to the air.

The trees are thin enough for me to fly, he said in her mind. *I'll wheel around and see if I can lay fire behind you to keep the imps from swarming.*

Fire at the fae gate?

I feel no fae presence here, he said. *This gate has grown wild.*

It felt like forever, but Carys heard the change in the underbrush before she lifted her face. The crackle of dry leaves and branches gave way to softer steps, soil and moss and the smell of rich verdant life.

Duncan slowed his steps, his chest heaving as he continued to grip her tight. Carys hugged his shoulders and finally lifted her head to see they had reached a wide outcropping that looked over the hills of dark fae country.

Naida was standing on a line of boulders along the edge of the clearing, looking between the sloping green hills in front of her and the shadowy forest behind.

Laura panted beside her, the light she'd been holding nowhere to be found, but the pearlescent grey sky of the Shadowlands lit the dewy morning.

Lachlan still battled in the trees, slicing and beating back a dark swarm of imps that flew up the path.

Tell Lachlan to join you, Cadell said. *I'm going to clear the edge of the forest.*

She could feel him turning and flying back to her, their connection like a tether between his dragon heart and her own.

"Lachlan, get over here! Run!" She pointed to the sky as Duncan set her down. "Run!"

Lachlan turned and must have seen Cadell approaching. He slid his sword into the scabbard at his waist and waved at them all.

"Behind the rocks!" he shouted. "Get behind the rocks!"

Naida slipped behind the boulders and virtually disappeared. Duncan ran up and threw one leg over a low spot before he reached out his hand. "Come on!"

Without a word, he hoisted Carys over with ease, then turned and lifted Laura up and over.

"Down!" he yelled.

Lachlan was right behind them, flinging himself over the edge of the hill just as Cadell flew low, his emerald-green throat glowing with fire.

He gave a loud roar, and Carys heard high-pitched screaming from the shadowed tree line.

Naida, crouched underneath a grey boulder, covered her ears and closed her eyes. Her face a pained grimace at the chittering and clicking that came from the trees.

Cadell let out a spurt of fire, a warning shot, then lifted up over the forest, turned, wheeled around, and flew low over the edge of the trees, laying down a precise line of fire where the imps were still swarming.

The trees exploded, and the branches popped. Carys hid behind the boulders, looking through a crack in the rocks as Cadell exterminated the nasty crowd of imps and sent small creatures with blood-red hats disappearing into the safety of the forest.

"What are those?" Laura pointed to the small, gnome-sized creatures.

"Redcaps," Lachlan said. "I've never seen them so bold before." Despite the fire, the blood, and the imps, he grinned at Laura. "Welcome to Alba."

Laura laughed a little bit. "Thanks?"

Duncan poked his head over the wall. "The ruins of the old castle exist on this side of the gate too," he said. "The redcaps usually hang out there. I've never seen them in this part of the forest before."

Cadell was flying overhead. *Ask the fae woman.*

Carys turned to her. "Naida, what's going on?"

Naida still had her eyes closed. "I feel no high fae here. The only presence are the small wild ones, and they can't control the imps or the redcaps."

Lachlan's face was sliced by scores of tiny cuts the imps had inflicted on him. "Algar of Dalriaden is the nearest fae lord," he said. "His patrols are the ones that guard this gate. He's an ally of my father's."

"That explains it then," Naida said. "Lord Algar always hated Dru. It's possible that since Dru is king now, he is refusing to patrol the gates to keep the wild fae in check."

"That's the last thing we need," Duncan growled. "Fucking fae politics when the Morrígan is already making life complicated on the other side."

"I'll talk to him. Tell him the gates are already under threat from the Brightlands." Lachlan stood and looked at the smoking black line of forest. "Duncan, you take Carys to see Angus, and I'll go to Algar's fort and tell him that now is not the time for petty resentment."

Nêrys, I will fly you to Duncan's cottage to make sure you arrive safely, but I can only take two of you. The rest will have to walk.

"Do you need a fae escort?" Naida was looking at Lachlan. "Algar doesn't hold me in any particular esteem, but I am fae and a healer. And I am known as the king's former lover. Whatever else Algar is, he is not immune to storing up favors when it might benefit him."

"Your help would be... good," Lachlan said. "I am Robb's son, but you make an excellent point."

"Plus I can help you with those wounds." Naida winced. "They look painful."

Laura was looking around. "What happened to Godrik?"

Duncan shook his head. "I don't know. Something in the woods must have spooked him. I saw him shift and disappear."

"I have a feeling he'll find his way back to us," Naida said. "Wolves can track at great distances."

Nêrys, who do you want to take with you? I would prefer Laura, but I realize that Duncan may be the better choice.

Carys looked at her friends. "Where are we going?"

"Should we wait for Godrik to find us?" Laura asked.

"I should get a salve on those cuts now." Naida was digging in her pack. "Or they're likely to scar."

Nêrys?

"Okay, wait!" Carys pressed her fingers to her temples. A fae lord absent from duties, a missing wolf, injured Lachlan. There were too many voices. Too many moving pieces.

She pointed at Lachlan. "Where is this Lord Algar?"

Lachlan glanced at Naida. "It's several miles, but we can go to the village, procure mounts, and—"

"Too much time." She pointed at Duncan. "I know the way to your cottage and the forge from there. It's walking distance." She pointed at the sky. "Cadell can take Lachlan and Naida to this fae lord, then bring them back to your place."

Cadell had other opinions. *I am not leaving you.*

Please, Cadell? Just go, take them, then meet us at Duncan's forge. This is the most efficient way.

"So Cadell is going to fly Lachlan and Naida to this fae lord," Laura said, "and we can walk?"

"It's a half hour at most," Duncan said. "And after we leave these woods, there are no other forests. We should be safe."

"Cool." Laura nodded. "Sounds like a plan to me."

Carys stood and started walking, ignoring the hissing remnants of fire behind her in the forest.

Nêrys —Cadell was still protesting— *my duty is to you.*

She turned and looked at the dark forest. *We're going to have to go back through that gate to get back, right?*

The dragon was slow to answer. *Yes.*

We need it to be safe. Getting this fae lord to stop pouting and control the gate is going to help everyone, including me.

The dragon had no response to that, but Carys could feel how dissatisfied he was.

Carys was trying to be practical. The line of Cadell's fire was precise and devastating. Though the forest was green and the fire had not spread, the edge of the woods was a black gash on the landscape.

There were no imps that flew after her when she started walking along the path, and she didn't see a single redcap lurking in the shadows. That didn't mean they were not there. She was positive they were.

She turned to Lachlan and Naida. "Cadell will fly you to Lord What's His Name. Duncan, Laura, and I will meet you at the forge."

Naida was already tending to Lachlan's face wounds. "Tell Cadell we are both grateful."

The dragon was grumbling in her mind, but she knew he could recognize the practicality of her plan.

Carys walked over and gave Naida a quick hug. "Thank you," she said with meaning. Then she pulled away and looked pointedly at Lachlan. "We will see you both soon."

CARYS WAS WALKING between Duncan and Laura, and it was nice to feel surrounded by humans. "I'm hoping Angus really can help me, because mostly I'm feeling lost and really, really guilty."

Duncan was shaking his head. "I realize a demigoddess told you that Angus was the key to resolving this, but I honestly don't know how that old bastard can help. Or even that he will help. He's not the generous type."

Laura frowned. "Why guilty?"

"Because this is all my fault." She stuffed her hands in her pockets. "I'm the one who traded passage to the Brightlands when Epona's daughters have been keeping the Morrígan contained for years."

"You're not the first human to be deceived by a goddess," Laura said. "From what I remember from all those lectures about mythology, you're actually in good company."

Carys shrugged. "It still doesn't feel good."

"I'll not try to blow smoke up your arsehole," Duncan said. "You are responsible for it, but Laura's right too. The Morrígan is a tricky one. She played the fae sorceress well. You're hardly the only one who was fooled."

"And if she was fae, she'd have very little power in the Brightlands, so it was a calculated risk," Laura said. "But not a stupid one."

"Does it matter?"

"Yes," they both answered at once.

They walked up and over a rise, and when they crested the hill, Carys paused to take it all in.

The Shadowlands spread out before her, Sgain Castle in the distance with Sgain Town reaching out from it, crawling along the gentle hills.

The main road met them, bordered by hedgerows and towering birch trees whose green leaves fluttered in the wind.

"Come, my lady." Duncan held out his arm. "Only a little more ways to go."

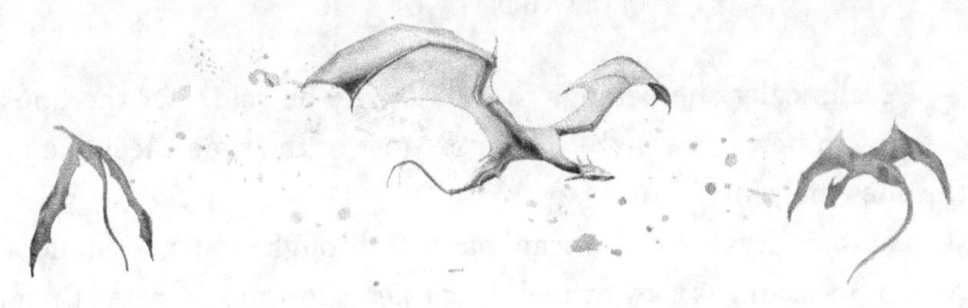

CHAPTER FOURTEEN

They passed a colorful penny tree and turned right to climb the wooden stile over the stacked stone wall that bordered Duncan's cottage.

"This is your house here?" Laura's voice was delighted. "I'm so jealous. I don't have a house in California. Well, not on the other side of the gate."

Duncan frowned. "Why not? You're a messenger, right? Like a diplomat? You have more of a role here than I do."

Laura shrugged. "I always sleep at Kere's when I'm there."

"I stay at the castle sometimes," Duncan said. "But I like having my own space, and this is a little more... private." He winked at Carys.

Carys's cheeks burned at the memory of a few heated nights in Duncan's cottage when the tension between them felt like it might set the thatch roof on fire.

"Auld Mags will have felt us coming," Duncan said. "She always knows when I cross the gate."

"Will I see her? Finally?" Carys turned to Laura. "Auld Mags is Duncan's broonie."

"Technically she belongs to the house," he said. "Or the house belongs to her, to be more accurate. Most of the time I feel like I'm the one who's intruding."

Laura, Carys, and Duncan passed through a dense stand of rowan trees, and as they turned the corner, a low moo greeted them.

Carys looked up. "You got her a cow."

There was a pretty brown cow munching on a few scattered flowers someone had thrown along the edge of the garden. She was wearing a straw hat that just covered the flop of long shaggy hair falling over her eyes.

"Ladies, meet Daisy."

"Daisy!" Laura was in raptures. "Look at her."

The cow trotted over and bumped Duncan's arm with her head. "She has a little one about somewhere." He craned his neck. "Come on now, lad."

There was a tumbling sound from behind the woodpile, and then a shaggy-headed calf with a white star on his forehead popped his head up and bleated a bright, small moo.

"Oh my god, I could die." Laura pressed her hands together. "I want one."

"I know. It looks like a fairy tale." Carys patted Daisy's side. "This whole place is like one of my—"

"Your mom's paintings!" Laura's voice rose. "Oh my god! It so is."

"Auld Mags won't come out until night," Duncan said. "So we should probably freshen up, grab some milk, then head to the forge."

"Milk?"

Carys nodded. "That's partly why Daisy comes in handy."

WALKING to the forge where they would meet Angus, Carys held a clay pitcher of fresh milk, and Laura had gathered a small bouquet of snowbells, daffodils, and a large clutch of bluebells under Carys's direction.

Duncan was holding a hefty bag nearly tearing at the seams. "Copper," he said bluntly. "Old copper wire. He loves messing about with it."

"Okay." Laura nodded slowly.

"So Angus is an ùruisg," Duncan explained, "which I always thought was some kind of fae, but Carys and the dragon tell me I'm mistaken, and obviously they're right, because he and I have…" Duncan cleared his throat and looked at the arched trees overhead. "I'll tell you later."

They had forged dragon steel, her boyfriend, her dragon, and the mysterious ùruisg who spoke in any language.

They walked through a forest and then down into a grotto-type area lined with stone where a small bridge crossed a brook of cold, tumbling water that danced over the rocks, singing along with the birds in the filtered light under the trees.

Laura noticed the difference as soon as they crossed the bridge. "No birds."

Duncan shook his head. "Don't know why, but sometimes Angus will throw out things like 'birds can't be trusted' or the like, so it's possible the fae watch him and he's wary of them."

"The fae wouldn't watch one of their own," Carys said. "Too nosy. Too rude."

"So Angus isn't fae." Laura was whispering. "What is he?"

"That's an excellent question."

They walked through the forest, keeping to the stone pathway that led through the trees. They passed the forge and the small hut where Angus slept, but Carys saw no one moving, and the forge was not lit.

"Huh." Duncan frowned. "That's odd."

"Should we keep walking?" There was something in Carys's chest, some instinct drawing her deeper into the forest where no birds sang. "We should keep walking."

She followed a narrow trail deeper into the woods where the only wild sound came from water running somewhere and an odd chorded music that sounded a bit like wind chimes.

With Duncan and Laura behind her, she reached a clearing where a waterfall tumbled over the rocks and a round pool had formed at the base.

This was no natural waterway; the pool was ringed by cut stones and cobbled rocks. The water flowed down the face of stacked slates, hitting copper bells that produced eerie, resonant notes that filled the air with their haunting song.

There was a clip-clop that sounded from behind the waterfall, and then a grey figure in a brown cloak appeared, walking through the water and tossing his hood back to reveal dark brown eyes narrowed in suspicion.

"You." He glanced sideways at Duncan and Carys for a second before he walked to Laura and lowered his face to hers. He spoke something in her ear, and Laura's eyes went wide.

Angus's hooded head bobbed up and down, examining Laura from her toes to the top of her head, murmuring too low for Carys to hear.

Laura put a hand on her chest and patted it, straightening and lifting her chin as she responded in her mother tongue.

"What's going on?" Duncan murmured.

"I don't know."

Angus passed a hand in front of Laura's face, and when she turned, Carys saw her chin had been painted with the thin lines the Yurok women in the Shadowlands tattooed to mark their clan and their status.

Angus finally spoke to her. "Daughter of two worlds, you bring me another shadow-walker. Why am I not surprised by this?"

Carys knew not to answer too directly. "I don't think you're surprised by much, Angus."

He kept his eyes on Laura when he spoke. "You are correct."

Laura's eyes were fixed on Angus. "How does he speak Yurok? Why?"

Carys had long suspected that Angus was some kind of god or demigod whose power came from the ancient messenger gods.

Mercury. Hermes. Thoth. Something even older than Thoth.

"Angus is good with languages," Duncan said. "And he usually speaks to you in whatever language you speak."

"For now I'll keep to Anglian, since that is the common" —Angus spat out the word— "tongue." He strode toward Carys with his loping gait. "Do you have a gift for me, Epona's daughter?"

She held out the clay pitcher of milk. "A gift from Daisy."

"And did you ask the cow for her offering?"

She'd thought it was a little odd at first, but she'd figured that it was Duncan's superstition, not Angus's. "I did."

"Good." He took the pitcher, lifted it to his lips, and drank deeply. "She's a good cow."

Then, without a word of warning, Angus put his hand on Carys's chest and shoved her backward, into the pool.

SHE FELL and she fell and she fell until her lungs were on fire and her clothes were dragging her to the depths.

She heard nothing but the chords from the copper bells, still striking over and over again by the falling water.

Carys was turned around, inside out, and had no idea which way to swim until a gleaming mirrored surface appeared in the distance.

She swam toward it, surfacing with a gasp into a dark grotto where water dripped from the rocks overhead into the pool where she had surfaced.

There was no cave, no opening, and the only light came from the surface of the water where she treaded. When she put her face under the surface, she saw the other side of the pool, and Laura's and Duncan's panicked faces as they searched for her.

"Do you have any idea what you've done?"

She pulled her head up, shook the water from her eyes, and saw Angus lurching toward her.

"What just happened?" She spat freezing water from her mouth. "Who are you? *What* are you, Angus?"

"You question me?" He leaned over her and shouted again. "Do you know what you have done?"

He was furious. She'd seen him cranky before, but now he was truly furious.

"I let the Morrígan into the Brightlands!" Carys was treading water, but her arms and legs were getting more and more exhausted. She was dressed in heavy canvas pants, a short-sleeved shirt, and a canvas jacket. "Then she used the fae battle on Saris Plain to give her enough power to raise a barrow."

Angus glared at her but said nothing.

"I fucked up, Angus. Big-time. But can I get out of the water before I drown?"

Angus jerked his head to the side, and Carys saw steps hidden in the rocks. She swam to them and crawled up the stones and out of the water.

No light. No sound. And once she left the water, the flickering reflection of Laura and Duncan faded until all there was on the surface was an eerie silver light.

"Goddess of war and chaos in the Brightlands. Legends coming to life," Angus muttered. "Your people have no idea what they are dealing with."

"I know, okay?"

"There was a reason the gates were built!" Angus snarled. "There was a reason the magic was contained."

"I know it's bad. I know." She held out her hands, which were shaking with both fear and freezing. "I need your help. The sea god's daughter said that one choice will lead the way."

Angus curled his lip. Had he always had fangs?

"One choice!" she said. "Angus. One choice. That's you. She spoke in prophesy. I've read enough to recognize it when I see it. She spoke in prophesy, and she told me that you—Angus—will lead the way."

"I could." Angus lifted his chin. "But Wada's daughter presumes too much."

"I need your help." Water dripped into her eyes, and she brushed it away again. "I fucked up and let a war goddess into the Brightlands. I know."

"You think she's simply a war goddess?" Angus let out a harsh laugh. "If all her power was contained in war, she could do no more harm to your world than you do to yourselves."

"I know there is more to the Morrígan than war, but—"

"*Your* people are acolytes of war. You revel in your bombs and your guns. In starvation and in suffering. You *worship* at the altar of violence. Nothing Macha could do would make your people's suffering worse."

Carys frowned. "Then why—"

"Why?" Angus strode to her, bent down, and stared into Carys's eyes. "Why does she bathe in the blood of her warriors? She is not evil no matter what your human heart might perceive. Her violence has a purpose, Carys of Baywood."

She racked her brain, but Angus's aggression was not exactly helping clear her mind. "Uh… she's a triple goddess. War and fate. She can…" Carys dug through her memory for everything she'd learned about Celtic mythology. "She can foretell victory in human battle."

"And that would be a useful trait for the vultures of your world who feed on the bones of war, but *that* is not her purpose."

Carys let out a harsh breath. "If she doesn't care about creating chaos or making war in the Brightlands, why is she there?"

"Think." Angus snarled at her. "Your Shadowkin would have

been a better hero for this battle, but then Seren would never have let a fae sorceress into the Brightlands in the first place."

"Well, she couldn't, could she?" Carys's felt heat flood her face. "Because she wasn't born in the Brightlands in the first place, and also, she's *dead*."

"Finally," the creature grumbled. "You have stopped your sniveling."

Carys felt like she was riding a roller coaster. Nothing made sense. She'd been hoping Angus would be her guide, but she'd heard nothing from him but disdain.

"You're not a warrior, Carys Morgan." He loped away from her, pacing. "And yet you're the hero the gods have chosen for this task."

The gods had chosen her? For what task?

She'd been the one who had caused all this in the first place.

Angus crossed his burly arms over his chest. "Why did the Morrígan want to get to the Brightlands?"

"I don't know."

If she'd been chosen by the gods for this task, was the Morrígan always going to cross the gates? Was Carys's birth, her life, Seren's death, Cadell's bond—was all of it simply the winding threads of a tapestry woven by the universe to put Carys in this exact place and time?

"You don't know?" Angus spat out. "I thought you were a scholar."

Carys's mind calmed; her body stopped shivering. "Macha is only one aspect of the Morrígan."

"Finally," Angus said. "She's thinking."

"She was Badb in the Shadowlands. The Crow Mother. She pretended to be fae."

Angus waved a hand. "The fae are not gods no matter how they wish they could be."

That wasn't strictly true considering the current king of the fae was the son of a Celtic sea god, but Carys wasn't going to argue with Angus about the squishy borders of myth at that exact moment.

"She chose the Macha aspect in the Brightlands," Carys murmured. "Macha is… from Ulster, I think?"

Angus waved a hand. "Doesn't matter."

Carys pictured the Morrígan's nubile, fresh body basking in the sun. The long hair and full figure. "She's a fertility goddess?"

What place did a fertility goddess have in the Shadowlands where the women could not give birth? She had *no* place here. The worshippers of the Shadowlands did not need her.

"You're finally on the path." Angus stamped one foot. "Not there yet."

I blessed this land by coupling with its king. Even their queens bear my mark.

"But it's not the fertility. Not *just* the fertility."

"War and sex. War and birth. Death and life," Angus muttered. "You have to think like the goddess, Carys Morgan. What does she want?"

"I don't know," Carys said. "You're supposed to give me answers, not more questions."

"What do all gods want?" Angus shouted. "You know this already!"

"Worship!" The moment it left her mouth, it was obvious. So obvious. "The Morrígan just wants to be worshipped."

Angus loped to her. "Your world is a twisted place that feeds on selfishness, greed, violence, and *attention*," he said. "And what is attention but worship in another form? The Morrígan's acolytes in the Brightlands are *begging* to be found."

Carys pictured the intoxicated young people who had come under her spell in Gorne Wood. "She's already started."

"Know this, daughter of two worlds, if there was ever a riper time for the Morrígan to take over your world, I have not seen it," Angus said. "She aims to break the gates, let the old gods rise in power again, and assert her sovereignty over a land that once *worshipped* her."

Carys finally met Angus's eyes, and her heart began to race. "I can't stop her. You said it yourself—I'm not a warrior."

"No, but part of you is." Angus lowered his head to look into Carys's eyes. "Light, dark, and beast. Like the goddess you face, you are also three, but you don't seem to know it. Haven't you heard her yet?"

A shiver creeped down her spine. "Heard who?"

"You know who I mean."

Break the enchantment. A voice on the battlefield, whispering in her mind. *You end the battle.*

Ogwen Valley.

"Ogwen Valley." Why had she shouted Ogwen Valley? What did it mean? "What is Ogwen Valley?"

"Ask your dragon, young hero."

"Are you saying..." Carys shook her head because the possibility was too much. Too confusing. Too... impossible. "Are you saying that Seren—"

"You and your sister were the gifts of a powerful goddess to one of her most devoted acolytes. Your mother was so beloved by Epona that she granted Tegan the gift of creating *life*." Angus shook his head. "Do you really think Epona would simply let your Shadowkin die?"

Carys's heart raced. Tears started to fall down her cheeks. "What are you telling me?"

Angus's voice took on an unearthly timbre. "There are worlds, pocket worlds, shadow worlds, and underworlds."

"Pocket worlds?" Carys looked around the strange unearthly cave that seemed to come and go from nowhere.

"There are realms of the old fae and the new, of demigods and demons. Before all this is over, you will have to learn how to walk between them."

Her stomach dropped. "I can't do that."

"Don't be foolish, child." He put a hand on her back. "You were born to do that. If you couldn't, you would have drowned moments after I pushed you into the pool."

"But you knew I wasn't going to, right?"

Angus shrugged. Then, without another word, he pushed her back into the water, and Carys was falling again.

CHAPTER FIFTEEN

She surfaced with a gasp to two hands reaching for her own as Laura and Duncan pulled her up and out of the water.

"Seren is alive!" The words burst from her mouth. "Seren is alive!"

She blinked the water from her eyes and saw Duncan fall back, his face pale as the moon, his eyes wide and dark.

Laura shouted, "What?"

The clip-clop of Angus's cloven hooves sounded on the stones, and Carys turned to see him emerging from behind the waterfall. "I didn't say that."

"You did," Carys sputtered. "You said—"

"I said she was in another realm, Carys Morgan." Angus clip-clopped over to Duncan and stared down at him. "She needs a guide on this journey. I won't be able to work at the forge for a while."

Duncan was still sitting on the ground, his elbows braced on his knees and his eyes staring into the distance. "Do you really think I care about the forge right now?"

"Perhaps not, but it would be irresponsible to not give you

notice." Angus threw a twisted grey wrap over his shoulders. "Now what have you to offer me, Tegan's daughter?"

Carys reached out her hand, and Laura helped her to her feet. "What do I... I already gave you the milk."

Laura reached down, grabbed the bouquet she'd gathered earlier, and stuck out her hand. "And flowers."

Angus walked over, bent down to sniff the bouquet. "Not a bad offering, but hardly enough to tempt me to be your guide."

"What?" Carys's head was still spinning from the revelations underneath the water. *Cadell?* She called her dragon in her mind. *I need you.*

She didn't hear anything audible, but a rush in her chest told Carys that the flying beast had immediately turned and was heading toward her.

The panicked fluttering in her chest died down. "You told me the gods had chosen me to be the hero on this quest, and Wada's daughter prophesied that you would be the one to guide me, but you want me to pay you?"

"Yes. I cannot work for free."

Cannot. Not would not.

Interesting.

Okay, Carys, think.

What would a not-ùruisg—because it was very clear to Carys at this point that the mythological fae identity was only a guise—want from her?

"I don't have anything to offer you," Carys said. "I have a house in California." It was her sole possession though, and not very portable. "I have tools. My father had a whole barn full of wood-working tools. Do you want—"

"I have no use for the belongings of a dead human from across the ocean." Angus waved a gnarled hand.

Carys felt her cheeks warm again.

"Hey," Laura snapped. "You may be a superpowerful creature who can speak any language, but maybe you should learn some manners." She put her hands on her hips. "What do you want? She's not a queen. She doesn't have a treasury."

"Then perhaps she should find another guide."

"I have…" Carys almost said a dragon, but Cadell wasn't a possession to be bargained with. "Do you want… passage to the Brightlands?"

"Really?" Laura's shoulders slumped. "Carys, after the last time—"

"What? He's supposed to go with us anyway!"

"Okay, fair point." Laura turned toward Angus. "So?"

Angus crossed his arms over his chest. "I have no need for passage through my own handiwork, Carys Morgan. Try something else."

"The forge," Duncan said quietly.

Carys turned. "No."

Duncan slowly stood up, brushed off his hands, and walked toward Angus. "Guide Carys on her journey, show her what she needs to do, and you may have the forge we've built as your own."

Angus's eyes gleamed. "So the forge and everything built there would be mine?"

"Everything built in the future," Duncan said. "That which is already made remains mine."

Angus was silent for a long time, then finally nodded. "This is an acceptable payment. I will guide you."

"Duncan, you can't pay for my guide," Carys said. "Isn't there some rule about that?"

"No." Angus was already loping away from the pool and back into the woods. "We have a deal, Carys Morgan. The forge is mine, and I will guide you to the druids."

"The druids?" Laura asked. "Wait, I thought we had to do this quest in the Brightlands because that's where the Morrígan is."

"Angus turned. "Yes, of course. Do you think druids only reside on this side of the shadow?" He shook his head and kept walking. "I would expect a shadow-walker to be more educated than this."

"Hey!" Laura frowned and started after him. "I am working in an entirely different mythological framework than I was raised in, so you can just—" She switched to Yurok and started telling Angus off in another language entirely.

Duncan walked over and tucked Carys's hand under his arm. "Don't think twice about it, lass. You don't owe me a penny." His dimple showed up. "In fact, you're saving me two hundred gold sovereigns a year."

By the time they arrived back at Angus's forge, Cadell was already waiting.

He had remained in beast form.

Nêrys, you smell of the otherworld.

"How can you tell that?" She walked over and immediately threw her arms around his leathery green neck. *Cadell, Seren is alive.*

She felt the fire rise in him like a flame hit with a bellows.

What?

What is Ogwen Valley?

Who told you she was alive?

"Angus." She stepped back and looked him in his great golden eye. "What is Ogwen Valley?"

There was a ripple along Cadell's skin, and moments later, he faced her in human form. "Come with me."

He led her to a round circle of tree stumps that had been cut and placed around a stone fire circle. He sat on one and Carys sat next to him.

"I heard Seren's call for the first time when she was eleven years old," Cadell said. "She was not my first nêr ddraig, but I had never..." The corner of his mouth turned up. "I had never been bonded to a human who fought me as Seren did."

"She was stubborn."

"*So* stubborn," he said. "Even as a child. I was the elder. Obviously I was battle-tested, but no matter how we trained or what we did, she had to do it her way."

"And you went along with that?"

"Not at first, and not always," he said. "Remember, I am your dragon, but I am not your servant."

"I remember."

"Seren took her power over me seriously, and she respected that, but I would always try to lead her in the direction I thought was the smartest or the safest. But she is her father's daughter." His eyes lit up. "As you are, Carys."

She blinked away tears when she thought about her father. Her steady, solid guiding light in the world. "But my father was a teacher, not a king."

Cadell nodded once. "Indeed. Seren grew up with a very clear path, and that path led directly to the throne." His voice dropped to a whisper. "And she would have made a remarkable queen."

"Ogwen Valley."

"It was a testing run," he said. "It is the final trial of the training school. The teachers and their dragons set up a series of trials—they're different every time—and hers was the most challenging I have ever seen. Marksmanship, tracking, hunting, ambushes. She was limping and had a spear through her leg by the time we reached Ogwen Valley. She was half delirious from blood loss, and there were more obstacles ahead. Spears thrown at my wings, sharpshooters in the hills."

"You couldn't fly over them?"

"Not if she wanted to pass the trial." Cadell folded his hands and looked at the ground. "I knew what was coming, and I knew she was in pain. She wasn't thinking clearly, so I had a complicated strategy planned to evade the sharpshooters and get us through the valley without her taking another hit."

"More dangerous for you, I'm betting."

He shrugged. "I am a dragon, nêrys. I heal much faster than a human."

"But Seren had another plan."

"'Fly as fast as you can, as straight as you can.'" He shook his head. "Low to the ground, well in range of the sharpshooters, leaving both of us exposed. Pure speed and nothing else. 'Just go as fast as you can. They're expecting strategy, let us give them power.'"

"You argued."

"Of course, but in the end, she reminded me that it was her trial, not mine. And that she knew she was right, and I needed to go along with it." He shrugged. "I did."

"And it worked."

"It worked. They knew she was injured, so they assumed we would be cautious. I took one spear to the wing, but it barely grazed me. Seren passed out as soon as we reached the castle, but her strategy—or her lack of one—succeeded. Her instructors unanimously agreed that she had passed her training."

"And she always reminded you of it?" Carys smiled a little bit.

"Ogwen Valley was our code, and she wasn't the only one who used it. It was a signal that one of us was sure—even if it didn't make sense—and we were asking for the other's trust."

"So when I said Ogwen Valley on the battlefield over Saris Plain—"

"I knew then that Seren wasn't entirely gone," Cadell said. "It wasn't my place to tell you that. I don't know how she is speaking to you from Annwn, but—"

"Annwn." The underworld of Welsh mythology was an alternate realm where the dead lived on, usually carousing with heroes of old and the gods. "But you said you felt her die."

"The dead may live on in Annwn, but they never return to the Shadowlands. They are lost to us. So when Seren spoke to you, I was confused, but do not take my confusion—or whatever the old one said—to mean that Seren is alive. She is not alive. I felt her die."

"But she's not really dead either."

Cadell looked up at the sky. "The prophets of your world write of a realm in the sky where human souls live in the presence of their god, do they not? How is it different? Don't you believe that is where your father's spirit resides? Does he not live on in some way?"

"I don't know." She'd thought about it after her parents passed, listened to the words of comfort from the pastor at the small Protestant church in the woods where her father had worshipped. "I know what my father believed, but how does that square with my mother being a devotee to a Celtic horse goddess?"

"People believe many different things," Cadell said. "Clearly it was not a point of argument for them." The dragon leaned forward. "My strategy would have gotten Seren and I through Ogwen Valley too."

The dragon's meaning was clear: There was more than one path. More than one belief. And clearly, in this place, more than one god.

Carys said, "Angus told me something strange when I was pulled into his little pocket world."

Cadell's eyes narrowed. "You were where?"

"I'll explain later." She leaned forward. "He said: 'There are realms of the old fae and the new, of demigods and demons. Before all this is over, you will learn to walk between them.'"

Cadell nodded. "So perhaps to finish this task and return the Morrígan to the Shadowlands, only a daughter of a Shadowkin and a Brightkin could succeed."

"Maybe. But what do we do now?"

Cadell cast his eyes at the forge where Angus, Duncan, and Laura were waiting. "I suppose... now we must listen to the goat man."

"You know you're thinking the same thing," Laura muttered.

"I am not. Stop."

Carys, Duncan, and Laura were walking back toward the gate, following Angus's loping, stilt-like lead while Cadell went to fetch Naida and Lachlan from the court of the local fae lord. According to the dragon, the meeting had been progressing well when he heard Carys's call.

With any luck, the gate would be a little less terrifying on the way back to the Brightlands. They were halfway there, traveling through the scattered woods of light fae country, and nearly to the heavier forest where the fae gate loomed.

Carys returned to her debate with Laura. "I'm sure a creature as powerful as Angus will have some way of cloaking his..."

"Hooves. You can say hooves," Laura said. "It's not like it's an offensive word. And okay, but if his magic is sourced from here, can he even use it on the other side? Or are we just picking up another random tall dude who's going to eat a lot?"

Carys leaped on the conversational tangent. "They do have huge appetites, right?"

Godrik had still not appeared. It was possible that their quest, as much as he'd been dedicated to it, was something he'd had to abandon. It wasn't like she could text the giant wolf. "Do you think Godrik is maybe waiting by the gate?"

"I have no idea, but I'm wondering if he found a local pack and heard something that made him head home." Laura nodded at Angus. "Okay, seriously. Let's say this dude has a glamour. Does he still look like he's walking upright on goat legs when we're on the other side? Like if he walked through mud, are there going to be little cloven hoofprints or footprints?"

"I feel like we're bordering on body-shaming now," Carys whispered.

"It's just his legs." Laura gestured at Angus and kept her voice at normal volume. "I'm not insulting them. They're perfectly fine, but we kind of need to know how much attention we're going to have to fight off." She looked at Duncan. "You hear me on this, right, grumpy?"

"I have no opinion." Duncan glanced at Angus. "If he agreed to guide us, he'll figure out how to blend in once we're in the Brightlands."

"I have my ways, human." Angus lifted his voice. "The imps have been here." He wrinkled his nose and stopped in the middle of the path. "Nasty creatures."

Nêrys, we are near.

They were closing in on the dense canopy of the dark forest when she felt Cadell approaching. Angus halted and looked up, watching the dragon circle and descend from the clouds.

Cadell set down on a clear rise a short distance away, and Duncan walked toward the landing party while Carys and Laura waited with Angus.

I am going to tell Lachlan that Seren is speaking from Annwn, Cadell said in her mind.

"So that's why Duncan walked over," she muttered.

Laura frowned. "What?"

"My boyfriend and my dragon are both protecting me from however they think Lachlan is going to react to Seren being... alive. Ish. Not completely dead."

"But she is dead," Laura said. "Cadell said—"

"Cadell is not hearing her in his mind." Carys pointed to her head. "Cadell did not hear it from the goat guide—"

"I heard that," Angus muttered.

"—that he was going to have to figure out how to walk to the otherworld before all this is over. So you can all say that she's not technically alive, but—"

"Seren is what?" Lachlan's roar erupted from beyond the trees.

"See?" Carys threw up her hands. "Alive-*ish* seems accurate."

Moments later, Lachlan was striding up the path with Duncan walking behind him. Cadell and Naida followed at a distance.

"Did you know?" Lachlan strode right past Carys and put his finger into Angus's face. "Did you know she was alive, you bastard?"

"She's not alive; she's in Annwn," Angus said. "And if you'd taken two minutes to think about it instead of rolling around in your own grief after she died, you would have realized it too. She was a warrior and heir to the throne who died in battle." The ùruisg leaned forward. "Just because you didn't know you were at war doesn't mean her mother's gods would have missed it."

"Not all humans who die go to Annwn," Naida said quietly to Carys and Laura. "But it does not surprise me that Seren would have been taken there after her death, considering who your mother was and the circumstances."

Carys kept her voice low too. "Angus told me ages ago. He asked if Seren had returned from Annwn when he saw me. I just didn't realize—"

"So she's alive," Lachlan said. "Seren is alive. Heroes travel back from Annwn." His voice was half-desperate. "It is written in the stories that—"

"The living are sometimes granted passage and return," Cadell said. "Not the dead." For once, the dragon's voice was soft with empathy. "If there is anyone whose grief is the equal of yours, it is mine, Lachlan of Moray. If I thought there was a way to return Seren to this realm, I would fly to Annwn and drink fire from the cauldron of Caer Sidi myself." He turned his gaze to Carys. "Even though I have found peace with a new nêrys."

Lachlan suddenly turned to Carys and his face went pale. "Carys."

"It's fine." She felt her cheeks burning. "Lachlan, we don't need to—"

"I love you both. Gods of old, I love you both so much." He wrapped his arms around her and folded her into a ferocious embrace. "What do we do, Carys? What do we do?"

Lachlan's shoulders shook with grief and confusion, and Carys felt his hot tears on her neck. She caught Duncan's glare over his Shadowkin's shoulders, but she couldn't find it in her heart to turn Lachlan away.

Seren was alive. Ish.

Lachlan had crossed a world once just to catch a glimpse of Seren's echo in the Brightlands. He'd abandoned a throne just to see her face.

What would he do now that he knew Seren lived in another realm?

"Enough of your human sentiments," Angus growled. "There is a goddess wreaking havoc on the Brightlands at this very moment. I can feel how weak the gates have become." He planted his staff in the dirt and pointed at Carys. "You have a task to fulfill, dragon lord. Until it is done, that is your only concern."

CHAPTER SIXTEEN

The passage back through the gates was less treacherous than the previous journey, but Godrik had not appeared in the forest, and Carys could see that his absence was troubling Naida.

They had just walked through the dense stand of rowan trees and the blue wisps were scattering into the predawn forest when Carys slowed down to walk next to her.

"I'm sure he'll find us," she told the small fae woman.

Naida nodded. "I think the imps triggered his true form, and it's possible he joined a local pack for a time." She glanced at Cadell and Laura on the path in front of them. "Creatures of all sorts usually prefer their own kind."

"Sometimes, yes." Carys nodded. "But not always."

Naida smiled. "Do you wonder if I have feelings for the wolf?"

"I'm sure you have feelings of friendship." Carys wanted to be nosy, but prodding at Naida—after knowing her history with Dru—just seemed cruel.

"Godrik is protective and loyal," Naida said. "Those are qualities I admire. They are not so common among my kind."

"He's blunt too."

Naida smiled. "He is."

They passed the ruins where Andy had said the redcaps hid, but there was no sign of the imps or the small wild fae that had pursued them on the way into the Shadowlands.

"Looks like your visit to Lord Algar was successful," Carys said.

"It was not unpleasant, and he was very respectful toward Lachlan. I believe seeing imp bites on the son of the Alban king brought the gravity of the situation into focus."

Lachlan.

Carys glanced over her shoulder to where Lachlan brought up the rear of the walking party. Angus had remained deeper in the forest to shore up the fae gate on this side.

The sky was a deep azure blue as dawn creeped closer, and Lachlan's pale face took on a moonlike luminescence as they walked out of the trees and into the rolling meadows that marked the boundaries of Murrayshall House.

Duncan turned, his face lighting up. "Carys, almost there."

She was shocked to realize that it had been less than twenty-four hours since they'd crossed into the Shadowlands.

She walked to Duncan and slipped her arm around his waist. "I feel like my internal clock is going to take a year to recover when all this is over," she murmured, leaning into his side as they waded through the long grass.

"We should rest at the house today," he said.

"Do you think we have time?"

Duncan said, "That fae lord seems to be doing his job, judging by how much easier it was walking back. Angus will harden the gate on this side so the imps and redcaps can't sneak through."

"That's one gate. Angus can't shore up every gate in Scotland."

It was fairly evident to Carys at this point that Angus was some kind of demigod or deity, which meant his power over the gates was at least as strong as Dru's. Good news for them, but hardly helpful for the hundreds of fae gates that dotted the British Isles.

"You need sleep, Carys." He glanced over his shoulder at the ragged group of travelers walking down the hill. "Even Cadell is exhausted. And he's probably hungry as fuck. I don't think he had time to hunt in the Shadowlands. At least let Mary feed him. Naida is looking peaked again, and Laura is dragging."

"Okay, fine." Leave it to the acerbic blacksmith to end up being the mother hen of the group. "You're right. We need to rest."

"Besides" —Duncan glanced over his shoulder— "Angus didn't change a whit when we walked through that gate, so I need to figure out how to disguise a goat man so we can move around the Brightlands without going viral."

A voice called from the trees. "I heard that."

"Christ, he's scary sometimes," Duncan muttered.

Carys couldn't help but check on Lachlan again; he seemed to be moving on autopilot. His face was locked down, and his normally bright eyes were fixed firmly on the ground.

"Stop it." Duncan squeezed her hand.

She turned her face forward. "I'm not doing anything."

"It's bad enough that he..." Duncan shook his head. "No, I'm not going to discuss this. Not when we're both tired and hungry."

"Fine." She didn't want to talk about it anyway.

Didn't want to talk about her fears that the voice in her head might come back.

Didn't want to talk about how hard it had been to let Lachlan go when he was so very vulnerable.

Didn't want to talk about the weird stab of jealousy in her chest when she saw Lachlan's haunted eyes.

It doesn't matter. It shouldn't matter. You're in love with Duncan.

She was in love with Duncan. He was an absolute rock and the one thing that seemed to make sense in this absolute fever dream that had become her life.

She loved Duncan.

And her feelings for Lachlan were complicated, but nothing was going to change the fact that she had made her choice. And that choice was holding her hand and holding her up when she was ready to fall over.

"Nêrys." Cadell spoke from behind her. "You need to rest."

"And you need to eat." She kept trudging along the path, and her spirits lifted when she saw a thin stream of smoke over the trees.

"Mary lit the fire," Duncan murmured. "We're almost home."

Carys glanced over her shoulder. "Hey guys, Duncan was just saying we should stay a day at his house."

Cadell nodded. "The surly human is not wrong."

Laura raised a hand. "I vote rest and recover too."

"The Morrígan—"

"Is not going anywhere," Naida added. "Whatever havoc she is causing at the moment will not be made better if the hero chosen to defeat her runs out of energy."

The hero chosen to defeat the Morrígan.

A daughter of a Brightkin and a Shadowkin who could walk through worlds.

Seren could walk through worlds too.

Carys reached back in her memory to the voice that had stayed with her through battle. The voice that had been as familiar as her own. *You never came to look for me,* she mused in her own mind as she walked on the path toward the house. *Why not? Duncan told me you crossed the gates, but you never came to look for me.*

Who says I didn't?

Carys froze.

"Carys?" Duncan shook her hand. "What's wrong?"

Her heart raced in her chest. "Nothing."

Liar.

Carys focused on the faint, thready voice in her mind. *Can you hear me? Seren?*

Nothing. Her mind was silent again.

Whatever magic that had allowed Seren to reach her from Annwn, it had run out of energy as the path widened and they approached Murrayshall House.

Within moments, the door opened and the smell of roasting meat reached her nose.

They were home.

CARYS SLEPT for what felt like an entire day. She woke in Duncan's bedroom and a note was on the pillow beside her.

There is food downstairs when you're awake.
—D

Perfect man. He was a perfect man.

Her stomach rumbled and she hopped out of bed, throwing on one of Duncan's massive robes and sliding her feet into slippers that were four sizes too big.

She was going to eat, then go back to sleep. The light outside her window looked like late-afternoon sunshine, so she knew they wouldn't be heading anywhere new until morning.

Carys walked down the stairs and froze when she saw a most surprising sight.

Laura on the stairs, Cadell a step beneath her, his eyes narrowed on her face as he leaned in.

He was either going to bite her or kiss her, and Carys didn't know which, but she turned and tried to hide.

Too late.

"Nêrys." The dragon straightened and cleared his throat. "Food has been prepared and is available in the morning room."

"Yeah." Laura's voice was as cold as the North Pacific. "You should eat something. Everyone else has been up for hours."

"Okay." She wasn't going to ask what was going on between

them because it wasn't her business, but as she walked past Laura, she caught her friend's expression and her eyes went wide.

Laura had been crying. There was going to be a conversation.

"Cadell, have you eaten?" Carys felt a little frosty. No one messed with Laura.

"I have."

She could read nothing from his voice. "Okay. I'm going to go eat. Laura?"

"I'm going to my room." She practically ran up the stairs, leaving Carys and her dragon in the middle of the massive front staircase of Murrayshall House.

"Explain," Carys said.

"I cannot." Cadell looked as irritated as Carys. "She is... recalcitrant."

Carys's eyebrows went up. Cadell was angry. Like... really angry. "Something happened."

He glared at her. "Are you going to eat or are you going to stand and gawk at me while your stomach churns in a most unpleasant way?"

Carys stood on her toes and stared into his eyes. "The fellowship is breaking..." she said in an eerie voice.

"If you continue to reference that movie, I will be forced to petition King Dafydd for redress."

Cadell continued upstairs while Carys shouted after him.

"Just because you don't like the way they portray dragons is not a reason to hate one of the most important works of fantasy fiction in the English language, Cadell!"

She walked downstairs and into the morning room off the main entry hall, where she remembered Mary serving breakfast in the past.

A table was laid out with mounds of roasted vegetables, platters of potatoes, and a half-carved leg of some massive beast. There was a grey-headed figure sitting at the head of the table, his head bent over the newspaper.

Carys muttered, "Surprised there's still meat left."

The grey-haired figure raised his head. "That's the second leg of venison the ogre has brought in."

Carys blinked. "Angus?"

Gone were the horns and the hooves, at least as far as Carys could see. The beard was brushed, and there was no grass or flowers sticking out of Angus's hair. The middle-aged man sitting at the head of the table looked kind of... professorial.

And Carys had to admit, it was the kind of professor who would attract attention.

She slid into the seat to Angus's right. "So this is your human face?"

It was recognizably Angus but without the trappings—his angular cheekbones, olive skin, and deep brown eyes read more dignified than wild.

He smiled, and the fangs were gone. "This is the face that suits my current task."

"It's not a bad face."

Angus smelled like cedar and fresh-cut wood. Something spicy with a hint of vanilla or chocolate. She was glad she hadn't sat on the other end of the table.

Carys reached over and spooned some roasted vegetables onto her plate. "This looks great. I'm surprised there's so many vegetables. Duncan's table is usually way more meat and potatoes."

"I do not eat flesh," Angus said, "of any kind. The matron of the house has been accommodating."

"Huh." Somehow that didn't surprise her. "You look like a hippie professor I had as an undergrad. Only more British."

He was Pan. Puck. A nature god of some kind or other.

It was no wonder that Angus could put on an attractive face if he wanted to. Pan was notorious for attracting women to him like flies to honey.

"I am not British." Angus raised his teacup. "Though I do like their tea. We are traveling to Sherwood Forest when the party has recovered."

"Like Robin Hood of Sherwood Forest?"

"That's one of my names, you know." Angus winked at her. "They sometimes call me Robin here. But we are not going to see Robin; we are going to see a man you may call Jack."

"Jack."

Angus nodded. "He goes by many names and many faces, but in this world at this time, you may call him Jack."

"And Jack is one of the druids I need to meet?"

Angus nodded. "He is."

"Okay." She was just going with this supernatural road trip. "A mystical druid named Jack. And what will the druids tell me? How to defeat the Morrígan?"

She'd already faced one challenge battling a sea monster. If myth was any guide, she had at least two more challenges to go.

Then again, myths in the Brightlands and the reality of the supernatural in the Shadowlands rarely lined up.

Angus flipped the paper around. "Did you see the headlines today?" He pointed at the top one. "'Mystery Mound: Still No Answers on Geological Anomaly in Salisbury.' Here's another one." He pointed farther down the page. "'The Fairies Return? How to Keep Your Children Safe.'"

Carys leaned forward. "Holy shit."

"Apparently there has been a rash of strange attacks on children in London parks. Bites that look like tiny teeth. Cuts and odd bruises that seem to come out of nowhere. The government is currently saying it's an invasive insect from overseas, but I can assure you" —Angus leaned forward— "this pest is very, very native-born."

"Okay, I get it." The potatoes turned dry in her mouth. "Things are getting weirder."

"Your task is not to defeat the Morrígan. That is impossible. But you must draw her back to the Shadowlands where her magic can be contained and keep her from rousing more of the old magic in this place."

Duncan stormed into the room. "Did you see the online" —he glared and waved a hand in the air— "things?"

Carys pulled out her mobile phone. "You really do not use a lot of social media, do you?"

"Fuck no," Duncan said. "Why would I choose to look at that depressing shite?"

Carys shrugged. "Funny duck videos?"

Angus said, "I like kittens."

Carys almost asked, *To eat?* But she resisted. He'd just mentioned that he was vegetarian.

"Look at it." Duncan pointed to her phone. "Mary was just showing me. She's everywhere. Macha, I mean."

Carys shot Angus a look as she pulled out her mobile phone and opened the first social app. She searched for the name Macha and was shocked but also not shocked to see a familiar nubile redhead dancing through a forest, wearing nearly nothing.

There were millions of views and the comments were...

"Wow." Carys scanned the hundreds upon hundreds of comments left on the dancing video.

> This is the kind of eco-warrior we need.

> Hot.

> When is she starting her OF?

Fire emojis and water droplets littered the screen.

Carys clicked on the profile, but the username was just macha.-girl and didn't seem to have any original content, just copy after copy after copy of pictures of the Morrígan, videos of the Morrígan dancing nearly naked through a forest. Another through a meadow. The Morrígan lounging in the grass with a flower crown and a come-hither expression. No clothes, just leaves covering the parts that would get an account banned.

Carys sighed. "Gee, I can't understand why she's so popular."

"I told you," Angus said. "Your world is ripe for her conquest."

Carys looked back at Duncan. "First thing in the morning, we drive to see a druid named Jack."

SHERWOOD FOREST NATIONAL NATURE RESERVE was a massive stand of old forest and contained the largest concentration of ancient trees in England. It was nearly a six-hour drive from Duncan's home in Scone, but since they'd started at the crack of dawn, the drive went quickly. They arrived before noon only a day and a half after they'd returned from the Shadowlands.

Naida was smiling when they left the highway and headed for the trees. "I'll be glad to be back in the forest."

"There are several gates nearby," Angus said. "I don't know how they have fared with the magic rising, but it's unlikely anything unfriendly or feral has leaked through in Jack's territory."

Laura was sitting next to Angus in the back of the van while Lachlan was brooding in the middle seat next to Naida, staring out the window of the van behind Cadell.

"Godrik would love this forest," Laura said. "Any news from him?"

Cadell said, "I would not expect Godrik to be able to reach us for some time. I believe he had business in the Shadowlands to attend."

"A wolf is not likely to send word at all." Lachlan's usually pleasant voice was acerbic. "He is not a child. It appears that Godrik has found something better to do than chase after a troublesome goddess. Good luck to him."

"You're in a foul mood." Angus peered out the window, watching the trees. "You should shut up. It's not our fault that your wife is beyond mortal reach."

Carys spun around, and even Laura sucked in a breath.

"Angus," Duncan said in a low voice. "Not helpful."

Lachlan's eyes were hollow, and he stared into space. Naida reached across the seat and slipped her hand into his. "I don't know if I ever expressed to you my clan's sorrow, and my own, about the loss of Princess Seren. She was greatly beloved in Cymru."

Lachlan looked down at Naida, and his expression softened. "Diolch o galon, Naida ferch Aled."

They slipped into a soft conversation in Cymric that Carys couldn't follow, and she was reminded again that Lachlan had this whole, massive life she barely understood.

If Seren had lived, he would have been the prince consort to the Cymric throne. Of course he could speak Cymric. Of course he knew fae lords and was familiar with wolf behavior.

"Hey," Duncan whispered.

She turned to smile at him, resting her head on the headrest. "Hey."

"He'll be fine," Duncan whispered.

It wasn't the first time Lachlan had grieved for his wife.

What a fucked-up situation.

The van wound through a small rural village before the land opened up and two hedgerows guided them south toward a dense stand of dark trees in the distance.

The hedgerows fell away, and there was nothing but waving wheat fields on one side of the road and dense stands of white-skinned birch trees glowing in the morning light as drifting fog dampened their soft green foliage.

"There." Angus slapped the window of the van. "On the left, idiot. Stop here. Don't you see that clearing?"

"Yes, but that's not a car park," Duncan said. "Do you understand what it means to be towed?"

"You'll stop here or you'll have to wait for tomorrow morning to find him," Angus said.

Grumbling, Duncan pulled the van over to the left side of the road. There was a wide spot on the grassy verge and a stile over a narrow fence where they could cross from the roadway into the forest.

"Why the hell do we have to stop here at this moment?" Duncan asked. "I swear to God, Angus, if this is one of your stubborn—"

"Girl." Angus crawled over everyone and yanked the door open. "Come with me."

Carys could only surmise that the "girl" that Angus was barking at was her. She rubbed her sleepy eyes and scrambled to follow him across the grass and over the fence.

"Hey!"

Angus's shaggy grey head was already disappearing into the trees.

"Will you" —she panted— "wait for me?"

Carys heard the others running after them. Cadell first, then Lachlan and Duncan. Naida had somehow run ahead of Carys and was already perched in a birch tree as Angus stabbed his walking stick into the soft ground underneath the ever-deepening shade of soaring pines.

He turned in circles, keen eyes scanning the trees.

Carys stumbled over grassy patches and dry creeks that criss-crossed the forest floor before she nearly ran into Angus's back. "Angus, what—"

"Hush." He loped forward into a circle of pine trees, staring at something in the distance.

"Jack of the Woods," Angus called. "Father of the Green!" He reached back, gripped Carys's hand, and tugged her to his side.

The moment she stepped next to him, Carys felt the world change around them.

The ground beneath her feet was soft and mossy. The summer forest grew dark and dense, and ferns nodded their heads in the shade.

Carys heard a voice behind her. "What in all the worlds..."

She turned and saw Lachlan had come to a halt, staring down at the leather armor that suddenly covered his body. In his hand was a bronze sword, and it gleamed with low gold light.

Duncan was beside him, clad in similar armor, an axe in his hands, and Cadell wore his leather dragon-skin armor and stared into the trees, his golden eyes fixed on something in the distance as the red glow of fire burned at his throat.

Naida appeared to be curled up and sleeping, nestled in the roots of an oak tree that hadn't been there a moment ago. Laura had her hands out, whispering to the air as the world around them grew green and verdant with violent speed.

"Youngling." A deep voice sounded from the trees, and a cracking sound reached Carys's ears. A heavy thunk. Then another thunk. "Little brother, you have come to visit."

Carys blinked, rubbing her eyes with her right hand as Angus kept her left firmly in his grasp. "What's happening?"

"Pocket world," Angus whispered. "Father of the Green, I bring a hero to your forest."

Thunk.

Creak.

Thunk.

The ground shook beneath her feet, and birds flew from the trees in a torrent of flapping wings.

Emerging from the trees was a creature as massive and as tall as Cadell, but unlike the sleek leather that covered her dragon in human form, this being was clad in leaves and vines.

His legs grew like thick pine trunks, and his body was covered in ivy.

His face was made of bark and flowers, and moss grew from his head, twisting with the vines that wound around his torso.

He was the Green Man, the Woodwose. A pagan folk figure.

Carys had little doubt this "Father of the Green" was far more than a druid. He was a deity and a very old one.

"Who comes to my woods?" The voice wasn't angry, but it was

low, rumbling, and curious. "I see a dragon, a knight, and a smith before me."

"Jack of the Woods." Angus took Carys's hand and lifted it over her head. "Here stands a hero in need of your help."

"A hero?" The creature turned his head from the three men and peered down at Carys with wide eyes as green as the leaves that sprouted from his shoulders. "This one does not look like a hero."

Carys felt words catch in her throat. "I... I—"

"Maybe not," Angus said. "But she is the one the horse goddess has chosen."

"Oh... Very well," His voice scraped over Carys like gravel over stone as he cocked his head and peered at her. "A hero must pass a test."

The Green Man drew a stone sword from his body, and the next step he took, the ground shook again. "Face me, hero. If you best me in a duel, I will help you on your quest."

Carys's eyes went wide when she saw the sword, which had to be at least as tall as she was. "Angus, I can't fight—"

"I will stand for her." Lachlan stepped toward the Green Man. "I am her champion."

The Green Man inclined his head and raised his sword. "Very well, Knight. We fight."

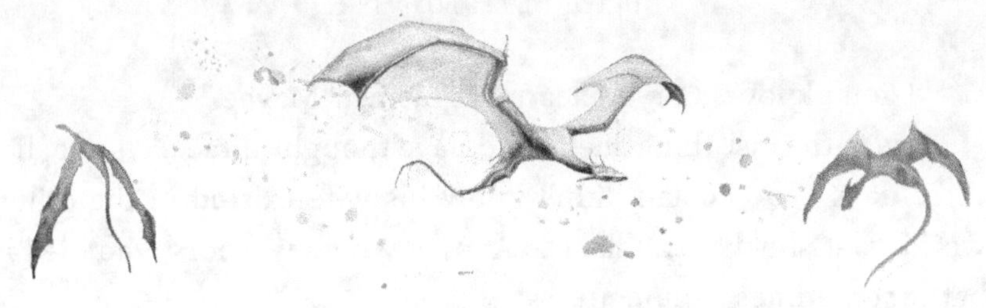

CHAPTER SEVENTEEN

"Lachlan, no!" Carys shouted, but it was too late.

The prince had lunged forward into a circle of light that illuminated the center of the clearing, going on immediate offense as his bronze sword clashed against stone.

"What are you doing?" Duncan shouted as he lunged forward.

Before he could enter the circle of light, Angus put a hand on Duncan's shoulder and yanked him back. "Not for you, Brightkin. Your brother has accepted this challenge. The old laws demand that he finish it before another can face the Green Man."

Duncan paced, raking a gloved hand through his hair, the axe swinging uselessly at his side.

Though the Green Man had appeared sluggish before, he now possessed preternatural speed, blocking Lachlan's every strike so smoothly he hardly appeared to be moving at all.

It was as if Lachlan was fighting a statue, only every time Carys blinked, that statue was in a different defensive position.

Laura ran to her. "Does Lachlan have a death wish or something?"

"I don't know." Carys's heart was racing. "Maybe."

It was the last thing she would have thought three days ago, but three days ago Lachlan didn't know his wife existed in the other-world, that she'd been taken to Annwn where warriors who died in battle sometimes wound up.

Oh Lachlan.

Cadell was circling the duel, his body moving in a reptilian crouch as the fire at his throat grew hotter and brighter. *Nêrys, what is this place?*

Carys looked around as Lachlan and the Green Man continued to fight. "Angus called it a pocket world."

Indeed, though the forest around them looked like any forest in any place, the air itself was laden with power.

When Carys looked at Laura again, she saw the tattooed lines on her friend's chin were visible, as if the magic of this pocket world had soaked into her very skin.

Carys looked down at her own hands and saw faint lines along her fingers, the tips of which appeared to have been dipped in blue ink.

Her mind flashed to her mother's hands.

Her hands. Her mother's hands.

Blue lines tracing down the center of her fingers.

Were her mother's hands tattooed?

She could no longer remember her face. When she thought of Tegan's face, another layered over it, a mirror image of herself.

...here. What is he doing? What did you let him do?

A familiar voice was whispering furiously in her mind again.

Carys answered without a second though. *I didn't* let *him do* anything. *He just charged in!*

Such a damned fool.

Lachlan spun around, trying to surprise the old god, but the moment he spun, the Green Man shifted and was already blocking the prince's blow.

...the best dualist in Alba.

What? Carys frowned, trying to focus on the voice.

He thinks he's the best dualist in Alba.

Is he?

Perhaps.

Cadell stood straight and threw his shoulders back. "Seren?" He scanned the tops of the trees, took a massive breath. "Seren?"

Lachlan's attention was caught, and he stumbled, looking at Cadell.

"Lachlan, on your left!" Duncan roared.

He brought his blade up just in time to block the strike from the stone sword, which broke in half with a great crack.

The Green Man's weapon in pieces, Lachlan tucked his shoulder, rolled to the right, and landed on his feet with his blade poised at the neck of the ancient forest god.

"I win," Lachlan panted. "Yield."

The Green Man's eyes narrowed on Lachlan, and then he angled his shoulders and sliced through his own neck while Lachlan stood frozen.

The moss-covered head thunked to the muddy ground and rolled across the sunlit clearing while the Green Man's massive body collapsed into a pile of leaves, bark, and vines.

Naida woke with a gasp.

"Fuck!" Duncan yelled, his hands going up as if warding off whatever disaster Lachlan had just unleashed. "What just happened?"

"No." Shock stole Carys's breath. "No. He can't..."

"Oh my god." Laura kept repeating it. "Oh my god. Oh... Oh my god."

Lachlan's eyes were wide as saucers as he stared at the pile of scattered vines that had made up the body of his opponent. His entire body was frozen.

"I asked him to yield," he whispered. "I only asked him to yield."

Angus leaned on his staff, his face screwed up in annoyance. Then he walked over and poked the mossy green head with the tip of his walking stick.

Carys winced. "Angus, maybe don't—"

Her voice was cut off by a burst of low, hearty laughter from the head on the ground. "The looks on your faces!"

Laura sat directly on the ground, and Carys watched with fascination as the sticks, the logs, the vines and the leaves slowly knit themselves together again.

A fresh green hand reached out, grabbed the head from the place where it lay at Angus's feet, and lifted it, plopping it back on the shoulders made of bark and twisted vines.

Lachlan looked like he might faint.

"That was seriously fucked up," Duncan muttered.

"As fine a duel as I've had in many years!" The Green Man landed a great slap on Lachlan's shoulder, which seemed to knock the prince out of his stupor. "Come then and let us share a meal, friends."

Lachlan lifted a trembling finger. "I gave you a touch. That was all. You're the one—"

"Who sliced off my own head?" The Green Man grinned, and his teeth were sharp white stones that resembled his sword. "But what a fine laugh it was, eh?"

Lachlan didn't seem quite as amused as his opponent.

"I'm Jack of the Woods, and I'd be honored to make the acquaintance of a such a fine group of travelers." Jack swept an arm out, motioning toward a break in the trees. "Come with me. You look hungry."

Laura leaned over toward Carys and spoke in a low voice. "Is this forest god making a giant pot of ramen in his cauldron?"

"Pretty sure that's a yes," Carys whispered.

They were sitting in a cozy house that was apparently still located in the pocket world because Laura's tattoos were still visible, Carys's fingers were still blue, and Cadell looked feral but still couldn't shift.

"I do not like this." He stood by the door, glaring at Jack, who whistled as if he hadn't a care in the world.

Which, honestly, was probably true.

Jack's cottage was a mishmash of ancient and modern. It was round, made of wattle and daub with a thatch roof and wooden beams crisscrossing overhead. There were bright open windows letting in light from all angles.

Which... didn't make sense. Light couldn't come in from all angles.

There were posters of bands and several framed photographs of a red-haired man who looked a little like Jack standing beside large trees. There was also a corkboard where various pictures were tacked up. The red-haired man with women. With men. With groups as large as five or six who all appeared to be fawning over him.

"You get a lot of company out here?" Carys scanned the corkboard, wondering if that was Jack in the pictures. Perhaps, like Cadell or Godrik, he could transform into a more human skin.

"Oh, I'm not lonely if that's what you're wondering." The cauldron Jack was puttering over sat in a large hearth where a cooking fire was burning and a kettle was steaming. "Who likes noodles? I like these noodles very much."

Angus grunted. "I'll have some."

"Knight?" Jack pointed at Lachlan. "Noodles for the victor?"

Lachlan's court training suddenly woke. "Of course. Thank you."

One by one, everyone except Naida agreed that they would love what appeared to be slightly watery ramen.

"So you just live here in Sherwood Forest?" Duncan was leaning against the curved wall. "I'm not going to lie—I'd be looking round here for your merry men if I didn't know better."

Another great burst of laughter from Jack, who was definitely still dressed in leaves and bark, though the longer they sat around his fire, the more his visage appeared human.

"You wouldn't be the first," Jack said. "Now, technically speaking, I'm a forest ranger."

"You're a forest ranger?" Laura was staring. "Like, you go and clear trails, guide tours, things like that?"

"Do you think they'd let me live here if I didn't?" Jack said.

"I am so confused right now," Laura muttered.

"Jack loves a joke." Angus's voice was testy. "Which explains the duel. But come now, Jack. You can't be surprised that the gods appointed a hero. Not when the old girl's running around in the Brightlands, undoing all our work in Briton."

"Undoing what?" Jack asked. "My gates are secure."

"Surely you've seen a few odd things. Heard rumors."

"Maybe she's just having a bit of a go right now," Jack said. "No harm done, is it?" Jack chuckled. "A bit of magic isn't a bad thing."

"But it's not just magic," Carys said. "She's calling sea monsters up rivers. She's casting enchantments over Brightkin and letting imps attack children in parks. She's trying to break open the gates so more magic can come through."

"We were attacked by redcaps in the woods behind my home," Duncan said.

Jack tsked but said nothing as he stirred the soup.

Angus leaned back on a wood-framed chair with a red-and-white blanket lying over it. "Jack, it can't be allowed. Epona's daughters were keeping her in the Shadowlands for a reason. Remember the last time she got loose?"

"That war was hundreds of years ago, and it was decades in coming," Jack said. "All she did was prod things on a bit."

"And do you think it's wise to let her roam free now? When she's raising barrows and calling up monsters? She's planning something, and you're feeling it too."

Jack narrowed his eyes.

"I haven't seen you take that form in few centuries, old man," Angus muttered. "Something has changed, Jack. Even you have to admit that."

"And if she did change things?" Jack nodded at Carys. "Why stop it, girl? Why not let people remember what magic could be?"

Carys glanced at Cadell. "Listen, as much as I love my dragon, I don't think it's a great idea to give modern human rulers a living weapon of mass destruction," she said. "I don't think dragons would want it either."

"The gates were never meant to protect them," Angus grumbled. "It was to protect *us*. Protect the weird and magical and mysterious. You want metal wires and electrical signals filling the Shadowlands? You want the wild creatures of the other side cowering as scientists in this world try to pick them apart?"

Jack sighed. "What do you want?" He dragged the pot away from the fire and turned.

And when he turned, it was no longer the Green Man Carys saw. It was no longer the crackling prankster with bark in his hair and leaves springing from his shoulders or even the red-haired man in the pictures.

Now Jack of the Forest was the ancient and the elder.

His grey hair hung to his shoulders in tangled waves, and a white beard fell down his chest. His eyes were stone grey, and when Carys looked into them, she saw not one druid but all the druids from every story. Merlin and Gandalf and Obi-Wan Kenobi.

The old man looked at Carys. "What is your plan, Daughter of Two Worlds? Because you cannot defeat the Morrígan. How can one defeat a god at all? If even one still believes in her—in either world— a kernel of her divinity remains."

"I don't know," Carys said. "That's why I'm asking for your help."

"Do you think you can persuade her to return? Because the only thing you can kill is their faith in her," Jack said. "And faith is a very hard thing to kill."

Kill faith in the Morrígan in order to rid the Brightlands of her?

Carys had no idea what might kill faith in the Morrígan, but she had a feeling that it wasn't something she was going to figure out that day.

"Will you help the girl or not?" Angus said. "There are other druids about. Others with a kinder face and more wisdom than you, Old Man."

"Oh hush, now you're just being insulting." Jack turned back to the pot and reached for a bright green pasta scoop that was shaped like a dinosaur head. "I suppose we could go visit the beekeeper," he said. "Might be good to hear what Jibril thinks. Check on what messages the bees have from other places."

When Jack turned with the first bowl of noodles in his hands, he had become a cheerful rogue with dancing eyes, curly red hair, ruddy cheeks, and just a few leaves stuck in his hair. "I serve you food, Carys Morgan. And I offer you respite in my home tonight."

Jack held out his hand and pushed the air. Within seconds, an entirely new wing of his house appeared. Rich wood panels clad the walls, and a half dozen doors appeared in the distance.

"That's kind of you, Jack." Angus rose. "We can get a good rest tonight, then drive down to Wyre Forest in the morning."

"That's fine for you all," Duncan said. "But if you're staying here tonight, I need to go move the van so we still have a car to drive tomorrow." He held out his hand. "Carys, you come with me. Anyone else prefer a hotel?"

"No need." Jack snapped his fingers and handed Duncan a bowl of ramen. "I pulled your vehicle over into my world. They won't find it there."

Duncan looked at the man, then at his finger. "You didn't even need to snap, did you?"

"I didn't, no, but humans seem to like some kind of gesture with their magic."

"And we're stuck here until you let us go, aren't we?" His jaw was tense. "Angus?" Duncan turned to the grey-headed man.

"To be fair, we didn't petition for entry," Angus said. "So broadly speaking, we are here until Jack decides otherwise."

CARYS TIPTOED through dusty grey rubble, leaning on the twisted frame of an old car that was crushed in the middle of the street. The remains of a building that had tumbled over were just past the car, and smoke drifted in the air like evening fog.

The air-raid sirens were immediately recognizable even though she'd only heard them in movies. There were buzzing sounds in the air that Carys realized were planes flying overhead.

Shouts and honks sounded somewhere far away. When she looked up, there was a light fall of flakes that looked like snow, but when she held out her hand, grey flakes landed in her palm.

Ashes. She was walking through ashes.

Carys saw a person standing at the end of the road, a slim figure with flowing red curls that fell down her back.

She was wearing a long gown made of black, and as she knelt down and put her hands on the rubble, the Morrígan threw her head back and let out an agonized wail that drowned out the sirens until the world around them went silent.

No sirens. No shouting. No buzzing planes.

Just the soft fall of ashes all around them.

The goddess wailed on and on, until the wails became screams so loud that Carys put her hands over her ears and closed her eyes to try to muffle the piercing sound.

She could not stop it. It drilled into her mind like an ice pick.

"Stop!" Carys screamed. "Stop it, stop!"

The screaming stopped.

She opened her eyes, and the Morrígan was still kneeling in the rubble.

Carys walked closer, and as she approached, she could see the dark robes that the goddess wore were dripping with blood.

"Macha?" Carys stepped closer with care. "Where are we?"

A whisper came to her mind. *You know. You have always known.*

Carys shook her head. "I don't know, because if movies are even a little bit accurate, we're in Blitz-era London, and I've never traveled to the past before."

Holy shit, had the Morrígan pulled her into the past? Was she stuck in a time loop? How did she get out of this one?

There was a low, grating laugh, then the Morrígan—still kneeling—turned her moon-pale face to Carys. "You're dreaming, you fool."

But it wasn't the Morrígan's voice, it was her own.

"Not yours, *mine.*"

Carys turned to her left, and she was looking at an image of herself, only this version had braids hanging to her waist and an ethereal blue glow to her skin.

"Oh my god, it's you."

"Which god are you talking about?" Seren asked.

"I'm pale." Carys stared at her near mirror image. "But I'm not *that* pale."

"You're also not dead," Seren said. "That helps."

What was happening? How was Seren here? Where was here?

Carys asked, "How are you here?"

"How are either of us here? Better yet, where are we?" Seren walked over and crouched next to the Morrígan. "What are you playing at, you saucy bitch? I always liked you, but this is a bit dramatic, don't you think?"

When the Morrígan blinked, tears of blood dripped down her cheeks. "If they had not trapped me, I would have prevented all this."

"Oh no, you wouldn't have," Seren said. "You would have probably made this entire war ten times worse."

"They attacked my people!" The goddess screamed long and piercing wails again.

"Is that the fairy tale you tell yourself?" Seren asked. "That you would have protected Briton if Epona had let you roam free?"

The Morrígan stood and spun around. "I would have protected my land!"

Since the wailing and weeping had died down, Carys stepped closer. "Her aspect is sovereignty too. Not just war, but war with a purpose. War with... an end."

Seren stood and turned to Carys. "Do tell, Professor." She scoffed. "We're not living in your books."

"Or are we?" Carys asked. "According to you, this is a dream. My dream."

"You dream about books?"

"Regularly, but that's not what's happening here." Carys walked away from them both and looked around her.

On closer inspection, the structure of the dream was sloppy. Far more like a film set than a real place. "Did she conjure this? Why? I've never dreamed about the war." Though her father's parents would have lived through the war, she'd never met any of them.

"Maybe this is better." The Morrígan brushed her hand over the burning scene of London, and it wasn't London anymore—it was a burning forest fire with a small cabin in the distance, smoke coming from embers on the roof.

"Now *this* is a nightmare." Carys turned back to the Morrígan. "What are you doing, Macha? Why did you pull Seren into my dream? Is she actually here or am I imagining it?"

The Morrígan was the Crow Mother again, and her smile was a mystery.

"I always knew you were out there." Seren walked around Carys, staring at the raging forest fire the Morrígan had conjured. "Is this your home? It wasn't a small thing to find you."

Carys turned to her Shadowkin. "You tried?"

"You and our mother were the ones to move across an ocean." The corner of Seren's mouth ticked up, and the expression was so like Dafydd that Carys took a step back.

"It's really you. This isn't just an illusion."

Seren turned in a circle, looking around at the fiery landscape. "She's managed to conjure your nightmare, which is no small thing in the Brightlands."

"I'm not in the Brightlands. Exactly."

"Where are you then?" Seren's eyes narrowed as she squared her shoulders with Carys. "Is Lachlan with you? What do you think you're doing? You're not a hero. You're not a *warrior*."

"I know I'm not," Carys stammered. "But Cadell and I—"

"Oh, that's right. It wasn't enough to steal my husband, you had to steal my dragon too?"

"What?" Carys's mouth dropped open. "I didn't *steal* anything. Lachlan came looking for me."

Seren started to circle her. "So why did you follow him?"

"What was I supposed to do?" Was she really fighting with a dead woman over her ex-boyfriend? "Pretend like my boyfriend getting stolen by the fae was normal?"

"In my world it would be."

"I wasn't in your world—I was in mine!"

"Fight."

They both turned and saw Macha standing, blood dripping from her eyes, her hands clenched at her sides. A wicked smile curved her lips.

"Fight," they said again, because Macha was two now, and Badb stepped from her sister's shadow.

Maiden and mother standing against Shadow and Bright.

"Fight," the Morrígan said, her voice echoing. "Fight. Fight."

"No." Carys reached for Seren's hand, and her Shadowkin wrapped her fingers around hers tightly. "No, but nice try."

"You brought us here so we'd fight, didn't you?" Seren clutched Carys's hand firmly. "Wrong again, saucy bitch. We're sisters. Sisters may fight, but they stick together. You'd know all about that, wouldn't you?"

Macha and Badb opened their mouths in unison, and the

piercing scream was bloodcurdling as a flight of crows flew from their yawning mouths, cawing and flying straight into Carys's eyes.

"Carys!" It was Lachlan's voice.

"Carys!" It was Duncan's voice.

Seren shouted, but then the crows surrounded them and she was gone.

CHAPTER EIGHTEEN

"Carys!"

She sat bolt upright in bed, sweat pouring from her body as her breath came in pants.

Duncan was already sitting next to her, his hand squeezing her own.

"Carys," he repeated. "You're having a nightmare."

"*Nightmare* is the last commonly used remnant of the Old English word *maere*," Carys mumbled. "It meant terror."

"Take a breath, Professor Morgan." Duncan brushed damp hair from her forehead. "What are you talking about?"

Carys's brain was on overdrive. "And *maere* comes from the Indo-European root for something crushing. Something terrible. *Maere, marōn, mara* is also..." She took a shuddering breath. "Also where the first part of the Morrígan's name comes from. At least they're pretty sure it's something... like that."

Duncan gathered her into a giant hug. "What the fuck were you dreaming about?"

"Macha and Seren. London was burning. Then Baywood..." She

turned her face into his chest. "There were planes buzzing in the sky. And sirens. Then the cabin and…"

He kissed the top of her head. "Christ, no more movies for you."

In the firm embrace of Duncan's arms, her heart began to slow, and her mind calmed. "It was a dream but not a dream if that makes sense."

"None of this makes sense." Duncan reached out to a pair of floating lights that emanated from the earthen walls of the room where they were sleeping. "Look at this place, Carys. I thought the Shadowlands was magical, but this?"

Jack of the Forest, the Green Man, the Green Knight, whoever he was, had stowed them in his strange pocket world in the middle of Sherwood Forest for the night. Jack's world was a place where tree roots had personalities, water babbled from an earthen pump, and leaves smiled when you walked past them.

It wasn't just touched by magic, it was made of the stuff.

Carys didn't feel unsafe in the least—in fact, she felt more than secure—but clearly the veil between Jack's realm was thinner than normal if the Morrígan was sending her dreams and her Shadowkin—

"Seren was there," Carys blurted out. "In my dream. Seren was there."

Duncan pulled back to look at her face. "You were dreaming about her?"

"No, like… she was *there*. In my dream. Still alive. Or kind of alive."

"I'm pale, but I'm not that pale."

"You're also not dead. That helps."

Carys shook her head. "It's hard to explain, but she was there, she realized she was dead, and she was talking to the Morrígan." She frowned. "She said she liked her because she was a saucy bitch."

"Oh aye, that sounds like Seren," Duncan muttered. "Carys, can you do me a favor?"

"Probably."

"Don't tell Lachlan any of this." He smoothed a hand down her hair. "Not right now. His head is already completely fucked."

She closed her eyes and fell back on the pillow. "Do you think he was trying to die?"

"When he challenged the... Jack? Earlier?"

"Yes."

"I don't know." Duncan scooted down next to her and put his arm around her waist. "Maybe. Maybe he was."

"He loves Seren so much." It was so obvious to her now. The love he had for Carys wasn't like what he'd felt for Seren.

Seren was Lachlan's person. Just like Duncan was hers.

Duncan kissed her forehead. "I understand his grief better now, because if anything ever happened to you..." His breath caught. "Just be careful, will you? Because if you get taken to Annwn, there's not a fae or a giant or a druid in the world who's going to stop me breaking through magical worlds to get you back. I'd make a deal with the devil himself. I'm not as polite as Lachlan, lass. I'd just end up burning everything down."

Carys had a vision of Duncan in the armor that the Green Man had given him, taking an axe to the forest behind his house and telling Cadell to light everything on fire.

"Don't burn everything down." The floating blue lights danced over her head, and she reached up to touch one with her fingertip.

The light shivered and darted away as if she'd tickled it.

She turned toward Duncan's chest and slipped her arm around him. "Don't burn anything down. I'm supposed to save the world, not burn it."

"Fine then," he whispered. "But no trips to Annwn for you."

"I don't plan on it." She lifted her face and kissed him, and the firm press of his lips on hers turned from reassuring to heated in seconds.

She still felt cold from her dream, so when Duncan slipped his hand under the oversized shirt she was wearing, she settled into the spreading heat, easing her leg over his hips as they lay on their sides and pulling him into the cradle of her body.

"Are you still shivering?" He trailed kisses along her cheek and whispered in her ear, "Let me take care of that."

She smiled. "I hear blacksmiths are good at heating things up."

"Och, that's almost enough to make me spank you." He playfully tapped his hand on her bottom.

Carys muffled her laughter in his chest.

Duncan's hand was running up and down her side as he kissed her and pulled her closer.

"Shhhh," he whispered. "When I say the walls have ears, they could literally have ears here. I've no idea."

"Neither do I."

Duncan's mouth covered hers as he teased his fingers between her legs, then slid them inside, stroking the channel of her sex as her body grew soft and languid in his arms.

He stroked her over and over until she was arching with pleasure, and then he released his erection and slid inside, making love to her with slow, devastating strokes.

He rolled Carys to her back, his mouth muffling her moans of pleasure as he braced his body over hers and rocked her back and forth in a bed made of twisted branches and living vines.

The chamber filled with soft lights, and when Carys came again, the air was redolent with the scent of jasmine.

Duncan planted his hand next to her shoulder and thrust into her with a sheen of perspiration glowing on his face while blue and white lights danced overhead. He came with a muffled exhalation, his jaw clenched in pleasure.

He fell forward, rolling to the side and gathering Carys into his chest as his lungs worked like a bellows.

She blinked at the shower of soft golden light that surrounded them and saw lilies, daisies, and daffodils blooming on the walls, the flowers nodding their heads as their soft scent filled the room.

A soft humming kind of music in the air lulled her to sleep as Duncan held her in his arms.

CARYS STEPPED out of Jack's cottage the next morning and into Sherwood Forest.

Not the magical forest where they'd been but the absolutely average and ordinary forest where she turned and saw what looked like a storage shack standing between two large pines. There was a sign on it, and in the distance she saw a trail marker and an early-morning hiker walking with a dog.

"Well, that'll do my head in if I think about it too much." Duncan walked ahead and scanned the area.

Cadell stepped out after them, then Laura and Lachlan and Naida and the rest. Each of them looked around as they stepped out of the shack and into the Brightlands.

Jack was last to leave. He ducked his green head under the doorway, and when he raised it on the other side, he was a jolly-looking young man with a ruddy red beard and bright green eyes, dressed in a flannel shirt and a pair of canvas utility pants.

He nodded at the trail in the distance as he slung a backpack over his shoulder. "Shall we? Your van should be on the road where you left it."

Laura cocked her head. "You need to teach me that trick, Jack."

He winked at her. "Can't give all my secrets away, shadow-walker."

Cadell was glaring at Jack, so Carys grabbed his arm and dragged him toward the tree line.

"Please don't murder the nice forest god," she muttered. "He's just flirting with her."

"He is an ancient fertility god," Cadell muttered. "He would like to do more than flirt."

Time to change the subject. "Seren was in my dream last night."

Cadell didn't question it. "What did she say?"

"Let's see, she called the Morrígan a saucy bitch, then started to fight me about Lachlan."

Cadell nodded. "Yes, that sounds like Seren."

"Duncan said the same thing. Well, about the saucy bitch comment. I didn't tell him we were fighting about Lachlan." She waved her hand. "We weren't fighting! I don't want Lachlan, obviously. But she was… kind of pissed."

"She could be quite jealous about him. He was a favorite of the women in the court."

Knowing Lachlan's charm and personality, Carys wasn't surprised. "She accused me of stealing you too."

Cadell cut his eyes toward her. "That's ridiculous. The bond of a dragon and their nêr is not as fickle as a mere romantic relationship."

Carys and Cadell stepped over a rotten log, which put them on a stretch of manicured path. "I think she was just pissed that the Morrígan had dragged her into my dream, and then it became obvious that Macha had ulterior motives when she started chanting 'Fight, fight, fight' like we were in a middle school hallway."

The dragon nodded. "So she was trying to divide you, which means that you and Seren cooperating across realms must be important in some way."

She looked up. "Oh, I hadn't thought about that. You're right."

"Well, I'm much older and wiser than you." He patted her head. "But you have your strengths too."

Carys rolled her eyes. "Thank you so much."

Cadell came to a halt in the middle of the path. "You had sexual relations with the blacksmith last night."

She felt her cheeks heat and immediately tugged on his arm to keep moving. "Uh, I know you can sense my moods and stuff, but if you could avoid broadcasting my sex life to a couple of strangers and the entirety of Sherwood Forest—"

"You had sex in a magical cottage that belongs to a fertility god," Cadell said bluntly, though he kept his voice low.

"Okay, not that it's any of your business," Carys said through gritted teeth, "but I am on birth control, so it's fine."

"Of course." Cadell nodded. "I'm sure your human chemicals are much more powerful than epochs of magic."

Well, that was the opposite of comforting.

The dragon patted her shoulder. "The surly human would make a fine protector and provider, and he has strong financial resources. You could have made a far stupider choice to be the father of your offspring."

"It is so obvious that dragons have arranged marriages," she muttered. "Please stop."

"Matings is more accurate." Cadell looked back at Duncan. "He is physically fit as well. And you are in your prime reproductive years. The more I think about this, the more I think it was a good decision."

"Nothing was decided!" Carys hissed. "Please be quiet."

"I see the van!" Duncan shouted from behind them on the path. "Good job, Jack—it's still there."

Jack laughed. "I told you it would be."

Duncan trotted ahead, clearly delighted to be back to his vehicle and back in the driver's seat where he could control the world at least a little bit until they ran into the next random god or goddess.

Carys stared at her boyfriend as he leaped over the stile and opened the van, walking around the vehicle, patting the hood, checking the tires.

It was exactly the way her father always checked his truck before she and her mother got inside.

"Yes." Cadell nodded. "The more I consider this, the more I am pleased with the idea."

Carys spun toward Cadell and grabbed his arm. "I'm going to

need you to shut up so much, especially when we are in that van that's going to be very crowded now with my *very* new boyfriend and yet another magical creature with supernatural hearing."

"Very well," Cadell said. "But understand that my protective instincts will likely become even more pronounced if you are with child."

She was dying. Cadell was going to kill her, and then he'd have to find another nêrys.

The dragon was beaming. "It will be delightful to be in the presence of small children again. Babies love me."

Maybe Cadell's next nêrys would be more immune to death-by-embarrassment.

THEIR DRIVE to the next druid would take them past Birmingham and toward a place called Wyre Forest. It was only four hours, but it felt longer with rowdy Jack poking fun at everyone in the van and shouting random recommendations for pubs and restaurants in every town they passed.

"That one!" he'd shout as they passed an exit. "Crown and Barrel Pub. Excellent fish pie."

"The most beautiful girls I've seen in a hundred years in that town. There's something in the water."

"You like beer?" He elbowed Angus. "You want the Three Friars Restaurant. I'm telling you, you can't go wrong."

It was like road-tripping with a slightly inebriated college kid with the voice of a radio DJ.

Duncan was whistling as they drove, clearly happy to be back on the road and headed toward something more familiar than a tiny alternate universe popped in the middle of an old forest.

"We should take a weekend in Birmingham sometime," he told

Carys. "I had a restoration job down there a few years ago. Excellent town. Great music scene."

She smiled. "You're sounding like Jack a little."

"I mean..." He glanced over his shoulder and lowered his voice. "He's better than a brooding prince and a stoic dragon glaring at cars and sunshine, isn't he?"

"I cannot disagree." Carys glanced at Lachlan again, wondering if his victory over Jack—though symbolic—had put him in a better mood.

He was staring out the window with his arms crossed over his chest.

Carys wanted to have a conversation with the man, maybe tell him about her dream with Seren, but she didn't know if that would help him or hurt him. Duncan had told her not to say anything but...

Maybe she should ask Cadell.

"Turn off in forty miles," Jack said. "You're an excellent driver, Laird Duncan!"

"Thank you."

"With the most beautiful copilot, eh?"

Carys saw his reflection in the window and caught Jack winking at her.

"I'm the luckiest of men." Duncan grabbed her hand. "Now if I can just keep her from starting another magical war, life will be easy sailing."

That led Jack to let out another raucous laugh, and Carys decided it was time to take a nap or at least close her eyes.

What seemed like moments later, she felt the van exit the highway, but she kept her eyes closed as they twisted and turned on city streets.

They'd reached Birmingham in the middle of the day, and Carys wouldn't have expected much traffic, but the roads were clogged and she saw two vehicles pulled over to the side of the road. The drivers were out of their cars and shouting at each other, fingers in each other's chests.

"Whoa." Laura followed the fighting men with her eyes. "I guess I assumed the States had more road rage than England."

Cadell frowned. "These days, it does not."

"That's intense for a fender bender."

Another few miles and they passed another accident and a man and a woman yelling from across the hood of a small sedan.

After the third accident in a few miles, Carys sat up straight and opened her eyes. "What the heck is going on in this town?"

Jack's smile had fallen. "She loves a good fight, that Macha."

"Why provoke humans to violence?" Naida asked in a small voice. "What purpose does it serve?"

"She feeds on it," Jack said. "You'd never understand, dear one. Your people fled from the Brightlands epochs ago to avoid this."

"Fae can be violent too," Lachlan said.

"Yes, but it's a different, quiet sort of war they have perfected," Jack murmured, watching another two cars collide and pull to the side of the motorway. "They sneak, they don't shout their intentions for anyone to hear them." Jack sat back in his seat. "Jibril will know what's going on."

"Jibril is the druid we're going to visit?" Carys asked.

"Jibril is many things, but you can call him a druid," Jack said. "His bees will have told him everything that's happening in this part of Briton."

"Bees are the worst gossips," Angus concurred. "If you need to know the news, always ask the bees."

Eventually the city turned to country again, the roads grew narrower, and buildings gave way to trees, orchards, and a distant dark forest that appeared as old and venerable as Sherwood.

"The Wyre is an old wood," Jack said. "But we're going to the village on the edge of it where Jibril lives. He doesn't like to live alone."

The sun was slanting, casting afternoon light from behind the trees as they turned onto a narrow lane where neat cottages lined a small road and a few grey-haired neighbors chatted in front gardens.

"That house." Jack pointed ahead. "That's his place." The old god looked around, shaking his head. "Never understood why he wants to live in such a busy place, but there you go."

"Busy place?" Laura shook her head. "You remind me of my grandmother. If there's not at least five acres around her, she feels like she's living in someone's backyard."

"She's exactly right," Jack said. "Wise woman."

Duncan pulled the van in front of a beautiful little thatch-roofed cottage with a bright blue door. The door had a moon-shaped window cut into it, and there was an abundant vegetable garden in front of the house within a border of apple trees.

The moment they parked, the door opened and a slim man with long dark hair walked out. His hair and beard were longer than Jack's, his clothing was immaculate white—a beekeeper's jumpsuit —and his face gleamed in the sunlight.

His entire bearing was radiant and warm. Carys wondered what kind of god he was if he worked with bees.

Almost all folk traditions had unique mythology about bees, dating back to the ancient Egyptians, who were the first to build hives to collect honey. The San people of the Kalahari had creation myths about bees, and the Greeks believed they could move between worlds.

"Jack Green." Jibril walked over and shook Jack's hand. "My bees told me you were coming today."

Jack glanced at Carys. "Did they tell you I was bringing a hero in need of help?"

The slim man frowned. "They told me you were bringing a hero, but I assumed that she was here about my bees."

Carys looked at Cadell, who looked as confused as she was. "Your bees?"

"Yes," Jibril said. "Something in the forest is bothering my hives."

CHAPTER NINETEEN

"Do you know that bees are not limited to the boundaries between worlds?" Jibril asked as he and Carys walked down the lane. "That makes them the perfect messengers."

The beekeeper had changed from his white coveralls, but his new clothing, a pair of loose white pants and a cream-colored shirt that buttoned up the front, was no less radiant.

"What are the bees telling you about the Shadowlands right now?" Carys carried a basket of honey jars and freshly made bread in brown paper bags. "If the Brightlands are getting more magical, are the Shadowlands getting less?"

"Hardly." He smiled. "There are many whispers and rumors. One of the old gods has returned to the Brightlands, and power may be shifting from the fae."

"Would that be a bad thing? In my experience, the fae tend to look out for themselves and aren't really worried about anyone else."

"Would you say that about Naida?" Jibril looked at her from the corner of his eye. "She is your friend. She has sacrificed much to accompany you to this world, and yet she makes that sacrifice without complaint because she believes in your mission."

"Naida isn't like other fae." As soon as she said it, she heard herself. "I'm prejudiced against them, aren't I?"

"You have reason to be suspicious, but yes." Jibril turned at a gate that had a sign clipped to it, then walked up to the front door. "Anna and Paul have a new baby," he whispered, holding out his hand. "We'll leave the bread and honey in the basket here."

Carys handed him a bright jar of liquid gold and a brown bag. Then they retreated from the front door without ringing the bell.

"The fae are a unique kind of creature," Jibril said as they continued walking down the lane. "Closer to my kind than yours."

"They're supernatural beekeepers?"

"A beekeeper?" Jibril shook his head. "I am a beekeeper by hobby. No, I am... a messenger."

"Jack called you a druid."

Jibril smiled. "Of course he would, because he is an ancient of this land."

"And you're not?"

Jibril looked at Carys with kind eyes. "I am as you are. An immigrant. Born of one world but thriving in another."

"Where did you come from?" Carys asked.

"Nearer and farther than you might think." He opened another gate and left another jar of honey and bag of bread, only this time he rang the bell before he backed away. "Do you know why your parents crossed an ocean after you were born, Carys Morgan?"

She had a flash of another dream.

"The Brightlands was both too familiar and too foreign for your mother. Better a place that was new to both of us."

She smiled a little bit at the memory of her father's voice. "I think my parents wanted to live in a place that was new for both of them. A fresh start, kind of."

"Then they have followed in the same path as countless others through history," Jibril said. "I hope their life there was a blessed and prosperous one."

"I think they were happy," Carys said. "They seemed happy. Why did *you* move?"

Jibril shrugged. "I was drawn here when people who believed in my god arrived. There is no faith without an object of faith, Carys Morgan."

"So you're a god like Jack?"

Jibril shook his head. "I am only the servant of a god. A messenger as the bees are."

"And what does your god want me to know?"

Jibril paused in the middle of the lane. "Briton walks along the edge of a knife. There are many gods on one small island. Old gods, new gods. Demigods and magical creatures sneaking through the gates."

"We knew that already."

"The gods of other lands have noticed. The gods in Europe and Asia are not pleased. They worry that instability in Briton will spread to their lands."

"They think the Morrígan is going to set her sights on other places after she wreaks havoc in England?"

"She is a goddess of conquest," Jibril said. "Born in the east, yet she and her sisters moved with their people, and now she is pressed against the sea, limited by the vast kingdom of Aegir. She can no longer move any farther west."

Aegir was the old Norse god of the Atlantic. More of a personification of the sea, not so much an individual. The Morrígan was trapped by the sea itself.

"So they're concerned she might look east and think it wouldn't be so bad to return?" Carys asked.

Jibril nodded. "Just so, Carys Morgan. The world is interconnected in a way that it has never been before. Ideas spread faster than my bees can fly. And ideas are all that is needed to create a god."

Carys nodded. "You're talking about deification of... what? Modernity? Science?"

Jibril walked to the right and opened another gate, stepping up a path through a lush cottage garden. "Humans will deify anything, given enough time and popularity. There are gods of the internet and gods of greed. Gods of beauty that are never satisfied, and gods of the mind that do nothing but lie."

"So the moment that enough people start worshipping an idea or a... pop culture phenomenon even... a god is formed?"

Jibril shrugged. "Of course."

"I've never thought about gods like that," Carys muttered.

Jibril frowned. "Why not?"

"I study mythology, so I mostly think about gods that have existed for a long time, but I guess anything could be a god if it's worshipped enough."

"A hero who is a scholar. The Builder would appreciate you." Jibril set two loaves of bread on a small table near the front porch and knocked on the door. "Mrs. Havers does not eat honey, so I bring her extra bread."

An old woman quickly opened the door and waved at them. "Thank you, Jibril."

"You are very welcome, Margaret. This is my friend Carys."

"Oh hello, dear." Mrs. Havers took the bread and disappeared inside.

"She lost her husband last year." Jibril's voice was soft. "A sacrifice to one of my least favorite deities. Despair."

Carys felt her heart sink. She was familiar with despair. "Despair is a god?"

"Of a sort. Despair is a god of the mind. Its worship takes many forms." Jibril turned to Carys and took the basket from her arm. "Now that we have made our deliveries, do you think you can help my bees?"

"I have no idea," Carys said. "But I can try."

THE APIARY JIBRIL tended was in the middle of a clearing in the forest, and Duncan, Naida, Laura, and Lachlan were happy to join Carys when she went to watch it that night.

Cadell waited back at Jibril's spacious house. The beekeeper had forbidden the dragon from approaching his hives as more than one queen had fled a hive when a dragon came too near.

"Did you know that?" Laura asked from her perch on a fallen log. "About dragons and bees?"

Carys shook her head. "That would be yet another topic that was not covered in my world mythology curriculum."

"Maybe they're afraid that dragons might steal their honey." Duncan was leaning against a tree, his eyes scanning the dark forest. "It is gold, after all."

Lachlan frowned at Duncan. "Dragons don't hoard gold; that's a myth."

"Have a sense of humor, for God's sake." Duncan sighed.

"Which god?" Laura asked.

"What?" Duncan asked.

She turned to him. "You said, 'for God's sake,' and I was just wondering which one."

He shrugged. "Fair question these days."

"Oh my god, it's you."

"Which god are you talking about?"

In the silence of the forest, Carys debated how much she should tell Lachlan about Seren and her dream. Would it make him more reckless? More angry? She should have asked Cadell, but it was almost impossible to get the dragon alone.

Cadell? Carys reached out for the dragon. *Can you hear me?* She heard nothing in response.

They must have been too far away from the house. Even with the Morrígan's magic causing chaos in the Brightlands, Carys's connection with Cadell only extended so far.

She and Laura, Duncan, Lachlan, and Naida had parked themselves behind a hedge that bordered the apiary and were waiting to see what happened when the world went quiet.

Naida sighed. "I love the sound of sleeping bees. So restful."

"Okay, so the pictures of bees that fall asleep in flowers that you see online," Laura said. "The ones with their little fuzzy butts sticking out. Are those real?"

"Oh yes." Naida smiled. "Some pixies keep bumblebees like a sort of pet, not that they are tame. But they are lovely flying companions."

For some reason it made sense that fae would like bees.

"What do you think is bothering the hives?" Carys asked Naida.

"My first guess would be imps," she offered. "I sense multiple gates in this forest, and if imps have found a way through one of them, they will do nothing but cause trouble for anything and anyone they come across."

"I remember." Duncan rubbed his neck where he still bore tiny teeth marks from the imps in the forest behind his house.

As the night grew darker and stars appeared in the sky, the forest came alive.

Far from the quiet place that Carys had been expecting, Wyre Forest at night teemed with activity. Carys heard foxes yell and owls hoot. She could hear bats in the distance, sweeping over the neighboring fields as they hunted for insects.

Duncan walked to a lookout position closer to the hives, with Laura circling the other direction. Lachlan remained alert, his eyes fixed on the wooden boxes in the distance, and Carys watched him.

"You are worried about him," Naida said quietly. "Worried about his mental state now that he knows his wife exists in Annwn."

"Yes," Carys whispered. "He thought she was dead. Gone. He grieved for her." She pointed at her own chest. "He even moved on in a way."

"Do you wonder if he really moved on or if he just transferred his love for Seren to you?"

It was a fair, if piercing, question.

"You know, when we were together, I used to worry about that. Even before I knew about the Shadowlands," Carys said. "I worried Lachlan was just missing his wife and wanted someone to love." Carys turned to Naida. "But I do think he loved me. So maybe it doesn't matter."

Naida frowned a little bit. "Maybe love is like faith. It only needs an object for its energy to focus on. If one god is lost, another one will do."

"Do you really believe that? That you could fall in love with anyone if you just focused?"

Carys hated that idea. Not that she was overly romantic about destiny or anything, but she didn't just decide to love Duncan. If anything, she kind of fought against it.

"I don't know," Naida said. "I never wanted to love Dru, but I did anyway. Maybe his love was so overwhelming I just gave in."

Carys didn't know where Naida's head was at, but she had a feeling that the melancholy expression she'd been wearing since Scotland had at least a little bit to do with a certain wolf missing from the party.

"I hear something," Lachlan said. "Coming from the east." He pursed his lips and hooted like an owl.

"Give me directions," Carys whispered. "East means nothing to me here."

"That way." Lachlan jabbed his finger toward the right.

Carys held up a hand and signaled to Laura on the other side of the apiary.

Laura nodded and started tiptoeing back.

By the time Laura got back to their first position, Duncan had also returned, his long strides surprisingly quiet in the forest. "I heard something. Did you?"

Lachlan drew his short sword. "Yes, if you'll..."

"Of course." Duncan lifted a cricket bat he'd grabbed from Jibril's house as Lachlan crept from the bushes and went to explore.

Duncan parked himself by the side of the hedge and watched the apiary.

"Does that ever drive you crazy when they talk in pieces like that?" Laura whispered.

"I'm kind of used to it now."

And it made her a little bit jealous.

"We're sisters. Sisters may fight, but they stick together."

What would Carys's life had been like if she'd grown up in Wales? Would her mother have taken her across a fae gate when she was young? Would she have grown up knowing Seren?

Don't be silly. She was a princess.

Right.

Lachlan had disappeared around the hedge, and the night birds fell silent as something crunched on the ground.

"That was not a human footstep," Laura whispered. "If I didn't know better..." She eased off the log and stepped lightly toward Duncan, who had already poked his head around the bushes.

Carys stood and looked for Naida, but the fae woman was already gone, halfway under the hedge and moving silently, as stealthy as a mouse avoiding an owl.

Carys peeked from behind Duncan's back and saw a dim figure moving in the shadows where the bees were now zooming and angry as an intruder violated their peaceful sleep.

There was an unmistakable huffing sound, and then the massive creature moved farther into the clearing and moonlight fell on the dark brown fur that covered his massive back.

Carys's breath left her body.

Laura said, "Weird. I thought you didn't have bears in England."

"We don't," Duncan said. "At least not in the Brightlands."

"You mean—"

"I recognize that bear," Duncan muttered. "He has one ear that's very noticeably cut. Right side, about a third of it taken clean off."

Laura squinted. "Good eyes."

"Easy to recognize because I'm the one who cut it." Duncan looked at Carys. "That's the Morrígan's bear. The one from the Crow Mother's mountain, remember?"

"I'm not likely to forget."

Lachlan appeared in the shadows, then slipped behind the trees and returned to their hiding place behind the hedge. "It's just the one bear, but he's not from this world. Somehow an enchanted bear is loose in the Brightlands."

"What do you want to do?" Laura said.

Lachlan shook his head. "I don't think a cricket bat and a short sword are going to do much against an animal that size other than make it mad."

Carys turned to Duncan. "We have to get him back to the Shadowlands."

Duncan crossed his arms over his chest. "Excellent idea. And how do you propose we do that?"

"Fire." Cadell nodded decisively.

Jack frowned. "We're not setting Wyre Forest on fire, dragon."

"Fire will work," Cadell grumbled. "Bears hate fire."

Carys was back in Jibril's cozy sitting room with Duncan, Cadell, Angus, and Jack. Laura had remained in the forest with Lachlan and Naida, keeping an eye on the bear while Carys and Duncan had a short consult with Jibril and Jack.

"We can't burn the forest," Carys said. "But what about smoke? You have smoking equipment, right?"

"Smoke will calm the bees," Jibril said, "but will do nothing about the bear."

"Fire will," Cadell offered again.

Jack stood up. "No fire!"

"Do you have any ketamine?" Duncan asked.

Carys and Jibril turned toward him.

"What? It's a large-animal tranquilizer."

Angus scooted forward in his seat. "This is no mere bear, boy."

"One, I'm not a boy. And two, what if he is?" Duncan pointed at Cadell. "That one can't transform on this side. Godrik couldn't either. What if the Morrígan's beast is really just a bear on this side of the gates?"

Angus frowned. "The boy could be right."

"We could tranquilize it, drag it to the nearest gate, and dump it in whatever forest is on the other side." Duncan nodded at Jack. "Then Jack can reinforce the gate so it can't get through again."

Jack lifted an eyebrow. "It's not the worst idea."

"I still don't have any ketamine," Jibril said. "I have herbs that might soothe an animal, but nothing narcotic in my house."

"But if the Morrígan's bear is just a bear on this side of the gate, that means that it would hate the same things that any bear would hate," Carys said.

Shockingly, she had an idea.

"Yes," Cadell said. "Like fire."

"*Not* fire." Jack turned to Carys. "Do you know about bears?"

"I mean... I grew up in Baywood. There are tons of black bears in the forest. I may still have a lot to learn about magical parallel worlds" —she glanced at Cadell and Angus— "but I do know about bears."

Jibril cocked his head. "Fascinating."

"Do you have any ammonia in the house?" Carys stood up. "I have an idea."

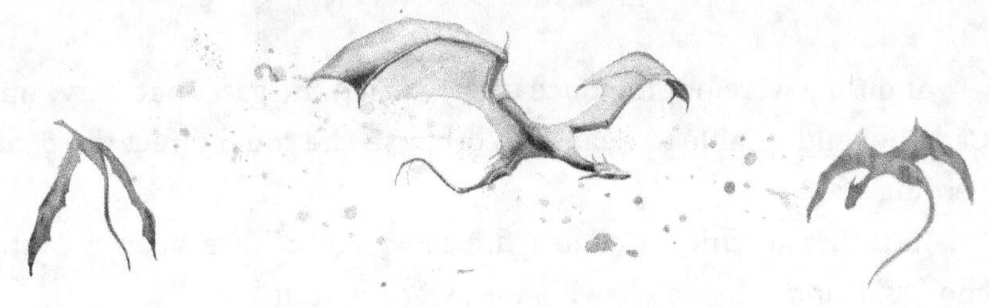

CHAPTER TWENTY

Even with a bandanna tied around her face, the rags soaked in ammonia made Carys's eyes water. "This better work because if all we do is make a magical bear mad, we're screwed."

Or Lachlan was going to get his wish to join the afterlife.

"Ugh." Laura was wearing a bandanna and holding a bucket of ammonia. "I can't believe you're using my mom's old trick to keep bears out of the trash."

"Does this really work?" Duncan held the sprayer that Jibril used to treat his trees with neem oil. They'd filled it with a highly concentrated mix of ammonia and water.

"Oh yeah." Laura nodded. "Bears hate the smell of ammonia. Pine cleaner too, but ammonia is worse. Or better. Depends on your point of view."

Naida, Cadell, and Jack had already taken a roundabout path into the forest to search for the fae gate where the bear had snuck through. Naida was hoping to guide the animal back through the gate while Jack reinforced the wards against the Morrígan's creeping magic so it couldn't enter the Brightlands again.

And they were hoping once they reached the gate that Carys and Cadell would be able to hear each other so she could direct the bear-herding.

"Starting to think Cadell's fire idea might have been a better choice." Duncan looked like his eyes were watering.

"We don't want to hurt the bear," Laura said.

"It's really not his fault for messing with the hives," Carys said. "It's just a bear."

"It's a possessed fae bear," Duncan said, "that tried to kill me once."

"And you took half his ear off," Carys said. "Don't you think it's kind of even?"

"No." Duncan strapped the sprayer pack on his back and covered his face with another bandanna. "This smells vile."

"According to Jibril, too many fumes will be harmful to the hive," Carys said. "So Lachlan will scare the bear away from the hives, get it back into the forest, and then we start chasing it toward the gate, waving the rags at it and spraying the underbrush."

Duncan was looking a little more than skeptical.

"I'm telling you, they really hate this smell." Laura held her arms up. "Be big and loud and make a lot of noise." She looked him up and down. "Easier for you than us probably."

Duncan rolled his eyes. "Once we get into the forest, how are we going to know where the gate is?"

"Jack said he'd make it clear," Carys said.

"How?"

"I don't know, okay?"

Duncan leaned down. "It seems there are a lot of unknowns in this entire operation, Carys."

"The one I planned with literally like an hour's warning?" she whispered. "Yeah! I'm not surprised!"

She dunked her gloved hands in the bucket of ammonia and grabbed a rag. Oh. That was terrible. "Will you just signal Lachlan now? That bear is going to lose interest in the hives and wander off if we wait too long."

Duncan glared at her, but he pursed his lips and hooted like an owl.

An echoing sound came from the hedges.

"Okay," Carys whispered. "Good luck, everyone. Let's go scare a bear."

By the time they crept from behind the hedges, the bear was lolling on the ground, drunk with honey and batting at the angry bees that buzzed around his face, so when Lachlan popped out from behind a bush and yelled at the beast with a great roar, the animal started and jumped back.

Lachlan ran at the bear with reckless bravado, banging his sword against a piece of metal he must have found in the brush. "Get out!" he shouted. "Back where you came from, beast!"

Laura ran beside him and raised her gloved hands in the air. She started waving two stinky rags over her head. "Hey!" she shouted. "Hey, you! Get out of here!"

Duncan took the right flank of the clearing while Carys went left.

The massive animal rose on two legs for a moment before it let out a roar and turned in circles, knocking over half a dozen boxes before it lumbered away from the hives and into the forest.

"It's working!" Carys shouted.

"Hey, bear!" Duncan waved one arm and boomed with a thick brogue, "Away an' bile yer heid, ya numpty!" He started spraying the underbrush in an attempt to corral the bear.

Carys was shouting and waving at it. "Get out of here!" She clapped her hands together, which only made the ammonia scent worse. She nearly gagged, but she kept shouting. "Out, out!"

The bear seemed more confused than anything as it ran on all fours. It paused at the edge of the clearing and nearly looked like it would turn back, but Lachlan raised his sword and shouted again.

"Away, foul beast!" He yelled like a marauder, banging his sword against the metal. The clattering sound had the desired effect, and the bear started again, turning for a moment before it loped slowly into the trees.

"Keep it away from the hives!" Carys shouted.

Laura positioned herself at the edge of the clearing and waved her arms over her head, each hand holding a stinky, ammonia-soaked rag. "And don't come back!"

Carys couldn't smell anything other than the stinking scent of ammonia as she ran into the trees. Every sense was overtaken by the fumes and the adrenaline coursing through her system.

Every human instinct was telling her to run away from the bear, but instead, she was running parallel to it, trying to keep even with Duncan, who was shouting and spraying ammonia on the other side of the animal. Lachlan continued at the rear, banging his sword and shouting.

Her eyes swept the dense forest in front of them. *Jack, where is the gate?*

They ran farther into the woods, Lachlan pursuing the animal, Duncan and Carys corralling it as the trees grew thicker and all light from the moon disappeared.

Carys stumbled over a root, fell to the ground, and looked up, worried she was going to see the bear towering over her in a rage, but instead, when she lifted her head, she saw a greenish glow in the distance.

"There!" She scrambled up and pointed. "I see it!"

"I see it too!" Lachlan shouted.

She stood again, clutching her ammonia rags as she kept her eyes on the green glow.

"To the right!" Lachlan shouted.

"Aye!" Duncan called from the other side of the trees.

Carys saw the bear start to turn toward Duncan. "Duncan, watch out!"

Lachlan banged his sword on the piece of metal, and the bear turned in circles, confused by the noise and the smells. He reared up on two legs, but as he did, Duncan lunged forward and pointed the ammonia sprayer right at the bear's face.

The bear roared, bared his teeth, and swung his face into a tree branch.

There was a sharp yelp, and then the animal turned and galloped ahead, running right at the green light.

It was working!

Nêrys?

As they approached the gate, Cadell's voice grew clearer.

We're coming toward you.

Jack lit the gate. Look for the light.

We see it.

They must have sounded like lunatics as they ran through the woods, herding the huffing bear toward a fae gate while the animal sneezed and moaned in complaint.

As the bear neared the portal, a strange light shimmered over the animal, and it slowed from a run to a loping walk.

The bear shook its head, and Carys saw the blood covering one side of its face. Something had jammed in the animal's eye, and blood soaked its dark brown fur. The bear turned and scanned the trees wobbling back and forth in some kind of daze. Its eyes turned and fixed on Duncan, and it let out a low, angry huff.

"The enchantment," Jack called. "Her magic is waking again."

"Don't stop!" Carys shouted.

They needed to herd the animal back through the gate before whatever spell the Morrígan put over it became active again.

Duncan kept his eyes on the animal. "Hello again."

Carys almost felt bad. In the Brightlands, this bear was just a bear. On the other side, it might be enthralled to the goddess again.

"Back!" Lachlan slammed his sword against the metal again.

He and Duncan moved in tandem, charging the animal, surprising it and knocking it back on its rear end before it stood on all fours, turned, and started trudging slowly toward the gate, grumbling as it retreated.

There was a faint song in the distance, a siren call from the other side as Naida lured the creature through the glowing green portal that appeared in the trees.

Cadell stepped forward as the bear disappeared into the light, and in the eerie green glow of the fae gate, she saw the dragon's profile lengthen and the fire at his throat glow.

Moments later, the bear disappeared, the green glow had died down, and Carys, Lachlan, Duncan, and Cadell were standing in the middle of the forest alone.

"It worked." Carys felt high. She felt elated.

She felt... just a little bit like a hero.

Cadell looked at the three of them. "All of you stink. Very, very badly."

CHAPTER TWENTY-ONE

"Oh, the oak and the ash, and the bonny ivy tree. How I wish once again in the north I could be."

Carys looked up when she heard the familiar words. Jack Green, his beard just a little greener than it had been the night before, was singing under an apple tree in Jibril's garden, staring at her with a twinkle in his eye.

"Why are you singing that?"

It was the morning after their ammonia-drenched trek in the woods, and Carys was sitting in the garden, soaking in the morning sun and trying to gather energy for whatever the day might bring.

Possessed sea monsters.

Enchanted bears.

Another horrible and violent nightmare.

And she still felt no closer to figuring out what she was supposed to do.

Carys was waiting as the last of her friends washed up in the only bathroom of Jibril's tiny cottage. They had all hosed off in the garden the night before, but the pungent smell of ammonia lingered in her nose.

And after the elation of success had worn off the night before, exhaustion had hit and there was nowhere to sleep save for the floor of the cottage.

She was sore, stinking, and hungry.

And Jack was singing Macha's song, apparently just to tease her.

Despite her small victories, there was still a goddess roaming through the Brightlands, and she didn't feel any closer to understanding how she was supposed to fix it.

"While sadly I roam, I regret my dear home" —Jack's eyes were fixed on her— "where lads and young lasses are making the hay…"

Carys started to get angry. "Macha sang that song in Gorne Wood."

"Did she now?"

Jack knew she had. Somehow he seemed to know everything, and he still expected her to fight the Morrígan blindfolded.

She wanted to drive back to Scotland. She wanted to fly back to Baywood.

She was exhausted, and she wanted to be anywhere but the front garden of another enigmatic supernatural who just wanted to mess with her head.

The Green Man continued singing. "The merry bells ring and the birds sweetly sing—"

"Why are you still singing that?" Carys snapped. She was exhausted, confused, and losing her patience. "What are we doing here?"

"You needed to protect Jibril's hives and chase off that bear. Well done."

"Okay, why?" Not even the peace of Jibril's garden could soothe her temper. "You all seem to know things, but you don't tell me anything. So… what am I doing here?"

Jack leaned against the trunk of the apple tree. "What *are* you doing here, Carys Morgan? You're not a goddess. Not even a fae. You're a human and a Brightkin. You're barely a dragon lord at all."

At the slap of his words, Carys felt as small as a child being reprimanded in school.

"You were tricked by a goddess and fumbled the one task Epona gave you by letting powerful, magical blood spill on Saris Plain."

Her temper was piqued. "You forgot the part where Cadell and I broke the fae enchantment that stopped that battle from turning into an all-out war."

"Actually," Jack said, "the blacksmith did that."

He wasn't wrong.

"Face it," Jack continued. "You're no candidate to be a hero."

"Good point." She scrambled to her feet. "Well said. The good news is I have a passport. Why don't I get on a plane and fly out of here? Go back to California and let you all figure out your old-god politics without me."

Jack's voice grew deeper, and his skin flickered with a bark-like texture before it smoothed out again. "This is your mess, Carys Morgan. You let a powerful goddess into the Brightlands."

"Oh yeah?" She leaned forward. "And who locked her up in the first place?"

"Epona."

"So tell the horse goddess to come and get her."

"Oh, but that's not the way the story is written." Jack picked a dandelion and the stem grew in his hand, the bud blooming bright yellow, then immediately turning to white fluff that drifted away in the breeze. "I don't write, myself. They sang my songs long before they could write. But others came after. Jibril and the Builder. They love a good *word*." Jack looked up into the canopy of the apple trees. "Love a good scroll, those two. People of the books and all that. *Your* kind."

"Do you just love spouting nonsense?" Carys wanted to hit him.

"See, it's all about stories. Storytellers like you. Don't have to be written. But they can be." Jack stared into the trees, and his green beard grew longer as the ivy in the garden bed wrapped around his legs.

"What the fuck are you talking about?"

"Sit down, Carys Morgan." His eyes locked with hers.

Carys took a seat, but she glared at him the whole time.

"Bad stories weave enchantments," the wild man whispered. Then he smiled. "But good stories can break them."

He was finally telling her something important.

"I have to break another enchantment?"

How was she supposed to break an enchantment in the Brightlands? In the Shadowlands, steel could break fae magic. Dragon's blood could break fae wards. In the Brightlands? Steel was everywhere. And dragon blood meant nothing.

What had Jibril told her yesterday? *Ideas are all that is needed to create a god.*

"Macha is enchanting the world right now," Carys said.

"Is that what she's doing?" Jack picked a blade of grass.

"So how do I break that enchantment?"

"How?" The blade of grass grew between Jack's fingers until a nodding head of golden seeds bloomed from the end and those seeds fluttered away in the breeze, taking their grains to other parts of the garden. "You have to tell the right story."

"To whom?"

Jack shrugged. "That is not for me to say."

Once again, she was seconds away from throttling an ancient nature god.

Duncan opened the front door. "Carys?" He walked out, holding a cup of coffee. "Have a cup of coffee, lass. Jibril just brewed it."

She took the mug of coffee prepared with milk and a little sugar, just the way she liked. She looked up at Duncan, who winked at her and blew her a kiss.

Carys's heart eased just a little bit. She sipped the strong coffee before she spoke to Jack again. "This man just saved your life, Jack."

Jack threw his head back and laughed.

"My mother escaped all this, you know. The magic and the scheming." Carys stood up and brushed the grass off her pants. "And every day I'm pulled in deeper, I understand more why she wanted out." She started walking toward the van.

Jack called to her back. "There is no out for you, daughter of two worlds!"

Carys walked to the passenger side, only to see Jibril already in the front seat where she usually sat. "You."

The man in white nodded at the garden. "Jack will stay here and rebuild the apiary while I take you to the Builder. I believe we are simply waiting for the rest of your party to bathe before we leave."

"There is room for more than one bathroom in that house."

Jibril raised a single eyebrow. "I usually don't have seven houseguests."

She hated that he had a point. "Okay, so who is the Builder? Is he going to tell me how to defeat the Morrígan?"

Jibril slipped on a pair of dark sunglasses and raised a mug to his lips. It smelled like spiced tea. "Humans are such linear thinkers; you want things right away. Clear directions. But stories rarely work that way. I'll take you to Blean Woods. Then the Builder will point you to the next turn that you must take, just as I did last night."

"Last night I chased an enchanted bear into the forest while I was soaked in ammonia that still reeks—even after two showers— then I collapsed in a sleeping bag in your sitting room." She sipped her coffee. "I'm losing patience with the mysterious directions, Jibril."

He smiled demurely. "That may be, but you show great potential as a hero. I was impressed by your bravery and your inventiveness last night. Plus the bees approve of you."

"The bees approve of me?"

"It's a great compliment, to be admired by bees." He sipped his tea. "Not the dragon though. They still don't like the dragon."

THE DRIVE to Blean Woods was less than four hours, but it felt longer sitting in the back of the van instead of next to Duncan.

Especially because sitting next to a silent Lachlan made her already testy mood even worse.

Laura and Cadell were talking quietly behind them, and Angus and Naida were sleeping in the far back.

Lachlan was sitting next to her like a statue, staring at the passing motorway.

"Are you ever going to talk to me again?" Carys finally asked.

Lachlan glanced at her from the corner of his eye. "I'm talking to you now."

"You're sulking."

He turned to her, and a corner of his mouth turned up. "I'm sulking?"

"Yes."

"*Sulking.* Like a child?"

"Sulking like a man who didn't get what he wanted," Carys said.

"And what do you think I want?" He leaned closer, and it was impossible to resist the wave of memories that his scent and his heat provoked. "Hmm?"

Lachlan in her bed, his arms around her.

Lachlan holding her up when she could barely function.

Lachlan swinging her around the dance floor at the pub in Baywood, laughing as he sang.

"I don't know anymore. I just don't want you to be so angry." She looked up and saw that he wasn't sulking anymore. His lips were parted, and his eyes were locked on hers.

"I never thought of you, you know. Before she died. I never thought of you once." His voice was bitter, but his eyes were aching. "And now I'm realizing that Duncan must have thought of you every day after seeing Seren and me together."

I never thought of you once.

"That's hurtful," Carys whispered. "Whether you realize it or not, that's hurtful, Lachlan, and I know you're grieving again, but—"

"I don't know why I'm still alive," Lachlan continued. "When he realized what I'd done—how I went looking for you—I don't know why I'm even alive."

"I'm not some kind of prize for you to fight over." Oh, she was just picking winners today. "Laura?"

"Yeah, hon?"

"Can you trade places with me?"

Her best friend didn't even hesitate. "Sure."

Carys moved to the side, allowing Laura to sit beside Lachlan while she moved back to sit next to Cadell.

He was close enough that his mental voice came through. *I can kill him for you.*

No.

It would be like a favor. He would be with Seren again. Well, probably not, because he didn't die in battle, but at least he will not put that look on your face.

I was trying to be nice to him.

Don't be.

She swallowed the lump in her throat and nodded.

Cadell's mental voice grew softer. *He does not have the space in his heart for kindness right now. All he can feel is his own selfish grief. This has nothing to do with you.*

I want to go home. I want to take Duncan and go home.

Call your uncle's man in Cardiff and he will send a plane for you.

She leaned her head against Cadell's shoulder. "I can't," she whispered.

"Why not?"

"Because there are sea monsters in Yorkshire and enchanted bears outside Birmingham." She looked up. "I have to fix this."

"Then I'm with you," Cadell said. "Wherever this angel leads us."

Angel?

Oh. Of course. Of course Jibril was an angel. A *messenger.*

Carys blinked. "Not a god. But definitely not just a beekeeper."

"Most definitely not."

"And this last druid that Angus mentioned?"

Cadell shrugged. "We shall see when we arrive in Kent."

Jibril wanted to drive directly to Blean Woods, but Duncan insisted on spending the night in Cambridge.

"I'm putting my foot down as the driver of this expedition or quest or whatever you want to call it," he told Jibril. "Carys needs to rest, and she's the hero of this whole business, isn't she?"

Jibril nodded. "She is."

"Then she's getting a full meal," Duncan growled. "Not travel center crap. She's getting a decent shower or bath or whatever the fuck she wants, and she's getting a good night's sleep." He glared over the rest of the van. "Anyone have a fucking problem with that?"

Carys felt like crying a little bit. "That sounds really great actually."

"I have a friend in town with a house we can borrow." Duncan looked straight at her. "I already called him."

"Fine," Jibril said. "But please know that according to the radio news, another fae fort just rose in Avebury that is nearly identical to the fort near Stonehenge."

Laura raised her hand. "And the Morrígan is trending on social media again." She glanced at Carys with a guilty expression. "I just wanted to let you know. People are starting to put Macha's appearance together with the fae forts and all the other supernatural stuff that's been happening."

Jibril nodded. "She is gathering believers."

Carys's heart sank. "Duncan, maybe we should—"

"Deal with that in the fucking morning?" Duncan snapped.

"Agreed. Because you're getting a decent night's sleep and a full meal." He glared at the rest of the van. "Do we all understand?"

Cadell said, "I approve of this plan, and I am happy to physically restrain anyone who does not."

"Thank you, dragon."

There was nothing other than vague murmuring after that, and the van fell silent.

Jibril did, however, turn on the radio, which was full of excited clamor about current events.

"—followers of the newest social media sensation, a young woman named Matcha—"

"I believe it's pronounced Ma-ha, Emily." A man with a slight Welsh accent interrupted the announcer. "Her appearance has taken the internet by storm with brands around the world purportedly clamoring to strike deals with the young, provocative redhead. We'll be talking later to a marketing pro. Does *sex* still sell?"

"In more somber news, we'll have a report at the top of the hour about the serious uptick in road crime, Gareth."

"Good to get more information about that, isn't it?" The male presenter responded in a deeper voice. "And of course we'll return to our local correspondent in Wiltshire where another extraordinary structure has risen that resembles something you might see out of a Hollywood blockbuster."

"Is this a geological phenomenon," the female presenter asked, "or have vandals pulled off the prank of the century? After this break, we'll be back with geologist Dr. Avery Khan from the Royal Geographic Society to get her insight into the exciting possibilities."

"What were you and Lachlan talking about?" Duncan was sitting at the foot of the tub, rubbing Carys's feet as she soaked in a bath filled with lavender-scented water.

She shook her head. "Nothing."

"Don't lie. You were upset."

"He was..." She closed her eyes. "I was just trying to be nice, and then he said he never thought about me at all before Seren died. And logically, I know that makes sense. Why would he? But for some reason it hurt."

Duncan's hand held her foot firm, but he stopped rubbing.

"It doesn't matter," she continued even though tears filled her eyes. "I don't love him, so it doesn't matter. I don't even know why it upset me."

"Because you did love him once," Duncan said. "And you knew he'd been married and widowed, and you probably had a lot of feelings about that. It was a cruel thing to say even if it was true. And I've a mind to go and bash him on the head for being a brute. There's no excuse for it."

She pulled her foot away and scooted to the side of the tub, throwing damp arms around Duncan's shoulders. "Why are you so good?"

He ran his hands down her back and hugged her even though she was soaking wet. "Well, it makes me look really good when Lachlan's being an arse, doesn't it?"

She laughed into his shoulder and blinked away her tears. "Yeah."

"I should probably thank him for being such a royal twat."

"He's *literally* a royal twat, isn't he?"

"He is." Duncan kept his arms around her, and her breathing calmed. "I thought of you," he whispered. "I didn't even know your name, but I thought of you nearly every day."

She turned her face into his neck and kissed it.

"I thought about what you must be like. With Seren being so fiery, I thought you might be calm and steady." He ran a hand up and down her back. "Softhearted maybe. I worried about people hurting you. Worried that if you were as kind as Seren was mean, they might see that as weakness."

"Was she mean?"

What are you doing in my world? It wasn't enough to steal my husband, you had to steal my dragon too?

Seren's words from her dream slapped Carys's memory.

"Oh yes, she could be mean," Duncan said. "But not for no reason. She had little patience for stupidity. She felt the weight of her role, I think. And that could make her harsh. And she was fierce about the people she loved."

He kept stroking her back, up and down, soothing and warming her up.

"He said that you probably thought of me," Carys whispered. "That he didn't know why he was still alive when you realized he'd gone looking for me after Seren's death."

Duncan's hand stopped, and his fingers dug into her back. "I was very angry."

"Probably with me too."

"Carys... it's not important."

She pulled away so she could look at his face. "Were you?"

"No." His voice was harsh. "How could I be? You had no idea about any of this. Had no idea about the Shadowlands. Had no idea about Shadowkin or Brightkin or any of this at all. How could I be angry with you?"

But Carys knew he had been. Maybe he still was.

It wasn't logical for her to resent Lachlan for not thinking about her when he was married to Seren.

It wasn't logical for Duncan to resent her for falling in love with Lachlan when she didn't know any of this existed.

She pulled away from Duncan and shrugged. "Sometimes feelings aren't logical."

"You're tired." His voice was rough. "You should finish your bath and go to sleep."

And suddenly that was all she wanted to do.

MACHA WAS LYING next to Duncan on the bed, her fingers floating over his temple. "Sleep, my fine human."

Carys sat bolt upright in bed. "What are you doing here?"

"Did you forget" —Macha climbed over Duncan's body and crawled toward Carys on all fours— "that I am a *goddess*?" She shrieked the last word. "Goddess!" She shoved a finger in Carys's face. "Mortal. Who do you think you are?"

Carys fell back on the bed as if pushed down by an invisible hand.

Her body was frozen, and tendrils of cold trickled from her nape down her spine. "You're not real," she whispered. "This is a dream."

If this was real, Cadell would already be in the room. Duncan would be awake. Lachlan would be swinging a sword.

"Oh, you *are* dreaming, Epona's daughter, but I'm real enough to kill you." Macha lay next to Carys and placed a hand on her chest. She pressed her hand against Carys's skin, and cold spread over her body; fingers of ice pierced her chest.

Carys tried to breathe but she couldn't, and crippling pain built in her lungs.

She was swamped in darkness; all she could hear was the Morrígan whispering in her mind.

"I could kill you now because I am a god. And you are nothing but a woman."

"Duncan." With the last of her breath, Carys whispered his name. "Duncan."

"He will not wake from the sleep I sent to him." Macha leaned over Carys, studying her as if she was an interesting specimen. "Imagine if I killed you." Macha smiled a little. "He would wake next to your dead body. The dragon would lose another lady. The prince would lose another love. Their grief would feed me for *days*."

The darkness around her pressed in, closing off her vision until she saw nothing. She felt only dry winter cold freezing her lungs and a burning sensation at the back of her throat.

"You tamed my beautiful sea monster. You frightened my bear. And what do you have for it?" Macha continued to whisper. "Nothing. I'm still here. You have been driving in your metal carriage, chasing rabbit trails around this little island, and you... have... nothing."

Cold lips touched Carys's cheek, and when Macha breathed on her skin, ice cut her.

"You have nothing. Because you are nothing." Macha sounded sad now. "They told you that you are special—you're not. You will fight me, and that is all I will need to break open your world so that the monsters pour in. The battle will be beautiful, Carys Morgan, and it will be everything I need."

Carys opened her mouth to speak, but her teeth started chattering.

"Look at you, poor thing." Macha's voice was pitying. "All you wanted was your lover back, and they drew you in, didn't they? Epona's machinations. The Pan's meddling." Macha's cold fingers stroked Carys's hair back from her forehead. "And all you wanted was to find your pretty man."

The kiss that Macha brushed across Carys's cheek was damp and cold.

"Poor little thing," the Morrígan repeated. "You're not capable of defeating a god. How silly of them. They needed a warrior, and instead they have you."

Carys felt like she was dying. She saw nothing but black, and her lungs were frozen. She sensed nothing around her. Not the bed she was lying on. Not the press of Macha's body. All she felt was cold.

It was so, so cold.

The tear that formed at Carys's eye froze on her cheek.

"Oh, shhhhh," Macha continued to whisper. "Poor, poor Carys."

She wanted to die. All she wanted was for the cold to end. Moments passed, or maybe it was hours.

"Sleep, little human," Macha murmured. "But when you wake up, remember... you cannot kill a god."

CARYS JOLTED AWAKE, her hand grasping her throat as she drew in deep, warm breaths of air. She looked to her left to see Duncan still sleeping, and a clock on the mantel over the cold fireplace ticked, ticked, ticked.

Somewhere in the house, a single clock struck one.

Carys bolted for the bathroom, vomiting the dinner she'd eaten before bed.

She curled on the floor, shaking from her toes to the top of her head. Then she grabbed a damp towel hanging over the edge of the bathtub and covered her face as she sobbed.

CHAPTER TWENTY-TWO

Carys sat next to Cadell in the van the next morning, leaning against the dragon's broad shoulder and trying to forget the nightmare that had woken her in the middle of the night.

Nightmare or vision?

"Poor little thing... You're not capable of defeating a god... They needed a warrior, and instead they have you."

The dream had been meant to terrorize her and make her give up, but where was the lie? Macha was right. Despite her small victories, Carys was wholly unequipped for a battle against an ancient Irish war goddess.

This wasn't the battle on Saris Plain where she had the entire Cymric dragon horde, a powerful fae prince, and Anglia's armies backing her up.

This wasn't even hunting down a half-fae sorceress with Duncan and Lachlan at her side.

No, she was in the Brightlands where she had no power at all, and an ancient and powerful goddess was trying to raise a new cult so that she could break the gates between worlds.

And the hero chosen by the old gods was a human mythology professor with raging anxiety.

What the actual fuck?

Carys was probably not the only one doubting their mission, because while everyone in the van was rested and well-fed, the mood was somber.

Duncan reached over to the radio and turned up the music—a classic-rock station that really loved the Eagles—and Carys's dragon took the opportunity to pry.

"What's wrong?" Cadell asked softly. "I tried to speak to your mind, but you're very closed off this morning."

"It's nothing." She shook her head. "Just tired."

"You are lying to me." His voice was stiff. "Did you have an argument with the surly human? Do I need to speak to him?"

"No. And no. Just..." Carys didn't know what to say. She was a grown woman. She shouldn't need a dragon to fight all her battles for her. "Leave it."

And it wasn't like she could send Cadell after the Morrígan. He couldn't chase a goddess into her dreams.

"I will find out what is bothering you," Cadell said, "and then I will deal with it. Or him. Or whoever has caused this melancholy."

"Can we talk about this later?"

Cadell's jaw was tense. "If you insist."

"I insist."

Ironically, the only cheerful member of the party seemed to be Jibril, who had not wanted to rest the night before and was now clearly eager to see the man he called the Builder.

"He might be working today," Jibril said, "but we'll visit his cottage first. It's on the edge of the forest."

West Blean Wood was a vast conservation area just a few miles outside Canterbury, so it only took them a few minutes from town to be in the middle of forest. Duncan drove up Thornden Wood Road, looking for a place to park.

"So does this builder live in a pocket world like Jack?" Duncan asked. "Can us regular humans enter this one?"

"No, he lives in this world as I do," Jibril said. "He is a simple man."

"He's a builder?" Carys asked.

Jibril nodded. "Of a sort."

They were nearly through the forest when Jibril pointed to the right where a nearly hidden driveway appeared between two trees. "There. Turn there."

Duncan waited for a car to pass, then turned in to the narrow, two-track drive that cut through a dense stand of chestnut trees and brush. Beyond the trees, they entered a clearing where a bright white wattle-and-daub house backed up to the forest. It bore a thatch roof, and at the peak of that roof, Carys saw a man working.

Duncan parked the van, and Carys immediately opened the side door and slid out of the car, her eyes fixed on the man working on the roof. There was something very familiar about him. Something about the way he moved.

The Builder turned and brushed the hair out of his eyes. He smiled when he saw the angel exit the van. "Jibril, old friend. Who have you brought to meet me?"

Carys had never seen the man before in her life, so why did she have a sense of recognition?

He had high cheekbones and a longish nose. His face was a sun-warmed brown, tanned from working in the outdoors. His dark brown hair was long and curly, pulled back into a messy knot at the back of his head.

The man—druid or god or whoever he was—sat on the roof, setting a bunch of long dry reeds next to him, and bent his knees, resting his elbows on his knees as he scanned the party exiting the van.

Kind brown eyes landed on Carys. "It's Gareth's daughter."

"Oh!" Tears immediately came to her eyes when she realized who the Builder had to be, and she could barely hold back a laugh. "You're..." She sniffed. "My dad knew you. And you knew my dad?"

His voice was resonant though his face was plain. He spoke in a rich South English accent with hints of something far more ancient. "I *know* your dad, Carys."

"So you're... I mean, you're really—"

"You can call me Joshua." He turned and started climbing down the ladder that was propped against the house.

"Joshua?" Duncan asked. "Joshua." He nodded slowly. "Oh fu— Uhhh. No." The tall man seemed bashful. "My... goodness."

"Oh, I get it!" Laura pointed to him. "Joshua. Yeshua. Jibril. Gabriel. That's unexpected, but I guess it shouldn't be."

Joshua reached the ground and turned, walking over to Jibril as he pulled off the thick leather gloves he'd been wearing to repair the thatch roof. "Welcome, friends."

"Old gods." Angus lowered himself from the van and ambled over, his back bent and his eyes keen on the man. He pointed his walking stick at Joshua. "New gods." He gave Joshua a curt nod. "Builder."

"Shepherd." Joshua crossed wiry arms over his chest. He looked at Carys, and his eyes softened. "You visit me with stories in your eyes, Carys Morgan."

Carys was still wondering at Joshua's existence in a small cottage on the edge of an old forest outside Canterbury. "How are you... here?"

Joshua glanced at the angel next to Carys. "Jibril and I exist where the faithful exist."

"But that's not *just* here," Carys said. "I mean... Both of you—"

"Are here because we need to be here," Joshua said. "And we are elsewhere when we need to be elsewhere."

Jibril turned to Joshua. "I feel that you must know the Morrígan is loose in the Brightlands."

Joshua nodded. "I have felt her rising power, but now I see the old gods have given us a hero." He gestured toward Carys, and his eyes landed on someone behind her. "And she has a dragon. George is turning in his grave, but there you are." Joshua's eyes were dancing.

Jibril leaned against the corner of the van. "A dragon's not much use in the Brightlands, old friend."

Lachlan and Duncan, Cadell, Laura, Naida, and Angus, all came to stand beside Carys.

Joshua nodded in approval. "Loyalty and love are useful everywhere." He angled his head toward the open door of his house. "Come. There are seven of you. Seven is a good number." He started walking to the cottage. "Come, friends. Let's eat, and we shall speak about many things. Let us see if we can find a way to help the hero the old gods have chosen for this task."

Laura was craning her neck as they sat in the surprisingly roomy living space in Joshua's cottage. "It's bigger on the inside."

Lachlan stretched his neck from one side to the other. "Pocket world."

"Is it?" Carys turned to Cadell. *Is it?*

The dragon stretched out his arm, and just under the surface of his skin, she saw a ripple of green pebbled skin. "It appears that it must be."

"None of that now." Joshua handed Cadell a large mug of tea. "I can make the place bigger, but you transforming would really ruin the roof."

Jibril looked up. "You're always working on your roof."

"The work relaxes me."

Duncan was sitting against the back wall, staring at the man. He kept looking between Carys, then Jibril, then Joshua again.

Joshua nodded at him as he sat across from Carys. "You have a faithful protector in that man. Your father would be pleased."

Carys couldn't handle thinking about her father and what he would have thought of Duncan right now. Her emotions were all over the place.

"How does it work?" Carys asked. "I mean, my dad is dead, but you said you know him and—"

"There are some questions that I cannot answer for you right now. Not because I don't want to but because the human mind is limited," Joshua said. "Can you accept that?"

Carys nodded numbly. "I guess I have to."

"But I can assure you that the gifts you have been given—from your father and your mother—encompass everything you will need to complete your task." Joshua kept his voice soft. "Do you believe me?"

"No," she blurted. "Right now I feel like I'm going to fail." Her cheeks heated.

Joshua waved a hand, and in the blink of an eye, the world around them froze.

Carys sat up straight. "What did you just do?"

"I simply gave us some privacy." Joshua shrugged. "Let us exist on another plane for a moment. You were embarrassed to speak the truth in front of your friends because you believe they are looking to you for leadership."

Okay, obviously he was a god, but how did he see her so clearly?

"The Morrígan sent me a dream last night," Carys said.

"Did you tell anyone?"

"No."

Joshua nodded. "You don't want to appear frightened."

"But I am."

"Which I'm sure you must know was her intention." He spread his hands. "You are a very intelligent woman, so I'm sure you realize that fear and discouragement was her objective."

"Logically yes, but... right now I am doubting everything," Carys blurted out. "I don't think I'm a hero. I don't even know what that looks like for me, you know?"

Joshua nodded thoughtfully.

"Like, maybe Seren was supposed to be the hero. Maybe that's why she was killed at the beginning of all this. *She* was a hero. She was a dragon lord—a proper one! And I'm just kind of the really bad substitute teacher." Tears began to well in her eyes. "I'm the substitute for a lot, I think."

Joshua spoke softly. "You are not the substitute."

"Really? Are you sure about that? Because I'm also worried that I'm going to get Laura killed while she's here just trying to help me. And she is my best friend, and honestly Kiersten—our other best friend—and Laura's family would never forgive me, and with my parents gone, they're basically all I have left."

Carys couldn't seem to stop herself from baring her soul, and Joshua just nodded along as she did it. "I *don't* know how to stop the Morrígan. I have *no* ideas. None. Jack said something about breaking an enchantment, and Angus said something about walking between worlds, but vague pronouncements are not a plan. And I'm just a mythology professor. I know all this stuff from *books*, and let me tell you, the reality of all the different parallel mythological worlds is not captured in books!"

"I understand," Joshua murmured.

"And Duncan is... the best! But I might be completely messing up his life by loving him. I mean, I'm pretty sure his mother hates me already, and he may say that's not important to him, but it is. It just is. Added to that, we live in completely different countries and cultures, and we both have lives where we live."

Joshua nodded in understanding. "All these worries are valid."

"But also! It feels super-selfish to even be talking about my love life right now because there is a literal war goddess loose in the world, and my romantic problems are like the least relevant thing right now."

Joshua smiled. "Carys, *love* is never irrelevant."

Carys cried. She wasn't proud of it, and she wasn't going to wallow in it, but the weeks of travel, the supernatural battles, frightening dreams, and the pressure of the unknown came crashing down on her.

So with her friends frozen around her and a kind god sitting across from her, listening to her bare her soul, she just let it out.

When her shoulders had stopped shaking and her nose was running, Joshua handed her a plain cotton handkerchief with the initials GM embroidered in the corner along with a red dragon.

Carys stopped crying. "This is my father's handkerchief."

"It is." Joshua sat back on the sofa, Jibril still frozen beside him.

"I'm so sorry I just laid all that on you." She sniffed and pressed the handkerchief to her nose. "I'm really sorry."

Joshua shrugged. "I can take it."

"Still."

"You're doubting yourself, Carys." He leaned forward and rested his elbows on his knees. "That's perfectly understandable. But you can accomplish everything the old gods expect from you. Otherwise, you would not have been chosen for this task. Do you believe me?"

"I guess" —Carys stared at her father's handkerchief— "I have to believe you?"

"You *don't* have to. All of this is a choice."

"Is it?"

"Yes." Joshua shrugged. "You have a passport. You have money. You could get on a plane today and fly away from here."

She let out a slow breath. "I could run away."

"Yes, you could. Take Laura with you. Cadell would follow. Duncan would too."

"And leave all the consequences of letting the Morrígan into the

Brightlands for someone else to clean up?" Carys felt a pit form in her stomach.

"It's a choice," Joshua said. "I'm not going to tell you what the right thing to do is because you have to decide that for yourself."

Carys sat back on the sofa and thought hard.

She could run.

She would be safe. Maybe forever.

But Naida and Godrik wouldn't be safe.

Her uncle wouldn't be safe.

Cadell's children, his whole horde, would be in danger.

Winnie and Elanor and Eamer. Lachlan and Angus and every human born into the Shadowlands.

They would all be caught in whatever chaos the Morrígan had planned.

"I have to defeat the Morrígan. I let her out of the Shadowlands—I have to figure out a way to get her back."

"Then I will help you." Joshua's face was encouraging. "I have faith in you, Carys Morgan. Faith in Gareth's daughter."

Carys looked at Angus, slightly amazed that he was still frozen. "Are you more powerful than Angus?"

"I currently have more faithful in this place, so right now?" Joshua nodded. "Jibril and I are two of the most powerful gods in Briton even though we are not the oldest."

"Right." So what did that mean for the Morrígan? Did she have enough followers to be a major power yet? Was that her aim? How would she gather followers, and could Carys take them away?

Was that how she could defeat the goddess?

"You need to reframe what victory means," Joshua said. "You have been told that you cannot kill a god."

"Dru—Diarmuid. The fae king," she said. "I'm not sure if you..."

Joshua nodded. "I know the fae of old."

"He told me that if even one person believes in a god, they exist."

"He is not wrong, but that is not the whole story." Joshua spread his hands, and the world around Carys came alive.

Laura leaned toward Cadell. Jibril finished his sip of tea, shooting a side glance at Joshua, and Lachlan and Duncan leaned against the cottage wall like twin sentries with solemn expressions.

"We're going to talk later, young man," Angus muttered.

Joshua continued speaking as if he hadn't literally frozen time while Carys had an emotional breakdown. "You *cannot* kill a god, nor should you want to."

"I don't know," Duncan said. "Defeating a goddess of war and bloodshed doesn't seem like the worst idea."

"I am not saying you should not thwart her," Joshua said, "but you should not equate victory over the Morrígan with her defeat. Those who follow me choose to do so. Those who follow the Morrígan have their own reasons for that as well."

"She used to live in the Brightlands, right?" Laura asked. "All the worlds were once united."

Jibril cocked his head. "I think it is more correct to say that worlds were once more fluid. The gods have always had their own realms, but magic once filled the world. The gates were created when humans began to doubt. When they looked to reason more than the gods."

"Who created them?" Lachlan glared at Joshua. "It was the fae, wasn't it?"

"The fae are creatures of the Shadowlands." Angus piped up from the back of the room. "They can't create gates—they can only manage them. And lately they haven't been doing a good job of it."

"This isn't about the gates," Joshua said. "Or not entirely about them. The gates protect the Shadowlands. The fae would not survive in the modern world." Joshua turned his eyes toward Naida. "At least not for long. You are creatures of old magic and the earth. This place is not your home."

Naida shook her head. "No."

"So the Morrígan once lived in the Brightlands," Duncan said. "Once upon a time and all that, all the gods did. And obviously there are gods in the Brightlands now." He gestured at Jibril and Joshua. "So can you explain why it's so damn important that the Morrígan goes back to the Shadowlands?"

"She is breaking down the gates that protect our world," Cadell said. "And she is drawing in monsters and imps and creatures that humans have confined to folk tales."

"Gates can be fortified," Jibril said, "And creatures can be contained. But the Morrígan is voracious."

"She can't help it." Joshua spread his hands. "Macha is a goddess of many things, but blood and battle combine with a thirst for conquest and sovereignty in her nature."

"The Morrígan's nature drives her toward war," Jibril continued. "She cannot stop herself, and all the gods across the world would end up rising to meet her should she continue in her quest beyond Briton." Jibril took a long breath and looked around the room. "If the Morrígan is not contained in Briton, chaos and magical war will spread across the world."

"And I'm supposed to stop that?" Carys rose to her feet and pointed at Joshua, her heart racing. "You said my parents gave me gifts, but my parents are *gone*. And they never explained any of this before they died. So how... I mean, how am I supposed to—"

"Your mother's not any more gone than your Shadowkin is," Angus growled.

Silence filled the cottage, and Carys sank to the sofa again. "Not gone?"

"What did you think, girl? That Tegan—Epona's most beloved daughter, the one the goddess gifted the power of life to—was just going to get stuck in a corner of the underworld for eternity?"

Carys gripped her father's handkerchief in her palm. "So it's not just my sister who's in Annwn?" She looked at Joshua, then Jibril. "My mother is there too?"

"When she died, your mother asked to join her other daughter in Annwn," Jibril said softly. "The goddess granted her petition. They are both there."

"Ha!" Lachlan burst out with a harsh laugh. "Both there and both completely out of reach."

"For you?" Angus barked. "Maybe. But not for her." He pointed at Carys. "She's of two worlds. Maybe the only child alive born to the Shadows and the Light. If there's another, I don't know one."

Carys remembered what Angus had told her in the world beneath the silver pool. "How do I get to them?" She looked at Angus, then at Jibril, then at Joshua. "If I'm supposed to walk between worlds, how?"

"I can't tell you," Joshua said. "That is a mother's wisdom."

Jibril turned to Joshua, his eyebrows raised. "You want to take her to the Mothers?"

Joshua nodded. "The Mothers will know how to get her where she needs to go."

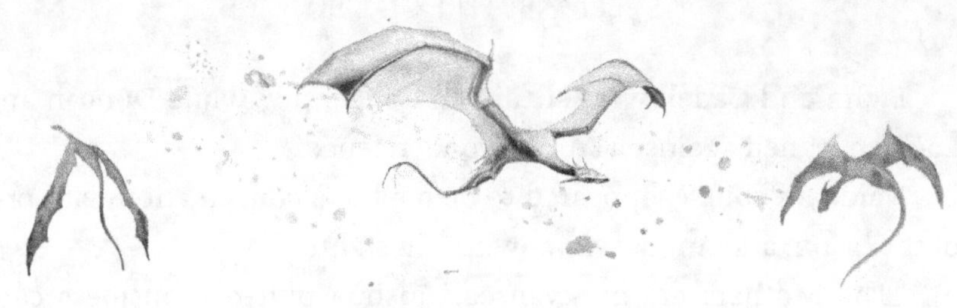

CHAPTER TWENTY-THREE

Joshua guided them through the forest, and Carys walked beside him, trying to find peace in the chaos of her mind.

"At least you got *some* answers, right?" Joshua asked.

Carys's mind was clearer, but her heart was heavier. "I don't suppose you're going to just give me an address where I can look up these Mothers, right? Or do you have to guide me to a bridge where, in order to find them, I have to battle a serpent or demonic cow or something?"

"Well, these are the only cows we have." Joshua gestured at the small herd of European bison that lived within the forest. He'd been walking with Carys and explaining the ecology of forest restoration that the bison and wild pigs in the land trust were part of.

"They're terrible about fence destruction," he continued, "but I'd have a hard time calling them demonic."

In fact, the bison grazed calmly in the underbrush beneath the trees. One of the calves nursed, and the lone bull in the group appeared to be taking a nap in the sun, dust floating around his thick brown fur.

Laura and Cadell were sitting on a fallen log while Duncan and Lachlan leaned against a sturdy wooden fence.

Naida, of course, appeared to be having a conversation with one of the bison, and Angus was nowhere in sight.

"The Mothers are in Swansea." Joshua pulled a business card from his pocket and handed it to her. "They have a shop on High Street."

Carys looked down and read the card. "Pages and Portals? There are three mother goddesses in Wales, and they run a bookstore in Swansea?"

"Books *and* records, but there's also a tea shop in back and a corner that's reserved for Oshun's jewelry. Stunning goldsmith, that one."

"Oshun?" She was a goddess from West Africa and a powerful fertility goddess. "She's one of the Mothers?"

Joshua nodded. "The Mothers are... well, old. Older than all the rest of us, I think." He glanced over his shoulder, back in the direction of the cottage. "Maybe not Angus."

"What *is* he?"

Joshua laughed a little bit. "He's a character."

"To say the least."

Joshua paused and turned to her. Carys stopped and faced him.

"Can I give you some advice?"

"Everyone else seems to, and I like you more than most of them."

Joshua smiled again. "Your father has a family in Wales. He left them behind because they found your mother too strange. They were very... conventional people."

"So they did know my mom?"

Joshua nodded. "You can't know your future unless you understand your past, but I would encourage you to focus on your mother in this chapter of your story, Carys Morgan. Not all mysteries can be solved in one tale."

She flipped the business card in her fingers. "Pages and Portals?"

Joshua nodded. "The Mothers will be able to guide you where

you need to go. I think Jibril brought you here because he wasn't sure about you. But I am."

"Well…" Carys sighed. "Thanks. It was great to meet you, and…" She took the handkerchief from her pocket. "I appreciate this."

"Your mother made these for him, didn't she?"

Carys nodded. "Yeah. She did the embroidery in the corners."

"So you have a bit of both of them in that talisman." Joshua smiled. "I'm glad I could give it to you."

She glanced at Duncan where he stood leaning against the wooden fence.

"You're not going to mess up his life," Joshua said. "You two belong together."

"How do you know?"

"Well, I don't like to brag." Joshua threw a wiry arm over Carys's shoulders. "But I'm kind of all-knowing about most things. Not everything, mind you. But most."

Just then, he froze. His arm dropped from Carys's shoulder, and he turned to face the herd of bison.

There was a huff and the bison bull rolled up to his knees, then his feet, grumbling and turning in circles.

Naida stepped away from the female she'd been talking to. "Something is happening."

A lone crow landed on a low oak branch overlooking the dry creek bed where the bison were grazing.

Joshua narrowed his eyes on the crow. "Hello there."

The bird angled his head toward Carys, peering at her from its branch and blinking one round eye.

There was a high-pitched squeal from the underbrush, and a group of large furry pigs darted from the forest, crossed the dry creek bed, and escaped into the dense wood that stretched out behind them.

"Carys?" Lachlan stepped toward her, followed by Duncan. "Carys, walk over here."

"Good idea." Joshua put a hand on her shoulder and urged her toward the distant fence where Duncan was waiting. Lachlan had stepped away from his Brightkin, squaring his shoulders against the small herd of bison and drawing his sword.

"Knight of the Shadows," Joshua warned, "you will not harm these animals."

Lachlan shot Joshua a look but said nothing.

Cadell and Laura were also on their feet, and Cadell was backing away slowly with Laura shoved behind him. "Something has disturbed them. Naida, step away."

There was a whispering wind that curled through the trees; then in a rush, a massive flock of crows swept in from the east, cawing and screaming as they swooped down and startled the bull, whirling around him as the animal let out a low, rumbling bellow that seemed to shake the ground.

The bull turned, lowered his head, and began to run directly at Carys.

"Carys," Naida screamed, "run!"

"The fence!" Joshua shouted. "Run for the fence!"

Carys didn't question it—she turned and ran.

The rumbling groan of the male bison transformed into the stampeding of heavy feet as the small herd began to chase them down.

"Can't you stop this?" she shouted at Joshua.

"Not without hurting the animals!"

Carys wanted to shout, *What about me?* But she was too out of breath.

Joshua was a god. He was going to be fine, but there was no way Carys was going to outrun a herd of bison. The most she could do was hope to climb up a tree or get over the wooden fence she could see in the distance.

Duncan had climbed up and was holding out his hands, ready to pull her over. "Don't look, just run!"

She heard Cadell shouting, and the rumbling came closer. The ground shook like an earthquake.

Just then, a low, eerie howl echoed from the forest.

She turned to look only for a second, but she saw a streak of white and black weaving through the trees, heading straight for the herd.

The bull swerved away from the dry creek bed where Carys and Joshua were running, wheeling to the left to face off against the predator.

A massive wolf ran straight toward the bull, snarling as it leaped, fangs bared, on the shoulder of the young male.

The bison shook its body, tossing the wolf away, and the animal flew through the air, striking a tree before he fell to the ground.

"Godrik!" Naida screamed. The fae put her hands to the ground and glared at the bison, and then her determined expression fell when she realized...

The ground here did not speak to her.

The battle was not finished though, because the wolf struggled to right himself, bared his teeth, and ran straight toward the bull again.

As they fought, the females of the herd encircled the younger animals and ran back toward the forest, leaving the two battling animals behind as they protected their young.

Godrik held the bull off as the crows cackled from the branches and clouds of starlings whirled overhead.

There was snarling and bellowing, howls and barks.

"They're not stopping," Joshua said. "They will kill each other."

The bull charged at Godrik with his head down, knocking him over and stomping his massive hoof on the wolf's leg. But Godrik struck, twisting his body to clamp his jaws around the bull's front leg, shaking his head until Carys heard an audible snap.

"No!" Naida cried.

The bison huffed and roared. It stumbled back, limping.

Then, just as suddenly as the bull had become aggressive, he stopped. The animal backed away from the wolf on the ground, shook his head and twitched his ears. Then a second later, he walked into the trees on unsteady legs to follow his herd into the forest.

Carys turned to Joshua to see the god holding up a hand and whispering something under his breath.

"What did you do?" Carys asked.

"A natural bison stampede I can't do anything about," Joshua said. "Sometimes the world works that way. But that bull was possessed." He nodded at the crows, who cawed at them one more time before they flapped away. "And I do know a little bit about animals being possessed."

Godrik lay on the ground, his leg at an odd angle and his side heaving as he struggled to breathe.

Naida ran to him. "Godrik!"

Cadell, Duncan, and Lachlan sped toward Carys.

"Are you safe?" Duncan wrapped her in his arms. "Christ, I was terrified."

Joshua cocked his head at Duncan. "I know."

Duncan blinked. "Oh. Right."

Laura and Naida were kneeling by Godrik on the ground.

"He needs help!" Laura shouted. "There's a lot of blood."

"Godrik?" Naida was cradling the wolf's head in her lap. She looked up at Joshua. "If he's here in wolf form, there must be a gate nearby. Help me get him to the gate and I can heal him."

"There is." Joshua looked at Lachlan, Duncan, and Cadell. "You three, carry your friend. I'll show you the way."

"I can't believe I found you." Godrik's shaggy silver and black hair seemed even darker in the pale light of the fae gate. "I heard Naida screaming, and I just ran. I don't even know how I found the gate or why it let me through."

Naida hadn't even taken the time to get them out of the forest. The moment they'd crossed into the nighttime world of the Shadowlands, Joshua had disappeared, as had the sun, and the blue lights of the wisps were the only thing that illuminated the world around them.

"How are you feeling now?" Naida brushed Godrik's hair off his forehead.

"Better." His grey eyes were soft on her. "I went back to the gate in Alba. The moment we went through, I heard a pack of young wolves crying for help, but I never found them."

"A trick." Angus was back in his natural form, loping around the clearing in the dark forest and stretching his goat legs. "No doubt the dark fae wanted to draw you away."

Naida sat on the ground, putting her back against a fallen log and sinking her hands into the forest soil.

Godrik nodded. "I wandered for hours and hours. By the time I returned to where I last remembered you, all of you were gone." He looked at Naida. "And then I couldn't find you anywhere."

The ellyllon's face was pale and drawn.

"She needs living water," Godrik said. "And food."

Cadell stood up. "Let me. I can stretch my wings, listen for news from any dragons in the area, and find food for Naida."

"No deer," Naida said.

Cadell smiled. "I have learned, small friend." He looked at Carys for her approval.

She looked at Naida. "We're here for a few hours at least, right?"

Naida nodded. "Godrik needs to rest."

"Good." Carys nodded at the dragon. "Then Cadell's plan sounds good."

Lachlan drew his bronze sword. "I'm going to check the perimeter." He cast his eyes around the forest. "This gate seems lightly traveled, but we should make sure there are no redcaps or imps in the forest."

"Thank you," Carys said. "Good thinking."

"I'll stay with Godrik and the women," Duncan said.

He and Lachlan exchanged a loaded look; then Lachlan disappeared into the trees and Duncan paced around the clearing, his hand on the cricket bat he'd stolen from Jibril's cottage.

Men.

Yes, Nêrys?

Carys hadn't realized that she'd thought that toward her dragon. *Not you. There's just a lot of testosterone floating in the air.*

They are in an unfamiliar place. It is to be expected.

At least Lachlan looks happier with a job to do.

Cadell was silent for a long moment.

We all need to feel purpose, he finally said.

She knew he was right, but the silent hostility between the two brothers felt like a weight hanging directly on her shoulders, and Carys didn't even know why.

She turned back to Godrik, whose color was improving by the minute.

"I have to ask, how did you end up here?" Carys asked. "Thank you, by the way. Your timing was perfect."

"When I couldn't find you in Alba, I headed home." He sat up, carefully moving the leg the bison had stomped on. "I searched for word of you, but it wasn't until I ran into a fae beekeeper in Eskari territory that I heard you were in the south."

The Blean Woods was denser in the Shadowlands, and the trees towered over them, blocking out any light save for the glowing blue lamps that Naida hung in the air over Godrik's body.

"Bees," Carys said. "Never taking them for granted again."

Godrik nodded. "They are the best messengers." He looked at Laura. "Shadow-walker, you are well?"

"Uh... yeah." Laura took a deep breath. "Still kind of freaked out from that bison stampede, but I'm fine."

Godrik frowned. "I thought the great beasts were common in your homeland."

Laura's eyebrows flew up. "Bison? In North America, sure. In Northern Europe? Not so much."

"We did run into a bear near Birmingham though," Carys told him. "That was unexpected."

Godrik reached for Naida's hand and wove his fingers through hers. "Truly, you have had many adventures without me. I shall try not to be jealous."

"How do you feel about a few more?" Carys said. "Because the Morrígan is still out there, I still have to stop her, and I'm pretty sure I can use all the help I can get."

The corner of the wolf's mouth turned up. "I wouldn't want to miss it."

NIGHT WAS FALLING by the time Carys and her friends walked back through the fae gate and into the Brightlands. Joshua and Jibril were nowhere to be found, so they looked for a path through the woods and started to make their way out of the forest, hoping the van wasn't too far away.

Laura patted her pockets. "Freaking fae thieves."

Naida frowned at her. "Excuse me?"

"Not you," Laura said. "I forgot to drop my phone before we went through the gate, and something must have snatched it." She looked at Duncan. "You?"

"With all the pocket worlds and realms and gates we've been dropped through lately," the man said, "I've taken to leaving my mobile in the van." He patted Laura's shoulder. "I'll buy you another one when we get back to town."

Laura turned to Carys. "Again, I do really enjoy that you have a filthy-rich boyfriend now."

Duncan laughed and Carys smiled, but she didn't miss Lachlan's stormy look.

As they walked, Cadell filled them in on the news across Shadowlands Briton, where little had changed save for a surprising lull in dark fae activity as Dru consolidated power.

"Most of the dragons seem to approve his actions, though they note that many of the fae dislike the new king."

Naida was conspicuously quiet as she walked beside a newly healed Godrik.

"King Diarmuid has spread power among the wild fae clans," Cadell continued, "giving them control over many of the gates in their territory, and some of the ruling lords don't like it."

"Are the barriers thinning?" Lachlan asked.

"There is speculation that the Morrígan's actions are having some effect in the Shadowlands as well as the Brightlands." Cadell nodded. "Four Chinese tourists were found wandering along the Tamis embankment a few days ago. They had no idea what was going on, but the Kingsguard was able to return them to the Brightlands quickly."

Laura shook her head. "That story is going viral."

Cadell looked at her. "Like you, they seemed mostly concerned with their electronic devices."

"Hey," she said. "Not everyone has a Duncan who can just buy them new phones. That's fair."

Duncan muttered, "London police are going to have a hard time taking that report."

"The barriers between the worlds *must* be thinning," Godrik said. "Otherwise, I would not have been able to cross into the Brightlands in my true form."

Carys turned to look at him. "How about now? Do you feel like you can shift?"

He shook his head. "The moment we went through the gate this time, I felt the magic leave my body."

Cadell, Angus, and Godrik were all back in human form, and none of them seemed very pleased about it.

"Thank you for coming with us," Carys said softly. "We missed you."

He glanced at Naida, then offered Carys a subtle wink.

"One more thing of note," Cadell added. "The spells the Frisians were using to ward away the sea monsters appear to be less effective. There have been few ships crossing the channel in the past two weeks. Briton is becoming increasingly isolated."

"Are the spells becoming ineffective?" Angus growled. "Or is the continent cutting Briton off? They're reading the stars. The bees visit their lands too."

Lachlan nodded. "They're worried about the Morrígan, just as Jibril said."

After an hour of wandering along the road, they finally reached the turnoff for Joshua's house. But though they found the van and the cottage, no one appeared to be at home. The windows were dark, and the chimney was cold.

"Well." Carys pulled the card for Pages and Portals from her pocket. "I guess next stop Swansea?"

"Back to the house first." Duncan opened the van door. "Let's get some rest and get a decent meal before... whatever comes next."

CHAPTER TWENTY-FOUR

"What are you reading?" Duncan rubbed a towel over his head as he walked back into the massive bedroom in the house outside Canterbury where they had returned after leaving Joshua's cottage.

Carys lifted two books. "I found a copy of the Bible and the Quran in the library, but the moment I opened them, I started falling asleep."

She'd collected a massive file of notes over the past couple of weeks, from the translation of the manuscript that Dr. Beck had given them in Oxford to a copy of *Sir Gawain and the Green Knight* that she'd found in a bookshop in Scone.

She picked up Laura's mobile phone. "I went online and found some information about Oshun because it's been years since I took a class in African folklore, but I can't print anything out and my eyes are so tired." She pressed the heel of her hand into her right eye. "Maybe I can find a printer in the morning."

"Carys." Duncan wrapped a towel around his waist and sat on the edge of the bed. "What are you doing, lass? You don't need to study; you need to rest."

"This is all I can do though." She stacked the books in a pile since her brain was too tired to read. "I don't have any superpowers in the Brightlands. Cadell can't help me be special here, so all I can do is research stuff." She threw up her hands. "And obviously I'm not even very good at that right now."

"You don't need a dragon to be special." Duncan's voice was hoarse.

He lifted a hand to the small of her back and rubbed small circles.

They hadn't made love since Jack Green's cottage. And since then, they'd met an angel, chased off a bear, met a thatch-repairing messiah who doubled as a forest ranger, and nearly been trampled by a herd of bison.

Carys's mind was a whirl of conflicting emotions, but after her breakdown in Joshua's cottage, she was clearer about a few things.

"I'm in love with you," she blurted. "You are kind and generous and strong. Physically, yes, but mentally and emotionally. You feel... solid. In the best way."

His voice was soft. "Thank you, lass."

"And you have this life that feels... massive—and I'm not talking about your money because I feel like that's not something I should be thinking about even though it's kind of *right there* and it's hard to ignore, but that's like... maybe the fifth most interesting thing about you."

The corner of his mouth turned up. "I cannae lie, I'm curious what numbers one through four are."

She looked straight into his eyes. "Why do you love me? Because I honestly can't figure that out."

Duncan frowned. "Carys, what?"

"I'm not special." She cleared her throat. "I mean, it's been made clear that on some kind of genetic level I am unique because of who my parents are, but if you take away the magic—because it doesn't exist in our world—I'm just a somewhat cute adjunct college professor at a moderately ranked state college with no family and a Subaru in desperate need of new tires."

Duncan was still frowning. "If you need new tires, we'll get you new tires. What are you even—"

"You're special in the Shadowlands *and* in the Brightlands, Duncan. And you look like an advertisement for Visit Scotland too. I mean, you're just..." She looked him up and down. "It's almost ridiculous how sexy you are."

There were drops of water on his shoulders, reddish-brown hair curled on his neck, and his arms looked like they were chiseled from marble. Carys had never seen a man as perfectly made as Duncan Murray.

"Why the fuck are you talking about the Scottish Tourist Board?"

"I just need to know that when all this is over..." She felt her heart racing. "I love you, and I need to know that you're not going to fall out of love with me when I'm just my regular boring self."

Duncan's mouth fell open. He stood up, dropped the towel, and walked to the duffel bag on the settee.

His ass was glorious, and Carys was very afraid that this was the last time she was going to see it naked, so she made no attempt to hide her stare.

"You're pissing me off." He pulled on a pair of grey flannel pants and dug around in his plaid duffel bag. "Stop this nonsense."

Murray plaid, of course. Because he was the freaking laird.

"I am not trying to piss you off, I'm trying to—"

"Are you fucking daft?" He spun on her, his face red and angry. "Are you really that fucking daft, Carys?"

Her stomach dropped, but her anger piqued. "Apparently yes! You are an aristocrat who owns half of Scone and restores castles, Duncan. You know people who" —she looked around the room— "I mean, I'm fairly sure that this house belongs to James Bond or at the very least a British spy who travels all over the world."

"It belongs to my friend Jeffrey, and he's a stockbroker in the city." Duncan threw his duffel bag on the ground. "You are a college professor from California who was so determined to find her missing boyfriend that you crossed a *fucking ocean* and walked into a parallel fucking world." He pointed randomly at a window. "You have taken on a dragon, stood up to fae kings and mad queens, survived a kelpie attack, learned archery, and you know how to scare off bears, for Christ's sake. Are you absolutely fucking daft?"

When he listed her accomplishments like that, Carys didn't sound as boring as she had in her mind. "But those are all..."

"All what?" Duncan spat out.

"None of that stuff would have happened if Seren hadn't died," Carys said. "All the interesting things in my life happened because my Shadowkin died and Lachlan came looking for me."

"And Frodo was just a hobbit until his uncle gave him a ring!" Duncan put his hands on his hips and glared at her. "Superman wasn't super on his home planet, was he? He was just an ordinary guy. Alien. Whatever."

Carys froze, and all the anger drained out of her. "You think I'm Frodo?"

"In the sense that you're a small man with hairy feet?" Duncan growled. "No. In the sense that you're a hero who stepped up when the world was in danger, absolutely."

THERE WERE moments in life that Carys knew she would remember forever, and this was one of them.

Angry Duncan Murray, shirtless and superhot, standing in a bedroom straight out of a spy novel—she was not wrong on that one; the stockbroker story was a cover—had just told her she was one of the most heroic figures in modern fantasy.

"When I defeat the Morrígan," she said softly, "and life can go back to normal, I really want you to move to California and maybe marry me. Or I could move to Scotland if you really can't move to Baywood. I'm pretty sure your mother is not going to like me, maybe ever, because I'm American, but if you're okay with that, we'll work through it."

Duncan walked over to her. "She'll love you if you give her grand-children." He narrowed his eyes. "Do you want children?"

"Yes. In fact, I was an only child, so I want more than one."

"Brilliant. We'll work out the details later." He dipped down, lifted her in his arms, and walked her to the bed. "Right now I think I have to remind you why I fucking love you and think you're the sexiest thing on two legs. 'Somewhat cute,'" he spat out. "Are you fucking daft?"

"Are you still mad at me?"

"Yes," Duncan growled. "Boring fucking college professor, Dr. Morgan? Did you really say that?"

She clung to his neck and peppered kissed on his shoulder. "But then you called me Frodo."

He tossed her on the bed. "You're going to have to drop that when I get you naked."

She wiggled out of her sweatpants. "I can be Sexy Frodo."

"Please." He nearly snorted. "Please no."

She quickly took off all her clothes and pulled Duncan onto the bed with her. She fell back into a mountain of pillows and then was covered with a mountain of a man.

A still slightly grumpy man who had decided to take out his frustration with her by pinching her very bare ass.

"Ordinary?" He pinched her and spread her legs, slapping the inside of her thigh lightly before he bent down and gave her a biting kiss. "I'll show you ordinary, Professor Morgan."

If the ferocity and focus of Duncan Murray between her thighs could only be provoked by anger, she was going to have to figure out how to make him angry on a semiregular basis.

He scraped his teeth up the inside of her thigh, from the knee to the soft swell of flesh just beneath her sex, then laved his tongue over her skin and sucked the tender flesh into his mouth, finally releasing it with a pop that Carys suspected was going to leave a bruise.

Then Duncan went and did the exact same thing on her other thigh, marking her with his mouth.

She was squirming under him, but he'd planted his elbows on either side of her body and had both his hands on her breasts, teasing the nipples to the point where she was practically weeping from frustration.

He lifted his head. "Tell me you love me."

The words burst from her mouth. "I love you so much."

"Good." He gave her one long, slow lick up the center of her sex. "Now tell me you're the sexiest woman in all the worlds."

"Oh my god, I can't." Tears leaked from the sides of her eyes. "Duncan, please."

"Yes, you can." He murmured the words against her softest flesh. "Daughter of two worlds," he whispered, "queen of my world. Tell me."

"I'm..." Her entire body was shaking. "I'm sexy."

"Fucking right you are." His hand left her right breast and slapped the side of her hip lightly. "Tell me to make you come with my mouth." He licked her again. "With my tongue."

She was going to die, and then the bad guys might win, but she'd be dead, so who cared?

"Make me..." She arched up when he slapped her hip again and pinched her left nipple. "Oh God, make me come!" she yelled.

He gripped her ass, lifted her body to his mouth, and feasted on her.

The orgasm that ripped through Carys was so intense she felt her entire body seize, her muscles quaked, and her toes curled so hard she was worried she was going to break her foot.

She had no words. No consciousness. She was pretty sure she blacked out.

When her eyes opened, Duncan was braced over her, his intense green gaze fixed on her face. "I love you so much," he whispered. "Thank you for calling me your man."

She could feel his erection pressing against her thigh, so she shifted until he was at her entrance, and then Duncan slid inside and rocked into her with an aching, easy rhythm that made more tears fall from the corners of her eyes.

Duncan kissed them away and whispered something. It took her a moment to understand what he was saying because his accent was so thick.

"...sweetest woman. God love me, you're so brave, Carys. Never imagined..."

"I never imagined love like this." She wrapped her hands around his wrists and turned her face so she could kiss his arm. "I thought it was only in books."

He let out a harsh laugh, and then his body tensed and the pace of his thrusts increased.

Carys lifted her legs and wrapped them around his hips, drawing him closer until they were a single creature of flesh and heart and tangled limbs. She was he and he was everything and she could not imagine a time when loving Duncan was not part of her soul.

"I love you."

Duncan came with a harsh breath and buried his face in Carys's neck.

She trailed her fingers along his nape, kissing his temple and pressing her cheek to his. "You are the dream that I was too afraid to dream."

And tangled with her lover, Carys fell asleep.

"He always loved you." Seren was sitting on the side of the loch where the kelpie had tried to kill Carys. "Or I guess he loved the idea of you. And then he met you, and he fell in love with the real you, not the idea."

"Was that how you loved Lachlan?"

"I love Lachlan." Seren swallowed hard, her fierce gaze pointed into the distance. "Just because you're dead it doesn't mean you stop loving someone."

"I'm sorry." Carys was sitting next to her on a fallen log not far from where Aisling had been taken by the kelpie, where Lachlan had lost yet another woman who had loved him. "I didn't know. I mean, I knew that he'd lost his wife, but I didn't know about..." She spread her hands and looked over the shimmering loch, the pearlescent sky, the forest where she could see unicorns grazing along the verge. "All of this. Or you. Or who you were to me."

Seren turned to Carys. "If you had known?"

Carys frowned. "Then it would have been like... I don't know, sleeping with my kind-of-dead-sister's husband." She shook her head. "So that's a no."

Her Shadowkin nodded. "I can accept that."

Carys watched Seren's face, which was like looking into a mirror if that mirror was distorted by time, experience, and death. "It's very strange."

"What in particular?" The curl of her lip at the corner was her father's.

"Looking at you. It's my face, but it's not." She smiled. "I see King Dafydd in you."

Pain streaked across Seren's expression. "Did you pull me into your dream so you could torment me?"

"Okay, no." Carys stood up. "And I didn't pull you into any dream."

"Didn't you?"

Carys looked around, but she didn't see any crows. No starlings. No darkness or cold. "I don't know why you're here. I'm not in any special place. I was in the Brightlands with Duncan; then I was here. I haven't seen a sign of the Morrígan since she drove those bison into a stampede."

Seren stood and started pacing. "It's possible that the crow goddess is thinning the barriers between all the worlds," she said.

"Not just the Shadowlands and the Brightlands. Valhalla could meet Hades. Elysium collide with the Duat. Gods and monsters would be thrown together if she succeeds."

"And what would happen then?"

Seren turned to her. "I don't know. No one knows because there has never been a time when the Morrígan could collect acolytes like she can now."

"I'm supposed to find Annwn," Carys said. "I think the plan is for me to find my way to Annwn."

Seren's eyes went wide. "No."

"I'm just telling you what I'm being told, okay? If you think I have control over any of this—"

"Mortals who visit Annwn do not return."

Shit. That was not ideal.

"Okay... Well, a druid told me—or kind of implied—that's where I need to go."

"Find another way." Seren crossed her arms over her chest.

"You can help me somehow," Carys said. "And so can my mother."

Seren's chin went up. "Our mother."

She was there. Tegan was there. "She's really there, isn't she?"

"It doesn't matter who is here. Arawn is the king of this place, and he will not permit your passage," Seren said. "Tell me what knowledge you need—what secret you must find—and I will find it. No doubt that is what the druid meant. No doubt that is why our dreams have been joined."

"I don't know what knowledge I need. I have to go and visit the Mothers."

Seren frowned. "Which Mothers?"

"One is Oshun, and I don't know the others."

"Where?"

"Wales." She shook her head. "Cymru."

Seren froze. "You're meant to visit mother goddesses in Cymru?"

"That's what it sounds like. They have a bookshop or something and—"

"Dôn's domain," Seren said.

Carys mentally skimmed the Welsh gods and goddesses she knew, but this one wasn't hard. "Dôn is the mother of all the Welsh gods? The matriarch, right?"

"Not for Arawn," Seren said. "Dôn and Arawn hate each other. It's a very old fight." She took a deep breath. "Talk to these Mothers and find out why they want you here, but talk to *me* before you attempt to enter the underworld."

"How am I supposed to ask you anything?"

"The same way you called me into your dream this time."

"I don't know how I did it this time!" Carys said. "How am I supposed to—"

"You will find a way." Seren walked over and slapped her shoulder. "You've proved remarkably hard to kill, but the last thing our mother would want is another daughter trapped here before her time."

"You act like it's a punishment," Carys said. "I thought Annwn was supposed to be a paradise."

Seren looked at her from the corner of her eye. "No place is a paradise when it takes you away from the ones you love." She walked to the edge of the loch and snarled. "That fucking traitor Aisling. I'd kill her myself if she was in front of me, then I'd cut her into pieces and feed her to the fish of the sea she loves so much."

So clearly no love lost there.

The last thing Carys wanted was to get her Shadowkin on the subject of the woman who'd killed her. "Annwn is the place where warriors go when they die, right? So when Lachlan dies, he can join you, can't he?"

"Doubtful." Seren's blue eyes were hollow. "He's a son of Alba. He has his own gods. His mother serves Frigg, and his father serves himself."

"So maybe—"

"I have no interest in speaking of Lachlan's death," Seren said.

"Lachlan needs to live. For many, many more years."

Carys thought about telling Seren about Lachlan's reckless behavior, but what good would it do?

"Treasure your love." Seren stared over the loch and toward castle hill where the ruins of the old tower still stood, even in Carys's dream. "I was a fool, you know. I could have loved him for more years, but I fought it because of duty."

"Lachlan knows that you loved him."

Seren turned to Carys with tears in her eyes. "Tell him that I love him still. That I might have died but my love never did."

Carys's heart ached, looking into eyes that were a grieving mirror of her own. "I will," she said. "It'll probably make him sad, but I'll tell him."

Seren walked over and stood face-to-face with Carys. "Perhaps it will give him some comfort as well as sorrow."

"I hope so." Carys smiled.

"Also tell him" —Seren put a hand on her shoulder— "that I am excusing his transgression with you because you are my Brightkin and the living image of me in the world, but if he takes another lover, I will return from the dead, haunt them both, and see that his lover flees from him in misery."

Carys froze. "Uh…"

"Joking." Seren smiled a little bit. "I am joking."

Well, that was a dark sense of humor.

"Right."

"Really." Seren nodded at the forest that had crept closer until the trees surrounded them. "It was a joke. Wake up, Carys."

"What?"

She turned and was in darkness. The loch was gone, and she was in the forest behind her house. The scent of pine and redwood detritus filled the air. There was a deer ahead of her, its short antlers glowing silver as it walked down a narrow path.

"Wake up, Carys." The voice was her mother's. "It is not time yet. Wake up."

CHAPTER TWENTY-FIVE

"Carys?" Duncan was shaking her arm. "I wish I could let you sleep for days, but the dragon is about the break into our room to check your breathing."

She blinked awake to see Lachlan leaning over her. No, it was Duncan. Obviously it was Duncan and they were in the spy's house and...

"I just had a very weird dream."

Duncan frowned. "Was it bad?"

"No, it was with Seren."

Duncan sat on the edge of the bed. "What did she say?"

"That I can't go to Annwn. That mortals don't return from Annwn. Which is not strictly true—some of them have returned in stories, but it's rare."

His eyes went wide. "Then you're not going."

Carys sat up slowly and rubbed her eyes. "Why don't we head to Swansea today and see what these Mothers have to say? How far away is it?"

"Not close. Four and a half hours minimum, and that's not

accounting for all the stops that Naida and Godrik are going to want to make at travel centers so they can feed their slushy addiction."

"So all day."

"Likely yes."

Carys stretched her arms up, then looked around the room. Her arms fell and her heart jumped. "Duncan, where are my papers?"

"I put them in the library this morning," Duncan said. "Relax. Just give your mind a rest. Have some food. Breathe. Go walk in the garden a bit. Maybe it will give you some perspective. Clear your mind."

Carys smiled. "If I'm Frodo, are you Sam? That would explain why you're always trying to feed me."

Duncan crossed his arms over his chest. "I'm not a fucking hobbit."

"But I am," she whispered. "I'm Sexy Frodo."

"Fuck me, I'm going to be hearing about this for the rest of my life, aren't I?" Duncan shook his head. "Get out of bed, Frodo." He pulled back the covers and slapped the side of her thigh. "Come on, lass. Get up and let me feed you."

"Okay, but only if there are potatoes involved."

"Is that another Sam reference?" Duncan asked. "Because I haven't read those books in ages, and at this point, I'm going to actively avoid them."

Carys slid off the massive king-size bed. "Dear Sam." She patted Duncan's shoulder. "Frodo wouldn't have made it very far without her Sam."

"Don't make me strip you naked and fuck you again, woman."

"Is that supposed to be a threat?" she muttered. "Because it's really not."

Duncan shoved her toward her duffel bag. "Get dressed or the dragon is going to break into our room."

She did not want Cadell breaking into their room when she was naked.

"Fine." She wrangled a bra from the tangle of her jumbled duffel bag. "But know that underneath my modern armor" —she nearly tripped over a heavy wool rug while trying to fasten her bra— "I am still Sexy Frodo."

THE HOUSE BUTLER, Franklin—no doubt a man who also doubled as a driver and majordomo for the undercover spy—delivered a rolling tray of breakfast to the library.

"Poached eggs and bacon," he said. "Roasted tomatoes and potatoes from the garden. The cook just took these scones from the oven." He lifted the last tray. "And of course a rack of venison for the" —he glanced at Cadell and Godrik— "for the gentlemen."

"Thank you, Franklin." Duncan picked up a scone. "I'll let Jeff know how helpful you've been."

Franklin didn't look like he gave two shits about impressing Duncan, but he was clearly more than a little bit worried about the library. He glared at Duncan before he closed the double doors and left them alone.

Laura had attacked Carys's file of research and spread it into very engineer-coded piles.

"Okay," she said. "I've separated the files on the Morrígan from the research you've done on other gods."

Naida added, "And we also have another pile of papers on various alternate realms."

"I had a dream with Seren last night," Carys said.

Lachlan's head popped up from his slumped posture in a corner of the room. "What did Seren say?"

"That I should absolutely not go to Annwn, but I was already kind of thinking that," Carys said. "I mean, the track record of humans returning from underworlds is not good no matter what world mythology we're talking about."

Godrik nodded. "The realms of Hel are only trespassed by the dead."

Angus muttered, "I could take you to several different other-worlds, but even as powerful as I am, I could not guarantee your return."

Naida sat at the table and looked at the spread papers. "But the druids did imply that Carys would need some kind of wisdom from Annwn to defeat the Morrígan."

Godrik walked over to the breakfast tray and took a plate. He piled it with roasted potatoes and tomatoes before adding a scone and taking it to Naida. "We should make a list of our assets for the coming battle."

Laura took out a notebook. "Let's start with what we know."

"Carys is the hero the old gods have chosen," Lachlan said. "That is without question. Wada confirmed it after the battle in Yorkshire, and his daughter gave Carys a prophesy that led her to Angus."

"Who led her to the druids." Cadell was leaning on the book-shelves and eyeing the side of venison.

He kept glancing at Naida.

"Just go ahead," she said quietly. "Both of you need to eat too."

Angus muttered, "You all could have found the druids on your own most likely."

Duncan cleared his throat. "Oh, I'm sure that finding our way to an alternate realm in the middle of Sherwood Forest where the Green Man lives would have been no problem, ye daft old creature."

"You could have found it." Angus pointed a gnarled finger at Carys. "Well, not you, but she could have."

"Luckily, Angus led us to Jack and saved us some time." Carys tried to redirect the conversation before it turned into an argument.

Cadell and Godrik started to wolf down the rack of venison, and the smell of roasted meat filled the room.

"So what did Jack tell us?" Laura said. "That's the important part."

"Uh..." Carys frowned. So much had happened that it felt like months since they'd been in Sherwood, but it had really only been a week or so.

"Jack confirmed that we cannot kill the Morrígan," she said. "Which Dru said too. Jack didn't seem all that upset about her being here, but he also didn't deny that his power was different with her influence."

"Truly," Angus said, "it has been centuries since I have seen him so fully transformed into his old form."

Lachlan spoke from the corner again. "I think we have to acknowledge that there will be gods who might not mind the Morrígan's actions. They may even be supporting her."

Lachlan wasn't eating. In fact, Carys hadn't seen him eat in days. His face was wan and his eyes were tired. The only time he seemed animated were the times that Seren's name was mentioned.

"Tell him that I love him still. That I might have died, but my love never did."

Would telling him that Seren still loved him bring him comfort or just make him more reckless and desperate?

Angus shook his head. "Gonna have to disagree on that, my boy. The gods who want to live as their true selves have the Shadowlands to command. Magic is real there. Humans believe in them. Jack lives in the Brightlands because he loves humans and this world."

Laura said, "You can love humans and still think we've done a pretty shit job taking care of the planet."

"He won't harm people." Angus was adamant. "The Morrígan will."

"Okay." Carys raised her hands. "Let's move on. Jack also said something about enchantments and breaking them."

Bad stories weave enchantments. Good stories break them.

"We scared off an enchanted bear," Laura said.

"No, this was after the bear."

Duncan said, "What about Jibril?"

"He's a messenger," Carys said. "Angels are messengers."

"If we don't stop the Morrígan here," Lachlan said, "magical war is going to spread. In all the worlds."

"The barriers between worlds could fail completely," Carys said.

Godrik chimed in. "That means more Brightkin wandering into the Shadowlands, possibly with deadly consequences."

"And more magical creatures creeping out here. Creatures like imps and redcaps can be vicious," Naida said. "And they don't need magic to harm people."

"My horde confirmed what Jibril said," Cadell added. "Briton is being cut off from the rest of the world. The other kingdoms are watching what happens."

"So we stop the Morrígan on this side," Carys said, "before she breaks down the gates. Or other countries might step in to try to save themselves."

"War," Godrik said. "Magical war on both sides of our world."

Angus pointed at Carys. "The Builder. He took you to another place, didn't he? When we were at his cottage."

Every eye swung toward Carys.

"What?" Laura said. "No, we were there."

"We were there, but they were somewhere else," Angus said. "At least for a moment."

"It was more than a moment," Carys clarified. "I had kind of a... slight mental breakdown. And Joshua was kind enough to freeze time for a little bit."

Laura's mouth dropped open. "Okay, how cool is that?"

Duncan frowned, "What did Joshua say?"

"After I blabbed every single fear I've been holding in about all this mess, he reassured me that I am capable of defeating the Morrígan." She glanced at Duncan. "Even when I don't feel like I can do it, I have to remember—"

"If you tell them..." Duncan started.

"—that I'm basically Frodo." She smiled at Duncan. "Because this is a burden that came to me, but I can carry it with the help of my friends." She looked around the library. "With your help, we are going to succeed."

Laura gasped. "I know I'm human, but can I be Arwen?"

"She wasn't part of the fellowship," Lachlan said.

When Lachlan had lived in Baywood, he'd become completely addicted to the movie series. So much that Carys thought he could probably quote it from memory.

"There were like, no women in the fellowship, so I feel like that leaves it open to creative casting." Laura pointed at Lachlan. "Aragorn. So Aragorn. You're royal and you ran away from your duties!"

"Thank you so much for interpreting my life that way," Lachlan said. "How insightful and sympathetic."

"You're the only one who regularly carries a sword, Lachlan."

Cadell shot Laura a look from the side. "If you even start—"

"Smaug!" Laura's eyes lit up. "Yay! We even have our own dragon, but he's a good dragon in our fellowship."

The dragon's nostrils flared, but he remained silent.

Naida raised her hand. "I do not know this Frodo, but did he also release a harmful god into an alternate realm?"

Godrik was also frowning. "That is what Carys did, so it must be."

Duncan snorted.

"Okay…" Carys shrugged. "The parallel might not be perfect."

THEY STARTED on the road before noon, but it was still going to be five hours before they hit Swansea.

Carys spent her time in the car reading as much as she could find online about the Welsh goddess Dôn, whom Seren suspected was one of the Mothers, and Oshun, the Nigerian fertility goddess Joshua had mentioned.

Mothers.

Fertility.

The Morrígan had aspects of fertility in her power.

Sovereignty. Wealth. Fertility of the land.

There were many scholarly interpretations of the Morrígan's powers and hardly any of them agreed with each other.

The parts that did agree were those about war, battle, and bloodshed.

At the second stop, she started feeling sleepy, so she let Laura sit in front, and she moved to the back of the van where she fell asleep on Cadell's shoulder.

"Carys."

At first she thought Cadell was nudging her mind.

What?

It is not me disturbing you from your rest, it is the prince.

Carys opened her eyes to see Lachlan sitting in the seat in front of her, completely turned around.

"Hey." She blinked. "What's up?"

Lachlan had been avoiding her for days, and now he was shoving himself into her space?

"Do you have a moment?"

Cadell was less patient than Carys was. "She was sleeping."

"I know that but—"

"It's fine." She lifted her head and wiped a tiny bit of drool from the dragon's shoulder. "Sorry about that."

"It is to be expected." Cadell moved to the right next to Laura, leaving the seat beside Carys empty.

Lachlan moved back and sat next to her. "This van is huge."

"Almost more like a bus than a van."

Lachlan smiled. "I'll make sure to remind Duncan that he was a bus driver on this quest."

"And I'm sure he'll appreciate that."

Leave it to a brother—or a doppelgänger—to needle you about the stupidest things.

"You said you had a dream about Seren last night."

Ah, yes. That was why he was talking to her. "We were mostly talking about what Joshua told me about going to Annwn and visiting the Mothers so they could point us in the right direction."

His face fell. "Was that all?"

"No."

Tell him that I love him still. That I might have died, but my love never did.

"We talked about you too," she said softly. "She was really angry with me."

"About us?"

"What do you think?" Carys shrugged. "I told her that if I'd known she existed, I wouldn't have ever fallen in love with you."

"So she was even more angry with me." Lachlan sighed and sat back. "The Cymric underworld is not open to me. If it were, I would have followed her there instead of searching for her mirror in the Brightlands." He looked at her. "I'm sorry, Carys. Searching for you was unfair to both of us. My feelings were never a lie—I did love you —but it was..."

"Not the same." She looked at Duncan, who was glancing at them in the rearview mirror. "I understand." It wasn't painful. Carys felt more... wistful.

For the woman she'd been. For the love they'd shared.

In another life, they could have been happy.

"You really would have died?" Carys whispered. "Because I don't think she would be happy to hear that. She wants you to live a long time."

"So I can finally enter an eternal realm without her?" Lachlan asked. "My ancestors reside on the distant isle of Tír na nÓg. When I die, I will walk the golden path over the western sea to meet them." His voice grew thick. "But Seren will not be there to meet me."

Who knew what the battle with the Morrígan would bring? Maybe she would die. Maybe they all would.

Carys finally told him. "Seren said that she loves you. That even though she's dead, she never stopped loving you."

Tears filled his green eyes. Lachlan swallowed hard and nodded sharply.

"I shouldn't have told you." Her heart hurt just looking at him, and his tear-filled eyes were even more hollow than they'd been before.

Lachlan shook his head. "Seren may be dead, but if her love still survives, a part of her still lives here too." He wiped his eyes with the back of his hand and pressed a hand over his heart. "As long as she speaks to you, I want to hear any message that she sends."

"Okay." She winced. "She also said she was excusing your mistake with me because I'm her Brightkin, but if you ever take another lover, she'll return from the dead, haunt you both, and make sure your lover flees from you in misery."

Lachlan must have had the right sense of humor, because he threw his head back and laughed long and hard.

When he finally stopped laughing, Carys said, "Okay, so you got the joke. Good. I was a little worried."

"Oh, that wasn't a joke." Lachlan smiled. "She would definitely do that." He shook his head and wiped his eyes. "Gods of old, I love that woman."

Okay, well... Okay. Carys nodded.

Apparently there really were people who were meant for each other.

Iᴛ ᴡᴀs after dark when they finally arrived in Swansea and pulled up to a purple-painted shop on High Street. The light in the sky was just starting to dim, but there were plenty of bright lights in the shop, so Duncan found the nearest parking lot and pulled the van into it, parking and then opening the door as their party poured out like menacing and magical occupants of a clown car.

First Godrik, glaring as he escorted Naida toward the sidewalk. The fae woman was red-cheeked and appeared much happier now that the wolf was back in the Brightlands with them.

Then Laura and Cadell, both sniping at each other as they argued about modern interpretations of dragons in pop culture.

"I'm telling you" —Cadell's nostrils were flared— "it's ridiculous and insulting."

"Riding dragons would be so cool though." Laura was adamant. "It wouldn't be like a horse at all."

"How would it even be possible?" Cadell was equally stubborn. "You've seen me in my natural form, Laura. You're an engineer. Think of the practical configuration. Where would a rider sit? There are massive muscle groups along our back to power our wings, and—"

"I don't know! Like maybe a..." Her cheeks got red and her voice dropped. "Like a... harness or... support or—"

"Saddle." Cadell crossed his arms over his chest. "You are describing a saddle."

"*Not* a saddle."

"As a horse would wear." He stormed off.

"Cadell!" Laura jogged after him. "It definitely would not be a saddle."

Finally Lachlan got out of the van, nodding at Duncan and Carys before he checked his sword under the back seat and then followed the rest of the group.

Duncan frowned. "Did we manage to leave Angus somewhere?"

"No!" A cranky voice came from the back of the van. "I was changing my jacket, that's all."

"Well, we're here."

"Good." Angus folded himself in half as he exited the van, then lingered for a moment, attempting to tame his wild grey hair in the window of the vehicle.

"Angus, are you trying to..." Duncan frowned. "I'm confused."

"Mind your business, human," Angus growled.

He gave Duncan one last glare before he loped down the sidewalk.

"What was that about?" Duncan asked.

Carys shrugged. "I don't know, but Angus is an old god."

"Okay yes, but—"

"And we're going to see three ancient goddess." Carys took Duncan's hand and started walking. "Matriarchs. Mothers. Fertility goddesses."

Duncan's eyebrows went up. "And if I remember correctly, Pan got around in his day."

"I mean..." She lifted one shoulder. "It's possible he knows exactly who we're going to visit."

"Huh." Duncan smirked a little bit, then walked down the road toward the brightly lit windows of Pages and Portals, the bookshop where the Mothers lived.

All of them waited until Carys arrived, and when she opened the door, a bell chimed over her head.

Then another bell sounded and another and another until the cozy shop rang with echoing chimes that sounded like rain falling on crystal.

A round-faced woman with a cloud of curly, nut-brown hair popped out from between two bookshelves, a smile creasing her face. "Oh, look who it is, sisters."

Another woman came from the back room, thick black hair braided and decorated with flowers. The lights twinkled on the gold ring on the left side of her nose.

"Oshun, she's here!" the second woman called.

Descending from a circular staircase in the back corner, a woman who could only be a goddess appeared. She wore a pair of flowing yellow overalls and a bright blue head wrap, and the scent of jasmine followed her.

She walked forward, and the two other goddesses flanked her.

"Hello, Carys Morgan," they said in a singular voice. "We have been waiting for you."

CHAPTER TWENTY-SIX

"More tea?" The woman—or goddess—Lakshmi held out a pot.

Carys dutifully nodded. "Please."

Lakshmi glanced at Angus. "More tea for you, Pushan? Or is it Nomios again? What name do you go by these days?"

"Angus." He cleared his throat. "Just Angus."

"Well, just Angus, we have no wine in the shop tonight."

"Tea will do nicely." Angus held out his mug. "Thank you."

"An oversight for company, I'm afraid," Oshun said. "We usually keep a case." She looked pointedly at the third woman.

"That's my fault." The round woman raised a hand, her wild curls bouncing. "I drank it all yesterday. See, I thought you'd be coming then, and I got very excited, but then you didn't come." She winked at Carys. "Well, I shouldn't say that, because you did. A number of times."

"Oh dear God." Duncan wiped a hand over his face. "There're more of them."

"We're fertility goddesses, love." Oshun might be a Yoruba deity, but she spoke in a swinging Swansea accent. "No secrets about sex here." She looked pointedly at Laura. "But dragon? You're taking on more than a bit with that one, mush."

When Oshun moved, the gold and silver around her neck and in her ears tinkled brightly. She was draped in jewelry, from brightly colored beads to rich, nearly orange gold chains.

Lakshmi was the most demurely dressed, in a flowing pink dress with embroidered flowers. She moved in silence, serving tea to all of them, as the intoxicating smell of jasmine and sandalwood drifted in the air.

And the first goddess, the one with the soft Valleys accent, wore earthen brown and deep green scarves around her plump neck. Her bright blue eyes were the color of the ocean, and silver and grey mixed with the deep-walnut-brown curls.

"Oshun, don't warn the girl away from dragons," she said. "Dragons are lovely. Just lovely. Very loyal mates."

"I wasn't warning her, I was warning *him*." Oshun smirked at Cadell. "So what are you here for?" She turned her attention to Carys. "We knew you were coming, but we weren't sure why."

"Sorry." Carys leaned toward the brown-haired woman. "Are you... Dôn?"

She waved a hand. "Go by Donna here because, well, the humans mostly speak in the new tongue, don't they? No shame in it, no shame, but it makes for fewer questions if I go by a modern name."

That meant Carys was having tea and biscuits with the goddesses Lakshmi, Oshun, and... Donna.

"So... uh, Joshua said I should come here," Carys started.

"*Love* Joshua," Lakshmi said. "Such a sweet god."

"So young but so wise." Donna nodded. "Softhearted, that one."

"He's popular," Oshun said. "I'll say that for sure. I wonder if part of it is the lack of sacrifices."

"Physical sacrifices, she means," Donna added. "Sacrifices of the self are more challenging in their own way, but I can't lie." She smiled. "I do love a good grain offering."

All three goddesses nodded and hummed in approval.

"Oh yes." Lakshmi's accent was soft Indian-British with a slight Welsh lilt. "Something about roasting barley when it hits the nose."

"There are just not enough humans who appreciate roasted barley these days," Donna said.

Oshun narrowed her eyes. "But why would Joshua direct you to us? You are the hero appointed by the gods to face the Morrígan in this chapter of her story, but I don't know that we have much knowledge that will help you." Oshun looked at Donna. "She's a very accomplished scholar."

"Oh, I've heard." Donna nodded.

Naida chimed in. "I would just like to say that this tea is wonderful and very nourishing."

"Little sister, we miss your kind," Oshun reached over and enveloped Naida in a hug. "Seeing you makes me want to walk straight through those gates."

"Can't you?" Duncan said. "You're goddesses."

"Why, thank you." Donna winked at him.

Duncan's cheeks turned a little red. "I just mean you could walk on either side."

"We could," Lakshmi said, "but we don't."

"Why not? The gates were created by the gods, weren't they?"

"In a sense, yes." Lakshmi looked at her sisters. "But it's not that simple."

"Who else could create them?" Lachlan asked. "The fae may tend them, but Angus has said they are not of fae construction."

Godrik spoke from the center of the room. "Who else but the gods has the power to create entirely different realms?"

The three mother goddesses had placed Godrik in the center of their circle, as if drawn to the fundamental masculinity of the wolf. It was impossible for Carys not to notice.

The three women were utterly feminine in every way, three earthy, creative forces of nature in entirely different forms but with deeply feminine energy.

Carys felt as if she'd been plugged into an electrical outlet the moment she walked through the door.

"We didn't create the realms," Donna said. "We wouldn't do that. We gave them shape, we created passage. But the lines between worlds were not built by the gods."

"Who then?" Laura looked around the bookshop. "Who would have that power? Who would even want to?"

The three goddesses were silent. They turned their eyes toward Carys and let their stillness fill the room, the shop, the very air that she breathed.

She was steeped in their silence until every other sense faded away and her vision turned inward. In her mind, she saw the worlds she had traveled, the twin worlds of light and shadow, and from that twin trunk sprouted other branches.

Branches of dreams and pockets of vision.

Worlds of the dead and amorphous realms of the infinite.

A sorceress's cottage on a misty mountain and a green hovel in the middle of the forest.

A still silver pool with no end and no beginning.

"We created them." The realization sank into Carys like water into thirsty ground. She looked at Laura. Then at Duncan. "Humans did it. Brightkin."

Oshun raised one eyebrow. "They were wise to pick this one. You are closer to understanding the nature of the gates now. Why they must be. How they must be protected."

"Carys." Duncan's voice was hoarse. "What are you talking about?"

"We stopped believing in magic." She looked at Naida. "We stopped believing in you. And the moment we stopped believing, we started pushing all the magic in the world away."

Carys moved back from Naida and stood.

The three Mothers were sitting in a triangle with Godrik in the center, and Naida, Lachlan, and Cadell angled like spokes from him.

Duncan, Carys, and Laura stood on the outside with Angus in the periphery.

Three ordinary humans looking at the circle of magic in the center of the room.

Awareness dawned in Laura's expression. "We turned to science and modernity and forgot the past. More than forgot—we *rejected* it. We rejected... you."

"The wheel turns and turns again," Lakshmi said. "It has not happened once but a thousand times, as long as human belief has existed."

Donna looked at Carys. "The barriers formed gradually and then all at once."

"Long, long ago," Oshun said. "Before human history was written, the first walls between the worlds were formed."

"And things that were once real in the Brightlands," Lakshmi said, "drifted into the shadow as humans stopped believing."

Duncan cocked his head. "So then every time we stop putting our faith in something—started thinking it was a myth or folklore—it moved from our world into the Shadowlands?"

"We are born in halves" —Carys looked at Duncan, then Lachlan — "because we continually reject parts of our own nature."

"Shadowkin have always existed." Donna brushed the back of her hand along Lachlan's cheek. "Because the human mind cannot survive in contradictions. Not as the gods can."

Oshun looked at Carys. "There are worlds within worlds within worlds. You see the Shadows and the Light, but we see all of them."

"And they are all beautiful." Lakshmi's face took on a radiant glow. "But the tender creatures of magic" —she put a hand on Naida's shoulder— "would be crushed out of existence if the worlds collided as the Morrígan desires."

"She wants all of them." Oshun's dire words echoed through the bookshop. "One world is not enough for her."

"She can't help it," Donna said. "She can only be as she is."

"She is three and she is one," Lakshmi said. "She must have everything or she would have nothing."

Duncan murmured, "Gods are contradictions."

"That is why the horse goddess bound the Morrígan to one world," Donna said. "And that is why she must be bound again or none of the worlds will be safe."

"So the Morrígan can't help herself," Lachlan said. "She *must* try to conquer the world and create war."

Laura added, "And it's not like it's a hard push for humanity these days."

"As it has ever been," the three goddesses said in unison.

"I understand that," Lachlan said. "But how does that help Carys?"

"Because in the circular way of things, the heroine has already defeated the goddess," Lakshmi said. "She simply has to realize how."

"Not. Helpful!" Carys paced around the library of their borrowed house in Mumbles, a small town just south of Swansea.

Duncan had called another friend from school, and that friend had an oceanfront "cottage" with five large bedrooms that sat empty for most of the year and a garden house in the back that Angus had claimed as his own.

Floor-to-ceiling windows lined the front sitting room, which also contained a decent library where Laura had spread out their research, again in neat piles.

"I've already defeated the goddess in a 'circular way'" —Carys's air quotes were more than sarcastic— "so why not just tell me how?"

"Carys." Laura tried to calm her down. "We're going back in the morning. Maybe this is a… thought exercise. Like learning how to picture the worlds. Maybe they want you to just think about what that could mean, but they're going to give you the answer tomorrow."

"Really? Has anything over the past month been that easy?"

Laura opened her mouth, then closed it.

Lachlan was looking oddly cheerful since their visit to the bookshop. "Maybe it means that you'll only have defeated her once you *realize* how."

"That could be." Laura pointed at him. "It's like... Schrödinger's victory. You'll have defeated the Morrígan when you realize how, but until then, she still has power. She is both defeated and undefeated at the same time."

Godrik frowned. "That does make an odd kind of sense."

"No, it doesn't!" Carys felt like she was losing it. "How does that make sense?"

Duncan cleared his throat. "I would like to point out that if we've learned anything over the past couple of weeks, it's that god-type things are full of contradictions. The three Mothers admitted as much tonight."

"Exactly," Laura said. "Our brains would literally break if we tried to understand all of it at once, which is why our natures split in two when we're born."

Carys muttered, "I feel like you're all as completely lost as I am, but you're trying to say things that sound like they make sense to make me feel better."

Naida raised her hand again. "I would like it noted—if Laura is taking notes—"

"I am."

"—that I also feel that no one understands what is happening," Naida finished.

"Thank you!" Carys turned to Naida. "But did *you* know that humans created the two realms? Like, the fae control the gates as they are now. Do you all have your own stories about their origins?"

"No, but I never thought about it much." Naida shrugged. "And I don't know that the three Mothers truly know either. I suspect that all this is a story. There may be other stories equally true."

"The fae woman is correct," Angus said. "Sure, those ladies are older than me, but multiple worlds have existed as long as humans have."

Cadell sat up straight. "Which would imply..." He saw the glare that Carys pointed at him. "Nothing. It implies nothing." Silently, he said, *It does imply that humans had something to do with the division of the worlds.*

Why can we talk here?

Cadell shrugged. "I feel very powerful." He turned to the wolf. "Do you feel it?"

Godrik nodded. "I do. I don't know that I could shift, but I definitely want to."

"Maybe because the Mothers are here," Naida said. "I also feel very *well*."

A bright full moon shone on the water of Swansea Bay, lighting a path in the smooth water that led out to the depths of the Atlantic Ocean and the vast realms of the deep.

"I need to figure out how to get to Annwn," Carys said. "It's a place where people are both living and dead."

"Another contradiction," Laura whispered.

"I do not advise it," Cadell said. "Especially not after the news this morning."

They all turned to the dragon.

"What news?" Laura asked.

"There is a new barrow risen on Glastonbury Tor," Cadell said. "That makes three places of power for the Morrígan. Three seems to be an important number for her."

"Triangles are inherently stable," Laura said.

"The Morrígan is three-natured," Angus said.

Carys looked at Cadell. "I don't know what I'm supposed to do," she admitted. "You all were there today. Do any of you have ideas?"

Dead silence in the room.

"I don't like the idea of you going to Annwn," Duncan said quietly. "But I also hate the idea of the Morrígan taking over the world and provoking a giant supernatural war that would absolutely thrill her." He took a deep breath and let it out slowly. "So whatever you decide to do, lass, I'm behind you."

Carys walked over to Duncan and wrapped her arms around him. "I'm going back to the bookshop in the morning," she said softly. "I think maybe just me."

"No," Laura said. "We're all in this together, Carys."

"She's the daughter of two worlds," Angus croaked from the corner. "She's the only one who can go where she needs to go."

Carys curled up next to Laura on the sofa in front of the fire.

Lachlan had spread a UK road map on the table, and the others were gathered around it.

"Carys will do whatever she thinks is best," he said, "but I think it would be prudent for us to think of plans to confront the goddess." He glanced at Carys. "Just in case you don't realize how you have already defeated her."

She shrugged. "Fair."

"Agreed," Cadell said. "A forceful response can be a last resort, but at least it gives us options."

Duncan grabbed a red marker. "She's raised mounds on Glastonbury Tor." He put a large red dot on the map. "Around Stonehenge. And Avebury."

"What's in Avebury?" Laura asked. "I forgot about that one."

"In the Shadowlands, there is a large fae fort there," Naida said. "It's been empty for many years, but it was once the home of a powerful queen."

"I think in our world, there are three stone circles," Duncan said. "National heritage marker on the map."

Naida said, "So it's a place of great power in both our worlds."

"Apparently yes."

"Okay, so in each world, these points represent old power." Lachlan took the edge of a large book and drew a line between each one. "What is in the middle of this area? What of note?"

Duncan walked over and looked at the map. "Some nice woods around there, but nothing that I can remember."

"What is the white horse?" Godrik asked. "That is marked on the map. What is that?"

Duncan shook his head. "I think it was put near an ancient burial spot nearby, but it was made later. It's not very old."

"But the barrow is," Godrik said.

"There are barrows and earthen mounds all over Salisbury Plain," Duncan said. "It's impossible to say if the Morrígan is going to use one for... I have no idea. Naked maypole dancing? God knows."

"The plain is also a place of Epona's power," Naida said. "The horse goddess is worshipped on the plain. Even today there are probably followers of her cult. The Morrígan would avoid it, don't you think?"

"Or that may be part of the attraction," Laura said. "Wouldn't that be like a little extra eff you from the Morrígan? This is what you get for keeping me locked in the Shadowlands for so long?"

None of this felt right. None of this made sense.

A third barrow had risen on Saris Plain, so clearly there was a reason, but the Morrígan had her sights set higher than a few stone circles in Southern England.

Carys walked over to Duncan. "Can you look at the social media feed for Macha?"

Duncan nodded. "That account you sent me?"

"Yes."

He quickly pulled up Macha's feed while Lachlan, Godrik, Naida, and Cadell argued in the background.

"There." Carys spotted Macha's distinctive red hair from over Duncan's shoulder. "There she is."

When Duncan had searched for Macha, a flood of images poured over his small phone screen.

Macha in fields.

Macha in trees.

Macha half-naked and riding a horse.

Ironic or a statement?

There was a video posted just a couple of hours ago that showed a topless Macha from the back, walking up a hill as the sun set. As she reached the apex of the hill, she turned, covered her breasts, and coyly curled her fingers in a come-along gesture.

"That one." Carys pointed at it. "Look at the comments on that one."

When Duncan clicked on the post, there was no location listed for the video, but there was comment after comment that all said roughly the same thing.

I'm there.

I'll follow you anywhere.

On my way.

Coming. LOL.

"Okay," Carys said. "Click on the profiles and see if any of them look like they're in that location or something similar."

"You think they might actually follow her?"

"You remember her in Gorne Wood, don't you? She's inviting the whole world to follow her. She wants acolytes to build her power, and she's using the internet to gather them."

Duncan nodded. "Right." He started clicking on profiles while Carys walked over to grab Laura's phone.

"We have an idea," she said. "Macha posted on her socials this afternoon. She's walking up a hill. We're trying to figure out if anyone in the comments knows exactly where she is. It could be in this area." She pointed to the triangle on the map.

Duncan was sitting in a chair, his feet kicked up on an ottoman, scrolling through his phone. "Come on, one of you horny nerds is into geography, aren't you?"

"Cley Hill!" Laura shouted. "Does that sound familiar to anyone?"

"Cley Hill is named on this map," Naida said. "It appears from the legend that there is a monument of some kind there."

"Two of these guys in the comments are certain that she's walking up Cley Hill," Laura said.

Lachlan stood over the map and marked Cley Hill with a question mark. "It does fall within the boundaries of the triangle."

"Tomorrow," Carys said. "Tomorrow morning I'm going to go to that bookshop and get some real answers. I'm going to figure out how to get to Annwn so I can talk to my mother and Seren." She raised her chin. "Because something tells me that they're the ones who can tell me how I've already defeated the Morrígan."

She turned to Duncan, who nodded. His face was grim, but he nodded.

It was the nudge of confidence she needed.

Carys looked around the room. "So if I manage to return from Annwn alive, I'm pretty sure we're all going on a trip to Cley Hill."

CHAPTER TWENTY-SEVEN

When Carys pushed open the door of the bookshop the next morning, Duncan and Angus were waiting in the van and three patrons were in line to buy books from Donna, who was behind the antique desk that served as the sales counter.

"Carys?" Lakshmi called her from the back where a table was set up for coffee and tea. The goddess waved her over. "Come sit with me until Donna is finished. We're almost ready for you."

Carys walked over, and Lakshmi handed her a pretty teacup that smelled of oranges. "Ready for what?"

"White tea with orange and lotus flower," Lakshmi said. "It will help you to find unity in your journey."

"I need some very direct answers this morning," Carys said. "I need to go to Annwn. I need to talk to my Shadowkin."

"Seren does not have the answers you seek," Lakshmi said. "She is just as lost as you are, though she will be with you in the journey. But you are correct that you must go to Annwn to seek answers."

"Who then?" Carys asked. "Epona?"

"Epona is a goddess of the Shadows now." Oshun spoke from the top of the stairs. "I'd ask forgiveness for ignoring you, but I don't need it. I'm finishing a special piece right now."

Carys could see Oshun on the landing above, bent over a wooden table. She couldn't see what she was working on, but there was a blue light glowing under her hands.

Carys glanced at the customers lining up at the desk. "Do any of them have any idea who you three are?"

"Probably not." Lakshmi sipped her tea. "Though there is a lovely coven who meets here on Thursdays for feminist book discussions, and two knitting clubs show up every other week."

"Knitting clubs?"

Lakshmi nodded. "The fiber arts are some of the oldest forms of worship still left in the Brightlands. I always feel very energized after they visit."

"Nice." She sipped her tea and started to feel a little lightheaded. "Uh... Lakshmi?"

"Yes, my love?"

"You didn't..." The world around her started to swim. "Uh..."

"Yes, Carys?"

She was definitely not herself. "Did you *drug* my tea?"

"Not really." The goddess's voice sounded hollow. "Well, maybe a little bit. It depends on what you consider a drug."

Carys was woozy and very relaxed when Donna joined them in the tea nook.

"Sometimes," Donna said, "it's good to dull the rational mind when you need to visit a spirit realm."

"Is... Annwn a spirit realm?" Her blinks were long, and everything felt like it was underwater. She didn't feel drunk. No, everything was extra clear, but it was as if she was watching all this from outside her own body.

Her mind's eye drifted up to Oshun's loft, and she saw a blue flame glowing over the goddess's table.

"You've probably been wondering why Angus has been hanging around, haven't you?"

"Yes."

The blue flame sparked again, and Oshun lifted a shining gold chain in front of Carys's face. "This the collar of Dôn, made of gold from her own body, purified by Lakshmi's fire, and woven into a chain by my hand. Do you accept this gift?"

"What does it do?"

"Do you accept it?"

All of this is a choice.

"Yes." Carys pushed the words from her mind to her mouth. "I accept it."

"Good." Oshun put the chain around her neck. "The shepherd will guide you to the otherworld, Tegan's daughter."

The gold collar felt light and heavy at the same time.

"What are you doing to me?"

"I am anchoring your spirit to your body." Blue fire sparked from Oshun's fingertips when she took the two ends of the chain and pressed them together. "So that Arawn's hounds do not sniff out the scent of a living soul."

Carys felt the warm weight of the gold sitting on the back of her neck. "Okay."

"Keep Dôn's collar around your neck," Oshun said. "It is now tied to your life, and it is yours to do with as you will. So until you are ready for death in this world, you must not take it off. That is the cost of your passage to the other land."

"So if I remove this chain, I'll die?" Carys would have panicked if she were capable of panicking. "What if it breaks by accident?"

Oshun smiled. "A chain made by the goddess will not break. Say 'I accept your gift, Mother.'"

She opened her mouth, but nothing came out.

Oshun waited in endless silence.

"I accept your gift, Mother." It was the only thing Carys *could* say.

Her mind drifted back into her body, and she was sitting on the couch again.

Donna was there, pressing a finger to her lips. "Listen before all else. Your time will be brief. Trust the shepherd and trust yourself."

Lakshmi leaned forward and presented a teacup. "Drink and wake, Carys Morgan. Time runs swiftly, and the worlds within the worlds begin to blur."

CARYS BLINKED and was in the van, sitting in the back seat with Angus beside her.

"Is she awake yet?"

"Yes." She cleared her throat. "Where are we going?"

"I've told Duncan where to go," Angus said.

"It's a sea cave, lass."

"A sea cave?" She blinked and tried to sit up, but her entire body felt heavy.

"Never thought you were one for tattoos, but it suits you," Duncan said.

"What?"

Angus touched her shoulder. "Don't touch it. It'll settle."

Carys glanced down and saw the edge of a braided design, glowing red-hot beneath her skin.

"To the rest of them, it'll look like ink," Angus whispered. "Only those with eyes to see will know the Mothers' mark."

Carys nodded. "We're going to Annwn?"

"We're going as close as I'm permitted." Angus shook his head. "But she should be able to reach you."

Carys understood more than she knew. "I'm not going to talk to Seren, am I?"

"No, you are not."

The rest of the drive passed in silence as Duncan took a twisting coastal road around the southern edge of the Gower Peninsula, driving past small seaside villages and bright beaches filled with holiday makers.

It was midmorning, and the air was crisp and cool.

"Turn right here," Angus said.

The world around Carys was a blur of blue and green. She could smell the salt air and a metallic tinge that she suspected came from the heated metal under her skin.

"Up this road?" Duncan asked. "This isn't even a road, man."

"It's where we need to go."

The way grew rocky, and the van bumped along what felt more like a goat trail than a road. Carys heard waves crashing in the distance, echoing along the rocks that jutted from the earth's crust where the ocean met the land.

"Here."

"There's no car park here," Duncan said. "It's just a wide spot in the road."

"Because no one comes here, you idiot," Angus said. "Stop the car and get out. I need your help for the first part."

Carys felt like her body was weighed down with sand. She felt everything, but it was nearly impossible to move. Even lifting her legs to get out of the van when Duncan opened the door was a monumental effort.

"Come here, lass." His gruff voice was as soft as it could be. "I'll carry you."

"I'm heavy." It took effort to speak too. As if her tongue were weighted like her legs.

"Don't be daft." Duncan chuckled. "You're nothing but a bit of thing, Carys Morgan."

"She feels the weight of the Mothers' blessing." Angus hobbled out after Carys. "She'll grow accustomed to it with time."

"The tattoo?" Duncan peeked down her shirt. "It's beautiful, but how does it look healed so quickly? I mean, I know they're goddesses, but human skin is human skin."

"Not a tattoo," she managed to say. "Chain."

"Aye, it's beautiful." He turned to Angus. "Where?"

"Follow me."

Duncan carried her in his arms, climbing up a rocky trail between two fingers of land that jutted into the ocean. There was a rocky beach below them, and the sound of crashing waves echoed around her.

The world was a wash of gold and grey rock, vivid blue sky, and green brush that covered the tops of the hills. Everything moved in sacred rhythm.

Leaves caught by the wind.

Waves on rock.

The heart of the world breathing in and out.

In and out.

"Here."

"Here?" Duncan ducked his head, and Carys was enveloped in darkness.

"Put her down."

Carys smelled the pungent mineral scent of salt water on stone.

"She can barely move, Angus. I don't know what they gave her, but—"

"Put her down!" Angus barked. "And stay here. You're not to go a step farther, do you understand me? No matter what you hear, you stay here, boy."

"Why?" Duncan lowered Carys carefully to her feet, bracing her until she found her legs. "I don't like any of this. They gave her something back at that shop, and she can barely walk. If she falls—"

"I won't." She patted his shoulder, gripping it when she swayed. "I'll be okay. But if you go farther..." Carys breathed deeply when she found her feet, inhaling the scent of cedar and iron that always clung to Duncan's skin. "The hounds of Arawn would probably find you."

She pulled him down and pressed a kiss to his mouth. "I'm kind of out of it, so don't make me fight off otherworldly dogs, okay?"

Duncan's eyes met hers. "I don't like any of this."

"I know," she whispered. "But I have to go."

"Carys—"

"Love you so much." She held out her hand and knew that Angus would take it. "Trust me. Trust Angus."

"I trust you." He glared at Angus. "I don't know about this one."

"Let me go."

Duncan slowly released the grip he had around her waist, and Carys moved away from him. Her legs still felt heavy, but she was getting used to the sensation. It was a little like those heavy exercise weights people wrapped around their legs when training, only the sensation was all over. As if her own bones had been turned to lead.

"Are you with me, Carys Morgan?"

She walked through the damp cave, holding Angus's hand. "I'm with you."

"Not much farther now."

There was a narrow passage with a glowing silver light at the end.

Carys saw shimmering waves of light painting the walls, and as she emerged, she saw a familiar sight.

It was another silver pool, like the one in Angus's own cave, but this one had a blueish-green, swirling light beneath it.

"This again?"

"All your clothes," Angus said. "Off. Take nothing from the mortal realm."

"You want me to strip naked in front of you?"

Angus rolled his eyes. "You think you have anything I haven't seen before?"

She looked down at the chain that was glowing beneath her skin. "I don't know. Have you seen a glowing gold chain embedded beneath someone's skin before?"

"That one I'll give you, Carys Morgan." Angus sounded amused. "But the rest is fairly boring to me."

"Thanks, I guess." She pulled off her shirt and saw Oshun's mark more clearly.

It was a twisting and intricate chain that dipped below her collarbones and just above the rise of her breasts. When she reached back, she could feel the metal just below the base of her neck and saw the edges embedded in her shoulders.

The weight of her limbs was still noticeable, but she felt lighter than before. And as she stripped the rest of her clothes off, she noticed warmth creeping over her skin that seemed to emanate from Dôn's golden collar.

Angus waited for her to be completely naked, then stood at the edge of the pool and held out his hand. "You know what happens next."

Carys walked over and looked down at her reflection. The chain was glowing with a warmer light than the silver pool. "Do you have to push me in or—"

THE WATER ENVELOPED HER, sucking her under the surface and pulling her down and down and down until she opened her eyes and saw the mirrorlike surface below her.

Carys swam toward it, her lungs burning and her body aching until she reached the other side and surfaced with a gasp, shoving the water from her face and pushing her hair back where it covered her eyes.

She looked around the glowing silver pool, then up at the glowing blue lights that hovered over her like wisps at the gate.

"Hello, cariad."

Carys turned and saw her mother bending down at the edge of the pool. "Mom?"

Tegan smiled at her daughter. "You followed the lights."

"Mom!" Her heart felt like it was going to burst. She swam to the edge of the pool and let Tegan pull her from the water, then wrapped her arms around her mother and sobbed into her neck.

"There you are," Tegan whispered. "There you are, my love. My precious gift. My lovely girl."

Tegan rocked Carys as if she were a child, hushing her and gripping her tightly by the shoulders. She rocked her until Carys's tears had stopped and the weight on her heart was a little bit lighter.

Carys pulled away to look at her mother, but it was a face she's only seen in pictures. As young as she was in that moment. "Wow."

"Hello." Tegan couldn't stop her smile. "Look at you. You look the same."

"You don't."

Tegan laughed. "I'm here, Carys. I hope you've forgiven me. I always thought we'd have more time."

"So you were going to tell me about... all of it?"

"Oh yes. I wanted you to know your sister if you could. I'd hoped..." Tegan's eyes were filled with regret. "I can't think of it now, because there's no helping it. I could never go back, so I thought it would be better to wait." She shrugged. "Then I ran out of time."

"You and Dad—"

"It was a deer," she said softly. "Just a deer in the road. A little thing, no? A drop of rain falling in water instead of the ground. We were gone. But I'm so sorry we left you, my love."

"But you're not together."

Tegan's smile was sad. "We are and we're not. It's hard to explain. But I always feel your father near me."

"I saw him in a dream, and he said you were just in the house. He was in—"

"His workshop?" Tegan laughed. "Of course he was, my love. Of course."

Her mother brushed her hair back, tucking it behind her ears and brushing drops of water from Carys's face. "Look at you. So beautiful." She ran her fingers over the gold chain embedded in Carys's skin. "And bearing the mark of the mother goddess."

"Oshun made it."

"But it is Dôn's collar." Tegan's voice was reverent. "I do not know who placed the chain on you, but the mark belongs to the mother of our gods." She leaned forward and pressed a kiss to the chain. "A gift I could have only dreamed of wearing."

Carys blinked and took a deep breath. "So I'm in Annwn now?"

"You're in a very small corner of it." Tegan glanced over Carys's shoulder. "And right now no one is watching. But we don't have much time. If Arawn's hounds catch the scent of a mortal in this realm, the hunt will be on. They will keep you here." Tegan lifted her eyebrows. "You'll have a great time, but I don't think that's really where you want to be, am I correct?"

"No, I need to go and defeat the Morrígan so she doesn't start a magical war."

"Oh." Tegan sighed. "Yes, that sounds like her. Where is she?"

"Southern England. She's raised three points of power on Salisbury Plain, and we think she's heading to Cley Hill to gather her acolytes."

"Okay, but you've given her three wounds, have you not?"

"What?" Carys shook her head. "No, I don't think so."

Tegan frowned. "Haven't you?"

"No, I've only seen her in dreams."

"Hmm." Tegan pushed away and looked at Carys. "I see that you need new eyes."

"What?" She put a hand to her temple. "What do you—"

"Not literally, Carys." Tegan sighed. "You were always strangely literal for a girl who loved fairy tales. You have wounded her, but you're not seeing it for some reason even though you've met her in battle three times."

"I am telling you, I have not met the Morrígan in battle. She's been wandering around Southern England, posting videos online and probably getting brand deals, and I've been chasing bears covered in ammonia and nearly getting drowned by sea monsters in Yorkshire."

Tegan stared at her.

"What?"

Her mother was giving her the "you know what you've done" stare, and it had always confused Carys.

"A sea monster in Yorkshire."

"Yes."

"And a bear in..."

"Wyre Forest, I think?"

"And there will have been another battle as well."

Carys's eyes went wide. "The bison in Blean Forest."

"Cariad, all of those were the Morrígan."

"But they all survived."

"Yes, but every time you battled one of them and drove her from their bodies, you dealt her a wound."

Carys sat up straight. "The Mothers said I've already defeated her, I just don't know how."

"You haven't defeated her." Tegan put a hand on Carys's shoulder. "And Carys, you cannot defeat her. But you can force her back to the Shadowlands, and Epona will bind her again."

"How?"

"I can't tell you that." Tegan's eyes narrowed when she smiled. "But I can tell you how to acquire the vision you'll need to see her wounds and exploit her weaknesses. You already know what you need to do."

In the distance, there was a sound, and then an echo came.

The howl of a baying hound.

Tegan's smile faded. "We're out of time, so listen closely."

"Mom—"

"No more questions." She pressed a kiss to Carys's forehead. "Listen to me and remember, because I can only tell you once."

She grabbed her mother's arm. "I changed my mind. I want to stay with you."

"No, you don't." Tegan's eyes were bright. "But I love you for saying it. I'm with your sister now. And it's everything I dreamed of, but it's not your time yet."

Carys blinked, and the cave was gone. She was walking through the forest, and a doe was leading her. Blue lights were guiding her in the darkness, and hounds were calling in the distance.

She opened her eyes, and Tegan had her hands on her shoulders. "It's not time yet."

Carys fell backward into the water, the dark ocean pulling her from Annwn.

Her mother's voice followed her.

She will gather at Cley Hill. Go to Hogg's Well, take the water in your left hand, and put it in your right eye. Do not drink it. Do not put it in both eyes. Only in one.

A rushing sound as violent water buffeted her body and pressed against her, shooting her from the land of the dead and into the living world.

When you see as she can see, your sister will be with you, and your eye will be opened. Then you will see the wounds you have dealt the crow goddess so you can send her back to the Shadows.

Carys surfaced in the cave where she had started, shaking the water from her ears.

I love you, cariad. Know that I love you so much.

She spat salty water from her mouth and searched the cave for Angus, but the old god was nowhere to be found. "Angus?"

She spun in circles, but there was no one with her, and the water in the sea cave rocked with the tide. The light below the water was dimming quickly.

"Seriously?"

Carys climbed out of the cave pool and managed to get to her feet on the rocky ground. Her entire body was shivering as she found her damp clothes and quickly pulled them on before the light was gone.

She stumbled back through the narrow corridor until she saw the glow of the cave entrance and the silhouette of the man waiting for her.

Duncan.

"Carys, is that you?"

"We need to get to Cley Hill!" Carys said. "And I need to find some place called Hogg's Well."

Duncan held out his arms. "I'm not sure if I can come and get you. Can you keep walking?"

"I'm okay. My legs feel normal now—I'm just cold." She stumbled to him and threw her arms around his solid warmth. "Let's get out of here."

"You're freezing." He rubbed her back. "And soaking wet. Where's Angus?"

"Gone." Her teeth were chattering. "I think that was all he was meant to do, so he's gone."

"Fucking arse," Duncan muttered. "He could at least have said goodbye."

CHAPTER TWENTY-EIGHT

Duncan was on the phone with Laura as soon as they got back in the car, so by the time they reached the house, everyone was ready and waiting to go.

"Where is the goat man?" Cadell scanned the car. "Did he remain in Annwn?" The dragon leaned into Carys's neck and hissed. "Which god has branded you?"

"Okay, the sniffing thing is weird; please don't do that." Carys knew Cadell had trouble with boundaries, but she hated when he smelled her.

"Nêrys."

"The Mothers, okay?" She pulled back her shirt so Cadell could see the gold embedded in her skin.

His eyes softened. "A gold collar from Dôn. My lady—"

"Don't start with the 'my lady' thing, okay?" She blinked back tears. "I've already seen my mom today, heard the hounds of Arawn, and lost Angus. I need to focus."

Laura nearly fell out of the van. "You saw your mom?"

"Yes, and I'm still cold, I've got sand in my underwear, and I'm emotional, but we need to get to Cley Hill."

"No." Duncan turned off the van. "Go inside," he said. "Take a shower and get warm. Change your clothes."

"Duncan—"

"It's going to be a long fucking day. It's a three-hour drive from Swansea to Warminster. There's no point in your being miserable the entire drive."

"He's right." Lachlan opened Carys's door. "Carys, you need to take care of yourself. Battles are lost because of boots."

"I don't know what that means." And she was tired again.

Go to Hogg's Well, take the water in your left hand, and put it in your right eye.

Do not drink it. Do not put it in both eyes. Only in one.

"It means," Godrik added, "that a warrior whose feet are sore will fail in battle even if he is the greater power."

"Okay, that makes sense."

"They are right," Naida said. "You didn't sleep well last night. I could hear you pacing. We'll get the car ready. It's not even noon, and you're already exhausted."

She was going to cry, and she didn't want to break down in front of her friends.

Laura got out of the car and helped Carys down from the passenger's seat. "Come on, dummy, listen to them. Take a breath. And take a shower. You smell kind of weird. Like realm-of-the-dead weird, which is its own special kind of funk, and I don't think we want it getting into the upholstery of your boyfriend's nice new van."

Carys burst out laughing and crying at the same time.

"Oh." Laura laughed. "I think I saw a snot bubble. Yeah, you're going inside for a shower. Come on."

Carys nodded and let Laura and Cadell lead her back into the house.

Her best friend started a shower that was so hot steam was billowing out of the bathroom when Carys walked in.

When Laura closed the door, Carys stripped off her clothes and let them fall to the ground. Sand was gritty beneath her feet.

She walked to the mirror and swept a hand over the glass so she could see her reflection, only to find a black-haired woman with a bleeding right eye staring at her from the corner of the shower.

Carys screamed, and a second later Cadell burst into the room.

She looked again, and the woman was gone.

She collapsed into her dragon's arms, and he eased her to the ground. Cadell held her in an iron embrace and let her cry.

"Nêrys, she is not here."

"She was in the mirror."

"I do not doubt your vision. Dôn's collar has opened your mind in a way that most Brightkin never experience. You have traveled to a realm of the dead. You will see things that other humans cannot."

She clutched his arm and felt his skin pebbling beneath her fingers. "Are you going to shift?"

"No, but your perceptions have." He brushed the hair back from her forehead. "Clean up and eat something."

"Find Hogg's Well and take the water in your left hand," she whispered. "Put it in your right eye. Don't drink it. Don't put it in both eyes."

"Is that what your mother told you?"

Carys nodded.

"Then that is what you will do." His voice was grim. "Did she tell you anything else?"

"I've already wounded her," Carys said. "The sea monster. The bear. The bison. All of them were her."

"So with each battle, you wounded the Morrígan." Cadell nodded. "You have already won, but you must understand how."

"But I have to see the wounds to understand how to defeat her."

"The collar has opened your mind," Cadell said. "The water from the holy well will open your eye."

Carys looked up into the dragon's warm gold eyes. "Cadell, I don't think I want to see."

"I know." He frowned. "But you are a nêrys ddraig of the Cymric throne. You are the Brightkin of Princess Seren of Cymru. You wear the mother goddess's collar. You will do what you must."

The traffic started at the roundabout north of Cley Hill, a stop-and-go mess of cars, vans, and a few small trucks, all of it leading into the city and none of it coming out.

"What the hell is this?" Duncan muttered from the driver's seat.

It was nearing sunset by the time they arrived, and this time Duncan didn't have a rich friend with a country house nearby, but he had secured lodging at a swanky mansion turned hotel on the south end of town.

"It's her." Laura was staring at her phone. "Cley Hill is trending. There are millions of hits."

"Millions?" Godrik's jaw dropped.

"Even if only a fraction of them come to her in person," Naida said, "that is an enormous show of worship."

Carys looked out her window, and it appeared that they were stuck in traffic headed to a music festival or something like that.

There were cars decorated with red ribbons and white flags. Every type of bumper sticker from Earth First to Save Gorne Wood to Vegan and Proud. There were also bumper stickers from primary schools and local churches. Plenty of Dog Moms and Cat Dads were represented too.

"It's like a Grateful Dead festival," Laura said. "Remember those, Carys?"

The Grateful Dead fans loved Baywood for some reason. Probably had to do with lax marijuana laws back in the day, but the spooky forests and Bigfoot rumors likely helped.

"If this is what the traffic is like from here to the city," Duncan said. "It's going to take hours to get through."

"We should walk," Godrik said.

"What?" Carys turned to look. "It's miles from here."

"It'll still be faster than sitting though this," the wolf said. "Lachlan, what do you think?"

"I would tend to agree, but Carys has another task before we meet Macha again, does she not?"

Go to Hogg's Well, take the water in your left hand, and put it in your right eye. Do not drink it. Do not put it in both eyes. Only in one.

"I have to find a place called Hogg's Well," she said. "But Laura can't find anything definite online. There are a couple of theories but—"

"I wonder if it's the same Hogg's Well as in the Shadowlands," Naida said.

Every eye save Duncan's turned to her.

"There is a Hogg's Well at the base of Cley Hill in the Shadowlands," Naida said. "It's an underground river that empties into a sort of pond, but it might be different here. The water is not good."

"It might *not* be that different though." Laura turned to Carys. "New plan. Duncan takes the van to the hotel whatever way he can find through this traffic. Lachlan and Godrik scope out Macha's gang. They're tall. They can walk faster." She pointed to Naida and Cadell. "You and me and the dragon find the nearest fae gate."

Naida perked up. "There is one not far from here."

"Your mum didn't say anything about going to the Shadowlands," Duncan said.

"No, but she also didn't say not to," Laura said. "And if it's the same water, maybe it works either way."

"I think I'll know pretty quickly," Carys said. "It's supposed to give me magical vision."

Naida's face was solemn. "There are stories about humans with magical vision, but I'm sure you'll live longer than they do."

"That is not helpful, Naida!" Duncan was fuming.

"Pull over." She put a hand on Duncan's arm. "Do you really think my mom is going to have me do something that might result in my death?"

"Your mum is dead," Duncan said. "Maybe she thinks having both versions of her daughter in Annwn is not such a bad idea."

"It's not my time." Fear had been riding her since the cave, but the moment she thought about going through the gate, she felt calm again. "It's not my time, Duncan."

He clenched his jaw but pulled the van over to a wide spot on the side of the road while massive honks and whoops sounded from the cars around them.

Lachlan and Godrik jumped out of the van, helping Naida and Laura out as well before they crossed the road and trotted off into the woods that bordered the motorway.

"They don't have phones," Duncan said. "How the hell do they think they're going to figure out where they're going?"

"They'll follow the crowd," Cadell said.

It wasn't a bad strategy. They were far from the first people who had decided to walk. Carys could see small groups of travelers dressed in everything from festive clothing to business suits walking along the road, and a few of them had wandered into the forest just as Lachlan and Godrik had done.

"Her power is growing," the dragon said. "I feel the urge to shift into my natural form even now."

"The gate is in those woods." Naida pointed across the road where Lachlan and Godrik had already disappeared. "It's small, but it's old. I don't think anyone is guarding it."

Cadell climbed out of the car and slid the door shut before he opened Carys's door. "Blacksmith, I have charge of these women, and I will bring them back safely."

Laura raised both her eyebrows. "You have charge of us?"

Cadell straightened to his full height and looked down his nose. "You have another protector in mind?"

Laura's cheeks turned red. "No, you're fine." She grabbed Carys and Naida by the hand. "Duncan, call me when you get to the hotel."

"You're going to lose your phone when you go through the gate," he said.

"Oh, for fuck's sake, those freaking fairies!" She threw her phone on the passenger seat.

"Ludlow House," Duncan said. "Southwest end of town. Good luck."

Carys walked over, squeezing between a slow-moving minivan and a convertible with red streamers flying off the windshield.

"Woo-hoo!" the driver yelled. "The new world is coming!"

There were cheers and shouts from everywhere, and the stopped traffic erupted in cheerful honks.

Duncan had his window rolled down. "You know, people want something to believe in."

She stood on her toes and kissed him. "Let's hope we can find something better than an ancient Irish goddess of war."

Squeezing through the gate in the woods took little more than Cadell scaring off a few angry badgers and lifting some rocks, which the dragon also did with ease.

Then Naida led them through what could only have been the narrowest, dirtiest fae gate in Southern England.

Carys crawled out of the other side to see two spears pointed directly at her face. They were held by two fae with silver sigils on their face, backed by a unicorn.

As soon as they saw Carys, they stepped away.

"The ellyllon tells the truth," one said. "She is King Dafydd's niece. I have seen her portrait in the great hall."

"Okay." She scooted out from the hole in the ground and brushed off her legs before she reached down and held a hand out for Laura. "I have a friend coming too. She's a shadow-walker from across the sea, and pointing a spear in her face would probably be like a diplomatic taboo, so please don't."

"Of course, my lady." The two fae spear holders backed off, and the unicorn tossed his head in the air, whinnying as he did.

"Cyrus would like to know your business in the Cley Forest."

Carys looked at Laura, then Naida. "I need to find a place called Hogg's Well."

Cadell climbed out of the hole, and the fae looked up and up until their faces went pale.

"You have a dragon," one of them said.

"She's the king's niece," Naida said. "I told you she is nêrys ddraig."

"Hogg's. Well." It was the only thing Cadell said.

"Not a mile south, lord dragon," the fae guard said, pointing in the direction behind them. "Just beyond the woods."

Carys asked, "Is there any unusual activity around Cley Hill on this side of the gates?"

The unicorn transformed in a shower of silver and gold, and a tall, beautiful man stood before them. "I am Cyrus of the Blessing of Wor. There *is* a disturbance. Epona's daughters have gathered on the plain. Our seers saw a great rip between the shadow and the light. A gathering of powers in other realms. It is the only reason I have joined the fae patrols in this area."

Unicorns loved peace, but if there was a blessing nearby, they were fiercely protective.

"Smart move," Laura said. "There's a conflict, but it's not on this side."

"I see the mark of Dôn on this one." Cyrus looked at Carys. "The old mother has given you a hero's collar. Is war coming?"

"That's what I'm trying to prevent," Carys said. "The Morrígan is trying to gain power in the Brightlands. That's why I need to get to the well."

Cyrus nodded. "To give you a vision."

"Something like that.

"Then follow me." Cyrus looked at Cadell. "Brother Dragon, take your natural form and fly behind. I can see that you have a need to shift. Your ladies will be safe with us. I will vouch for the honor of these fae."

Cadell looked at Carys. She gave him a nod of approval; then, in the space of a heartbeat, his human body disappeared and he was a beast again, spreading his wings and rising from the forest floor, taking to the predawn sky as Carys watched him fly overhead.

Nêrys!

You're so relieved.

It feels like weeks, not days.

I know.

Laura was already speaking to the fae guards, one of whom led a horse from behind a copse of chestnut trees.

"I will stay here to guard the gate," the fae said, "but you may borrow my mare. She is bred of Epona's blood and as gentle as the moon."

"I am grateful for the loan," Laura said.

"Nêrys Ddraig, you must ride with me." Cyrus transformed back into unicorn form and knelt down so Carys could mount him. It wasn't the first time she had ridden a unicorn, but the height and power of the animals always gave her pause.

"Come on." Laura urged her on. "It's almost sunrise here, which means that the sun is setting in the Brightlands."

They took off through the forest with the unicorn and the fae as Carys felt Cadell soaring overhead. He swept over the landscape of Saris Plain, narrating what he saw.

The scars of war have been completely healed. I see nothing from Dru and Cian's battle save for some memorial mounds.

That was only a month ago.

Yes.

It feels so much longer.

Only a month for the Morrígan to set her plan in motion. But of course, it had been far more than a month. The goddess had probably been looking for an opportunity for centuries.

Carys had just given her one.

I am feeling your guilt again, Cadell said. *Stop. You had no way of knowing what she was.*

I should have been paying better attention.

Cadell ignored her. *There is a large group of women wearing white gathered on top of a hill. I think they must be Epona's daughters.*

What are they doing?

They are in a circle. That is all I can see.

The unicorn slowed and then started walking when they came to a spring that flowed from a small rise of the earth before it tumbled over a pile of rocks and landed in a large round pool lined with cobblestones.

"Beyond those trees is Cley Hill." The fae pointed to the right. "A giant named Hogg lives under that mound. A long time ago he grew angry that the humans feared him and fled from his territory, so he redirected a stream under the hill to feed the land."

Carys dismounted from the unicorn, who immediately transformed.

"But it was the blessing of a giant," Cyrus said, "so the water is bitter. It is useful only for bathing and a few plants that are able to tolerate it."

The ground around the spring was rocky, and there were only a few plants growing. And while Carys could see the water coming out of the ground, the pool had no outlet.

"The fae dug a deep well here centuries ago," Naida said. "That way the water can return to the earth and join other springs that will cleanse it."

"Got it," Laura said. "So this water here is old."

Naida nodded and bent down by the edge of the spring. "It's very, very old."

Carys approached the well with a pit in her stomach. *Cadell?*

He circled overhead, then came to land in the clearing beside the well. *Do you need me in human form?*

"No." She looked into his great gold eyes. "I just need you here."

Go to Hogg's Well, take the water in your left hand, and put it in your right eye.

Do not drink it.

Do not put it in both eyes.

Only in one.

Carys knelt down next to Naida, and for a moment, she felt the heat of Dôn's collar burning around her neck.

Your sister will be with you, and your eye will be opened. Then you will see the wounds you have dealt the crow goddess so you can send her back to the Shadows.

Carys dipped her left hand into the water, bracing herself with her right. Then she carefully brought the bitter water of Hogg's Well to her right eye, as he mother had told her.

She blinked, letting the water enter her eye, then lifted her head, careful not to let any of it touch her lips.

"Carys?" Laura called out to her, and Carys turned. "What do you see?"

"Whoa."

It was more than disorienting at first.

When Carys turned to look at her best friend, there were two images laid overtop of each other. Laura in her ceremonial clothing;

Laura in her traveling clothes. Laura with her face painted with traditional tattoos. Laura with no tattoos.

And when Carys closed her left eye, she saw a massive bird on Laura's shoulder, a giant black raven, silent and watching.

"Laura, when you did your initiation as pauwau inwe, what was your personal totem?"

"Honey, you know I can't tell you that. I can't tell anyone that."

"Was it kwe gok?" She used the Yurok word for raven to keep things private.

"Yes." Laura's voice was soft. "How did you know that?"

"I can see it." She covered her right eye. "And now I don't."

She turned to Cadell. When she looked through her right eye, she saw a massive green dragon with pebbled skin and a fire burning at his throat.

And when she looked through her left eye... she also saw a massive green dragon with fire at his throat.

"Yeah," she muttered. "That figures."

She stood up with Naida's help and wobbled a little bit. "This is very disorienting."

"I have an idea." The ellyllon dug into the pack she carried and quickly ripped some fabric to form a sort of eye patch. "Try this."

Carys pulled the band over her right eye, and everything looked like it had before. Then she tugged it over and covered her left eye, and the world shifted.

The fae looked as they always did, but the unicorn was covered in scars invisible to her other eye. And when she looked at Cadell, she also saw wounds that had been long healed. A piercing through his wing and a great gash below his neck where he had once bled so Duncan could forge dragon steel.

"Okay." Carys nodded. "I think I know why my mom wanted me to do this."

Your vision is now touched by the gods, Cadell said.

Sister.

Carys blinked at the sound of Seren's voice in her mind.

I'm with you. It's time.

"I can see magic," Carys said. "And Seren is with me." She turned to look at her dragon. "We're together now. It's time for me and the Crow Mother to meet face-to-face."

CHAPTER TWENTY-NINE

When they crawled back through the fae gate, Carys was curious if the enchantment over her right eye was still going to work. But the moment she moved her eye patch to observe the dark woods around them, the more she realized it not only worked but was as much curse as blessing.

Cadell, back in human form, held her by the arm. "Are you all right?"

"Yeah, just... adjusting."

I see what you see, Seren said in her mind. *Give ourselves time to adjust.*

"We don't have time," Carys responded to the voice in her head.

The forest around them was alive with magical creatures. There were wisps and nymphs floating in the trees. Pixies danced along the long grasses, and sly, furtive creatures skittered along the forest floor.

"We need to find Duncan," Carys said.

And Lachlan.

A long howl broke the silence of the forest.

Naida's head went up. "Godrik."

"How is he in wolf form?" Carys asked.

The magic is powerful here. Can't you feel it?

A massive white wolf with dark grey shoulders bounded toward them. Carys was almost afraid he was going to roll right over them until he circled once, then transformed.

She blinked her right eye. "How?"

Godrik was a man with her human vision, but when she closed her left eye, he was all wolf.

The wolf has his power in this place. Seren spoke in her mind, and it was like hearing her own thoughts. *The Morrígan is thinning the barrier between the realms of Shadow and Light.*

"Duncan is at Cley Hill," Godrik said. "Everyone in the village is at Cley Hill. Along with who knows how many people from all over Briton. The chalk plain is covered with her acolytes."

"In like... half an hour?"

Naida cocked her head. "I hear no vehicles as I did before."

"All the roads are clogged. People eventually just got out of their cars and walked," Godrik said. "That's why Duncan is with Lachlan and me."

Laura looked him up and down. "What is going on? How can you shift?"

"There must be a gate nearby or some old power rising, because the magic..." Godrik looked at Cadell. "Can *you* shift, brother?"

Yes.

"I think if you can, he can," Carys said.

The dragon stretched his neck to the side, and Carys saw the glow of red fire at his throat.

"Yes." The word was more of a hiss than a statement.

Careful. Seren spoke in her mind. *His natural form is the beast, but violence will only feed the Morrígan now.*

"Agreed."

Cadell's eyes flashed like fire. "Nêrys, let me loose and I will burn the goddess where she stands. There will be no shelter for her, no place to hide. There will be—"

"So, so, so many humans who die," Carys said.

Cadell went still.

Can Seren hear me?

Cadell!

The dragon's face was a torment of emotion.

Seren. I have... missed your voice.

We need to be careful, old friend. Listen to your nêrys now.

"We need to get to Cley Hill and confront her," Carys said, "but we are not killing hundreds of random people who have fallen under her spell. That would be exactly what she wants."

Laura took Cadell's hand. "She's right, and you'd feel horrible about it later. There has to be a better way."

There is.

Carys pulled the eye patch over her left eye and started walking. "Come on. We've got a walk ahead of us. Let's go."

THEY WALKED THROUGH THE FOREST, encountering various people as they made their way to Cley Hill.

Some were laughing as if they were drunk, and others were weeping. Carys looked at a weeping man with her right eye and saw a crouching, mud-brown creature perched on his back. It was whispering in the man's ear as he cried.

"Despair," she whispered.

The Brightlands are not at all as I remember.

"Jibril called Despair a god," Carys said softly. "I think that might be it."

I believe you are correct.

"So we can see spirits now," Carys said quietly. "Maybe hidden gods."

As they walked, she encountered more.

What are the lights around them? Pixies? Wisps?

Many of the people they saw had bright sparks swirling around their heads. The lights buzzed like bees, but no matter which way the humans looked or who they were talking to, the moment they started focusing on anything but the buzzing lights, a spark would go off like a bug zapper.

A girl pulled out her phone and checked something on the glowing screen.

"It's the internet," Carys murmured. "Social media. That's what she worships."

There were humans with feet that seemed to sink into the earth and humans with angry red skin and ears that literally steamed. Nature lovers. People who lived in pure anger.

I would not mind being a tree. But the red-skinned humans are dangerous. Be wary of them. They will ignite with the smallest spark.

Sprinkled among the spirits and what Carys could only think of as demons were familiar marks of other gods. Crosses and crescent moons, prayer beads or the scent of incense.

"It's everyone," Carys said. "It's not just people with no religion or belief. She's enchanted all of them."

Not all of them are enchanted. Some are simply... interested.

"Either way," Carys whispered, "they're giving her attention, and attention—"

Means power.

Godrik led them out of the forest and into a wheat field where deep paths had been laid down through the nodding golden heads.

You have formed your own wing.

"What?"

Though you are a nêrys ddraig, you were never trained as I was. These people—the wolf, the fae, your friends, along with Cadell—they are your wing.

Carys smiled a little bit, glancing at Cadell.
He nodded.

He hears me too.

I do, old friend.

Don't use that voice, lizard. You act like I'm dead.

You are *dead.*

Only from one perspective.

"Okay, you two are going to have to stop having conversations in my head," Carys whispered, "because it's going to get way too confusing."

They stopped at the edge of the wheat field and looked back toward the forest at all the humans who were following them.

"I hate to say this," Laura said as they watched the throngs of people all walking toward Cley Hill, "but this almost feels like a zombie movie."

"You're not wrong," Carys said.

She lifted her eyes to Cley Hill in the distance, and the sky above it terrified her. She stumbled in the field.

Gods and goddesses of old.

Cadell rushed over. "Nêrys?"

"The sky is broken," Carys whispered. "Don't tell the others, but there's something wrong with the sky."

I have never seen anything like this, Cadell.

Where stars should have shone over the peak of the hill, instead there was a dark, blood-red gash, and no one—not the humans trudging toward it and not even the magical creatures by her sides—seemed to realize it was there.

"I see nothing," Cadell said. "Are you sure?"

Dark waves of magic floated over the land, flowing upward and toward the violent tear like blood flowing into a wound.

"I'm sure." She leaned on him and felt his skin pebble under her fingertips. "Resist, Cadell. We have to get to the top of that hill."

She's gathering power from those who are giving her worship.

"I want to protect you more than anything." The dragon's voice was deeper, more like the beast within him. "My instincts tell me that I could protect you better in my natural form."

Not yet, old friend. You must resist.

"She's right." Carys put a hand on Cadell's cheek, anchoring him to his human body. "Remember who she is."

The Morrígan was a goddess of war, bloodshed, and chaos.

Seren said what Carys was thinking.

The moment you give in to the violence that your instincts are telling you to unleash, she will use that violence to add to her power.

Cadell nodded, but his jaw was clenched tightly.

"You have this." Carys nodded. "You have this, Cadell."

Massive crowds had gathered to the Morrígan. Most of them seemed peaceful, but it was no coincidence that gods of despair and anger were among them.

The Morrígan had gathered a brush pile of acolytes around her, and all it would take would be one spark to make this situation explode. One spark, and there would be violence and chaos.

And all that violence and chaos would only feed her power.

"I can't kill her," Carys said to Laura as they walked. "But Seren and I can defeat her."

"How?" Laura asked. "With love and understanding?"

The hillsides were singing with magic. Bright wisps flew overhead, and the humans watching them seemed to delight in the show.

"They probably think it's some kind of trick or special effect."

Most of them were recording the play of light and the dancing pixies with their mobile phones.

"We have to... dampen the power she's gathering somehow." Carys knew it was going to be difficult. Even she felt the seduction of the magic dancing through the air, though she could also see the dark energy pulling from the crowd and up toward the gash in the sky where crows were circling and cawing.

"I know the magic she's gathered is dark," Naida said, "but the little ones don't know that." She was smiling at the delighted pixies that danced along her fingertips. "The world is so beautiful."

"It's dangerous," Godrik said. "But I cannot deny that seeing so many Brightkin surrounded by magic is seductive."

That's exactly what she wants. She wants the worlds to merge so she can create war in both of them.

"We've got to resist the urge to join them." Carys couldn't argue that on the surface, the crowd felt like the biggest party ever thrown.

There were musicians playing music when they reached the base of the hill and started on the winding path upward.

"Flowers from the goddess?" Young men and woman were handing out yellow and white flowers near a bonfire where people were dancing. "Flowers to celebrate Macha?"

"Thanks." Laura took a flower.

One of the tall young men handing out flowers put one directly in Cadell's short hair.

"Joy, brother," the young man said. "Macha has returned."

Seren snorted when Carys looked at the dragon, the yellow flower tucked behind his ear.

I heard that.

Cadell's jaw was tight. "Do you even know who Macha is?"

The young man smiled with bright white teeth. "She's love. And magic. Don't we need more of that in the world?"

Carys looked at the man with her right eye and saw the swirling lights of the internet gods were still hovering around him, but he seemed completely oblivious to anything but Macha's enchantment.

He's enthralled by the idea of her. How long until he pulls out his phone?

As if on command, the moment Cadell stepped away from the young man, the human pulled his phone from his pocket and posed for a selfie with one of the other young people holding flowers.

It's not her they love. Not truly.

"Agreed," Cadell said quietly.

Godrik glared at a young woman with flowers when she approached him, and the girl backed away. "They believe it is a game."

"It is," Laura said. "From their perspective, this is just fun."

Carys kept walking, leading them from the front but covering her right eye so she didn't get distracted walking up the narrow clay path that wound from the base of Cley Hill to the summit.

All around them, revelers sang, danced, and more than one couple was having sex under blankets or right out in the open. No one around them seemed to care.

Men and women dressed in everything from beach dresses to business suits were dancing and singing around campfires and bonfires. The revelers blanketed the slopes of Cley Hill, laying out tents and tarps. A few had even set up camp underneath the swirling, blood-red sky.

"How do we defeat her when she's pretending that it's all love and joy and peace here?" Laura asked.

"She has enchanted the humans," Naida said. "There is great

power in this place, and the more people come, the more attention they give her, the greater her power grows."

Carys nodded. "More people means more enchantment means more and more people and so on."

We must break the cycle. Kill their belief in magic.

Carys knew Seren was probably right, but it made her sad.

Naida shook her head. "These humans don't understand magic. They have no idea that some of it is dangerous. They're just drawn to anything that seems greater than themselves."

Someone shouted: "They want to be part of something!"

Carys heard the familiar Scottish voice above her and looked up. "Duncan!"

Lachlan.

Duncan and Lachlan were standing near the summit of the hill, and humans pressed around them. Carys felt a well of deep and overwhelming love as she looked at Lachlan.

It nearly made her weep.

It wasn't the bright, fresh passion that she and Duncan shared but a tested and deep love that had seen decades.

Carys experienced a flash of memories that she knew had come from her Shadowkin.

Lachlan holding her hand and running through a field when he was no more than a boy.

Watching his bright face from above, safe in the hold of her dragon's claws.

The thrill of a stolen kiss.

The anguish of a fight and the comfort of his embrace.

She was crying when Duncan and Lachlan pulled her up to the summit of the hill.

"Carys?" Lachlan bent down. "What's wrong?"

Don't tell him. Seren's voice was hoarse. *Not yet.*

"I'll tell you later." She patted his shoulder. Then she turned and threw her arms around Duncan. "You found us."

"Are you okay?" Duncan hugged her tightly. "There was no getting into the village. I parked the van and walked with the rest of them. It was sheer luck that I found Lachlan and Godrik at all."

The summit of the hill was teeming with people. Revelers from below who were dancing and beating drums. People walking on stilts through the crowd.

There was a fire-eater and several acrobats. It looked and felt like a circus.

"Thank the gods you are here," Lachlan said. "Carys, did you have a vision at the well?"

Carys pointed to the eye patch. "More like supernatural, god-fueled night vision."

Duncan frowned. "What does that mean?"

"I'll explain later." She stood on her tiptoes, but she couldn't see anything through the crowd. She had to set her eyes on Macha. "Can you lift me up so I can see?"

Duncan nodded and waved Lachlan over. "Get her up."

Carys grabbed both their hands, and the twin men lifted her to their shoulders, standing shoulder to shoulder so she could see what was going on at the summit of the hill.

Macha was sitting on a small grassy knoll in the distance while humans lay around her. There were flower bouquets surrounding her along with wads of cash, jewelry, mobile phones, and anything that seemed valuable.

"They're giving her offerings," Carys shouted.

"They have come to worship her," Naida said. "They are completely under her control."

Carys looked to her right and saw Naida on Godrik's shoulders and Laura on Cadell's.

More than one person was holding up their phone, live streaming the event to the rest of the world, and on every screen she saw, hearts and small thumb emojis littered the screen like bubbles floating in the air. Tiny animated presents and kiss emojis.

Thousands of people were watching. Maybe millions.

With a deep breath, Carys slid her eye patch to the left and looked at the gathering with her right eye.

"Oh." Her breath caught. "Oh, this is bad." She spoke to Seren in her mind. *Do you see this?*

I see it.

It wasn't only humans on the hill but thousands of spirits, shadowy twisted creatures, and wave after wave of dark magic, all flowing up from the slopes around them and feeding into the red-gashed sky.

And from that red gash, power fell down on the summit where Macha lay.

The goddess was bathing in dark worship.

CHAPTER THIRTY

ad stories weave enchantments. Good stories can break them.
A good story might break an enchantment, but Carys knew that first she had to break the endless cycle of attention, worship, veneration, and power that was enabling Macha to keep an entire hillside in thrall.

"We have to pull the plug. Somehow we've got to pull the plug."

Pull the plug?

Electricity, Cadell answered Seren.

We must break the current of her power.

Carys had to grab the crowd's attention somehow. She had to stop this insanity before it all boiled over. Boil. Heat.

How do you kill heat?

What are you thinking, sister?

"Hey, Laura!" Carys shouted. "Remember that Grateful Dead festival in Baywood they ended up canceling a couple of summers ago?"

"Yeah!"

It had been a gorgeous summer interrupted by a freak rainstorm that had driven the old hippies back to their trucks and camper vans.

"We need to break up this party!" she shouted.

It was a glorious summer night in Southern England with balmy air and a warm breeze wafting over the countryside, which meant that everyone was prone to being outdoors to enjoy the weather anyway.

Even people who hadn't seen Macha online were probably hearing about the party happening at Cley Hill. They were followers, not worshippers. The people camping on the hill and grilling hamburgers and sausages on the hill. But followers or worshippers, their energy fed Macha just the same.

"We need to rain them out!"

Someone walked between Carys and Laura with an honest-to-God boom box on their shoulder.

"What did you say?" Laura yelled.

"Rain!" Carys yelled. "Can you make it *rainy* and *cold*?"

Duncan grunted and shifted under her. "Rain has to be the least magical thing about England. You're probably on to something there."

"Rain?"

Carys nodded.

That's actually quite brilliant.

"You don't have to sound so surprised," Carys muttered.

Naida's eyes brightened. "Macha has thinned the barrier between the worlds here. I believe the earth will listen to me. I can help."

Laura patted Cadell's shoulder. "Okay, dragon. Get me to anyplace that has some water, bare earth, and open sky."

That woman is in love with Cadell.

"Go!" Carys ignored Seren because wow, this was really not the time to gossip about that subject. "Find someplace that's away from here."

Cadell turned and started back toward the slope of the hill where they had walked up.

"Wolf!" Duncan tossed Godrik a phone. "Give that to Laura."

Godrik nodded, then moved through the crowd with Naida on his shoulders.

"What do you want us to do?" Lachlan shouted.

"How secure am I on you two?"

"You weigh nothing," Duncan said. "What do you want?"

"Let's see if we can get closer." Carys needed to see Macha up close. With her right eye open, Duncan and Lachlan moved her through the crowd, and Carys had a chance to scan the spirits and demons the war goddess had called.

There were the now-familiar internet worshippers and so many demons of despair. The muddy-brown creatures were draped over people's shoulders and whispering in their ears.

Carys's heart hurt, especially when she saw the longing, hopeful eyes of the people they tormented.

You have a soft heart, sister.

"They just want to be part of something." Carys repeated Duncan's words, feeling her eyes fill with tears. "They want magic. They want something beautiful."

The Morrigan will not give them that. She will only feed on their attention.

Duncan and Lachlan held Carys on their shoulders and waded through the crowd, moving like a living wall through the flood of people as crows and starlings circled overhead.

The chain around Carys's neck heated. She looked up to see Macha's eyes on her.

"Epona's daughters." The goddess's voice came to her ears. "What are you doing on my hill? I feel your sisters on the other side, but their prayers are useless and futile."

Epona's cult must be gathered in the Shadowlands. They might be trying to pull her through as she thins the barrier.

"Did you come to worship me, daughters of Tegan?" Macha stood and lifted her arms, raising them to the blood-red gash in the sky where black crows circled and power rained down. "Shall I show you how to dance?"

Carys yelled down at Duncan and Lachlan. "She spotted me!"

"What should we do?" Lachlan asked again.

Just keep walking.

"Keep walking."

Cadell spoke to her mind. *Naida and Laura are calling the rain, but I feel the goddess's attention on you, nêrys. I should come.*

Stay with Laura and Naida! Protect them. I'm safe with Duncan and Lachlan.

The Morrígan began to dance to the drumbeat of two men on either side of what could only be described as an altar.

There were flowers and offerings of food. Bags of drugs and wads of cash. People had thrown clothing and mobile phones while others danced naked around the altar.

Carys saw a woman rake her fingernails across her breast, and blood welled from the scratches.

Blood offerings. The Morrígan's favorite.

"She's getting more powerful."

And the red gash in the sky was widening. Through it, Carys could see darkness swirling like blood spreading through water.

The Morrígan lifted her hands to the sky and danced, turning in circles to show off her half-naked form to the worshippers around her.

Everyone who hadn't had their phone out before pulled it out and started recording.

"Millions of people will see her," Duncan said. "That's going all over the world."

As Macha turned, Carys saw all three of the goddess's aspects fully—the nubile young woman, the lush mother, and the wrinkled elder. Her hair flashed from red to black to white as she turned, whipping around in the wind.

"Macha," the crowd began to chant. "Macha. Macha. Macha."

"What the fuck is happening?" Duncan asked. "Carys, are you okay?"

"Wait." She narrowed her eyes, pulling the eye patch back over her left eye so she could focus her vision on what she was seeing.

Red-haired maiden.

Black-haired mother.

Silver-haired crone.

And round and round she went, the one turning to three turning to one whirled vision in Carys's eye.

But as she turned into one and three, another vision became clear too. The nubile body was scarred with a deep bruise over her abdomen, purple and green, weeping blood from under the ribs.

Her dark eyes were bleeding, but not to cause terror. One eye was completely destroyed, the socket empty and dripping blood.

And as she turned, she leaned a little, as if one of her legs was broken. When Carys looked closer at the whirling dancer, she saw deep punctures in the Morrígan's leg.

Wounds from a wolf's bite.

"She *is* wounded." Carys couldn't laugh because the sight before her became more horrible by the second, but she did feel a sense of relief. "You guys, we did hurt her. Badly."

Carys flashed back to the days immediately after the Morrígan's barrow had risen and a conversation with the son of a god. *"I assume you've heard of* The Cattle Raid of Cooley...*"*

The eel.

The bear.

The bull.

"It's not the same story, Carys Morgan, but it just might rhyme."

Each battle had weakened the goddess, and now all Carys needed to finish her was...

A story.

Carys felt a drop land on her shoulder.

The dancers worshipping in front of Macha's altar slowed, then stopped. They looked at the sky, turning their faces up to the clouds that had gathered over Cley Hill.

And a loud groan came from all of them.

"Stop!" Macha screamed. "Where are you going?"

It wasn't everyone, but while the crowd at the top of the hill continued to dance and sway and chant, some of them even more enthusiastically than they had been before, the Morrígan wasn't looking at the worshippers closest to her.

She was looking at the phones being turned off and stuffed into pockets.

She was looking in the distance at the crowds that were no longer pushing up Cley Hill.

Macha stomped her foot. "Stop it!"

Nothing stops a party like rain.

I see it. Carys smiled. *I feel it.*

The crowds on the hillside were breaking up. Fires were going out, and the few people who had brought rain ponchos were holding them over other revelers, joking as their attention shifted from Macha to the people around them.

"Look!" Macha screamed like a petulant child. "Look at me! Look at me!" She stamped her foot and lifted her arms to the bloody sky.

Carys followed her hands and saw the crows and starlings massing over Cley Hill, but even the birds were having trouble flying through the rain that was growing ever harder, soaking the hillside and turning the fine clay soil into mud.

Nêrys, I am not shifting, though with Naida and Laura's magic around me, the urge to do so is very strong.

Wait! Cadell, you can do this. The crowds are still worshipping her up here. We need to drain her power.

"You!" Macha pointed to Carys. "Get them and bring the horse goddess's daughters to me!"

"Daughters?" Lachlan looked up and their eyes met.

My love.

"Not now!" Carys was worried the crowd would riot. "Put me down! Quick."

Duncan and Lachlan slowly lowered Carys to the ground as muddy revelers turned on them, reaching for Carys.

"I don't think so," Duncan growled. "Back off, boy."

The two Scotsmen stood on either side with Carys between them, blocking the people from reaching her.

Carys saw Lachlan reach for the short sword hidden in his coat.

"No!" she shouted. "You have to let them take me!"

"What?" both men shouted.

"Fuck no!" Duncan said.

"I will defend you unto death itself!" Lachlan's eyes were flashing.

"That's what she wants!" Carys yelled over the thunder that was rolling across Salisbury Plain. "She wants violence, remember?"

Nêrys...

Cadell's voice was low and bestial.

Not yet, old friend!

Carys tugged on Duncan's arm, forcing him to listen as a muddy hand grabbed her wrist. "She *wants* violence," she said. "You can't give it to her. It will only make her stronger."

"I can't." Duncan's eyes went wide as two young men covered in mud walked over to Carys and grabbed her by the shoulders. "Don't ask me to let you go!"

The gold chain in her skin burned, and when she turned to look at Macha's servants, she saw the red flush of anger covering their skin.

"It's okay." She kept her voice calm. "I'll go to Macha. I'll go."

Duncan roared and raised his fist. "Absolutely fucking not!"

"No." She turned to him and put a hand on his arm. "Let me go."

His eyes were wide and crazed with fear. "Carys—"

"I have to go," she said. "This is what I'm supposed to do, remember?"

He shook his head. "No."

"Please." She felt them start to drag her away, and she sent one last look to Lachlan before she went with Macha's servants. "Don't fight them, f'anwylyd. That's what she wants. Put the sword away, my darling. Let me go."

Lachlan's eyes went wide, and he froze. "Seren?"

Nêrys, I am shifting. She cannot—

Stop. Seren's mental voice was firm.

Peace settled over Carys's body.

Wait.

Carys whispered to Cadell, *We will tell you when it is time.*

The two men took her by the arms, dragging her up to Macha's altar. She slipped in the mud and nearly fell, but they lifted her, carrying her up and over fallen humans that Carys forced herself to ignore.

She ignored the tug of her heart as she left Duncan and Lachlan behind her.

Gods old and new, protect them, Seren whispered in her mind.

The rain continued to fall, and the waves of dark magic that had streamed from the hillsides up to the gash in the sky had turned to more of a trickle than a flood.

The men flung Carys onto the altar, and she fell to her knees on the grassy knoll.

Macha stood over her, glaring down her nose.

"Epona's daughters." Macha sneered. "What exactly do you think you're doing?"

Carys looked up, and as she did, the Morrígan's gaze fell on the glowing gold collar around Carys's neck. "No!"

Macha ripped the rag from Carys's head, and twin visions swam in front of her eyes.

The young social media sensation, still glowing as if untouched by the rain.

The wounded goddess, blood pouring from an empty eye socket.

"You're hurt, Morrígan." Carys managed to get to her feet. "We can see your wounds."

"You interfering bitches," the Morrígan sneered. "You think you can stop me?"

"No." Carys shook her head. She looked over the crowd, a jumble of mortals and magic drenched in rain.

Far from a fearsome crowd, the humans still shuffling around at the top of Cley Hill looked cold and wet and tired. They didn't look angry. Just a little disappointed and confused.

And bored.

Nêrys. I see you.

Carys had to force her eyes to remain on Macha even though she longed for the safety of her dragon's presence.

"You can't win." Carys looked up at the red gash in the sky. It was starting to close as the dark magic that fed it thinned and dissipated.

"I have already won!" Macha threw out her arms. "Look at my Fianna come to serve me!"

"All these people?" Carys stood. "You think they're your Fianna?" She shook her head. "They're just regular people, Macha. They just want something to believe in."

You're provoking her. Is that wise, Professor?

Oh, now you know what a professor is?

"Most of them are already leaving." Carys pointed at the people walking down the hill in groups, following the footpath back to the village, returning to their cars or taking shelter from the rain in the forest below. "Look."

The goddess watched the humans walk away, and the crows over her head circled and called.

She is growing angry. I hope you know what you're doing.

Carys kept talking in what Laura called her "professor voice." "They didn't really believe in *you*, Macha. Modern humans want something to distract them, and you gave them that."

The internet worshippers left next. Carys saw them and their buzzing blue and pink lights heading toward the back of the hill where the downhill path started. The rain was too heavy to keep their phones out, and Macha had stopped dancing naked.

Without the feedback from their live streams, they quickly lost interest in the woman on top of the hill.

"They will come back!" Macha spun back to Carys. "You can't keep up the rain all night."

Carys sighed. "Morrígan, this isn't the Shadowlands. By the time you dry out, they'll be distracted by something else."

"What?" The Morrígan threw up her arms. "What could possibly match the thrill of the goddess of war?"

Cadell, Seren whispered. *Now.*

With a roar and a great crack of thunder, Cadell took his true form in the Brightlands, and a dragon spread its wings over Salisbury Plain.

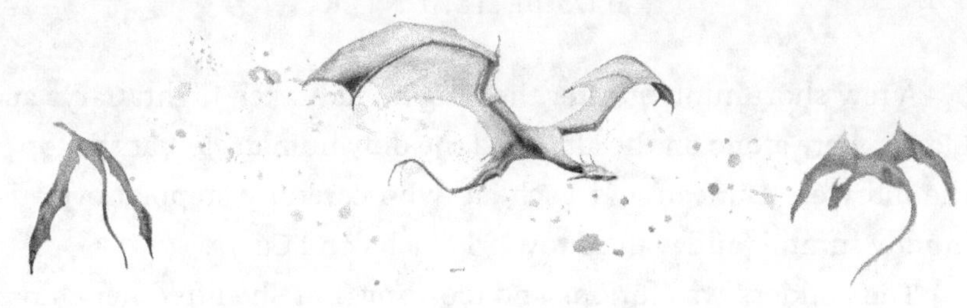

CHAPTER THIRTY-ONE

"Dragon!"

The Morrígan's acolytes ran for the edge of the drop-off where Cadell had mounted the sky, pulling out their phones and trying to capture the flight of an honest-to-God dragon flying over Wiltshire.

"Holy shit," someone yelled. "That's a dragon!"

"Oh my god!"

"Is that real?"

The crowd surged down the hillside, tumbling over each other and rushing to capture the vision of a dragon flying before it disappeared into the darkness.

The moon was full, and the wingspan of the great beast blocked out the stars.

Nêrys, are there humans taking pictures of me?

It's fine. For once, give them a show.

Cadell grumbled in her mind, but he kept flying in circles, drawing Macha's followers away from Cley Hill and down across the wheat fields.

"This is the best music festival ever!" a woman shouted.

A few short minutes after the dragon had taken flight, Carys and Macha were alone on the altar and the only humans left at the top of the hill were Duncan and Lachlan, who carefully stepped over the muddy summit and walked toward Macha and Carys.

The goddess was furious and bleeding, but she lifted her chin in defiance. "Do you think you have defeated me?"

"I think I've wounded you at best." Carys spread her arms. "And Morrígan, I'm not your enemy."

"Oh?" Macha smiled slyly. "I see you have unleashed your beast in the Brightlands."

"Carys?" Duncan called. "Are you okay?"

"I'm fine!"

"Your warrior sister sits on your shoulder," the Morrígan whispered, "and you wear a powerful collar from the mother goddess." Macha stared at the gold glowing through her skin.

She is going to try to tempt you with power.

"Yeah, I caught that."

"Perhaps our plans are not unaligned." Macha stepped closer. "Wouldn't you enjoy seeing your dragon fly over the city?"

Duncan and Lachlan came closer.

She's going to bring up laying waste to your enemies now.

"You could be a queen here." Macha pointed at Duncan and Lachlan. "Take both these men as your lovers. Why should you choose one over the other?"

Ew. Seren sounded like she was gagging. *Didn't see that one coming.*

"No offense, but not my style," Carys said. "But thanks, I guess?"

"I would let you lay waste to those who have wronged you and your people!"

Ah, there it is. Knew she'd offer to lay waste.

"Good call," Carys murmured.

"Good?" Macha smiled.

"I wasn't talking to you," Carys said. "What I meant to say was that I'm not your enemy, but I do happen to think that having dragons flying around in the Brightlands is not a great idea."

"What do you want?" Macha shouted.

"I want..." Carys took a chance. "I want to tell you a story."

Macha blinked. Her furious face went blank.

Seren was shouting in her mind.

You want to what?

"Once upon a time..." Carys started. "There was an ancient king in Eíre." The words slipped from her mouth. She was going on instinct and hoping those instincts were correct. "He wronged you, so you cursed his men. But while his army was sick, a hero rose up."

Macha was staring at her now, but Carys couldn't read her expression.

You're telling her the story of Cú Chulainn? I think she might know it already!

"But this hero didn't displease you. In fact, you tried to give him a blessing, but in his youth and his arrogance, he scorned you." Carys smiled a little bit. "So you took your revenge and thwarted him three times."

The eel.

The bear.

The bull.

Carys saw each parallel now. She knew the story she needed to tell, and it rhymed with the old myth that Luna Beck had given her weeks ago, the story of a hero who had bested a god.

And that tale of the Morrígan didn't end with a triumphant defeat in battle.

Carys smiled, "But even after all of the wounds that hero gave you, you still got the better of him."

"You tell me tales I already know." The Morrígan raised her chin. "I ask you again, daughters of Epona, what do you want?"

Carys held out her hand. "I want to heal you."

Seren erupted in her mind.

Are you fucking kidding me, Carys?

As soon as she uttered the words, the gold around Carys's neck warmed, and she knew the Mothers approved.

The only hero who had ever bested the Morrígan hadn't challenged her in battle. He had healed her wounds by inadvertently blessing her three times.

Macha's face fell. "What?"

Duncan froze. "What did she say?"

Lachlan cocked his head. "Carys?"

"I want to heal you." Carys lifted her hands and felt the power of Dôn's collar flowing through her. "That's what this collar really does, Morrígan. It protects me. It protects my life."

Don't do it.

"But I think... I can give you a little bit of that life to heal you," Carys said.

"Carys, do not do this!" Lachlan said.

"I don't know how much it would take." Carys's voice was thick. "A couple of years? A decade? I don't know."

"No!" Duncan roared and lunged forward, but though he tried to climb up the knoll, something held him back. "Carys, no!"

The Morrígan stood before her, and her wounds were grave. Her eye socket was gaping and bloody. The wound on her side wept pus and blood, and the punctures on her leg were angry and red.

"You are offering to heal me?"

"You're not going to heal here." Carys looked around—not a single one of the Morrígan's faithful was left on the summit of Cley Hill. "Think about it."

"Carys, are you daft?" Duncan shouted. "We can kill her!"

Lachlan lifted his sword and walked toward them, and Carys saw the Morrígan's eyes light up.

Carys spun toward them. "No! That's what she wants. She feeds off violence, Lachlan." She turned back the Morrígan. "One condition. I will only heal you in the Shadowlands."

The Morrígan lifted her chin. "No."

"Then suffer here," Carys said. "Your acolytes are gone. Your Fianna has fled. No one believes in you anymore, Macha. Everyone who was following you is watching a dragon fly right now." She shook her head. "You can't compete with a dragon."

"Curse you!" The Morrígan stomped her foot, but she collapsed with pain, falling to the ground.

Carys knelt next to her. "Come back to the Shadowlands where you are feared and powerful," she whispered. "Don't waste your life in this place where distracted humans flit from one god to the next. Your believers are there, not here."

The Morrígan stretched out on the ground and stared into the sky as Cadell soared over her, the shadow of the dragon shielding her from the rain for a moment before he was gone.

Her blood leaked into the soil beneath her. "Fine."

Wait... it had worked?

"We have a bargain?"

"Yes." She turned her eye on Carys. "I will return to the Shadowlands if you use your life to heal me."

Do not do this. You don't know how much of your life she will take.

"There was always going to be a price." Carys looked at Duncan, then at Lachlan. "We have a deal."

A moment after that, the Morrígan plunged bloody hands into the ground beneath her, and the earth fell away below them.

WHISPERING INCANTATIONS FILLED HER MIND. She was wrapped in soft, dry clothes that smelled of rosemary and rue. She felt gentle ministrations over her skin and a cool cloth pressed to the burning gold collar at her neck.

"Welcome back," a soft voice said.

Carys opened her eyes, and she was lying in the soft glow of the Shadowlands, a pearl-grey sky overhead and a woman with flowing brown hair and dark brown eyes kneeling beside her in the long waving grass of Saris Plain.

"I know you."

It was the goddess she had seen by the loch, confiding in the dark man who became a kelpie. She was the woman who spoke to her in dreams, whispering Rhiannon's name into her ear. She was the goddess on a horse, warning her at every turn that danger was coming.

"Epona."

The lovely woman brushed Carys's hair back from her forehead like a mother soothing her child. "What a wise gift you were, Carys Morgan."

"You gave me to her."

"The only gift she asked for." Epona smiled. "Well, that and being released from her vows, but her vows were always a choice, though she didn't seem to know it."

Part of Carys wanted to sit up, but part of her was enjoying the soft ground beneath her and the calm, clear vision of the goddess's face. "My mother loved you so much."

There was no half sight. No double images.

Maybe it was the goddess or maybe her half vision had fled. She was praying it was the latter.

"When she came to me and told me she had fallen in love…" Epona sighed. "How could I not grieve the loss of Tegan? Her love had been the sweetest of any servant in my memory."

"Wow." Carys's heart swelled. "You're a really old goddess. So that's a lot a lot of servants."

"Yes, it is." Epona smiled. "But I blessed her for her years of love. And I offered her one gift."

"She wanted to be a mother."

Epona nodded. "She wanted to be a mother."

Carys felt tears at the corner of her eyes. "But nothing is born in the Shadowlands except by magic."

"So you had to be born in the Brightlands, and she could not return. For there is always a price to be paid. My only condition was that she bear you in Cymru so that your father's Shadowkin could raise her other daughter in the land of Tegan's birth, where I could watch over her."

"Because Tegan didn't have a twin in this world."

"Correct." Epona stroked Carys's hair. "You offered a sacrifice as well. In order to get the Morrígan to return to the Shadowlands. Unlike the hero of Ulster, you are not a demigod, so you offered part of the goddess Dôn's gift to you."

"Yes. Did it work?"

Epona nodded. "It did."

"Oh, thank God." Relief flooded Carys, and she sat up and looked around, but there was nothing and nobody on the grassy hills except for her and Epona. "I don't suppose there's a way that you already healed the Morrígan without me having to give up part of my life?"

Epona shook her head. "A bargain struck must be met, Carys Morgan. And as you wisely said, there is always a price."

Carys felt her throat tighten. "Any idea how much of my life I handed over? She was... pretty damaged."

Epona frowned. "That? That was nothing." She stood and offered a hand to Carys. "The minute she entered the Shadowlands, the magic of her believers here started to heal her."

Carys paused. "So you mean—"

"If you want a number..." Epona put a hand on Carys's chest, just under the gold collar and right above her heart.

Carys held her breath and felt her heart racing.

"Five months you have given to heal the goddess. Five months of your mortal life."

Carys let out her breath. "Not too bad."

Epona smiled. "Not bad at all."

They started walking, and the wind was silent, moving over fields of golden grain.

Carys looked around. "Are we...?"

"We're not in the Shadowlands exactly. You're still healing there. You did give five months of life to a war goddess. That's hard on a body."

"So this is a dream?"

"Of a sort."

But Epona probably had at least one answer she could share. "Am I still going to have the two different eyes when I wake up?"

The goddess raised an eyebrow. "You know, many people seek magical vision. They want to see the true nature of things."

"Well, I am not one of them."

Epona laughed softly. "It's not always a blessing."

"It's very disorienting."

"At least you have an eye patch." Epona lifted a finger. "That was good thinking from the ellyllon. Keep using that."

"So it's still there?" Carys was stuck with the magical vision? Forever?

Dammit.

Epona smiled. "It will not last forever, Carys Morgan. I promise that one day you will wake up, and your vision will be as it was unless you go back to Hogg's Well."

"Are you sure?"

"I am sure." She cocked her head. "I can't tell you when though."

"Great."

As they walked, the goddess's voice grew fainter. "You have unfinished... the Shadowlands."

"Unfinished what?" Carys turned, but she was alone.

She spun around, looking for direction, but there was nothing around her save for silent heads of nodding grain.

A drifting voice was all that was left of the horse goddess, and it was barely a whisper on the wind. *Tell him that when he is ready...*

"What?" Carys shouted, but there was no one. She was utterly alone. "What am I supposed to tell who?"

...he may join the one he loves.

CARYS WOKE with a deep breath to find herself in an unfamiliar room with grey stone walls and a fire crackling. She sat up and felt the cool press of rough linen sheets on her skin.

"You're awake."

She turned and saw Duncan in the chair next to the bed.

Where's Lachlan?

Seren was still with her.

"I'm awake, and so is Seren." Her voice was hardly more than a croak.

Duncan jumped up and offered her a silver goblet. "What's that?"

Cool water touched Carys's lips, and she drank deeply. "Where am I?"

"Cadell felt you shift worlds with the Morrígan when she left this one. She'd ripped some kind of hole in the barrier between the Shadowlands and the Brightlands and dragged you through."

"So the ground—"

"Apparently the entire hill was like a huge gate, but we couldn't get through. Luckily, Epona's daughters were waiting on the other side. According to your uncle, those women had her wrapped and warded as soon as she set foot in this world." Duncan refilled her water and handed the goblet back to her.

"Cadell?" Carys croaked. She took another long gulp of water.

He's close. I can feel him.

"Laura just made him go eat something. Naida got all of us through the nearest gate," Duncan said. "And as soon as we were on this side, the dragon took off. Said he picked you up from the top of the hill and flew you straight here. The rest of us had to wait for other dragons."

You're in my father's castle. You're in Cymru.

"I'm in Cymru." Carys smiled. "Finally."

Duncan smiled too. "About time, isn't it? What about you? Do you remember any of this?"

No, we were passed out and talking with a goddess. Where the hell is Lachlan?

"Seren, just give me a minute, okay?" Carys pressed a hand to her temple.

Duncan went pale. "So it's true."

Carys looked up at him. "What?"

"Lachlan said... He thought maybe Seren was with you somehow. On the hill with the Morrígan."

"He's not wrong. When I took the water in Hogg's Well, she..." Carys pressed her fingers to her temples again. "She came to me. To my mind."

Duncan's voice was rough. "So when you called him darling—"

"That was her." She tapped her forehead. "Not me, Duncan. That was Seren."

The burly Scot stepped backward and angled his head, peering into Carys's eyes. "Seren?"

When Carys closed her left eye, she saw him as the gods did, his great heart glowing with a golden aura and a shimmer of transparent silver armor covering his body.

Carys smiled. "You're a knight, you know. In your heart. You're just as noble as he is."

Duncan's eyes went wide. "Seren?"

Oh for fuck's sake.

Carys laughed. "No, that was me. She thinks I'm a sap."

He doesn't need any more confidence. The stubborn bastard has it in spades.

"She said she missed you and it's good to see you," Carys said.

Duncan frowned. "No, she didn't."

"You're right, she called you a stubborn bastard."

"Ah, there she is." The corner of his mouth inched up. "Fuck me, Carys, is she stuck in there or something?"

No. In fact, I don't have much longer. I can hear Arawn's hounds in the distance. Mother can only hide me for so long.

"No," Carys said softly. "She doesn't have much time. It sounds like our mother has been hiding her."

Let me say goodbye to Lachlan.

Carys swallowed hard. "She wants to say goodbye to Lachlan."

Duncan's smile fled. "I'll find him."

He left the room, and Carys tried to stand up, but her legs felt heavy again, like when the Mothers had first given her their collar.

Just stay still. He's coming.

Lachlan must have been close, but so was Cadell. Both men rushed into the room with hopeful expressions.

"Is she still here?" Lachlan burst out. "Why didn't you tell me?"

Carys took a deep breath. "She told me not to."

"Dammit, Seren!" Lachlan burst out in anger. "How could you? How *could* you?"

Carys, let me speak.

"I don't know what to do," she whispered.

Let me.

"I don't know."

Let me...

A wave of dizziness swept over Carys, and she fought to stay sitting.

Please, sister. Let me say goodbye.

Carys gave in to the utterly foreign sensation of another's mind layered on top of her own. When she opened her eyes, it was as if Seren were standing in front of her, using her mouth to speak.

"F'anwylyd," Seren said. "My darling husband."

Carys felt her heart break when Lachlan looked into her eyes and collapsed into her lap. His shoulders shook as he clutched her around the waist, and she stroked his hair as he cried.

"How could you?" He moaned. "How could you not tell me?"

"You would have fought the Morrígan and spoiled the whole plan." Seren sniffed. "You idiot."

"Stop." Lachlan straightened, and his eyes were fierce. "Is it you? Truly?"

"Only for a moment."

He took her hand. "I couldn't say goodbye when I lost you."

"Of course not. I was murdered," Seren said. "But thank you for killing Regan."

"Aisling—"

"We will waste no words on that woman."

Lachlan nodded. "How much time do we have?"

"Enough time to tell you not to be reckless with your life," Seren said fiercely. "Enough time to tell you to live and be happy."

He shook his head. "I will live the rest of my life knowing that you are gone from me forever. Not even when I am dead will we be together."

"Then there's no reason to rush death, is there?"

Carys realized what the goddess's parting words meant.

Tell him that when he is ready, he may join the one he loves.

She struggled to force the words into Seren's mind.

He can be with you! Epona has given him passage to Annwn, the same as you and our mother!

"Be quiet, Carys, it's my time now, and he doesn't need to know that."

"I don't need to know what?"

"She'll tell you later because she won't be able to keep her mouth shut." Seren put her hand on Lachlan's cheek. "I hear Arawn's hounds, Lachlan. The hunt is coming. I have to leave."

"If I kiss you," Lachlan said, "then I kiss you goodbye."

"You're not going to kiss me," Seren said, "because this is still her body."

Thank you.

"Carys, shut up." Seren kept her hand on Lachlan's cheek, but she turned to Cadell. "Hello, old friend."

Cadell smiled. "Hello, my lady."

"I miss our flights together."

He nodded. "As do I."

"I know you had other lords, but I was your favorite, right?"

Hey!

Cadell nodded with a hint of amusement in his eyes. "Of course you were, Princess Seren."

She turned back to Lachlan. "Don't tell Father about this. I have to go, and I couldn't bear to see him."

"No." He grabbed her hand. "Seren, please—"

"I have to go, my darling man." She pressed a kiss to his cheek. "But this is only farewell. I'll see you again."

"Seren!"

Carys felt a wave of nausea, and the sound of dogs bellowed in the distance. There was a wave of darkness and the whisper of her mother's kiss on her forehead.

Then Seren and Tegan were gone.

CHAPTER THIRTY-TWO

Carys recuperated in King Dafydd's castle for a week, nursed by Eamer and Laura, guarded by Duncan and Cadell.

And by the third day, she was going stir-crazy.

"I'm fine!" She threw off the covers and unwrapped the scarf from around her neck. "I feel fine. I'm not injured. My legs are still a little weak because of the goddess-collar thing, but I'm only going to get used to it if I get up and walk around."

Laura looked at Eamer. The maid looked at the queen.

Queen Eamer wore a pinched expression. "Carys."

"Aunt Eamer."

"You came to Briton expecting to attend a coronation in your uncle's company," she started. "And instead, you spent months navigating treacherous court politics."

"Which I was happy to do. After all—"

"Then you fought in a *battle* against my own niece."

"The point was that we avoided a war and made peace with your niece, which I hope—"

"Then you disappeared from your uncle's house and went on a

quest with only a dragon, a wolf, a fae, and a few humans to help you."

Laura piped up. "We got help from some gods and druids too."

Eamer ignored her. "*Weeks* in the Brightlands, fighting battles against the Morrígan. No word to your uncle—who only heard rumors about your whereabouts from various dragons—and then we find out you sacrificed months of your life to heal the same goddess who was trying to kill you."

Carys opened her mouth, then closed it.

Eamer leaned closer. "I don't care if you carry the collar of the Dagda himself around your neck—you can give your body and your spirit time to rest."

Laura pursed her lips, and her eyebrows went up. She shook her head vigorously behind Eamer's back.

"Yes, Aunt," Carys said quietly.

Eamer nodded firmly, then strode out of the room, pointing at Carys's maid. "She doesn't leave this room."

"Yes, my lady."

Carys wrapped the scarf back around her neck, took the warm broth the maid handed her, and pulled the blanket up.

"It's so hard when people love you," Laura said.

"Shut up."

SHE SLEPT in a warm chamber at the castle with Duncan holding her every night, and every day she felt a little more like herself.

Carys leaned against his chest one night. She'd been unable to sleep, and Duncan had woken up too. He pulled her closer and stroked her hair.

"Your eyes still bothering you?"

She pulled the eye patch more securely over her right eye. "I'm getting used to it."

"The minute you really get used to it, it'll be gone," Duncan said. "That's usually the way of it, right?"

"Right."

He leaned down and kissed her forehead. "Why are you sad, lass? You did it. You saved the Brightlands and the Shadowlands too. You kept another war from happening."

Carys blinked away tears. "It's really hard to explain."

Duncan was silent for a long time. "I'm here when you want to try."

"I feel... this hollow in my mind. There's this space where Seren was. And even though it was just for a little bit, when she was with me, I felt..."

"Whole?"

Carys turned and looked up at him. "Yes."

He frowned. "It's an annoying, shitty thing to feel like half of yourself lives in another person. Especially someone you don't always like."

She let out a long breath. "Is this how you feel about Lachlan? Like, all the time?"

"Something like that, yes."

"I'm sorry." She laughed a little bit. "I'm sorry, I shouldn't laugh. It's not funny."

Duncan's mouth turned up at the corner. "No, but it is a bit."

She swallowed hard and laid her head over his heart. "I felt it," she said. "What Seren felt for Lachlan. When she was with me, I could *feel* their love."

His voice was rough. "What's that like? To feel someone else's love?"

"It was overwhelming," she whispered. "And... clarifying. Years of memories. Years of loving him. This fierce devotion burning in the center of my chest."

Duncan's heart was racing under her ear. "Carys—"

"It's the way I feel about you, Duncan." She lifted her face to his. "It was the way I know I'm going to feel about you in ten years. Twenty years. That fire never left her even when she died."

"That's it then," Duncan said. "You're stuck with me, Carys Morgan. Even after we leave this life."

"If the past three weeks have taught me anything" —she settled her head against his chest again— "it's that there is way more than one world. And death isn't an ending at all."

IT WAS her last day of imprisonment. Or what her aunt graciously called her recovery.

Carys had been pacing around her room, eager to leave and explore her uncle's castle. Dafydd had assured her that all their travel arrangements back to Baywood were taken care of by his man in Cardiff and that when they were ready to go home, a plane would be waiting.

For the first time since she'd returned to the Shadowlands after her first journey there, she actually felt like she was enjoying a holiday.

Someone tapped on the door. *Nêrys?*

"Come in, Cadell."

She was alone in her room and sitting by the window, looking at the kitchen garden where workers were cutting branches, harvesting late summer crops, and enjoying a warm breeze.

She turned when she heard the dragon enter her room.

Cadell wasn't alone.

"Hey!" She smiled at the little girl in his arms. She couldn't have been more than three or four, and she bounced in Cadell's arms, speaking rapidly in Cymric.

"Yes," he said in English. "This is my nêrys." He smiled at Carys.

"This is Mared's youngest. She's been very eager to meet you, but she doesn't speak any Anglian, so I will translate for her. Her name is Eleri."

The little girl perked up when she heard her name and smiled at Carys.

Carys had no idea her father's dragon had a child so young. "She's adorable!"

Mared had a dark complexion and tight, curly hair, and Eleri shared her features. Her curls were pulled into two high buns that made it look like she had mouse ears.

"Oh my god," Carys said with a gasp. "She's a baby dragon."

The corner of Cadell's mouth turned up. "Yes," he said carefully. "She is."

She pressed her hands together, forcing herself not to grab the little girl. "Oh my god, she's a baby dragon!" she whispered.

"Eleri." Cadell lifted the little girl up and whispered in her ear.

She giggled and climbed down Cadell's legs, running across the room as her body erupted in a bright red shower of sparks.

The baby dragon nearly ran into Carys's legs before she could stop.

Carys immediately sat on the floor, and Eleri turned in circles, waving her tail and flapping her wings. She was roughly the size of a spaniel and made a chirruping sound as she showed off her beauty.

"Am I dreaming?" Carys whispered.

"You will never speak of this," Cadell murmured. "And as far as Mared is concerned, her daughter was never here."

Carys gasped and looked up. "Are you the bad-influence uncle?"

He lifted one shoulder. "My children are more mature. I can spoil the little ones."

"Oh my god, Cadell is a bad influence," she whispered at Eleri, who promptly shoved her spiky head under Carys's hand. "Yes, you're *very* beautiful, Eleri."

The little red dragon turned her head to Cadell.

Cadell spoke to her in Cymric.

Eleri made a clicking noise in the back of her throat, then turned in more circles and puffed out a small stream of fire.

Carys pretended to be shocked. She sucked in a breath and put a hand over her chest. "Oh no!"

"Gofal!" Cadell barked.

The chirping sound was back, but this time it had the timbre of a giggle.

"Oh Eleri, you're very scary." Carys nodded. "Very beautiful but very scary too."

The little dragon rolled on the ground, curling into a ball and rocking back and forth with her tail.

"They do that when they're happy." Cadell walked over. "I better get her back to her sire or Mared will hear of it."

Carys stuck out her lower lip, but Cadell shook his head.

"Most humans never get to see the younglings ever," he whispered. "Don't complain."

She ran a hand over Eleri's head a moment before the little girl transformed again. She immediately started babbling something in Cymric.

Cadell answered her, then turned to Carys. "She wants to come visit you again, but I said you are only here for a short time."

"Tell her I'll be back though."

"I will." Cadell lifted the little girl to his shoulder and pulled open the chamber door, ducking under it as Eleri continued to babble.

"Cadell!" Carys scrambled to her feet.

He paused in the corridor. "Nêrys."

"Thank you for showing me a baby dragon," she whispered.

"I have no idea what you're talking about." He shut the door behind him.

"Our riders have gone out to survey," Dafydd said. "There is no evidence of the Morrígan on Saris Plain. What has happened in the Brightlands, I have no idea."

Duncan said, "Lachlan and I walked through the Ynys Môn fae gate yesterday. We looked at the papers, but the only mention of a dragon in England was in the tabloids, and most people think it was some kind of prank."

"Someone called it the best drone show they've ever seen." Lachlan glanced at Cadell with half a smile.

Laura stifled a laugh.

Cadell grimaced. "I will try not to be offended."

Lachlan was smiling more. Not fully back to himself, but partway there. There was a peace in his eyes that had been missing for a long time.

Carys looked around the cozy library where Dafydd was sharing a new barrel of wine with them the day after Eamer had released her from her room. "Any news of Naida and Godrik?"

"Gone," Laura said. "A couple of days after we got here. You were still sleeping, and they said they needed to get back home, so..."

"I understand completely." Carys shook her head. "What's the date back in the UK?"

"August third," Duncan said.

"I have to go back soon." She took her uncle's hand. "I have classes starting in like two weeks, and I'm completely unprepared." She laughed.

Duncan said, "If you tell your students you were stopping inter-dimensional battles in the fae realm, they might cut you some slack."

"No, I think they'd very kindly call for a psychological intervention," Laura said. "And I have to say it's just a good thing that my uncle is my boss and is in the know about all this stuff, otherwise, I would be so fired."

"So you are returning to the Brightlands," Dafydd said. "For good?"

She cocked her head. "Uncle, you know I'm not suited to be queen here."

"On the contrary, you would make an excellent regent," Dafydd said. "You have negotiated with goddesses, fought in battles, and have the wise counsel of Cadell of Eryri." He looked at her solemnly. "Added to that, you bear the collar of Dôn, our oldest goddess."

Carys shook her head. "I know. But I don't *want* to be queen. Seren did. Seren knew her whole life she was going to be queen. She could prepare for it. Me?" She shook her head. "I'm a teacher. Just a teacher, Uncle Dafydd."

"There is nothing *just* about those who shape young minds." The corner of his mouth turned up. "And remember, whether as teacher or mother, you could shape the future of our kingdom, Carys Morgan."

She sat back. "What is that supposed to mean?" She looked at Duncan. Then at Cadell. "Hey, as far as I know—"

"We want children, don't we?" Duncan reached for her hand. "Someday. And when we have them, I think all your uncle is saying is that it might be prudent to be in Scotland."

Lachlan sat up straight. "Yes." His expression brightened. "Yes, of course."

"Any child born to you would be as my own grandchild." Dafydd glanced at Cadell. "And those of our line do have a very strong affinity for dragons."

"Of course." Carys felt tears come to her eyes, but she tried to hide them.

It wasn't sadness. It wasn't something she could ever be sad about.

But now she knew. Now she knew that whatever children she and Duncan might have someday, those children would have a shadow twin, another half.

But unlike Carys, those children wouldn't be strangers to the two realms. Because she was a daughter of two worlds.

And she would have a home and a family in both.

CHAPTER THIRTY-THREE

She dreamed of flying when she slept.

The cold wind cut through the leather armor that shielded her body, creeping down her neck like icy water over rocks.

She soared over mountains draped in fog where the dark tips of ancient giants jabbed the cloudy sky.

The only light that touched her face came from the glow of fire coming from the belly of the beast that carried her, and in the distance, she heard the thunder of the Tistilal's wings as the thunderbird flew north over the mountain peaks that bordered the great Pacific Ocean.

She dreamed of flying, cradled in smooth, curved claws that wrapped around her body and held her in their grip.

Nêrys.

Carys opened her eyes in darkness at the sound of Cadell's voice.

Duncan was sleeping beside her in the cozy house in the middle of the forest. The house Gareth had built for Tegan. The house where the blacksmith had come to live for a year, to try life in Baywood.

With more than a few flights back to Scotland for both of them.

Carys got out of bed and threw on a robe before she walked outside.

She saw the world in a hundred shades of grey but also in green and purple, pink and vivid blue.

"Hey." She slipped on her boots and walked to the edge of the forest where she could see Cadell waiting.

Her eyes were still seeing double, and the kids at school had taken to calling her the Dread Captain Morgan since she had to wear an eye patch or go crazy while she was at work.

Also because they were college kids and thought any joke about rum was hilarious.

"Look." Cadell pointed to the bushes. "I thought they might be gone by morning. I hope you don't mind that I woke you."

"No, it's cool." Along with her vision, Cadell's ability to speak to her mind had also lingered. Carys couldn't respond mentally, so the effect was definitely wearing off. But she knew she'd miss his voice when it was gone. Having Cadell close to her mind, even in the Brightlands, eased the hollow that Seren's voice had left.

Carys knelt down and saw a doe with two dotted fawns hiding in the brush. "Hello there." She kept her voice soft and slid her eye patch to the left. It was unusual to have young fawns this time of year, but magic could be at work. And sometimes nature simply didn't go by the rules.

Her right eye caught the dancing sprites hidden in the leaves around the fawns who both carried a single thumbprint on their forehead, the mark of the Deer Woman's protection.

"Two little girls, Cadell."

"Shifter?" It wasn't uncommon to find animal shifters from Pauwau Aki, even this far from the gates.

Carys shook her head. "Just regular deer."

"They're beautiful." He lifted his chin. "I scented a bear in the woods."

"That's normal this time of year." They were deep into fall, and the deciduous trees had lost their leaves, but the snow had not come yet, and the bears were lumbering around, gathering as much food as they could before true winter set in. "I don't think you need to worry."

"Hopefully their mother will keep them near the house during the winter." Cadell frowned at the doe. "It's very late in the season to give birth."

Despite the fact that Cadell hunted deer in his dragon form, he was softhearted toward the young. She didn't try to make it make sense. Every creature, even if they weren't gods, lived in contradictions.

"Well, if she keeps them near the house, we'll put out some food." Carys stood, leaving the two newborns in the bushes, thankful that no predator would come near the house with the scent of a dragon nearby.

Cadell looked up at the moon and the blue glow of morning that touched the horizon. "The day is ending in Pauwau Aki."

Carys narrowed her eyes. "Are you thinking what I'm thinking?"

Cadell smiled. "I'll race you to the gate."

"No fair!"

The dragon always won, but it didn't matter. Carys ran through the woods in her bathrobe and boots, her heart light in the forest that was as much her home as the cabin in the woods.

The scent of pine and cedar suffused the air as she ran, and when she reached the massive fallen log that guarded the gate to the Shadowlands, the mountain lion shifter perched on the granite rocks above winked at her before he laid his head down.

The voices that met her ears whispered secrets and greetings, recognizing her step and the goddess's gold collar that shone beneath her clothes.

By the time she reached the clearing beyond the gate, Cadell had already transformed.

Nêrys. His voice rumbled in her mind. *Are you ready?*

She threw up her arms when Cadell took to the air, waiting for him to reach down and pluck her from the frosty meadow.

She put a hand on her belly, whispering in her mind as the great claws closed around her. *Do you feel it?*

Cadell curled his foot back, creating a secure cage as he beat his wings and lifted into the sky.

Do you feel his power? Do you feel how he cares for us?

She rested her cheek on Cadell's claw as he flew into the soft gold-and-pink sky with no sun.

Because the Shadowlands would always remain the Shadowlands. A place of myth and story. A place where fairy tales were real and the world was a dampened echo of the harsh and brilliant Brightlands.

But with every month that passed, Carys knew that the name others had given her was true. She was a daughter of two worlds. She was home in the light and the shadow, and even though she'd started this journey alone, she had found family in both places.

Love surrounded her; she would never be alone again.

Do you see that thunderbird in the distance?

No racing, Cadell.

Cadell's mental laugh was low and wicked.

Cadell!

WHEN SHE WALKED BACK into the kitchen, her hair was a tangled mess, and Duncan was standing at the counter, dunking a cookie in coffee and peering out the window over the sink.

"Saw you walking in."

She loved seeing him in her space, his shirt untucked, wearing his flannel pajama pants and slippers that he kept under her bed.

He had his own mugs and his own messes. Little hairs in the sink when he shaved, and he was still getting accustomed to not having a housekeeper to pick up after him.

But the laird was getting the hang of commoner life.

Carys slid her eye patch to the right and tried to comb a hand through her hair, but it was useless. "Why does a relaxing morning flight always end up being a race with a thunderbird?"

Duncan's eyebrows went up. "Because your dragon is a daredevil?" He glanced at her belly. "All good?"

She had to admire his nonchalance. The Duncan of a month ago would have gone on a rant about his pregnant fiancée racing a thunderbird while clutched in the claws of a massive dragon.

"I'm good."

"No nausea?"

"I'll let you know when it happens so you can spoil me." She walked over and slid her arm around his waist. "Is there more coffee?"

"Yes. Half caffeine."

She stuck out her tongue at him, but he just winked and kissed her forehead.

"Just think," he said. "That means you can have two cups of coffee instead of one."

"Oh, good point."

Duncan was very much trying to be cool about the unexpected. Considering how many fertility deities they'd been hanging around with, in the end, neither one of them was all that surprised when Carys was late no matter what kind of birth control she was taking.

Magic had a mind of its own.

"Class at ten today?"

She nodded and poured herself a mug of coffee, adding some milk and grabbing a piece of shortbread that Mary had mailed them from Murrayshall House.

"You working on that gate for the Rothman Mansion?"

"I am."

In the months since they'd returned to the Shadowlands,

Duncan had started making friends with various restorers in Northern California, one of whom was more than happy to send work to an experienced blacksmith accustomed to working on historic buildings.

Duncan had quickly found an appropriate space in town for welding and ironwork projects, then dug into solitary projects with no need to run an entire metal shop.

He said it was like taking a vacation.

And Carys? She was doing exactly what she loved.

"Did I tell you my Celtic mythology class was full?"

"Full?" His eyebrows went up. "No joke?"

"No joke." She sipped her coffee. "Apparently there's some singer who's super popular that makes a lot of mythological references, so it's trending."

"Do you think viral videos of a dragon flying over England had anything to do with that?"

"Maybe." She pinched her fingers together. "Just a little bit."

Despite various attempts at debunking, there were still videos of Cadell flying in the Brightlands that even experts couldn't explain. And while #wheresmacha was trending on social media for a few weeks, the attention of the world had moved on.

Still, seeing as there was no way all those videos of a dragon were going to be contained, it was probably better that Carys and Cadell avoid the Shadowlands in the UK for a few months and gave everyone a chance to calm down.

"Everyone wants to believe in fairy tales," Carys said. "There's a deep and intrinsic need for the other within the human psyche."

"They *want* to believe." Duncan smiled and walked over to her, sliding his arm around her waist and drawing Carys up for a kiss. "What about you, Professor Morgan?" He kissed her right cheek, then her left. "Do *you* believe in fairy tales?"

"No need." She lifted to her toes and pressed her lips against Duncan's. "Because this is it. You and me. My friends and my family. My home here."

"And there." Duncan smiled.

"This is the fairy tale for me." Carys felt the contentment deep in her chest. "And it's real."

THE END
(For now.)

AFTERWORD

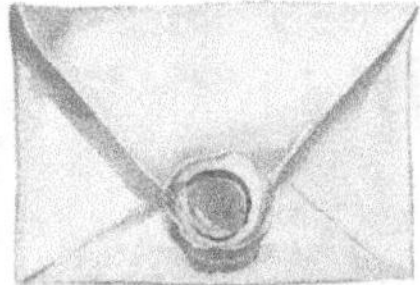

Dear Reader,

I hope that you enjoyed the conclusion of Carys's story! It was an absolute delight to give Carys and Duncan their happily-ever-after; I hope you found it as satisfying as I did.

Some of you may be wondering about other characters in the book.

- *What about Cadell and Laura?*
- *Is this the end of Naida's story?*
- *What will happen to Lachlan?*

There are definitely more stories that I would love to write in this world, but for now, I need a little break. I wrote all three of these (rather large) books over the course of about two and a half years, so I'm going to take some time to breath and work on other projects. But I love this world so much, and I definitely want to explore more.

So for those of you who are eager to return to the Shadowlands in other books... keep an eye out for more and please subscribe to my newsletter at ElizabethHunter.com.

My eternal gratitude to all of you who have taken the time to follow this journey with me. I wish you love, laughter, the family of your heart, and of course... I wish you dragons.

Best always,

Elizabeth Hunter

ACKNOWLEDGMENTS

I want to take a moment to thank everyone who encouraged me when I was writing this absolutely strange story idea that I couldn't get out of my mind.

Portal fantasy teases readers with the dream of a fantastical world just a step away, but this book series wasn't a step or a magical portal for me. Despite my lifelong love of high fantasy, writing the Shadowlands series often felt more like Carys's first passage through that fae gate in Scotland, roots tripping her and grasping fingers slowing her down.

This series taught me patience, though probably not as much as my incredible agent, Kimberly Brower, would prefer.

This series taught me perseverance, though not as much perseverance as my incredible editing team of Amy Cissell, Anne Victory, and Linda, who have to fight their way through plot glitches, confusing references, passive voice, and overenthusiastic comma usage.

This series taught me flexibility, like changing cover designers midway through. I am grateful to M's vision and patience. Thank you for your incredible work on the most beautiful and most purplest cover in fantasy romance history.

This series taught me innovation, like designing special editions with Jen and the team at Painted Wings Publishing, who worked with me to produce the stunning printed edges for the Shadowlands hardcovers.

I also want to give a shoutout to my narrator for the audiobooks of this series, Ava Lucas, who elevated my words with her performance of Carys's story. She is an artist, and I am privileged to work with her. *Broken Veil* audiobook coming soon!

So many thanks to my assistant Gen, who runs ElizabethHunter Shop.com and has worked tirelessly on our social media accounts to promote the Shadowlands series and all my work.

This book is dedicated to my husband, who is every hero I've ever written, in one way or another.

And finally, to my parents, who instilled in me—not only a love of all reading, but a particular love for the magic of Tolkien and L'Engle, Lewis and MacDonald.

Thank you for raising me to be a big nerd who is passionate about dragons and elves and time travel and fairies and tesseracts. Who loves myths and magic. Who still wants to learn about every new thing.

I'm so grateful that you always encouraged my curiosity. Thanks for never limiting what I could read. And thank you for filling our home with books.

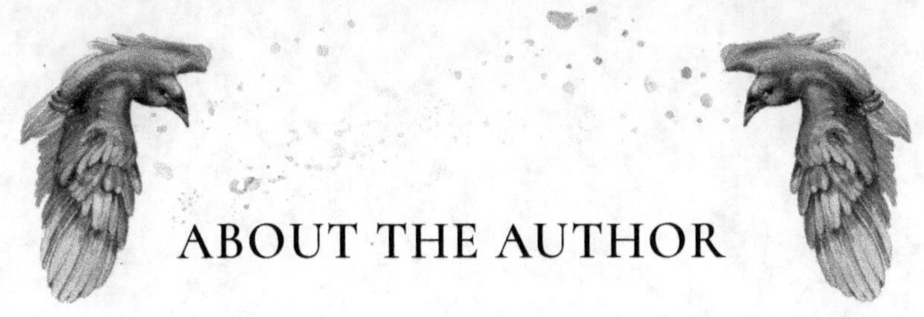

ABOUT THE AUTHOR

ELIZABETH HUNTER is an eleven-time *USA Today* and international best-selling author of romance, contemporary fantasy, and paranormal mystery. Based in Central California and Addis Ababa, she travels extensively to write fantasy fiction exploring world mythologies, history, and the universal bonds of love, friendship, and family.

She has published over fifty works of fiction and sold over two million books worldwide. She is the author of the Elemental Mysteries, the Irin Chronicles, the Shadowlands series, and other works of fiction.

LOOKING FOR MORE?

For more information about Elizabeth Hunter's fiction and upcoming work, please visit ElizabethHunter.com and make sure to also visit ElizabethHunterShop.com for special editions, signed books, and exclusive merchandise!

ALSO BY ELIZABETH HUNTER

THE SHADOWLANDS

First Light

The Shadow Path

Broken Veil

THE FIREBIRD & THE WOLF

Blood Mosaic

Crimson Oath

Obsidian Empire (February 2026)

THE IRIN CHRONICLES

The Scribe

The Singer

The Secret

The Staff and the Blade

The Silent

The Storm

The Seeker

THE ELEMENTAL MYSTERIES

A Hidden Fire

This Same Earth

The Force of Wind

A Fall of Water

The Stars Afire

Fangs, Frost, and Folios

<u>The Elemental World</u>

Building From Ashes

Waterlocked

Blood and Sand

The Bronze Blade

The Scarlet Deep

A Very Proper Monster

A Stone-Kissed Sea

Valley of the Shadow

<u>The Elemental Legacy</u>

Shadows and Gold

Imitation and Alchemy

Omens and Artifacts

Midnight Labyrinth

Blood Apprentice

The Devil and the Dancer

Night's Reckoning

Dawn Caravan

The Bone Scroll

Pearl Sky

<u>The Elemental Covenant</u>

Saint's Passage

Martyr's Promise

Paladin's Kiss

Bishop's Flight

Tin God

THE SEBA SEGEL SERIES

The Thirteenth Month

Child of Ashes (Coming 2026)

CAMBIO SPRINGS

Long Ride Home

Shifting Dreams

Five Mornings

Desert Bound

Waking Hearts

Stings and Arrows

Dust Born

GLIMMER LAKE

Suddenly Psychic

Semi-Psychic Life

Psychic Dreams

MOONSTONE COVE

Runaway Fate

Fate Actually

Fate Interrupted

VISTA DE LIRIO

Double Vision

Mirror Obscure

Trouble Play